# THE FINAL STAND

"I don't know if this is such a good idea," Hal said. "They're going to spot us here."

"I'm through running," Arthur said. "We're going to fight them."

"Are you kidding? We don't even have weapons, for pete's sake." They both turned toward the sound of hoofbeats. Four horsemen were galloping across the open meadow toward them, scimitars raised overhead.

"Then we'll fight them alone," Arthur said quietly.

*He's not even afraid*, Hal thought. The boy's eyes seemed to be made of steel. Arthur was right. Better to fight and die with honor than to flee and die ignobly.

## Praise for
### *The Forever King*

"*The Forever King* is a fresh and exciting view of the Arthur legend, full of adventure ranging from ancient Babylon to Camelot to the present day. I read it in one sitting because I didn't want to put it down."

—Robert Jordan,
author of the Wheel of Time series

"The Arthurian section is well written, with some clever new twists on familiar characters, especially Merlin and Nimue."

—*Publishers Weekly*

"It's a charming and most entertaining novel. I particularly enjoyed Saladin and the eventful history the authors created for him."

—Charlotte Vale Allen,
author of *Leftover Dreams*

"Echoes of *The Once and Future King* sound at many points....The book achieves its own distinctive approach to the Arthurian saga. A well-told tale."

—*Booklist*

"*The Forever King* is full of Molly Cochran's and Warren Murphy's best, by which I mean the pirouetting wit which has you twisting and turning from page to page."

—Gregory Mcdonald,
author of *The Brave*

"Once I started it I couldn't put it down. What an adventure! Cochran and Murphy are THE writing team of the nineties."

—Aimeé Thurlo
author of *Black Mesa*

# MOLLY COCHRAN
# WARREN MURPHY
# THE FOREVER KING

**TOR®**

A TOM DOHERTY ASSOCIATES BOOK
NEW YORK

THE FOREVER KING

Copyright © 1992 by M. C. Murphy

Cover art by Joe DeVito
Interior art by Mel Green

A Tor Book
Published by Tom Doherty Associates, Inc.
175 Fifth Avenue
New York, NY 10010

Tor Books on the World Wide Web:
http://www.tor.com

Tor® is a registered trademark of Tom Doherty Associates, Inc.

ISBN: 0-812-51716-4
Library of Congress Catalog Card Number: 92-2677

First edition: June 1992
First mass market printing: March 1993

Printed in the United States of America

0  9  8  7  6

This book is dedicated to
Tony Seidl

You were valiant, knight, and true.

# ACKNOWLEDGMENTS

We are indebted to many for their help with this novel, and offer our sincere thanks to those who generously shared their time, advice, and expertise with us.

Most particularly we wish to acknowledge:

Duncan Eagleson, for condensing his prodigious knowledge of ancient weaponry in order to teach us the difference between slashing and bashing;

Kent Galyon and Rev. Paul M. Corson, for their insights into the theological aspects of the book;

Melissa Ann Singer, our editor, whose brilliance helped us to write the best story we could;

And Megan Murphy Coles, who read and criticized the manuscript for this novel (and everything else we've ever written) before its submission, thereby giving us one last chance not to make fools of ourselves.

To these individuals, and to our friends, who have supported us with their kindness through the years, we are grateful.

MOLLY COCHRAN AND WARREN MURPHY
1992

# PROLOGUE

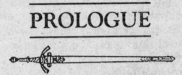

The king was dead; of that there was no doubt.

The old man had gone to the castle and had seen the knights in ceremonial armor carrying their ruler's body down to the lake where they set it adrift on a funeral barge.

Later, after the knights had left, the old man went to the lake and retrieved the king's jeweled sword from the waters where the knights had thrown it. He took it back with him to the cave where he now spent most of his time alone.

For many nights, in the flickering light of a campfire, he stared at the sword. And more than once he wept for the young man who had been his student and his friend and for whom he had had such high hopes. Once he had even dared to hope that the young man would reign forever.

But now that hope had died.

Everything died in time, the old man thought bitterly.

He mourned until the moon was new again and then walked back to the field outside the castle. There he mixed sand and pulverized limestone with water.

He dug a hole in the earth, lovingly placed the sword inside, then poured the mortar mix over it until it was covered.

The sword would never be found. In time, the castle too would be destroyed. There would be no songs or histories written of the dead king. It would be as if he never lived; as if none of this had ever happened.

And perhaps it was best that way. Perhaps it was best that dreams of justice be allowed to die.

So why was it that the bitter old man paused momentarily over the rapidly drying mortar in which the sword was encased and, with his finger, scratched a message into the cement?

It was, he told himself, because he was nothing but a superstitious old fool. Then he strode away, turning his back on the giant castle, back to his small cave where he bundled himself in animal skins and lay down to die.

But he only slept.

. . . and dreamed.

. . . and waited.

# BOOK ONE

## THE
## BOY

# CHAPTER ONE

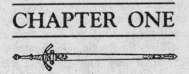

He was there again.

The bright orange blaze was scorching, suffocating in the July afternoon heat. Through the din of cracking timbers and the air-sucking whoosh of the impossibly high and angry gasoline flames the frantic voices of the firefighters sounded muffled and small.

Hal Woczniak swallowed. His hands rose and fell in a jerky motion. The features of his face were contorted, still wearing the expression of shock that had followed the explosion. Nearby, sweating and helpless, stood a small army of useless men—six members of the FBI, a fully armed SWAT team, the local police. A heavyset, balding man unwrapped a stick of gum and popped it into his mouth.

"Forget it, Hal," he told Woczniak.

The house blurred and wavered in the heat. Two firemen dragged a body—what was left of it—out of the doorway.

"Leave him!" Woczniak shouted.

The heavyset man raised a hand to Woczniak's chest, a gesture of restraint.

"Chief, there's a kid inside!" Woczniak protested.

"They know that," the Chief said placatingly. "But they just got here. They've got to move that body. Give them a chance."

"What kind of chance does the kid get?" Woczniak growled. He shoved the Chief's hand away and ran for the house. Into the thick of the smoke pouring from the building, his lungs stinging from the black air, his legs pumped wildly.

"Woczniak! Hal!" the Chief shouted. "Somebody stop him, for God's sake!"

Two firefighters flung themselves at him, but Woczniak

leaped over them effortlessly and hurtled himself into the inferno.

It was pitch-black inside except for high licks of orange flame that shed no light in the dense smoke. Coughing, Woczniak tore off his shirt and pulled it over his head as he crawled spider-like up the fragile, superheated wooden stairs. A timber broke with a deafening crack and fell toward him. He slammed against the far wall at the top of the stairs. In the blind darkness, a shard of glass from a broken mirror cut deep into his cheek. Woczniak felt only a dull pain as he pulled it from his flesh.

"Jeff!"

Stooped and groping, he found a door. He pulled it open.

*The boy will be there, tied to the chair. The boy will be there, and this time I'll get to him. This time Jeff will open his blue eyes and smile, and I'll muss his carrot hair, and the kid will go home to his folks. This one will escape. This time.*

But it was not the boy with the carrot-red hair tied to the chair. In his place was a monster, a fire-breathing dragon straight out of a fairy tale, with eyes like blood and scales that scraped as it writhed. It opened its mouth, and with its foul breath came the words:

*"You're the best, kid. You're the best there is."*

And then the creature, the terrible beast Hal Woczniak had somehow known all along would meet him in this room, cackled with a sound like breaking glass.

Screaming, Woczniak ran up to it and clasped the saurian around its slimy neck. It smiled at him with triumphant malice.

Then, fading as if it had been fashioned of clouds, it vanished and the reality of his life returned. In the monster's place was the red-haired boy, tied to the chair . . . dead as he had been all along, dead as he always was in these dreams.

Woczniak was still screaming. He couldn't stop.

He woke up screaming.

"Honey. Hey, mister."

Hal gasped for breath. His sweat was slick and cold.

"You musta had a bad dream."

It was a woman's voice. He looked over at her. It took him a moment to orient himself to his surroundings. He was in bed, in a dingy room he reluctantly recognized as his own. The woman was beside him. They were both naked.

"Do I know you?" he asked groggily, rubbing his hands over his face.

She smiled. She was almost pretty.

"Sure, baby. Since last night, anyway." She snuggled against him and flung her arm over his chest.

He pushed her away. "Go on, get out of here."

"Watza matter?"

*She's not even angry,* Hal thought. *She's used to it.* He pulled the filthy covers off them both, then saw the bruises on the woman's body. "Did I do that?"

She looked down at herself, arms spread in self-examination. "Oh. No, hon. You was real nice. Kind of drunk, though." She smiled at him. "I guess you want me to go, huh?"

She didn't wait for an answer as she wriggled into a cheap yellow dress.

"What . . . ah . . . What do I owe you?" Hal asked, wondering if he had any money. He remembered borrowing twenty from Zellie Moscowitz, who had just fenced some diamonds for a second-story man in Queens. That had been yesterday. Or the day before. He pressed his fingers into his eyes. Hell, it might have been last week, for all he knew. "What day is this?"

"Thursday," the woman said. She wasn't smiling anymore. Her shoulders sagged above the low-cut bodice of her dress. "And I ain't no hooker."

"Sorry."

"Yeah." She zipped up her dress. "But now you mention it, I could use cab fare."

"Sure." Hal swung his legs woodenly over the side of the bed and lurched toward a pair of pants draped over a chair. They reeked of stale booze and cigarette smoke, with a strong possibility of urine.

There were four one-dollar bills in his wallet. He handed them to her. "It's all I've got."

"That's okay," she said. "My name's Rhonda. I live over in Jersey. In Union City."

"Nice to meet you," Hal said.

"What's yours?"

As he replaced his wallet, he caught a glimpse of his reflection in the broken triangle of a mirror above the sink. A pair of watery, bloodshot eyes stared stupidly at him above bloated cheeks covered with graying stubble.

"I said, who are you?"

Hal stood motionless, transfixed by the sight. "Nobody," he said softly. "Nobody at all."

He didn't hear the woman let herself out.

*You're the best, kid. The best there is.*

That was what the chief said when Hal had turned in his resignation to the FBI. *The best there is.*

He turned on the tap in the sink. A thin stream of cold water trickled out, disturbing two roaches that had apparently spent the night in a Twinkie wrapper stuffed into a brown-speckled Styrofoam coffee container.

Hal splashed water on his face. Hands still dripping, he touched the scar on his cheek where the piece of glass had cut him during the fire.

That was the problem: Too much of the dream was real. If it were all dragons vaporizing on contact, he could handle it better. But most of it was exactly as things had really been. The fire, the boy, the laughter . . . that crazy bastard's laughter . . .

—*Look, Woczniak, nobody else could have saved the kid, either. You went into the burning building, for chrissake. Even the fire department couldn't get into a gasoline fire. SWAT couldn't go in. You've just spent five months in the hospital for that stunt. What'd you expect, magic?*

—*Maybe.*

—*Well, welcome to the real world. It's got psychos in it. Some of them kill kids. That's not the way we want it, it's just the way it is. I'm telling you, you did a good job. You're going to get a citation as soon as you're out of here.*

*—A citation.*

*—That's right. And you deserve it.*

*—The kid's dead, Chief.*

*—So's the psycho. After four months, you were the one who found him. You were the one who figured out why he went after the kids.*

*—I was the one who let him kill the last one.*

*—Nobody expected him to blow himself up.*

*—I could have stopped it.*

*—How?*

*—I could have shot him and covered the grenade.*

*—With what? Your body? Jesus Christ. How long you been with the Bureau, Hal? Fifteen years?*

*—Sixteen.*

*—That's a long time. Don't throw it away just because you got too close to one kid's family. Believe me, I know what it's like. You see pictures, home movies, you have dinner with the parents 'cause you've got nothing else to do at night . . .*

*—I'm out, Chief.*

*—Listen to me. You find a girl, maybe you get married. Things are different with a wife.*

*—I said I'm out.*

Hal Woczniak left the hospital five and a half months after the fire that killed Jeff Brown and his abductor. He left with no future and a past he wanted only to forget.

Funny, he thought as he walked down the glistening hospital sidewalk toward the bus stop. He had just spent half a year in the same hospital where the killer had found Jeff.

His name was Louie Rubel, Hal remembered. He had worked as an orderly in the Trauma and Burn Unit from which Hal had just been released. Using the Visitors' Registration records, Rubel would pick out boys of the right age among the visitors and then stalk them on their home turf. Before he got to Jeff Brown, he had already killed and

mutilated four other ten-year-olds. Each murder reenacted the
first killing, that of his better-favored younger brother.

Woczniak led the FBI team that cracked the case just as
Rubel was about to murder the Brown kid. It had looked like
a perfect collar, with evidence in place, the boy alive, and a
confession. No one had counted on the killer's own sense of
drama.

As the authorities approached the house, Louie Rubel
announced that he had sprayed the place with gasoline. Hal
ordered everyone on scene to freeze. When they did, Rubel
took a grenade out of his vest pocket and pulled out the pin
with his teeth.

The next few seconds were pandemonium, but Hal remembered only silence, a silence welling and gradually filling
with Rubel's high, shrieking, monstrous laughter. He
laughed until the grenade exploded. He blew himself to bits
in full view of the police, the FBI, SWAT, and an ambulance
crew.

A moment later the house went up like a torch, but Hal
could still hear the laughter.

He had run into the fire, run to save the red-haired boy,
kept running even after the shard of glass had ripped his
cheek in two and the flames burned away the hair on his arms
and chest and head, had run into the upstairs room where the
boy was sitting, tied to a chair. *You're safe, Jeff. Just a
second here, let me get these ropes off you . . . Jeff . . .*

And he carried Jeff Brown out the window and tried
mouth-to-mouth on him right there on the roof while the
SWAT boys nearly roasted themselves pulling a tarp over to
the wall beneath them. But it was too late.

Hal had come to in the hospital a week later. His first
thought was the memory of the boy's lips, still warm.

*You're the best, kid, welcome to the real world you'll get
a citation for this what'd you expect?*

Magic?

It had been almost a year since the incident.

The face in the broken mirror above the sink, the loser's

face, shook as if it were powered by an overheated engine. His eyes—a stranger's eyes—were glassy and staring. His teeth were bared.

He turned off the water. The roaches returned.

"Screw it," he said. It was time for a drink.

It was always time for a drink.

# CHAPTER TWO

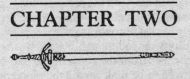

In the western part of Hampshire, on a hill turned black from a hundred fifty years of exposure to the soot-belching factories and oil refineries of industrial England, stood an asylum for the criminally insane.

Since the early 1970s, it had been called Maplebrook Hospital, but no one in the vicinity ever mistook the forbidding Victorian edifice for a place of healing. The Lymington locals knew it as the Towers, a prison whose thick walls exuded pain and madness.

The Towers housed fifty-eight patients on four floors, excluding the basement. There, in a dungeon reserved for lunatics of especially heinous dispositions, lived one lone inmate. He had no name.

Or so he claimed. One of the points that had irked all the legal personnel involved with his trial was that no legal document concerning the man's identity seemed to exist. In the end, the prosecutor charged that the man had made a life's work of so obfuscating his personal records that no one in Britain's legal network, including the defendant's own barrister, had been able to find a single fact about him that was not contradicted by some other fact.

The man was an artist of sorts, the creator of grotesque sculptures showing human beings in the throes of violent death. Although they had never been exhibited en masse, several of these works had been sold to private collectors around the world. One had been on permanent display in New York City's Museum of Modern Art. None had ever been signed by the artist.

It was when one of these—an eerily realistic statue titled *Washerwoman*, which depicted a plump, middle-aged female with an axe embedded in her chest—was en route to a buyer in Berlin that the search for the nameless artist began.

The delivery van carrying the piece skidded on a wet curve on the Autobahn and crashed through the guardrail. The driver of the van was thrown from the vehicle, as was the statue. Carefully wrapped though it was, *Washerwoman* was cleaved lengthwise, from the point of the axe blade.

The axe proved to be real. So did the blood on the edge of the blade. The corpse inside was almost perfectly preserved.

When the artist was arrested, he said only, "The point of entry was always a weakness in that piece."

After the ensuing publicity about *Washerwoman*, the New York museum donated its sculpture to Interpol to do with as it liked. Two other owners came forth, demanding to have the price of their statues refunded.

When asked how many pieces there were, Mr. X—as he had come to be known to Scotland Yard—smiled and said, "Twenty-three."

He was charged and convicted on four counts of murder, and sentenced to live out the remainder of his days in the asylum at Lymington.

The other nineteen sculptures were never recovered. In underground art circles, the price of an "X" skyrocketed into the hundreds of thousands of dollars.

Now, four years after his incarceration, the sculptor sat at a table in his basement cell, a threadbare blanket around his shoulders to ward off the perpetual dank chill of the place, reading an Urdu text. He had been a model prisoner almost from the beginning, and the nearest big library—at Bournemouth—had agreed to provide him anything he requested, as long as each order first received the approval of Maplebrook's director, Mark Coles.

Dr. Coles had never objected to the prisoner's reading matter. The doctor was, in fact, constantly struck by his patient's literary sophistication. The solitary inmate relegated to the basement was obviously a brilliant man and, from Coles' observation, a gentle and civilized one as well, with impeccable table manners, elegant, well-modulated speech, and a bearing which could only be described as regal. Were it not for the former director's written instructions that the man be kept permanently in solitary confinement, Coles would have moved him to a ward for less-disturbed patients long ago.

It was still something Coles considered every day. True, the man had allegedly killed an orderly with his bare hands on the day of his admission to Maplebrook, but even the most violent patients were capable of change. Besides, Coles often thought, the former director's methods were less than conducive to rehabilitation. Faced with life imprisonment in a place like the Towers, anyone might have attacked his jailer in a similar manner. The dead orderly's neck had been broken. It could well have happened by accident during a panicked scuffle.

Mark Coles was thirty-six years old, the youngest doctor to head Maplebrook in its century-and-a-half history. In the three months since his appointment as director he'd ordered all the interior walls painted, engaged a nutritionist, introduced music and television, increased the wattage of the lights, instituted recreational team sports, installed an auxiliary generator so that the inmates could stay warm during the winter when storms regularly knocked out the electricity, and paid daily visits to each of his fifty-nine patients.

But the lone prisoner in the basement was by far the most interesting of Dr. Coles' charges. He was, in fact, perhaps the most interesting human being Coles had ever met. Standing nearly seven feet tall, with black hair that grew past his shoulders and an Elizabethan-style goatee, he would have been physically imposing even had he possessed an ordinary mind.

But nothing about the man's mind was ordinary. He was a

psychological phenomenon, for one thing, a confessed killer who felt neither remorse nor a need to justify his crimes; yet he was unfailingly charming, a man whom Dr. Coles, in other circumstances, would have cultivated as a personal friend.

And although he would not speak about his crimes or his past, the man was completely forthcoming about neutral subjects. He was prodigiously knowledgeable about history, geography, biology, anatomy—naturally, Coles thought, given the nature of the man's artwork—weather, comparative religions, physics, chemistry, English literature, mathematics, medicine, and art, both Eastern and Western.

He spoke eight languages fluently, knew enough to get by in twelve others, and read in fifteen, including ancient Greek, Old and Middle English, late Celtic, and Egyptian hieroglyphic.

He had no interest, however, in anything mechanical. Coles warmed with amusement when he remembered the patient's first encounter with the lid of a paste pot. Others, he explained, had always opened and closed containers for him.

He had never driven a car nor operated a washing machine. He had never purchased anything from a vending machine. He could use a telephone, but usually left the receiver dangling when the conversation was over. He could not type. His handwriting was flowing and elegant.

Occasionally he played chess with Dr. Coles. He always won, usually within minutes, but sometimes he deliberately ignored one of Coles' blunders in order to draw the game out toward some dazzling endgame. It was on these occasions that Coles felt he was making real progress with the man, although he often wondered after these sessions why he, the doctor, was suffused with a feeling of privilege after being beaten in a game of chess by a diagnosed psychopath.

Still, the games were fascinating, and Coles sensed they were an avenue into the man's extraordinarily complex personality. With the right approach and the sensitive direction of a gifted therapist, the doctor was sure, that genius might yet be coaxed into productivity.

Coles whistled a tune to announce himself as he carried a folding card table down the basement corridor. The artist, sitting ramrod-straight in his chair, gave no indication of having heard him.

"Are you married?" Coles asked cheerfully.

The man looked up from his book and smiled. Even seated, he was so tall that his eyes were almost level with the doctor's.

Coles shrugged as he set up the small table just outside the bars of the cell and arranged a chessboard and playing pieces atop it. He always began his visits that way, with a disarming question which his patient was not likely to answer.

*What is your real name? Who were your parents? How did you earn a living? What games did you play as a child? What is your favorite food? How many women have you made love to?* Anything, anything to open the door to that hidden, vulnerable person behind the prodigious intellect and the bestial instinct to kill.

From the beginning, the man had ignored every question. Coles had nearly given up hope that he would ever answer one. Yet, perhaps someday . . .

"Yes," the man said.

Coles looked up, dropping one of the chess pieces. "I beg your pardon?"

"You asked if I was married. I was. At least a hundred times. But I do not remember any of their names."

Coles blinked. It was a lie, of course, but why? For its shock value? Surely a man who had murdered twenty-three people and then covered their still-warm bodies with plaster could come up with a bigger stunner than that.

He bent slowly to retrieve the fallen piece, a pawn. True or false, he knew, the statement had been terribly important. It was the first chink in the patient's psychological armor. He was beginning to trust the doctor.

"When was the last time?" Coles asked casually as he took a small notebook from his shirt pocket. *Don't frighten him, now*, he told himself. *Let him talk.*

"I believe it was in Mexico. She was a lovely creature, although rather stupid. But fecund."

"Is she alive?" Coles asked.

"Oh, my, no."

*Of course not. She's in a glass case in some art collector's parlor.* "Did you kill her?"

The tall man's eyes narrowed in thought. "No. I don't believe so. I did kill her parents, though. Tiresome people." He came out of his reverie with a smile. "That was some time ago, you understand."

Coles nodded uncertainly. "You said your wife was, ah . . ." He checked his notes. "Fecund. You have children, then?"

"Descendants."

"As you wish. How many descendants do you have?"

"Thousands, I imagine," the patient said with a shrug.

Coles exhaled. Sometimes he almost forgot that the inmates here were insane.

"Do you ever see them?"

"Of course. They are obligated to me by blood."

"But you've had no visitors."

The man half-closed his eyes. "I have not summoned them yet."

"I see," Coles said.

"By the way, I have a name."

Coles sucked in a rush of air. "What is it?" he asked softly.

"Saladin." He spoke the name slowly, aware that he was giving the doctor a gift.

"Is Saladin your first name?"

"It is my entire name."

Coles looked into his patient's eyes for a long moment, then wrote the name down. "Why have you decided to speak with me?" he asked at last.

"I want another cell."

Coles tented his fingers beneath his chin and nodded.

"I said I want another cell. There are rats down here. I dislike rodents."

"Do they frighten you in any specific—"

"Stop playing psychiatrist, you ass." Saladin's long fingers splayed out, just once, as if taking the first preliminary stretch before reaching out to strangle the doctor.

Coles flattened himself against the back of his chair. The move had been instinctive, a reaction to the lightning intensity of the man on the opposite side of the bars.

When Saladin spoke again, his voice was calm. "My name is of value to you, Dr. Coles."

Coles picked up the notepad which had fallen to the floor as he assumed a more casual posture, trying to erase the image of bald fear he had shown a moment before. "What do you—" He cleared his throat. "What do you mean?"

"Do you publish?"

"Well, I—"

"Probably not," Saladin answered for him. "You can't be very well regarded in your field if you've ended up here so early in your career." He observed the doctor flush. "Listen to me. I'm going to be here for the rest of my life, but you don't have to be. I'll cooperate with you. I'll tell you everything about myself—my past, my childhood, the murders . . . anything you want to know. I'll permit any kind of testing, if you wish to study me. My name alone will get you into the newspapers. A monograph on my case will make your reputation. Afterward, you'll be offered positions in the best universities and have a lucrative private practice on the side." He crossed his arms in front of him. "You can leave the loony bin, Doctor," he said in a whisper. His eyes were laughing.

Coles ground his teeth together. How was it that this mental patient could see through to the very heart of him?

"The lower level of this building has been designated the maximum security wing," Coles said, hearing the trace of pomposity in his own voice.

"Has any of my behavior, in your opinion, warranted my being kept in maximum security?"

"According to your file—"

"I asked for your opinion, Doctor, based on your own

observations. Not for a recitation of the prejudices of some quack who once worked here."

Coles did not answer.

"Have you read anything—anything at all—in the reports issued about me by your staff during the past four years to indicate I have been anything but an exemplary inmate?"

Silence. Coles was thinking. A monograph on Saladin— and of course he would insist upon knowing the man's real name—would put Mark Coles' name in the annals of psychiatry. A donship at Oxford. A practice on Harley Street.

"This is your only chance, Dr. Coles," Saladin said. "A warm room on an upper floor. That is all I ask in exchange for my information."

"I'll have to—"

"If you tell me you'll have to discuss this with some board or other, I'll never give you any further information about myself. I promise you that."

"Saladin—"

"*Now*, Dr. Coles." His black eyes were like a doll's, unblinking and hard.

"I . . ." Coles sighed. "All right. We can do that."

"Tomorrow."

"Yes. Tomorrow."

Saladin smiled. Through the bars he extended his long, slender hand and moved the white king's pawn. "Your move, Doctor," he said smoothly.

He won the game in ten minutes.

At 2:45 A.M., long after the doctor had left, a night orderly walked through the building to check the patients in their cells.

His name was Hafiz Chagla. He had been working at Maplebrook for eight months. Before that, he had worked as an electrician. Chagla was a squat young man in his late twenties, with flat feet and an inner tube of fat around his middle. His face was not particularly memorable, except for one thing which would not have been noticeable to any but the most trained and discerning of observers.

His eyes looked exactly like Saladin's.

Nobody in the asylum had noticed that.

As Chagla arrived in the basement, he passed Saladin's cell and looked inside deferentially, as if searching for a door to knock or a bell to ring.

Saladin glanced up from the Urdu volume. On the pocket on its inside front cover was stamped the date 6/1. On page 61 of the text were a number of scattered pencil dots. One of the assistants at the Bournemouth library, an Algerian named Hamid Laghouat, had put them there.

Mr. Laghouat had been working at the library for nearly four years, the same length of time Saladin had spent at the Towers. Before that, he had been a linguist at the University of Algiers.

He also had Saladin's eyes.

Each pencil dot on page 61 was below a letter in the Urdu alphabet. When the marked letters were written down consecutively, they formed a message.

Saladin did not need to write anything down. As his eyes scanned the page, they saw the message at once. Translated, it read:

> All is in place.
> Bless your name.

Four years. It had taken four years for him to receive that message.

Saladin nodded. The guard returned the gesture, but it looked more like a bow.

# CHAPTER THREE

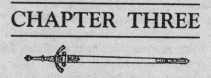

The steamy midtown air smelled somehow of meat—maybe from the sidewalk food vendors—and it nauseated Hal. He walked frantically, without direction, only wanting to get away, first from the frightening image in the mirror of the filthy room he now called his home, and now from the awful putrescent city smells that surrounded him.

His head pounded. If he'd had a dollar and a half, he would have gone directly into Benny's across the street from the transient hotel where he lived and ordered a shot of whiskey. But he had no money left, and while there had been a time when Benny would have fronted him the drink, those days were over. Benny weighed three hundred and twenty pounds, and he didn't have to toss you into the garbage cans in the alley very often before you got the point that you weren't welcome in his place without some ready cash.

As it was, his best bet was O'Kay's, a yuppie hangout way the hell uptown with enough ferns to choke Alan Alda. He couldn't get credit there, of course, but a Greek pimp named Dimitri Soskapolis sometimes dropped in for lunch around two or three in the afternoon, and he might be good for a short loan. Hal had fixed Soskapolis' Jaguar a couple of times, and the Greek swore he'd never let another mechanic touch it again.

So he owed him, Hal figured. At least a ten. For a couple of days.

Maybe.

As he walked, the scenery on Broadway changed from the peep shows and welfare dumps of his own neighborhood to the grand office buildings of respectable Manhattan, where young men with expensive haircuts traveled in herds and the women wore sneakers with their silk business suits.

It was lunchtime. The streets were packed with people in a hurry, striding incuriously between a glut of exotic street vendors, seedy-looking men slapping their thighs with pamphlets advertising massage parlors, earnest women passing out pink brochures with "PREGNANT?" on their covers, hucksters delivering their pitches while wearing miniature umbrellas on their heads, exhibitionists jerking off in the crowd, keys and change jingling, and pickpockets so deft that only a trained eye could spot them.

Hal watched one of them at work while he strolled. The thief was an Asian teenager, fifteen or sixteen years old. Good hands. He'd been trained by an expert, maybe even Johnny Chan, by the looks of his technique. Chan, who had begun picking pockets in Hong Kong back in the late forties, was a master of the art. Now in rich retirement in New York City, he supplemented his income by playing Fagin to a tribe of immigrant street urchins.

The kid was circling behind him. Hal kept walking, but he felt the intense, almost electrified presence of the boy's fear coming closer to him.

*Christ, he's not going to try me, is he?* he thought wearily.

Then he felt the hand go into his trousers pocket, fast as a bird in flight.

*Today of all days, with the mother of all hangovers . . .* He slapped his hand over the kid's wrist.

The boy dropped the wallet, his hand caked with debris from the inside of Woczniak's pocket. A crushed maraschino cherry dusted with loose cigarette tobacco dangled from his thumb.

"*Zhulo!*" the boy said, the look on his face changing in an instant from surprise at his capture to pure disgust.

"Don't mess with me in daylight," Hal said.

The kid let loose with a stream of angry singsong Vietnamese as he struggled to wriggle free. Hal picked up his wallet. Then, holding the kid by his collar, he brought the boy's face in contact with his own sticky hand and rubbed them together.

"*Dung lai. Dung lai,*" the boy shrieked. Stop! Stop! He was South Vietnamese, Hal realized. The youth had pronounced it as "Yung lie." North Vietnamese said "Zung lie."

"*Di mau,*" Hal snarled back. "Beat it." He laughed and pushed the boy away, sending him reeling down the sidewalk. "Give my regards to Johnny Chan," he called out after him.

The boy turned around long enough to give him the finger. As he did, he barreled full force into an elderly gentleman walking with a cane. The old man's feet seemed to slide out from under him. He fell on his back with a whoosh of expelled breath as the kid disappeared into a subway stairway.

Hal winced. A fall like that had most likely broken every bone in the old man's body. He bent over him to look for signs of life.

"You okay, Pop?" he asked softly.

The ancient eyes fluttered open.

"Take it easy. I'm going to get an ambulance for you."

"Quite unnecessary," the old man said with a smile. He sat up.

"Hey, maybe you'd better wait . . ."

"Nonsense. Where's my cane?" he demanded in impeccable King's English.

Hal retrieved it for him. When he got back a moment later, a fat man eating a hot dog was bent over the old gentleman.

"General bodily injuries, right?" the fat man said, wiping mustard from his chin with a paper napkin.

"I beg your pardon?"

"Here, take it." He handed him a business card. "That's LaCosta and LaCosta. Legal representation, easy payment terms. You definitely got a case here."

"Get lost, hairball," Hal said.

LaCosta took another bite of his hot dog. "Get this bozo's name," he mumbled, jerking his head toward Hal in a spray of crumbs before waddling away. "He's a witness."

Hal helped the old man to his feet. "Look, I'm sorry," he said. "The kid was running from me, but I didn't knock you down." He looked down the street at the retreating figure of Attorney-at-law LaCosta. "Besides, it wouldn't do any good to sue me."

"I'm planning nothing of the kind." The old man sprang to his feet with surprising agility. "There!" he said, grinning broadly. "Good as new." LaCosta's card sailed away, lost in the wake of a passing bus.

"Bertram Taliesin." The old man tipped his homburg.

Hal rubbed his hands together, afraid of soiling the exquisitely clean old gentleman with his touch. "Uh, Hal Woczniak. Listen, if you want, I'll take you to a hospital to get checked out. I mean, you look okay, but you can never tell."

"Oh, I'm in far too much of a hurry for that." He took a gold pocket watch on a chain from his vest. "In fact, I'm afraid I may already be late for my appointment, and I'm not quite sure where it is. Would you be familiar with the CBS building, Mr. Woczniak?"

"CBS? Sure, it's in Rockefeller Center. Just go east to Sixth—they call it the Avenue of the Americas on the street signs—then up to Fifty-second. Big black building. You can't miss it."

Taliesin frowned. "Go up to American Avenue . . ."

"Avenue of the Americas. Two long blocks up."

"Long blocks?"

"Blocks. Regular blocks, only they're longer than most. Then turn left, heading uptown."

"East, that is."

"No, north. You want to go uptown."

"But you said east."

"You'll *be* east," Hal said. He felt his headache returning.

The old man shook his head. "No, no, no. I remember distinctly that the letter said midtown Manhattan, not eastern Manhattan, not northern Manhattan. 'Midtown Manhattan, the core of the Big Apple.' "

The headache had come back full force. "This *is* mid-town,"

Hal explained. "Midtown's small. It's laid out on a grid . . . Oh, never mind. I'll take you there myself."

"Well, that's bloody decent of you," the old man said.

Hal spat onto the sidewalk. "Think nothing of it."

The old man fairly bounded across Broadway, with Hal struggling to catch up with him. "I'm going to one of your television game shows," he chattered amiably. " 'Go Fish!' "

"What?"

" 'Go Fish!' That's the name of the show. Have you seen it?"

"I don't have a TV," Hal said. *And if I did, I'd sell it for a drink just about now*, he added silently.

"Oh, it's delightful." The old man chuckled. "I watched it the last time I was in this country, visiting some Indian ruins in New Mexico. Laughed myself silly. So when I found I'd be coming to New York, the first thing I did was to write for a ticket. I've got a personal letter from the producer right here." He patted the front pocket on his perfectly tailored jacket.

"Uh," Hal said, his eyes lingering on a Sabrett stand. The air had dissipated his nausea, and his stomach, if not his brain, realized that it hadn't contained anything solid or nonalcoholic in a number of days.

"I say!" Taliesin whirled suddenly to face him. "Perhaps we could arrange for two seats!" His eyes were gleaming.

Hal could not think of anything he would rather do less than watch a taping of a game show called "Go Fish!" "No, no, really," he mumbled. "It's probably all sold out, anyway."

"Do you think so?"

"Oh, yeah." He nodded emphatically. "A hot show like that—you've got to get a reservation early, no question about it." He steered the old man away from the street corner, where two preppy college-age boys were trying vainly to give away free tickets to any number of midday game shows.

"Sir," one of the boys called out.

"Shut it, kid," Hal said. He looked over to Taliesin and smiled. "Probably muggers."

The old man looked back in confusion. "But they didn't seem—"

"There's the CBS building, right over there."

"Oh, I do wish you could come along," Taliesin said. "I owe you something for helping me after my fall."

*Did you hear me refuse money?* Hal thought. But he said, "Forget about it. Enjoy the show." He walked the old man up to the main entrance. A sign reading GO FISH! USE EXPRESS ELEVATOR stood on a portable stand in the lobby. Below it was a hand-lettered add-on. It said 6/1 FREE LUNCH TODAY.

"Hey, look at that," Hal said, hearing his stomach growl. "You hit the jackpot. Lunch and everything."

"Oh, good heavens!" The old man reeled backward.

Hal swooped in to catch him. "What? What is it? Lie down. Christ, I knew I should have taken you to the hospital . . ."

"No, no, it's not my health," he said, wriggling out of his grasp. "It's June the first."

"It is? I mean, so what?"

"I have an appointment with the curator of the Museum of Natural History on June the first at half past twelve." He took out his pocket watch again. "Oh, dear, it's half past now."

"The Natural History museum's way up in the West Seventies," Hal said.

"I'd best get a taxi, then."

Hal looked up the one-way street. Traffic was moving at a crawl. "That's not going to be so easy this time of day," he said.

The old man muttered something unintelligible and appeared to hold his breath. His face turned beet red.

"Hey, take it easy," Hal said. "You find a phone, you give this guy a call . . ."

Taliesin made a loud popping sound with his mouth. "That ought to take care of things," he said.

"You feeling okay?"

At that moment, the near lane of traffic suddenly cleared with the exception of a yellow taxi speeding toward them. Taliesin held up his cane, and the cab stopped.

"Works every time," he said with a grin as he opened the door.

"I'll be damned," Hal whispered. "A Checker, too."

"Oh, Mr. Woczniak." Taliesin took something from his jacket and pressed it into Hal's hand. It was made of paper. Soft paper. Soft and folded into a roll. Oh, yes.

"For your trouble. Please."

"Oh, no, I couldn't."

"I insist."

Benny's was calling to him. "Well . . ."

"Jolly good meeting you," the old man called as he slammed the door.

The cab sped away. Within seconds, the lane was again jammed up with cars.

Hal shook his head and laughed, then remembered the bill the old man had placed in his hand.

Screw Dimitri Soskapolis. Screw Benny. He was going to Gallagher's for a steak and a highball. Happy days were here again.

He looked at it. It wasn't money. It was a ticket to "Go Fish!", worn and crumpled after months of loving fondling.

"Sheesh," Hal muttered, truly understanding the meaning of despair.

He was about to throw it away when a sudden strong breeze toppled the sign in the lobby. It crashed onto the marble floor with an ear-splitting clang.

FREE LUNCH TODAY, it said.

Hal sighed. Well, what the hell. Nobody else was going to give him a free lunch.

# CHAPTER FOUR

Hal took the elevator up to the top floor, where a harried-looking security guard was checking the tickets of last-minute audience members pushing to get to their seats before the start of the show.

Hal flashed his ticket at the guard. "Where's lunch?" he asked.

"After the show," the guard said, scanning Hal with an air of disgust.

"You're kidding. You mean I have to sit through the whole thing?"

The guard wrinkled up his nose. "Yeah. And somebody's got to sit through it next to you. Keep moving."

Hal looked at the clock on the wall. Still an hour and a half before the Greek pimp would show up at O'Kay's. If he showed up at all.

He evaluated his options. True, "Go Fish!" was probably as entertaining as walking behind a flatulent horse, but the room was air-conditioned, there were comfortable seats inside, and nobody said he had to stay awake. Besides, the prospect of a hot meal in the CBS cafeteria was looking better all the time. With a shrug, he went into the studio and slinked over to a seat near the back as the curtain rose to reveal a stage set designed to look like a dilapidated hillbilly farm.

Hal had, in fact, heard of the show, as had nearly everyone in the country. "Go Fish!" was a phenomenon in the television industry, an incredibly corny game show featuring a hillbilly theme, impossibly difficult questions, and cruel stunts designed to humiliate the contestants who failed to answer correctly.

The stunts were clearly the highlight of the show and the

reason for its runaway success. From its beginnings as a local program in Birmingham, Alabama, TV audiences were entranced by the sight of middle-aged women and game old gentlemen wrestling with rubber cows or wading through vats of mud as punishment for failing to name the major weaknesses of the Weimar Republic. As the show went national, the stunts became more varied, although no less sadistic, and its regional host was replaced by a slick game-show veteran carefully dressed and made up to look like a mountain man.

The mishmash of elements in the show was weird but mesmerizing, and the fact that "Go Fish!" was broadcast live gave it an edge that shot it to the top of the daytime ratings almost immediately. Now, two years after its nationwide debut, it was already in syndication, and taped repeats of the show were aired several times a day.

Hal could not have avoided seeing it if he'd tried. At 12:30 P.M., every television in every saloon in Manhattan was tuned to "Go Fish!". And now, he thought with a sigh, his degenerate ways had finally reduced him to sitting through an actual segment. He closed his eyes and tried to sleep.

Seconds later, he was awakened by the din of strummed banjos blaring over the loudspeakers to usher in the show's host, a toothy urbanite named Joe Starr whose manner was completely at odds with the overalls and tattered straw hat he was wearing. Despite the fact that audiences had watched him for years on a number of other shows, Starr affected a Southern drawl while he explained the rules of the game.

Participants, he twanged, were selected from the audience at random, their seat numbers having been placed in a device known as the Rain Barrel at the center of the stage. When their numbers were called, contestants were given the chance to win fabulous prizes by answering "some itty bitty questions ever'body ought to know." The audience laughed.

"And if you don't answer 'em right, why then . . ." Joe Starr shrugged elaborately as the banjo music was replaced by the sound of chickens squawking. "You know what that means, folks."

A dummy dressed in a man's suit flew across the stage

behind Starr. The chicken squawks were drowned out by the sound of water splashing as the dummy landed offstage. The audience cheered. Starr pretended to wipe something out of his eye.

None of the first three contestants answered even one question correctly and were immediately smeared with cream pies, forced to chase a pig through a vat of gelatin or dunk one another in tubs of grapes in a quest for a brand-new frost-free refrigerator and fifty square feet of parquet flooring.

Hal settled back into his seat and folded his arms over his chest as he felt himself drifting. At least the music had stopped, and in his condition, the audience noise didn't disturb him much.

"Doesn't look like we got too many geniuses in the audience today," Joe Starr said, shaking his head as if it were perched on the end of a spring.

"Well, let's find a new contestant in the Rain Barrel, okeydokey?"

Hal half-heard the applause from the audience and the wobbling of some mechanical device onstage. He could smell himself, a combination of stale liquor and ancient sweat. His head felt as if bombs were exploding inside it. His hair, he thought briefly, hadn't been cut—or combed, for that matter—in weeks. His breath felt as if it were about to ignite.

"Two fifty-one!".

Benny's. That was where he would spend the evening. A few quiet hours, maybe watch the Mets on TV. No women. It was always too rough the morning after when a woman was involved.

"Seat number two fifty-one?"

Soskapolis owed him. That's the attitude. *Hey, Dimitri, you rich Greek bastard!*

A hand touched his shoulder. He opened one red eye. A gorgeous redhead in a Daisy Mae push-up halter and a minuscule pair of denim shorts beamed at him.

"Your seat number's been called, sir," she said through her immovable smile.

"What?"

"Here he is!" the redhead shouted cheerily, waving and bouncing up and down.

Hal followed the movement of her bosom with interest. In another moment, an equally ravishing blonde was also in the aisle beside him.

"No, no thanks," he said.

They ignored him, pulling and prodding him with the expertise of downtown bouncers until he was on his feet.

"Come on down!" Joe Starr called out. The audience applauded. A thousand banjos strummed.

"Shit," Hal muttered. As if his life weren't bad enough, he was now about to be terrorized on national television.

Onstage, Joe Starr clapped him on the back. "Howdy, pardner," he roared into Hal's ear. "What's your name?"

"Woczniak," Hal said.

"Whoa, Nellie. How's about a name old Joe can say?"

"Hal," Hal said.

"Now that's better. Where you from, Hal?"

"West Side."

"Oh, a real New Yorker, eh?"

" 'S'right."

"I see we got a man of few words here," Joe Starr said. "Ready to play 'Go Fish!'?"

"I'd rather go back to my seat."

Joe Starr led the audience in laughter. "This man looks like he's had a heck of a rough night, ladies and gentlemen." His head waggled precariously.

"Okay, Hal, I don't want to get you riled up. Know how to play the game? A hundred dollars for every *kee*-rect answer. Five *kee*-rect answers, and you win the Grand Prize. And just what is that Grand Prize, you may ask?"

At that moment, accompanied by "oohs" from the audience, a curtain opened to reveal a giant blow-up of Big Ben atop St. Stephen's Cathedral.

"A fabulous two-week, all-expenses-paid trip to London!" Starr boomed. "How's that sound, Hal?"

"Okay." He picked some mucus out of his eye.

"I can tell you're all excited."

"Yeah." *Let's get this over with*, he thought.

"Think you can answer all five questions?"

"Dunno."

"If you can't, you're going to be doing some fancy stepping up here, you know that?"

"Uh."

"Want to check and see if your heart's still beating, Hal?"

Laughter from the audience.

"He's going to wake up any minute, folks."

More laughter.

"Can we get on with this?" Hal said.

"He's alive!"

Applause.

"Okay, Hal, you're a good sport. Ready for the first question?"

"I guess so."

"Okay, then." Starr held up his hands as if conducting an orchestra.

"Go Fish!" the audience shouted in unison as the two beautiful girls who had forced him out of his seat jiggled onstage. They were pushing what looked like a well. It was made of Styrofoam and painted to resemble weathered wood, with the words Ole Fishing Hole scrawled across the front in antic letters. Inside was a wire-mesh basket half-filled with little pastel-colored plastic fish.

Joe Starr handed Hal a fishing pole of sorts. On the handle was a lever that manipulated a clip at the end of a long steel tube which served as the line. "Now you just dip that in the Ole Fishing Hole wherever you want, Hal, and pull us up a fish. Got that?"

Obediently, Hal extracted a pink fish. Joe Starr plucked it off the clip and opened it to reveal a small white envelope.

"Here's the question, folks," he said as he pulled a card out of the envelope. He read it silently, then laughed and placed an apologetic hand on Hal's shoulder. "Now, before I do this, I just want you to know I don't write these, okay?"

More audience laughter.

"You ready, Hal?"

"Yeah, yeah," Hal said wearily. "Go ahead." Unconsciously he squeezed his eyes shut in a grimace.

Starr cleared his throat, then read: "According to Malory, who was the legendary knight of the Round Table who actually found the Holy Grail and died with it in his possession?" He shook his head as if he were the clapper in a bell. "Well, I got to say that ain't something you read in the *National Enquirer* every day. Want me to repeat the question?"

"Re . . . no," he said, his voice hoarse with wonder. Weird as it was, he knew the answer to the question. "Galahad."

"Galahad is *kee*-rect!" Joe Starr shouted, slapping Hal on the back.

Banjo music swelled to an ear-splitting level. The two buxom women ran onstage to kiss Hal. The audience cheered.

"Now, how the Sam Hill did you know that, Hal?" Starr asked as the music died down.

Hal shrugged.

"Well, you just won yourself a hundred bucks, old buddy." He slapped a bill into Hal's hand.

It was not a real hundred-dollar bill. It was a certificate with a form on the reverse side. "Balls," Hal said, but his comment was drowned out by a new surge of music.

"Well, that's all the time we got today, folks. Hal's going to be back tomorrow, though, so you make sure you're on hand to watch him . . ."

"*Go Fish!*" the audience shouted.

Joe Starr waved to the camera.

"What do you mean, I'll be back tomorrow?" Hal asked crankily.

"You want the hundred, don't you?" Starr said from the side of his mouth, still grinning and waving.

"Yeah . . ."

The camera's red light went off.

"You don't get the money till your run is over," Starr said without a trace of Southern accent.

He walked into the wings. Hal followed him.

"How long's that going to take?"

Starr turned to face him. "Tomorrow. Count on it. And for God's sake, take a shower." He jerked his thumb at a young man wearing a ponytail. "Tell our contestant the rules about coming on for a second day."

The young man sniffed. "Got to change your shirt," he said.

"All right, all right," Hal said. As he left the studio theater, someone handed him a paper bag. It contained a chicken sandwich with a strip of wilted lettuce and a plastic cup half-filled with Hawaiian Punch.

"Enjoy," the security guard said.


Hal ate his lunch on a bench in Rockefeller Center, reliving his small triumph. Who would ever have thought that jerk would ask him about the knights of the Round Table?

He almost laughed aloud. They had been his first love. Ever since two broken legs in the fourth grade had forced Hal to read for pleasure, his alternate universe had been populated by the likes of Sir Launcelot and Gawain the Green Knight and young Perceval. They had become like friends to him, and more. They were the men who had raised him, with their code of chivalry, their ideals of courage and faith.

Hal's mother had died in the accident that broke his legs. A hit-and-run up on East 115th Street. She was spending the food money to see some fortune-teller in Spanish Harlem and had dragged Hal along, despite his protests.

"Didn't I tell you? Didn't I tell you she'd see that halo thing over your head, same as me?" she had asked him after they left.

"Jeez, Ma," Hal whispered, blushing horribly as two pretty girls chattering in Spanish passed them crossing the street.

His mother laughed and swung her beefy arm around his neck, further mortifying him. "I seen it since you was a baby,

Harold, and I always knew it was magic. Your life's going to be something special, believe me."

"Will you cut it out?" He wriggled away from her grasp. "She's a phony, Ma. She tells that to everybody. That's how she gets you to give her money."

"What do you know? You don't know nothing." She swatted him. "You're going to grow up to be President. Or a millionaire. Something. I seen it since you was a . . ."

"Ma!"

But the car was already careening toward them by then, moving too fast for either of them to get out of the way. Hal took a glancing blow that broke his legs, but his mother was hit straight on. Hal screamed as he watched her limp body, stuffed into its heavy black coat, fly in an arc to the other side of the street.

The driver slowed down momentarily, then sped off again. He was never identified.

Hal spent most of his time alone in the Inwood walk-up he called home during the months that followed, while his father, known as Iron Mike to his cronies, spent his evenings getting into fistfights in neighborhood dives.

Mike Woczniak wasn't a bad sort, Hal would begrudgingly admit years later. Sometimes, when he remembered, he brought home hot dogs for the boy, or a cheese sandwich, or a six-pack of soda. And on good days, when he wasn't snarling with a hangover, he sometimes took Hal with him by taxi to the garage where he worked. Weighted down by the double casts, Hal would sit on a couple of crates stacked together and watch as Iron Mike worked on a car's engine with the grace and precision of a surgeon, explaining as he went the intricacies of the internal combustion engine.

If Hal hadn't graduated from high school, if he hadn't gone to CCNY or joined the Bureau, if he hadn't accomplished any of the things that had so astonished and pleased his cabbage-eating relatives, he probably would have made a first-rate mechanic. As it was, Hal's skill with cars was currently the only thing that stood between him and starvation.

But the best things to come from the bleak months after his

mother's funeral were the books. The first was T. H. White's *The Once and Future King*, dropped off by the school librarian. At first, Hal had groaned at the size of the volume, but as the long days wore on and the images on the fuzzy black-and-white television in the apartment grew less and less visible, he began to read.

It was a revelation. Here was a world of honor, of magic, of mystery and truth and bravery, and it had been *real*. From the first page, Hal had believed in Merlin's outlandish wizardry and young Arthur's special destiny to unite the world.

In time, of course, he dismissed the more farfetched legends, but he never lost his interest in the castles and heraldry of the Middle Ages and the feudal system which had saved Europe from chaos after the retreat of the occupying Romans. And he had continued reading about the knights of the Round Table long after other boys his age had turned their attention elsewhere. Gawain and Gaheris, Lucan and Bohort and Lionel, Tristam the lover, and Launcelot, the noblest and, in the end, most human of them all . . . These were the men who had shaped his life, and they never stopped being real to him. *I make thee a knight; be valiant, knight, and true!*

Even now he remembered the words of the initiation ceremony which had so entranced him when he read them in his youth. To have grown up during those times! To have fought with the great men whom history had made into legend!

Hal smiled. How ironic that the Ole Rain Barrel had coughed up the one question he'd been qualified to answer.

"Be valiant, knight, and true," he said aloud.

"What, mister?"

A young boy stopped in mid-sprint in front of him.

"Nothing." Hal took another bite of his sandwich.

"Hey, watch me." Instantly, with the unselfconscious arrogance which only five-year-olds possess, the boy turned a somersault on the concrete walkway.

Hal applauded as the boy thrust his arms skyward, a blob of chewing gum stuck to his hair.

"Tyler! Tyler, come here this minute!" A young mother rushed up to the boy, brushed him off mercilessly, then wrenched him away, scolding loudly.

"Don't you *ever* do that again, you hear me? You could have fallen into the ice-skating rink. And I've told you a million times not to talk to strangers."

"But he was—"

"He was a dirty man, that's what he was. It only takes a minute, Tyler . . ."

Her voice faded away into the crowd.

Hal finished his sandwich. *Well, she's right, isn't she?*

Valiant and true . . . They were nothing more than words, read long ago by a boy who had never become a knight.

He was just a dirty man now.

He crushed the sandwich's cellophane wrapper into a ball and tossed it on the ground.

# CHAPTER FIVE

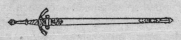

"What was the medieval English name for Scotland?"

"Albania," Hal said.

Joe Starr did a double take. He looked back at the card in his hand. "You're right." He held the card up to the audience and shrugged. "He's right, folks."

Wild banjo music played. Daisy and Mae, as Hal had come to think of the two generously endowed hostesses of "Go Fish!", slinked onstage to embrace him. The audience cheered, although not so loudly as before. They had come to watch zany sight gags, not an intellectual question-and-answer show. Joe Starr shot Hal a wary look out of the corner of his eye.

After the noise quieted, Starr pointed Hal to the Ole Fishing Hole again.

"Let's try this one," he said.

"Go Fish!" the audience chanted obediently.

After Hal went through the motions of retrieving an envelope from the Styrofoam well, Joe Starr opened it and frowned momentarily before resuming his Amos McCoy persona for the camera.

"Well, I'll be dipped," he drawled. "Looks like another question on medieval English history."

"Great," Hal said.

There was a mild rustle from the audience.

"Now, I got to tell you, folks, this is one heck of a coincidence, and I ain't lying. We got questions in the Ole Fishing Hole about everything under the sun, believe me, and for the same category to come up three times in a row . . ." He looked offstage at his producer. "Well, it just goes to show that lightning sometimes strikes twice. Up where I come from, we got the stills to prove it."

The producer waved him on. "Okay, Hal, old buddy. Here's the question: Before the Black Plague that devastated Europe appeared, there was another epidemic that raged through Britain. What was it?"

A loud clock began ticking.

"The Yellow Plague," Hal said.

Joe Starr signaled for the clock to stop. "What's that, Hal?"

"The Yellow Plague."

"By gum, that's it!"

"It came from Persia . . ." Hal began, but the raucous banjo music drowned him out.

"Be right back after a word from our sponsors," Joe shouted, extending his hand to Hal.

He dropped it as soon as the red light on the camera went out. "What the hell's going on here?" he demanded.

"Hey, it's your show," Hal said. "You ask me the questions, I answer them."

"If you've been tampering with these cards, buddy . . ."

"Look, butthead . . ."

"You're on!" the producer rasped from the wings.

Starr plastered a smile on his face and slapped Hal on the back, hard. "Well, folks," he said, "it looks like Hal here is on one heck of a roll, wouldn't you say?"

There was some desultory clapping from the audience. A few people booed.

"You've got three *kee*-rect answers. Two more, and you win an all-expenses-paid trip to London, England!"

He waited for an audience response, but there was none.

"So what do you say, Hal? Dip that pole down into the Ole Fishing Hole and . . ." He waited.

"Go fish," a few spectators said flatly.

Hal poked the fishing rod into the receptacle, pulled up a green fish, and waited for Joe Starr to take it.

"Just wondering, Hal," Starr asked as he fondled the envelope. "What happens if this is a question about rocket science?"

"Then I guess you get to throw a pie in my face," Hal said. The audience cheered.

"Oh, it'll be worst than that," Starr said with a grin. "Lordie, yes." He tore open the seal and took out the card. "Uh . . ." He tried a smile. "It's another question about Medieval English history."

The audience got to its feet, hissing and catcalling.

"This show is fixed!" someone shouted.

Joe Starr did his best to calm them down. "Whoa, there," he said with false heartiness. "Wait'll you hear this one, friends and neighbors. It's a doozy. Ready, Hal?"

"Shoot."

"Scam!" someone screeched.

Starr wiggled his head confidently. "The Western world's first tragedy, *Gorboduc* . . ." He pronouced it Gore-bow-duck. "Hey, he sounds like the Russian version of Donald."

He waited for the laugh, but there was not a sound from the audience.

"Think he knows Mikhail Mouse?"

Silence.

Starr cleared his throat. "Okay, Hal, this play *Gorboduc* told the story of two ill-fated brothers. What were their names?"

Hal grinned. He'd read *Gorboduc* as a freshman in college. "Ferrex and Porrex."

"You got it," Starr said wanly.

The sound technicians drove the level of the canned banjo music up to maximum in an effort to drown out the shouts from the audience, to no avail. The spectators were leaving their seats, marching up to the stage in protest. Daisy and Mae, en route to the contestant for their ritual kiss, suddenly turned and ran offstage, out of the way of the grim-faced army of advancing audience members being held at bay by the stage crew. The show's producer, with a telephone in his hand, motioned to Starr from the wings.

"We're going to take a little break here, folks, and when we come back, we're gonna . . ." Joe Starr put his hand to his ear, beckoning the audience to shout the name of the show. "Go . . ." he prompted.

"Go shit in your hat!" someone offered.

The producer rushed onstage and huddled frantically with Starr. Afterward, he approached Hal.

"Hi, Hal. Frank Morton. I'm the producer." He held out a clammy hand. "Look, we're going to switch to another contestant," he said, the sweat visible on his forehead. "The FCC's on its way."

"Oh, Christ," Joe Starr moaned.

Morton ignored him. "We've got a room where you can wait for them," he told Hal calmly.

"What for?"

"Because they think the game is rigged, you jerk," Starr blustered. "Oh, God. God."

"Take it easy, Joe," Morton said.

"Take it *easy?* Don't you understand? This is the frigging *Sixty-four Thousand Dollar Question* all over again!"

"No, it's not." The producer was struggling to keep his voice low. "This show is a hundred percent on the level, Joe, and you know that as well as I do."

"Then how'd this guy answer those questions?"

They both looked at Hal. "Just knew them," he said with a shrug.

"Just knew them? Four in a row?"

"Hey, it's a game, Jack. Somebody's got to win sometime."

"Okay, that's enough." Morton took off his glasses and wiped his face. "I'm sure there's nothing to worry about. It's just that with a live show, there are bound to be glitches once in a while . . ."

"Glitches! This is my career, Frank!"

"We'll talk later," Morton said. He motioned to the big guy with the ponytail to come take Hal away.

"You're dead, shitface," Joe Starr muttered.

Hal laughed. "You don't look so hot yourself." He waggled his head in a parody of the show host. "Old buddy."

Somehow Starr had managed to get the audience to sit down. On the greenroom monitor, Hal watched a man being dumped from a crane into a vat of water balloons. The audience roared with delight. The contestant had missed a question dealing with astrophysics.

Weird, Hal thought. There had to have been three or four thousand cards in that well. The odds of getting four questions in a row on the same subject were impossibly small.

And yet it had happened. Four questions on the one subject he knew anything about.

"That's not true," he said aloud. He knew other things. He knew automobile engines. He understood firearms, police procedure, a certain amount of law . . .

*Baloney. If somebody had asked you those questions a week ago, you couldn't have answered them.*

It was true. He had read *Gorboduc*, yes, but that had been more than twenty years ago. Ferrex and Porrex? Those names had been buried for two decades. Albania? Who was he kidding? He'd never even studied ancient Scotland. It might have been a footnote in a book he'd read somewhere along the line, something he'd researched for a junior-high essay, maybe . . .

*You've never heard of any Albania outside of Eastern Europe, lunkhead.*

He ran his fingers through his hair.

What had made him say *Albania*?

*And while you're being truthful, Hal, let's not forget to mention you don't know dick about any Yellow Plague.*

He reached over and turned off the television just as two men in suits entered the room.

They identified themselves as investigators for the Federal Communications Commission.

"Just a few questions, Mr . . ."

"Woczniak."

"All right. Do you realize that taking *any part* in the manipulation of results in a contest of this nature constitutes a federal offense?"

They loomed over him. "Yes," he said. "The FBI explained it all to me once."

Four hours later, when the two FCC men ran out of questions, Hal was permitted to leave the studio. Joe Starr and the producer of "Go Fish!" were on the stage with another pair of inquisitors, the contents of the Ole Fishing Hole spilled onto a table in front of them.

# CHAPTER SIX

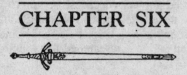

"We read every question in the barrel last night," the bleary-eyed producer told Hal the next day. "There were seven questions about medieval England in the entire she-bang. You picked four of them." He shrugged. "It was a wild coincidence, but that's all it was."

"I guess so," Hal said.

"The FCC guys want to supervise the final drawing, but that'll be the end of it." He smiled in a weary, businesslike way. "Sorry if we've put you to any trouble. The show's live, you understand . . ."

"Sure," Hal said.

"Good luck."

Hal nodded.

Morton was right, he told himself. Coincidence. That was all there was to it. A wild coincidence.

*And the wildest part was that you didn't know the answers until they came out of your mouth. But you didn't tell the FCC boys that part, did you, old buddy?*

He shook the thought away. When a man drank as much as Hal did, he reasoned, there was no telling what he did or didn't know. Things happened to your brain. You heard things, read things . . . For all he knew, he might have spent the past year reading up on medieval history after he'd drunk himself into a stupor at Benny's.

Speaking of which, Hal figured some of the old gang had probably heard of his TV success by now. A snippet of tape from yesterday's show had appeared on the evening news. It showed a swarm of angry people leaving the studio. A smiling man declared confidently that the fix was in. An irate woman blamed the government. The same news item showed

Hal, looking even more scroungy than he'd felt, pronouncing the names "Ferrex and Porrex."

*No wonder they think the game's crooked*, he thought, appraising his own image. Not that it would make a whit of difference in his circle of acquaintances; the guys at Benny's would be delighted that Hal had found a new way to steal money.

He could almost hear them all laughing around the bar, discussing Hal's relative indebtedness to each of them and the methods they would use to collect. He wouldn't have touched Benny's last night with a ten-foot pole.

Or at least that was the reason he gave himself for not going for a drink. He hadn't had a drink in two days.

"Ready, Hal?" The guy with the ponytail escorted him backstage as banjo music played. While Hal waited to go on, Joe Starr explained the presence of the FCC men onstage, although everyone in the country knew by now that this episode of "Go Fish!" would be under close scrutiny. "Revenooers," Joe called the two intimidating men who stood behind him like pieces of scenery.

Starr had objected strenuously at first to being monitored by Feds on the air, but after learning that the television audience for "Go Fish!" would be the largest in the show's history, he acquiesced. After all, Frank Morton told him, the news stories about yesterday's near-riot had boosted the show's visibility by a thousand percent.

"Are you ready for Hal?" Starr shouted.

The audience sounded as if it were assembled to watch a football game. There were cheers and boos, pneumatic horns, whistles, banners proclaiming Hal a genius, and others calling for his arrest.

"Come on out, old buddy!"

The FCC men scowled as the contestant walked past them. On their instructions, Hal was dressed in a short-sleeved shirt and plain trousers with no belt.

"What do you think I'm going to do, hang myself on TV?" he had asked. The Feds had not cracked a smile.

Joe Starr, too, made little attempt to hide his dislike for the unpersonable contestant who had jeopardized his show and his career with a bizarre streak of luck.

"Now, Hal," he said in his lazy, down-on-the-farm voice, "how'd a guy like you get so interested in medieval times, anyway?"

He shrugged again. "Just liked it."

Behind him, the two FCC men regarded one another.

"Well, I got to be truthful with you, Hal. Our friends the Revenooers have gone through every question in the Ole Fishing Hole, and they tell me there are only three cards left that have anything to do with medieval English history. So it's not likely you're going to get one of them, is it?"

"Guess not."

"Think you can answer a question on another subject?"

"Fixing cars, maybe."

Joe Starr chuckled.

"Then I sincerely hope you draw a question about fixing cars, Hal." His eyes glinted malevolently above dark circles. "Because if you don't give me this one last *kee*-rect answer, I got a mighty special treat for you here on the show."

The audience cheered.

"Oh, one more thing, Hal."

Daisy and Mae came onstage, carrying a length of black silk between them. Starr waved it with a flourish. "This here's a blindfold. Care to check it, gentlemen?"

One of the FCC men ran his hands along it, held it to the light to check its opacity, then handed it back with a nod.

"Just to show our good friends the Revenooers and our studio audience that there's no way on God's earth you could be reading the answers some kinda way, we want you to put this on, Hal. That okay by you?"

"Guess so."

The two women tied the cloth around Hal's eyes.

"See anything?"

"No."

"Good enough. Are you ready, Hal?" Starr shouted.

Hal nodded.

*"GO FISH!"* The command from the audience was thun-

derous. As Hal blindly thrust the end of the fishing pole into the container, the FCC men approached to stand on either side of him. The plastic fish he selected was immediately snatched out of his hand by one of the "Revenooers," who opened and read the card inside before handing it hesitantly to Joe Starr.

"Ready for the question, Hal?"

"Guess so."

Starr took the card from the FCC man, who looked strangely ashen.

"In medieval times . . ." Starr's arm dropped. He closed his eyes. "This just can't be," he said softly, his accent forgotten.

The audience exploded. The FCC men looked at each other. One made a helpless gesture of defeat.

"Should I read this?" Starr asked them.

After a short hesitation, one of them spoke. "Yes, sir," he said quietly.

It took two minutes plus a commercial break to calm the audience.

"Now, listen up, folks. The Revenooers say it was a fair draw, and I'm here to tell you they're right."

The FCC men were roundly booed.

Joe Starr waggled his head ferociously. "Man, oh, man, Hal, all I got to say is you are one lucky son of a gun."

"Just read the question," Hal said impatiently.

Froth formed at the corners of Starr's lips. "Oh, I'm going to read it, all right. But then *you* got to answer it."

A threatening clamor rose up from the spectators.

"In medieval times, legends spoke of a silk-like substance that often appeared magically in connection with extraordinary events. What was the name ascribed to this unusual and now-lost fabric?"

A clock began ticking loudly. Hal took a deep breath. His mind was a blank.

It was a relief, in a way, not to know the answer. For the past three days he had lived in an agony of uncertainty, knowing things without knowing them, wondering how information utterly alien to him had somehow leapt into his mind like magic. Now, at least, he knew he wasn't crazy. And he was four hundred dollars to the good. Four hundred dollars, plus one pie in the face, and it was filled with pheasant, pheasant pie with bread. . . .

The cooking smells of pheasant filled the great hall, along with the music of the singer and the barking of dogs. It was strange to hear the bird then, above all the other noise, but its song was so pure and sweet that Hal looked up, and then the bird flew in the open casement . . . *my God, this is a memory* . . . with its wild song bursting out of it and it came to rest on . . . *someone else's memory, not mine* . . . It came to rest on a man's finger, someone whose face Hal could no longer see, a man who gave the bird a piece of bread. And then the cup appeared, floating above the table.

Hal gasped. *Stop it! This is not my memory! I never saw any cup.*

All of them saw it. The cup, floating in air, reminding the knights that their work was not done. Hal's knife fell noisily to the table at the sight of it, but the bird did not stir from the long finger which had become its perch. It, too, watched the cup, the Grail, appear like a rainbow in mist, draped in samite, shimmering like water . . .

"You got an answer for us, Hal?" Joe Starr barked.

The vision fell away like a broken wall.

"Draped in samite," Hal whispered.

"Say what?"

"Samite," Hal said, feeling inexplicably on the verge of tears.

"*Kee*-rect! You win a trip to London!"

The audience screamed. Banjo music began to play. Hal heard only a few notes before he fainted.

# CHAPTER SEVEN

The man who called himself Saladin squinted against the bright afternoon sun streaming through the windows in Dr. Coles' office. It was the first time in Dr. Coles' entire tenure at Maplebrook that the prisoner had been out from behind the bars of his basement cell.

"Please sit down," Coles said, gesturing to an armchair upholstered in imitation leather.

The inmate sniffed in disdain. He lifted his patrician head, making the straitjacket which encased him look like an unnecessary barbarism.

"Are my new quarters ready?" he asked softly.

"Yes." The doctor smiled. "There was no room vacant, but then during the night one of our other patients died in his sleep. A curious coincidence," Coles said.

"It is of no interest to me," Saladin said. "I would like to move into my room."

"I thought we might talk for a while first," Coles said.

"A session of soul-searching before I'm allowed into the cell, is that it?"

Coles fidgeted uncomfortably. "Something like that." Even with a distance of several feet between them, the doctor's neck felt the effects of staring up at Saladin's imposing height.

"This garment is humiliating. Please remove it."

"I can't do that."

"Bring an orderly. If I attempt anything untoward, you can have me maced and beaten before sending me back to the basement."

Coles knew the drill. His predecessor had assured him that chemical spray combined with a stiff stick was the most effective method in treating the criminally insane. Coles had hated the man from that moment.

"I've abolished the use of mace here," he said.

"How humane, Dr. Coles." There was a glint of merriment in Saladin's dark eyes.

"Cruelty is not necessary."

"Not even if a patient tries to kill you?"

"I don't believe you'll do that."

"Then take off the straitjacket."

Coles blew a noisy stream of air through his nose, thinking.

"That enlightened manner of yours is really no more than a sham, isn't it, Doctor? For all your protestations, you're scared to death of me."

"Nonsense. Now suppose we chat about something else."

Saladin laughed, a deep and rolling laugh, a sound like music. Howard Keel in *Kiss Me Kate* came to the doctor's mind. "Of course." He coiled himself into the chair gracefully. "What would you like to know?"

Coles picked up a yellow tablet and balanced it on his knee as he leaned against his desk. He was looking down on his patient now and enjoyed the vantage point. "Oh, whatever comes to mind. Your name, perhaps."

"You know that."

"I meant your full name."

"Saladin is the only name I have ever known."

"Your mother called you Saladin?"

The tall man made a dismissive gesture with his face. "Perhaps not. But I have not seen my mother since I was five years old."

"Where was that?"

Saladin thought. From his expression, it looked to be a pleasant experience, mentally reaching back to realms long forgotten. "Somewhere warm," he said finally. "The women's breasts were exposed. Tall reeds grew by the river."

"Which river?"

Saladin concentrated for a moment, then gave up with an apologetic smile. "It has been many years, Dr. Coles."

"Quite all right. Do you remember the country where you were born?"

"No. Just a few mental pictures. As I said, it was so long—"

"Yes, yes. Exactly how old are you, Saladin?"

"I've no idea."

*Extraordinary*, Coles thought. *He's negated his entire personality. Whoever "Saladin" is, this man has invented him from the whole cloth.*

"Are there large segments of your past which you don't remember?"

The patient's eyes blinked lazily. "I know what I know," he said. "Which I suppose is what I need to know at the present."

"I see," said Coles.

"Dr. Coles?"

"Yes?"

"The straitjacket," he said softly.

"I've told you. I can't . . ."

"Please." Saladin looked down at the horrid device, then his eyes met the doctor's. "A little dignity."

Coles' mouth twitched. He had always hated straitjackets. In other institutions, he had seen the look on the faces of men forced to wear them for days on end, degraded beyond hope by their helplessness.

Almost angrily he picked up the telephone. "Send in an orderly," he said.

Within minutes, a man in white hospital scrubs entered the office and stood unobtrusively by the door. With a nod to the doctor, he folded his arms over his chest.

Coles walked behind Saladin and unfastened the restraints, then quickly returned to his desk.

"Ah, much better," Saladin said as he shrugged out of the garment. He stretched his long fingers and looked at them. "Thank you, Dr. Coles."

Then, in one convulsive motion, he lunged over the desk and snaked his fingers around Coles' necktie. Before the doctor could utter a sound in protest, Saladin brought his head slamming down against the edge of the desk.

Coles gurgled, his eyes bulging. Blood poured out of the horizontal wound across his forehead, where flecks of frothy gray brain tissue oozed. His fingers twitched.

He looked up at his attacker. Saladin was watching him with intense interest, and a touch of impatience. Behind Saladin stood the orderly, his hands still crossed over his chest.

Dr. Mark Coles' last, half-formed thought was that the two men had the same eyes.

Saladin's nostrils flared. He held on to the necktie for a moment, savoring the sight of the warm, dying object at the end of it.

"Get the secretary," he said at last.

The orderly peered out the door. "Doctor wants you," he said.

Coles' secretary, a young woman with a long mane of carefully styled blonde hair, rose quickly and strode past the orderly into the office.

"Yes, Dr. Coles?"

She barely had time to notice the blood spilling in torrents from the doctor's body lying across the desk before Saladin grasped her by a handful of her hair.

She screamed. It was almost pretty, the high, sweet sound of it, but of such short duration that, heard from outside the office, it might have been a laugh. Because just as the scream left her throat, Saladin took her small golden head in his elongated hands and twisted it, his eyes half-closing at the satisfying crunch of the small cervical vertebrae as they snapped.

A stream of the girl's saliva pooled on the side of his hand. He released her with a cry of disgust.

The orderly watched the scene dispassionately and dialed the telephone. At the same time he retrieved a shirt and a pair of long trousers from a package hidden behind a bookcase in the doctor's office.

Beside the package was a cube of plastique with two small

wires running from it to an electrical socket into which a timer had been fitted. Throughout Maplebrook, on every floor and on every wing, were identical devices, ultimately hooked up to the new auxiliary generator.

The man who had supervised the installation of the generator had also had Saladin's eyes.

"Clean this off me," Saladin said. He held out his hand as if expecting it to be kissed.

Dutifully, the orderly set down the telephone and wiped the dead secretary's spittle off Saladin's hand with a tissue. Then he picked up the receiver again and spoke into it.

"Five minutes."

The lights blinked off for a moment before the auxiliary generator kicked on.

A voice on the other end of the telephone answered, "Done."

Saladin held his arms out and raised his chin, a signal that he was ready to be dressed. As the orderly unbuttoned the blue prison shirt, a car pulled up on the pavement in front of the asylum. Another followed it.

The last item the orderly gave Saladin was a golden ring with a huge opal set in the center. Carved into the stone was an image of Saladin's own face.

Three men got out of the cars and walked into the building, herding between them a tall, cadaverously thin man, dressed in the rags of a tramp. The man looked around him, uncomprehendingly, as if he were drugged.

In the lobby, one man walked up to the security desk, stationed at a T where the east and west corridors met. Behind the desk were two elevator doors.

"Name, please?" the guard asked.

The new arrival drew an automatic Beeman P-08 with a long webbed silencer from under his jacket and slammed it across the guard's forehead. The *crack* of the blow echoed through the empty marble-floored hallway. The guard slumped forward, unconscious, his head split and bleeding. He looked as if he were napping.

The other men checked both corridors as the indicators

above both elevator doors spun downward. One bell rang as the elevator reached the lobby level. The two men froze in their tracks, their guns poised to shoot.

The door opened and a couple, obviously visitors, got out. The woman was dressed in a blue, puffed-sleeve Sunday-school dress. Her eyes were swollen and red. She sniffed once, bravely, before seeing the guard bleeding at his desk.

"Darryl," she whispered, clutching the arm of the man with her.

It was all she had time to say before she too was clubbed across the skull. Reflexively, her mouth opened and closed like a fish's as her legs buckled beneath her.

Her companion wasted no time on sympathy. He plucked her convulsive fingers off his sleeve and bolted for the front door and nearly made it to the rubber mat at the entrance before one of the men caught up with him and pounded him to the floor with powerful blows to the head.

The two men herded the tall tramp into the waiting elevator car. The door closed and the car headed down to the basement level of the building.

The remaining gunman checked his watch. The second elevator stopped in the lobby and when the door opened, Saladin and the orderly got out.

The gunman bowed to Saladin. Just then the other elevator returned from the basement. This time, the two gunmen stepped off alone. The reedishly tall man was no longer with them. They too bowed to Saladin.

Then all five men headed outside. Only Saladin, with his long legs, was not running.

The cars had just passed through Maplebrook's front gates when the building ignited like a fireball.

# CHAPTER EIGHT

Five months before Maplebrook Hospital burned to the ground, just after Hal Woczniak took early retirement from the FBI and began to drink himself to death, two crack addicts robbed the safety-deposit boxes of the Riverside National Bank in a suburb of Chicago.

The thieves left the bank with nearly ten million dollars' worth of cash and jewelry but were apprehended a few blocks from the scene of the crime. The loot, which was stuffed into green plastic garbage bags, spilled out of the getaway car onto the street when the police made the arrest. All but one piece, a hollowed lump of grayish green metal which resembled a bronze art-deco ashtray, was recovered.

No one noticed the vaguely spheroid piece roll beneath the car and into the gutter, where it gained momentum on its downhill run, floated for half a block in a rivulet of melting snow, then came to rest in a heap of cigarette butts in front of a draining grate.

It was here that a ten-year-old boy named Arthur Blessing found it. He wiped off the mud with his mittens and discovered that the ball was actually more like a cup, with a scooped-out cavity and an open end. It greatly resembled the tiny handleless cups in his Aunt Emily's Japanese tea set.

The cup was warm. Even though he could see his breath in the cold January air, Arthur felt its warmth through his soggy mittens. He held it to his cheek and experienced something he could not have explained, something like the feeling he got when he hit the home run that won the game at summer camp. It felt like *belonging*.

"Emily! Emily!" he shouted as he bounded up the stairs in the apartment building where he lived.

"You never heard of an elevator, Mr. Elephant Feet?"

An old man stood inside an open doorway on the first landing. He was wearing a plaid shirt and the yellow cardigan sweater he had worn every day that Arthur had known him. His white hair stuck out in peaks around the shiny bald center of his head. His hands were spotted. They hung down at his sides, quivering in a rhythm of their own. Through the coke-bottle lenses of his glasses, his eyes looked enormous.

"Sorry, Mr. Goldberg. I hope you weren't sleeping or anything."

"Sleep, who could sleep in this apartment? Always people talking on the stairs. Two feet away is the garbage dumper. All day and night they bring their garbage, then they stop and talk. The middle of the night, it doesn't matter. You want a cookie?"

"No thanks, Mr. Goldberg."

The old man pulled an oatmeal-and-peanut-butter cookie wrapped in cellophane from his pocket. "Here. You take it. I got two from the deli. They make you buy two, even if you only want one." He bobbed his offering again. "Go ahead."

"Thanks," Arthur said.

The old man smiled.

"Want to see what I found?" Arthur took the metal ball from the pocket of his wool baseball jacket.

Mr. Goldberg examined it, lowering his glasses to peer over them while he touched the ball to his nose. "What is it, an ashtray?"

"I don't know. I found it on the street."

"It's an ashtray," Mr. Goldberg pronounced. "You don't need it." He handed it back. "How's your aunt?"

"She's okay, I guess."

"She don't go out at night."

"Not much."

Mr. Goldberg shrugged expressively. "Who can blame her, with the crime?" He craned over Arthur's head. "Sooner or later, they're going to come in here and shoot us in our beds," he shouted for the benefit of the doorman, who ignored him. "We got no protection here. What we need is police security!"

The doorman shook his head and smiled.

"Me, I could protect this building better than some they've got."

According to Aunt Emily, Mr. Goldberg and the doorman had been feuding for the past nine years, ever since the doorman had let Mr. Goldberg's daughter-in-law into the old man's apartment to clean it while he was in the hospital.

"I guess I'd better be going, Mr. Goldberg," Arthur said.

"Okay. You say hello to your aunt. She's a good girl. Very pretty. She should find a nice gentleman."

"Sure," Arthur said and rolled his eyes. "Pretty" was not a word he would use to describe his Aunt Emily. He started edging up the stairs.

"I'm not talking about me, of course."

"No, sir."

"She should find a young man. With a good job."

"Yes, sir."

"Tell her I got a nephew thirty-six years old, a lawyer. Just divorced. It was for the best, believe me." He was leaning on the railing now, shouting up at the boy's retreating form. "Tell her to see me."

"I will, Mr. Goldberg," Arthur lied. There was no way he was going to sic Aunt Emily on some unsuspecting jerk looking for a date with a normal woman. "See you in the morning," he called behind him.

The old man waved to him abstractedly as he began a new tirade against the doorman.

"I'm home, Emily," Arthur said.

His aunt was seated at the computer, with her back to him. She nodded to acknowledge his presence.

"I found something . . ."

Emily raised her right hand, her index finger pointing upward, a signal for silence.

Arthur took off his hat and mittens and placed them on the radiator. They steamed, emitting a faint, oily wool smell. He went to the refrigerator, where the evening meal was set out on two paper plates, ready for the microwave. Tonight it would be green beans and braised fennel, along with some speckled brown noodles.

Arthur groaned. Emily Blessing had become a vegetarian years ago, but since she didn't cook, she hadn't imposed her eating habits on her nephew until a meatless take-out restaurant opened two doors down from their apartment building. Now, instead of the familiar TV dinner and Dinty Moore stew which had sustained Arthur through his childhood while Emily grazed on lettuce and raw carrots behind a newspaper, he was forced to eat piles of Cilantro Rice, Rutabaga with Nutmeg, and other delicacies which tasted even worse than they looked.

He poured himself a glass of milk and slammed the refrigerator door. Emily raised her finger again.

"Sorry," he muttered.

He carried the milk to the dining table at the other end of the room from Emily's computer. There was a small paper bag on the table, next to the stack of math worksheets and a freshly sharpened pencil. Arthur already knew what the bag would contain. Every morning at seven A.M., Emily bought a biscuit from the tea cart at work, and kept it in her purse all day to give to Arthur in the afternoon.

It was part of a pattern, Arthur thought. Everything was part of a pattern with Aunt Emily.

The boy was up every weekday at five-thirty, cornflakes for breakfast, downstairs to Mr. Goldberg's apartment at six-thirty, when Emily left for work. After an hour spent watching the news on television (to Arthur's delight, the old man had decreed at the outset that television had some redeeming qualities, despite Aunt Emily's ban on it), Mr. Goldberg would accompany him to the bus stop at 7:30, when Arthur left for school. Emily paid Mr. Goldberg a small sum of money each month for these services.

Every day, when Arthur returned in the afternoon, his aunt was waiting for him. Or, rather, she was in the apartment.

She usually worked on her own at the computer until five or six o'clock. She rarely acknowledged Arthur before then.

He eschewed the sour-tasting biscuit in favor of Mr. Goldberg's cookie and drank the milk while examining his new find. He hadn't been mistaken about the hollowed-out sphere. It was warm. Even in the apartment it felt warm.

"Em—"

She shook her head vigorously, her fingers flying over the keys.

Arthur set down his treasure with a defiant *clunk*. What did Emily care, he thought sullenly. She'd never wanted to raise a kid. When she was angry, she often reminded him that his bedroom used to be her office, as if she'd made the ultimate sacrifice for him.

And in her mind, Arthur knew, she hād. Emily Blessing was a brilliant woman whose work had helped to win two Nobel Prizes for scientists she assisted at the Katzenbaum Institute, a "think tank" devoted to the exploration of pure science. If Emily had not had to curtail her education in order to raise an orphaned child from infancy, those prizes might have been hers.

He ran his fingers over the sphere. The warmth was peculiar, comforting. He tried to balance it on his head but it fell and crashed to the floor.

Emily jumped. "Arthur, do you mind!" she shrieked.

"Okay, okay."

"I've left some work for you."

"Yeah. I see it."

"I beg your pardon?"

"I mean 'yes, thank you.'"

"That's better." Her fingers resumed their clacking on the computer keys.

With a sigh, he picked up the first sheet of math problems. They involved cube roots. Arthur solved them in his head, then went on to logarithms and binary functions. He used the pencil only for some equations on the last page.

"Done," he said in a monotone, knowing that Emily would ignore him. He flipped the final worksheet face down on the table. Beneath it was an airmail envelope with a British stamp. It was addressed to him.

Arthur tore it open eagerly. With no relatives except for Emily, he almost never received mail, certainly not anything from another country.

"Dear Mr. Blessing," it began.

> It is our sad duty to inform you of the death of Sir Bradford Welles Abbott . . .

Arthur frowned. *Sir who?*

> According to our client's Last Will and Testament, a parcel of real estate measuring approximately 300 meters square has been left to Ms. Dilys Blessing or her surviving descendants. As you are, to the best of our knowledge, the sole living offspring of the deceased Ms. Blessing, this property rightfully shall pass to you.
>
> The above-mentioned real estate, referred to traditionally as Lakeshire Tor, lies approximately three (3) kilometers southwest of Wickesbury, on the southern border of Somerset County. It is workable farmland, although quite rocky, due to the presence of ruins from a post-Roman hill fortification. . . .

"Emily!"

Her hands flew up from the keyboard. "Arthur, I have *told* you . . ."

"Read this! I've inherited a castle!"

"Stop shouting."

"Okay. Look," he said quietly, waving the letter as he ran to her. "Somebody died and left me a castle. Well, a hill fort, but that's practically the same thing. His name's Sir Bradford Welles Abbott. Isn't that a cool name?"

Emily's face froze in an expression of grim surprise.

"Did you know him?" Arthur asked.

His aunt took the letter without answering and read it silently. She had to clear her throat before she spoke.

"It says these lawyers can sell the property and forward the proceeds to you here." She tried a strained smile. "We can put it toward your college fund."

"But Emily . . ." His voice was a whisper. "It's my castle . . ."

"Oh, it's hardly that, I'm sure. 'Post-Roman ruins,' it says. It's probably no more than a few boulders."

"I want to see it."

"That's out of the question. My work . . ."

"You could take a vacation, Em. You've never had one. We could go to England."

"And what about school?"

"We could go in the summer when school's out."

"There isn't enough money."

"Yes, there is. I saw your bank balance on the computer—"

"Stop arguing with me!" she screamed. Her cheeks were a vibrant red. She took off her oversized glasses and brought a trembling hand to her forehead. "I don't want to discuss this," she said quietly.

But she held on to the letter, reading it again and again.

"Emily?" Arthur asked at last.

She looked up, as if startled to hear his voice.

"Why haven't you ever told me about my mother before?"

"It just never came up, I suppose," she snapped. "I never . . . never . . ."

Suddenly, inexplicably, two tears dropped onto the letter in rapid succession. Then Emily crumpled the letter into a ball and threw it across the room. "Keep it if you want," she said. "It's your property, not mine."

"Aunt Emily . . ."

"I've got work to do." She pushed him away with one of her narrow, shaking hands, put on her glasses, and turned back to the computer.

# CHAPTER NINE

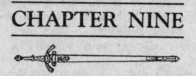

Since Emily had steadfastly refused to discuss Arthur's inheritance, the letter from Sir Bradford Welles Abbott's law firm remained unanswered through the winter and spring. Nevertheless, news about the boy's "castle" spread slowly through the apartment building and eventually into the pages of the *Riverside Shopper*, from which it was picked up by the *Chicago Tribune*.

The *Tribune* photographer took Arthur's picture in front of his All-State Spelling Bee trophy. It appeared in the Saturday edition, next to an article about cooking with pine nuts.

Five days later, Arthur and Emily Blessing were running for their lives.

It was the cup, of course. Arthur had known there was something unusual about the ball from the moment he first held it in his hands on that cold January day when he picked it out of the gutter. But Emily didn't give it a thought until the Day of the Bacteria, as they came to call it.

It was evening. Emily was reading one of the Katzenbaum physicists' treatises on the behavior of neutrinos in radioactive suspensions. Arthur was playing with the microscope Emily had bought him for Christmas. He prepared slides of everything he could think of: a scraping of broccoli from dinner, a drop of melted snow, oil from his own nose, a pink smear of Emily's lipstick, a hair from his head. Then he watched them under the lens, marveling at the life inside these innocuous substances, the motile one-celled organisms which lived invisibly at his own fingertips.

Beneath the microscope they seemed to almost dance, their

movements quick and jerky, like Mexican jumping beans on
a hot stove.

All except one. On that slide, the bacteria had lined up end
to end in precise parallel rows and moved slowly back and
forth in a display of absolutely tranquil motion.

"Holy crow!" he shrieked. "You have to see this, Emily."

His aunt got up with a sigh. "What is it?"

He stepped aside from the microscope and she peered into
the eyepiece.

"Good God," she whispered.

"Ham-*mer!*" Arthur said, imitating some of the boys at
school who were fans of a wild-dancing rap singer whom he
had never seen.

"What is this?"

"Tap water," Arthur giggled.

"What was its environment?"

He blinked.

"The container," she said impatiently. "Did you have it in
a clean container?"

Arthur held up the metal ball. Its hollowed center was
half-filled with water. "I used this."

Emily rolled her eyes.

"But I washed it out first."

She took an eyedropper, rinsed it in the sink, then filled it
with tap water. Expertly she prepared a new slide and placed
it under the microscope.

She looked through the eyepiece and then nodded.
"There," she said. "The water's perfectly normal."

Arthur looked. The bacteria was doing what bacteria were
supposed to do—jumping and dancing around the slide in
purely random motions.

"I know," Arthur said. "But what about the other slide?
Have you ever seen anything like that?"

"No," she said honestly. She tapped the ball disdainfully
with the back of her fingernails. "This thing must be filthy."

"I used Pine Sol," Arthur said. "And I boiled it, too."

One of Emily's eyebrows shot up. "How did you dry it?"

"I let it air-dry. I used the same method for all of the containers."

Slowly Emily's fingers wrapped around the spheroid cup. A distinct sensation of well-being spread through her body.

"It's warm," she said. "Did you use hot water?"

Arthur shook his head.

She inserted Arthur's original slide into the microscope carrier again, stared at it for a long while, then shook her head. "I don't understand it," she said. "Living bacteria, but in uniform motion."

She reached past the microscope to a pencil box on the boy's desk and extracted a steel compass. "Do you mind?"

"Guess not," Arthur said begrudgingly.

With the point of the compass, she scraped on the bottom of the object.

It did not make a scratch.

Arthur touched the point of the compass. The metal of the ball had blunted it.

"Wow," he whispered.

Emily dumped the contents of the ball into the kitchen sink, refilled it with tap water, made a new slide, and put it under the microscope.

She inhaled sharply as she saw the bacteria again lined up in perfectly uniform rows.

She stood up and held the sphere in her hand like a living thing. "Remarkable," she said. "Where did you get this?"

"I found it on the street."

"I want to have it analyzed."

"No," Arthur said, snatching it away. "They'll keep it."

"It might be some sort of experimental alloy. It might have very unusual properties."

"I don't care! The Institute's not going to have it."

There was a long silence before she spoke. "What if I do the analysis myself?" she offered. "I can go in early. I'll bring it home tomorrow."

"And you won't tell anyone?"

Emily hesitated. "It may be something of importance . . ."

"It's mine. That's the deal."

He had her, and Arthur knew it. Emily's curiosity was such that she would have to analyze the metal cup, even if it meant stealing it from her nephew; but she wouldn't lie. She didn't know how.

"All right," she said finally. "I won't tell anyone."

"Or show them."

"Or show them."

When Arthur got home from school the next day, Emily was not at her computer. She was sitting at the dining table, holding the sphere in one hand and writing furiously with the other. A strand of dark hair had escaped the severe bun on the back of her head and hung over one eye. She didn't seem to notice. The stack of papers beside her was covered with drawings and equations.

"It cleaves in a curve," she said immediately. "At least I think so. I was only able to get a fragment off the unit with the laser . . ." She shook her head impatiently. "Anyway, its molecular structure is unlike anything I've seen before."

Arthur had never seen his aunt so excited before. "What's it made of?"

"I didn't have time to run all the tests, of course. All I found out is that it doesn't contain lead, gold, silver, uranium, nickel, iron . . ." She breathed deeply. Her eyes were glassy. "It doesn't contain any known metal."

The silence in the room was palpable.

"Cheez-o-man," Arthur said at last.

"Dr. Lowry at the Institute is working with properties of base metals . . ."

"No!" He snatched the ball away from her. "You promised!"

"Arthur, my analysis doesn't begin to explain the activity of the bacteria . . ."

"It's mine! I need it. It's my good-luck piece."

Emily sank back in the chair. "Oh, Arthur, really."

"It is. It brought me my castle."

"How can you be so stupid?" Her hands clenched. "That

thing might represent something totally new. An absolute scientific breakthrough. You can't just keep it as a toy."

"It belongs to me," Arthur said stolidly.

Emily leaped up, prepared to take it by force, but the boy wriggled out of her grasp and ran down the hall.

"Arthur!" she called. "Come back here immediately!"

All she heard in answer were the squeaks of his sneakers as he bounded down the stairs.

She sighed and closed the door.

It had been the wrong approach, she knew. In her eagerness to find out more about the strange metallic object (*It cleaved in a curve!*), Emily had forgotten that she was dealing with a ten-year-old boy.

Not that she had ever known how to deal with him. Emily had never been comfortable around children. They were, to her, like Siberian tigers or polar bears—creatures known to her, but whose existence never touched her own life.

Emily Blessing was meant to be a scholar, not a mother. She had flown through school like a rocket. Two skipped grades, a Westinghouse Science Award at fourteen, graduation at sixteen, a bachelor's from Yale at twenty, a master's at twenty-two, ready to go on for her doctorate . . .

And then a note beneath the hanged body of a dead woman.

> *Dear Emily,*
> *Please take care of my baby. You are all he has now.*
>
> > *Love,*
> > *Dilys*

Love, Dilys. Dilys, with her flaming red hair so much like her son's. Dilys, the beautiful one, whose laughter always filled the room. She had come home only to die.

The police had cut her down. And after the questioning, after the funeral with its pitifully small group of mourners, after the item in the hometown newspaper saying only that Dilys Blessing, 19, of East Monroe township, had committed

suicide at her sister's Connecticut apartment, there was
nothing left of Dilys except for her infant boy.

She hadn't even given him a name. Emily named him
Arthur, after their own father who had died while Dilys was
living in London.

She had tried to raise the boy as best she could. She had
left the secure, mind-stretching atmosphere of the university,
shelved her plans to get her doctorate, and taken a research-
er's job in Chicago with the Katzenbaum Institute. She had
arranged her hours so that she would be home for Arthur as
much as possible. Through the years, she maintained a frugal
lifestyle in order to send him to the best private school in the
area. On weekends, she took him to *Kumon*, a Japanese
mathematics workshop. During the summers, she enrolled
him in computer courses at Northwestern University. Because of her efforts, she acknowledged with some pride,
Arthur showed every sign of developing a first-rate mind.

But he never confided in her, or shared a joke with her, or
came to her for comfort. They had spent the past ten years
like two trees in a forest, near one another without ever
touching.

That was her fault, she supposed. Emily had never been
close to anyone. That was Dilys' province. She had always
been wildly in love with someone or other. Passion had been
the hallmark of her life. And her death, as well.

Still, Arthur would not have run away from Dilys.

Emily began to walk over to her computer, realized that
she couldn't pull her thoughts together, and changed direction. She ambled instead into Arthur's room.

She had never paid attention to it before. There was a
poster of Bart Simpson taped to the inside of the door, and a
smaller picture of a Teenage Mutant Ninja Turtle shouting
"Cowabunga!" in a white cartoon bubble over his head. TV
characters for a kid without a TV. Above his desk was
Rudyard Kipling's poem "If," painstakingly printed in
Arthur's own hand. Next to it was a Gary Larson cartoon
depicting a cave man using a dachshund to paint on a wall,
with the legend "Wiener Dog Art" beneath. There was a

scuffed baseball in the corner of the desk, probably a memento from the summer Arthur had spent at camp.

He'd liked that, Emily remembered, but there was no time for camp and Northwestern's computer program too.

On the shelf above the desk stood the All-State Spelling Bee trophy, thick with dust, and a red plastic lunch box.

Where had he gotten this? she wondered, opening the box. It was filled with junk. Sparkling rocks. A piece of snake-skin. A magnet. A miniature magnifying glass. The dis-carded carapace of a summer cicada. The letter from Sir Bradford Welles Abbott's solicitors. All of Arthur Blessing's worldly treasures.

Tears filled Emily's eyes. Where had she been when he'd found the cicada, or hit the baseball? Had he told her? Had she listened, at least for a moment?

The doorbell rang. She closed the red lunch box hurriedly, as if she'd been caught snooping, then composed herself to answer the door.

Two men in good suits were waiting for her. They had curious, identical eyes.

"Emily Blessing?"

Her first reaction was panic. *Police*, she thought. *Arthur ran into the street, he's been hurt, they've come to tell me . . .*

"Yes," she answered quietly.

One of them reached into his jacket.

*Police I.D. Oh, God, not this, not this . . .*

The man pulled out a gun with a silencer. Then, before Emily could even sort out the intense, divergent thoughts that were screaming in her brain, two bullets slammed into her chest.

She fell back, tasting the blood that flooded into her mouth. The men stepped over her, one of them pushing her legs aside to close the door. Then, systematically, they ransacked the apartment.

Blinking to ward off the fog that was enveloping her, still unable to comprehend the outrage that had been committed against her body, Emily gasped for breath. Then a thought formed in her mind.

*Arthur's not here.*

The muscles in her neck relaxed. She closed her eyes and allowed the blackness to seal them. Her bladder released. She was dying.

*Don't come home, Arthur.* The words spun in the darkness of Emily's fading consciousness like living things. Marching bacteria. Her lips moved slowly. *Don't come home.*

# CHAPTER TEN

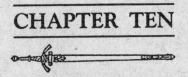

As the bullets tore through Emily's chest cavity, Arthur was downstairs in Mr. Goldberg's apartment, looking at the high school photograph of Goldberg's divorced lawyer nephew who, the old man insisted, was exactly the man for Emily.

"He don't look like that now, understand," the old man was explaining. "He's put on a little weight, lost some hair . . ."

"That's good," Arthur said, examining the wavy Beatle cut in the photograph.

"It was the style. Sloppy was in. You don't know how many times I said, you, get a haircut, look like a normal person for a change. But kids, they don't listen." He smiled and tousled Arthur's red hair. "Even you, am I right?"

"I guess so." Arthur stared at the metal globe in his hand.

"Drink your cocoa."

Arthur cringed. Mr. Goldberg made his cocoa with one level teaspoon of Nestle's Quik and one measuring cup's worth of tepid tap water in a dirty mug. He took a polite sip, then set it down.

"How is it?"

"Okay."

"So, Mr. Mad-at-the-World. You fought with your Aunt Emily?"

The boy's eyebrows knit together. "She doesn't understand anything," he said.

"Oy, if I could have a nickel for every time a kid said such a thing about his mother . . ."

"She's not my mother," Arthur said sullenly.

"That's right. She don't got to take care of you. She don't got to wear old shoes so she can send you to that fancy school. She don't got to stay home every night just so she can be with you." He was leaning close to Arthur, jabbing a gnarled finger at the boy's face. "She does it because she loves you."

Arthur turned away. "That's not why she stays home."

"Oh, it's not, is it?"

"No. She stays home so she can work. That's all she cares about. She doesn't even like it when I talk to her."

"So who needs a lot of talk?"

Arthur sat back in Mr. Goldberg's rump-sprung sofa and tossed the metal ball up in the air. "Not me. Not with her."

Goldberg caught it. "Don't play while we're making conversation." He examined the ball. "What are you doing with an ashtray, anyway?"

"It's not an ashtray. It's a good-luck piece."

Goldberg snorted. "You're so lucky, how come you're sitting here telling me your troubles?"

Arthur looked up at him. The boy's eyes were on the verge of tears. "She wants to take it," he said.

The old man was quiet for a moment. "You broke a window?" he ventured.

Arthur shook his head. "I did an experiment. It's . . . it's some kind of special thing."

Goldberg held the ball in front of his face. "This?"

"Emily wants to give it to the Katzenbaum Institute so they can figure out what it's made of."

"Ah," the old man said.

"Do you understand?"

"No. I should still be smoking, I'd put a cigar out in it."

Arthur's lips moved in the trace of a smile.

"Why is it so important to you?" Goldberg asked quietly.

The boy covered his face with his hands. "I don't know!" he shouted. "But it is. As soon as I picked it up, I knew it belonged to me. Or *I* belonged to *it*, if that makes any sense." Slowly his hands came down from his face, and his eyes focused on a spot outside the dirty window. "It was like I'd been looking for it for a really long time, even though I hadn't been. And I need it. That's just something I know." He wiped his nose with his knuckle. "That sounds really stupid."

"No, no."

Arthur stole a glance at the old man's face. Goldberg was nodding thoughtfully. "This, this is something I understand."

"You do?"

"Yes."

Arthur's face screwed up. "Why should you?"

The old man stood up and paced behind the sofa. "Do you believe in ghosts, Arthur? Spirits?"

The boy stared at him. "No."

"Well, they're with us, whether you believe in them or not. And every once in a while, when a person really needs something—and let me tell you, that person may not even know he needs it—one of the spirits looking after him will make sure he gets it."

"Are you serious?"

The old man nodded gravely. "Let me tell you something. My wife Ethel died in 1968. In that chair."

He pointed to an armchair covered by an old mustard-colored throw in the corner. "Stroke, the doctor said, very peaceful. She still had the book she was reading in her lap. *The Valley of the Dolls*, it was."

He came around slowly and sat beside Arthur. "Well, to make a long story short, about three months later I was visiting my sister and her family in the city. We ate a good meal, we played cards. By the time I left, it was after eleven o'clock. My sister says 'It's freezing, Milton, take a taxi.' I say 'Are you crazy, a cab to Riverside? I'll take the train,' I says.

"So I walk to the El stop. Almost as soon as I leave the

house, I find a paperback book on the sidewalk. There's nobody around, it's late, I think maybe I'll read something on the train, so I pick it up. As God is my witness, it's *The Valley of the Dolls*."

He held his hand up solemnly. "Now, Arthur, I am a Jew. Jews do not believe in ghosts. When a person dies, that's it. This is what our religion teaches. But holding that book in my hand, I knew it was Ethel trying to give me a message. We were married for forty-one years. We never talked. You know why?"

Arthur shook his head.

"Because we didn't have to. That woman knew what I was going to say before I said it. I'd think, it's cold, a little macaroni and cheese might be nice, and the next thing out of her mouth would be, 'Do you want fish or chicken with your macaroni and cheese?' Are you getting my drift?"

Arthur nodded. His mouth had fallen open.

"So I put the book inside my overcoat and walked on to the El. It's maybe a ten-minute walk. When I get there, the platform is deserted. The train just left. I'm standing there all alone, when a mugger in a ski mask comes up to me with a knife."

"Holy crow," Arthur said.

"Holy *shit* is what I feel like, let me tell you. This individual tells me to give him my wallet, which I do. He stuffs it into this jacket he's wearing, and then looks around to see if anybody saw him. Nobody. 'Go,' I says, ' I won't chase you.' 'That's right,' he says. But instead of running away, the bastard stabs me."

Arthur gasped.

"Right in the heart. Only my heart's not there, because *The Valley of the Dolls* is in front of it. All four hundred pages."

He folded his arms. "So I don't care what anybody says. That was Ethel looking after me." He pointed to the metal sphere. "And maybe this thing's come to you in the same way."

"It must be," Arthur whispered. "Maybe it's from my mother. She died when I was a baby."

Goldberg shrugged. "Maybe her, maybe someone else. But it's not Emily's fault she don't understand. She probably don't believe in ghosts, either."

"No, she wouldn't," Arthur said reasonably.

"Then you got to explain it to her."

"She won't listen to me."

"Not if you run away from her."

Arthur looked abashed.

The old man nodded. "Try again, Arthur. Do it now, before she can think of a better argument."

"Yeah."

"And tell her you love her. Women like to hear that."

He made a face. "Okay." He smiled. "Thanks, Mr. Goldberg." He got up and ran to the door.

"Arthur?"

The boy looked back, the excitement still in his eyes.

"Touch her with it."

"What?"

"The ashtray. She should touch it."

"What for?"

Goldberg flapped his hands to shoo him away. "Go, Mr. What-For. Who listens to an old man these days?"

Arthur ran up the stairs. "Emily!" he shouted. "Emily, I've got to tell you something . . ."

There was no answer.

The door was ajar.

And the first thing he saw was the blood spreading around Emily's body like great, red wings.

"Oh, God," he whispered. There were two gaping holes in his aunt's chest. Her lips were blue. "Oh, God. God."

He dropped the cup and ran for the telephone. As he dialed 911, the metal sphere rolled toward Emily. It came to rest next to her foot.

"What is your address?" the voice on the telephone demanded.

"Four twenty-two East Lansing Street, Number Three-A."

"What is the nature of the emergency?"

"My aunt . . ."

He gasped. Emily's eyes blinked open.

"Yes? Go ahead."

"My . . . Emily . . ."

Emily sat up, a look of bewilderment on her face. Her cheeks were flushed. Her lips were red.

"What is the nature of the emergency?" the emergency dispatcher repeated.

Slowly, Emily opened two buttons of her blouse and touched the smooth skin above her bloodstained brassiere.

"Sir! What is—"

"Never mind," Arthur said. "It was a mistake. Everything's all right." He hung up the phone.

He walked over to his aunt and knelt in the blood surrounding her.

"He shot me," she said.

"Who, Emily?"

"I don't know. Two men . . . two shots . . . I was dying." She looked into his eyes. "I was *dying*, Arthur, and now there isn't a mark on me."

"Did they take anything?"

Emily stood up shakily and looked through her pocketbook on the dining table. "My wallet's here. The money's still in it. There isn't anything else . . ." Her hand slapped the wooden table. "My notes. They've taken my notes."

Her eyes fixed on Arthur. He was holding the metal cup in his hand. They were both silent for a few moments that seemed much longer.

"He said to touch you with it," Arthur said softly.

"What? Who are you talking about?"

Wordlessly he went to the kitchen drawer and came back with a small steak knife.

"Arthur, what on earth—"

He sliced it across the pad of his index finger. Bright blood welled out of the narrow wound.

Emily rushed over to him, but he held up his hand. A day before, it would have seemed a ludicrous gesture, but the expression on Arthur's face was not that of a child. He commanded authority, and his aunt obeyed him.

Then slowly, tentatively, the boy touched the cup to his finger.

"Arthur?" she whispered.

His eyes rolled back into his head. His knees wobbled, but he willed himself to stand. The heat from the cup was coursing through his blood like liquid music.

When it subsided, he lifted the cup. The wound was healed, gone without a trace. Only the spilled blood remained.

"It can't be," Emily said.

"This is what they were after."

"Then . . . then we'll have to get rid of it. We'll give it to the police . . ."

Arthur shook his head. "No, Emily. It's mine. It belongs to me."

"You can't be serious. They'll come back."

"They'll come back anyway."

"Then we'll give it to them."

"Don't you understand, Emily? They'll kill us after they take it."

Her hand went to her mouth. "But there must be something . . ."

Arthur wasn't listening to her. "But how did he know?" he asked himself, unaware that he had spoken aloud.

"Who? How did *who* know?"

"Mr. Goldberg. He told me about *The Valley of the Dolls*."

"The . . . What are you talking about?"

He didn't have time to answer. He was running down the stairs.

"Mr. Goldberg!" he called breathlessly, his legs pistoning down the worn marble.

The old man was not at his usual post in front of his apartment. Arthur beat on the door with his fists. He made such a racket that the doorman peered around the corner.

"He's not there, son."

"Where is he? Where'd he go?"

The doorman shuffled uncomfortably. "Mr. Goldberg died this afternoon," he said finally.

Arthur felt as if he were going to faint. "What?"

The doorman took off his cap and wiped his forehead with his sleeve. "About three-thirty. He keeled over right here in the foyer. It looked like a heart attack."

Arthur stared blankly at him, unable to speak.

"Ambulance got here real fast."

Arthur bit his lip. "Yes, I . . . I saw it out front," he said.

"Yeah. I was going to tell you before, but with all the commotion and everything, I didn't even see you come in."

*Or the men who shot my aunt, either*, Arthur thought dimly.

"Well . . ." He put his hat back on. "I'm sorry, kid. Guess you kind of liked the old man."

"Can I see his apartment?" he blurted out suddenly.

The doorman made a face. "Gee, I don't know . . ."

"I won't go in. I'd just like to see it."

The doorman thought about it for a moment, then shrugged. "Sure, why not." He lifted the huge key ring attached to his belt as they walked up the few steps to Mr. Goldberg's apartment. "There you go," he said, swinging the door open.

A mug half-filled with cocoa was on the coffee table in front of the sofa. Beside it was Mr. Goldberg's photo album.

*Just the way it was ten minutes ago*, Arthur thought. He backed out of the room.

"Hey, you okay?" the doorman asked.

In the hallway, Arthur turned and ran back up the stairs as fast as he could.

Emily was on her hands and knees, staring at the stain of her own blood on the carpet. She looked up at him. For the first time Arthur could remember, his aunt's face showed fear.

Arthur put his arms around her. "We've got to get out of here, Emily," he said quietly.

# CHAPTER ELEVEN

The apartment's white curtains billowed with a tropical breeze that carried the faintly animal scents of Kowloon and the sea up to the thirtieth floor. Across the bay, bathed in early morning mist, stood the Hong Kong skyline.

Saladin crossed the white carpet without a sound, then folded himself like a long-legged spider onto a wicker chair. He was dressed in fine white linen, a tunic and loose trousers. As a servant brought him tea and a newspaper, he turned his face toward the sun.

How he had missed that, the sun and the warm air and the sounds of civilization! After four years of artificial light and endless solitude, he felt like a lazy insect crawling out of the soil.

He caught a glimpse of his reflection in the window, and it saddened him. Those four years had aged him. The lines in his face were deeply etched, and his head sprouted a scattering of gray hairs.

How old was he? Forty? No, forty-one. He had been thirty-seven when he entered the asylum. It was important to be specific.

Four years was a long time. He would get none of those days back. But he would lose no more.

Angrily, he turned away from the glass and picked up the London *Times*. Inside he found an article about the burning of Maplebrook the previous week. Firefighters and other experts had apparently determined that the explosion was not an accident caused by faulty wiring, as was originally thought, but a deliberate act of sabotage.

"We are working very diligently in sorting through the debris," the newspaper quoted a Scotland Yard source.

In other words, Saladin knew, the authorities had no clue. There was little reason to blow up an insane asylum. Even the IRA had not claimed responsibility for this one. Yet the work, according to all the evidence, was of professional caliber.

It was a crime without reason, the article concluded, against men whose faces society did not wish to see. "Yet these faceless men are dead," it read ominously. "Their deaths mark the final chapter in the tragic story of the Towers."

Saladin laughed, his momentary pique forgotten. He was completely free now. He filled his lungs with sweet air. The smile was still on his face when his houseman announced a visitor, a man named Vinod. Saladin had not seen him for years.

Vinod had traveled more than seven thousand miles to see him. He had made the journey because Saladin disliked talking on the telephone.

"Well? Where is it?" Saladin asked immediately.

The man trembled. "There have been complications."

The look that crossed Saladin's face would have been enough to turn Vinod's insides to jelly, had they not already been in that condition.

"We had kept it in a bank. But the bank was robbed. We didn't know about it. No one expected—"

"Where is it?" Saladin repeated, clapping the man around his neck in a death grip.

Vinod's limbs twitched. He could no longer speak. Desperately, he pulled a piece of paper from his pocket.

It was a clipping from an American newspaper. The headline read:

## LOCAL YOUNGSTER INHERITS CASTLE

Saladin released his visitor and read the piece. It was about a ten-year-old boy named Arthur Blessing who had come into a twenty-four-acre property in England upon the death of an unknown relative. The land, it said, held the remains of an ancient castle. The story was accompanied by a fuzzy photograph of a grinning redheaded boy.

He looked at the date. The clipping was several weeks old. "Why are you showing me this?" Saladin asked.

"Look . . . at the background," Vinod rasped, still unable to speak clearly.

Then Saladin saw it, on a shelf above the boy's head, next to a trophy of some sort: an object, obviously metallic, shaped something between a bowl and a sphere.

The cup!

Saladin's mouth suddenly felt dry. He struggled to contain his fury. "How did it get there?"

Vinod's breath was foul with fear. "We are uncertain of the details," he said. "It was not among the items confiscated by the police after the robbery. Perhaps it was misplaced, discarded . . ."

Saladin cut him off with a gesture. "What of this boy?"

Sweat was beading on the smaller man's upper lip. "We assumed you would want him eliminated."

"And?"

"We tried his aunt's apartment. The boy and the . . . the cup were not there. We thought the woman was dead, but . . ." He shrugged. "We found these."

He gave Saladin the notes Emily had made on the chemical and physical analyses of the metal ball. "I cannot understand them."

"No," Saladin snapped. "Of course not."

"After that, they left."

"With the cup."

"The . . . yes."

"Where did they go?"

"East. We made an attempt on the woman's car in Detroit, but it misfired. Someone stole the vehicle. The explosion occurred less than a kilometer from where the boy and his aunt were staying."

"So you killed a car thief."

Vinod's face was a mask of humiliation. "We did not wish to draw attention to ourselves by injuring bystanders. But we were afraid of losing them again, so we tried to kill them both as they left the hotel."

He paused for breath. Saladin's eyes narrowed. "Go on," he said.

"It was a freakish accident. An old man fell from a window . . . a suicide, perhaps . . . The bullet struck him instead of the child. We . . . we had to leave . . ."

"Impossible," Saladin muttered. His voice was low and feral, the growl of a wolf.

"Yes, sire. It seems impossible. It is uncanny. We found them again in Pennsylvania . . ."

Saladin waved a hand for him to stop. "Where are they now?"

"In England. They left on a flight to London two nights ago from New York. To see the estate, most likely. That is why I came here. My team was ordered to remain in the United States. If you wish, we will go to England, but we will need new identification, contacts for weapons . . ."

Saladin shook his head. "No," he said. "I won't need you there."

"Thank you, sire." Vinod backed away. Saladin smiled at him briefly, and the little man's face flooded with relief.

When he left, Saladin nodded to his Chinese houseman.

The servant understood. By morning, Vinod would be dead.

Surrounded once again by silence, Saladin studied the newspaper picture of the boy and the odd metal sphere behind him. How curious that his name too was Arthur.

The boy had found the cup by accident, no doubt, just as Saladin himself had found it all those long, long years ago. He too had been only a boy.

His first memory was fear. When the savages swarmed into his family's great house in Elam and the servant women screamed, he knew his father and older brothers were already dead.

His mother did not look at him. Years later, Saladin would realize, in retrospect, that her simple act of disciplined negligence had probably saved his life. Since the fighting had begun, she had dressed her youngest child in the rough clothing of a servant. She treated him as a servant now, ignoring his cries as she faced the soldiers from Kish and their black swords running with blood.

They cut off her head. They poured through the house like locusts, screaming their grotesque war cries, cutting down the helpless women and old men who were all that was left of the ruling family of Elam.

The few servants and their children who were spared were marched far north into the moated city of Kish. Saladin, who had never known anything but luxury and privilege, was taken on as a house slave in the home of a merchant. He was fed scraps from the table of the other slaves and slept on the kitchen floor. For three years, until he was eight years old, he brought water to the women's bedchambers and served at the dining table.

And then came the destruction of the ziggurat.

It was already centuries old. There had been temples in Elam, also, but none so grand or ancient as the ziggurat at Kish. It stood in the center of the city, surrounded in concentric rings by the public buildings and the residences of the wealthy, then by the mud shacks of the poor, and finally by the wide moat which protected the inhabitants from raiders.

From the merchant's house where he lived, Saladin could see the priests climbing the ziggurat's hundred steps to offer sacrifices to the gods, those immortal beings who bore the faces and bodies of men but shunned the company of those whose puny lives could be extinguished in the blink of an eternal eye.

There were those who claimed to have seen the gods. A farmer from beyond the protection of the moat came to tell the king of Kish of a terrifying encounter on the banks of the Euphrates. The god, he said, had risen from the water of the river, carried on the back of a great fish. He was naked, save for a miniature moon tied around his waist. His skin, in the moonlight, had been white as alabaster, and his eyes were made of jewels, sapphires so bright that they shone like stars in the night.

The farmer had not dared to speak to the god. When the moon-colored deity saw him, he had held up his arms, supplicating the moon to strike down the mortal. The farmer had prostrated himself then, covering his face. When at last he raised his head, the god had flown from his place in the water toward the dark sky, riding on a beam of moonlight.

"He has seen the moon-god," the elders agreed.

The farmer was given three casks of oil for this vision, and though he waited by the banks of the river each night for many years afterward, the god never returned.

Fish and meal cakes were sacrificed to the moon-god each month by the holy men who climbed to the top of the ziggurat by torchlight. They chanted the moon-god's name and asked for his blessing in the hunt.

Then came the earthquake, and when the ziggurat lay in ruins in the town square, the elders would whisper that their sacrifices had displeased the moon-god. He did not want fish and meal cakes but the life of the man who had dared to look upon his face. They dragged the farmer out of his home and forced him to climb the rubble of the ziggurat, where they tied him to stakes and cut out his living heart.

And the earth lay still again.

"The moon-god is appeased," said the elders.

No one missed the young slave boy who disappeared during the earthquake. The members of the merchant's household assumed that he had been killed by the flying debris which fell during the terrible moments when the ground yawned open and swallowed the massive ziggurat like a honey cake. No one looked for the boy.

No one saw the small footprints in the mud where the moat had buckled like a ribbon and spewed out its water. No one noticed the small figure running across the land that would be known centuries later as Babylon, toward the Zagros Mountains, far to the east of Kish. Even if he had been seen, no one would have thought of going after him. The mountains were the end of the world. Beyond them was nothingness. Everyone knew that because the priests and the elders had decreed it to be so.

In the Zagros Mountains, the boy shivered with cold and fear. When the earthquake had struck, his only thought was to flee from the house. He had been in the kitchen with the cook and her helper. At the first rumble, the oil-filled pottery jars tumbled off the shelves and crashed to the floor, coating the tile with a thick film that flared up in a blanket of flame when it reached the cooking fire. For a moment, Saladin watched the carpet of flame with terrified fascination as the two cooks shrieked and tried to beat out the flames with rags while the floor shifted crazily beneath them.

Then the cook's hair caught on fire. Her hands flew to her burning head, her eyes bulging.

"Help me!" she screamed.

Saladin backed away. She looked like a monster. He shook his head. No. No. She lurched toward him, toward the door. He ran from her.

The next shock caved in the roof. But by then Saladin was already running.

He stopped only once, at the moat. Until then, he'd had no plan to leave Kish; the sentries at the bridges would have known him for a runaway slave. But there were no bridges now. There was not even a moat. The water had vanished to flood the other side of the city. Here was nothing but a river of mud.

Tentatively, Saladin took one step into that mud with his small bare foot. Then he threw himself in, digging and clawing until he reached the other side. He would never be a slave again.

Hunger gnawed at his stomach. He had been running all day, but he would have to wait until morning to eat. His feet were badly cut from the rocks on the barren slope of the mountain he had climbed. As a house slave, he had not been given shoes to wear, but the soles of his feet were still not tough enough to endure a long trek through open countryside. The bloody footprints behind him were black in the moonlight. He could walk no farther. He must sleep now, he told himself, here beneath the stars at the end of the world. Saladin put his head down on the dry earth and closed his eyes.

He did not hear the old man's footsteps. He awoke to a sensation of exquisite pleasure that began at his feet and warmed his whole body. It was a dream, he thought. A lovely dream from a long sleep in a bed of feathers in his family's palace in Elam.

But Elam was gone. The barbarians of Kish had destroyed it.

Frowning, he forced his eyes open. At his feet, an old man was hunched over him. The man was dressed in a tunic of animal skins, and his hair was a tangle of long gray strings, like his beard. When he saw the boy's face, he smiled a toothless grin.

Saladin gasped. The man's eyes were blue, as blue as the sea. And his skin was white.

He shook his head and made a clucking sound with his mouth when the boy tried to scramble up, then gestured to an object in his hand. It was a small metal cup of some kind. He was rubbing it over the wounds on Saladin's feet.

Only there were no more wounds. They had been completely healed.

Saladin heard a low sound come up from his own throat.

He had met the moon-god.

# CHAPTER TWELVE

His name was Kanna, and he had lived, as far as Saladin could tell, forever. Kanna himself could not remember much of the time before the Stone, as he called the cup, had fallen to earth.

He did know that it was before the Semitic peoples had

wandered into the valley and begun the civilization known as
Sumer, with its weaving and pottery and trade. His people,
the people of white skin and blue eyes, had been hunters.
Hundreds of generations before Kanna, they had walked to
the valley from the high steppes of a land where ice rained
from the sky and coated the earth each year with a white
blanket that was colder than the river.

The Stone had crashed into the trees—for there were trees
in the valley then, before the sun had grown too warm—near
the place where he had built his fire. Kanna had been a holy
man, a healer who wandered from tribe to tribe in the valley
to tend the sick and sing to the families the stories of their
ancestors. But he had been old even then and did not often
seek the company of men. Most of his days were spent in the
mountains, gathering the herbs and roots to make his medicines. His children had grown and died, as had two wives. He
was already a very old man when he found the Stone.

He had seen the explosion in the night sky, a fireball
shooting sparks. When one of the sparks streaked down
directly toward Kanna, he had not attempted to move. It was
the tongue of the night come to eat him, and he would not
object. There was no point in running from death, especially
when one had lived as many years as he had.

But the fireball did not strike him. It slammed instead into
a massive cedar growing out of the hillside and severed its
trunk like a mighty axe swung by the moon itself. The place
where it struck the tree burst instantly into flame.

Had he been a younger man, Kanna might have fled from
the burning tree, yielding to the will of the gods. But he had
seen lightning strike before. In his lifetime, he had watched
vast tracts of forest burned to ashes by the fire from a single
tree. And so instead of running away, Kanna scooped dirt
onto the fire with his hands. The hair on his arms singed. His
fingers blistered with the heat. An ember burned his face. But
he put the fire out.

In the morning he found the Stone's mother, a pitted,
cratered boulder still smoldering with its own heat. It had

cracked open when it hit the tree, and its interior lay exposed and gleaming in the sun.

It was a thing of weird beauty, a mass of concentric circles interspersed with bumps so perfectly round that they might have been eggs growing out of the hot metal. Where there were no bumps, there were depressions of equal perfection. One of these was deeper and wider than the others.

Then he saw it, lying against a rock: a perfect sphere of a color unlike anything he had ever seen before. He bent to touch it. When he could feel, through his burned hands, that it was not hot, he picked it up.

He was disappointed. It was not a perfect sphere. Its top had come off and its interior was hollow, as if it had cradled another perfect sphere. He looked for the missing piece. If he found it, he would have not just one, but two spheres nesting together. A moon within a moon. A true gift for the gods. But he did not find the other piece.

Kanna stared at the Stone in his hand. It would be useful, he decided. He could drink from it, like a gourd. And it was beautiful. And it had come to him straight from the sky.

Suddenly he noticed his fingers. The blisters were gone. The hair on his arms had grown back. The sore spots on his face had healed.

Then he understood. The gods had given him the Stone to heal the sick. It was time he left the mountain.

Quickly he gathered up his things and set off toward the valley. He would tell the families there that the gods had smiled and brought them a gift.

Never did he consider that he would *become* their god, or that the gift he carried would make him immortal.

Saladin listened intently to the stories of the Stone. They had taken Kanna years to tell, since the two of them had begun with no common language. By the time Saladin was fifteen, he had learned all the skills the old hunter and healer could teach him and had surpassed Kanna in many ways.

He began to realize that the hermit was not only an old man, but a completely different type of being. And not a god;

not unless the gods knew less than mortals did: For while
Kanna could still heal most of the lame and injured creatures
of the mountain without the aid of the sacred Stone, he could
not fashion a net to catch a fish.

Saladin had tried to explain the purpose of a net, but the
old man had only stared at him, dull-eyed. It was not until
Kanna saw what the net his protégé had made could do that
he realized the boy had made a tool.

It was the same with numbers. No matter how many times
Saladin demonstrated it, the old man could not grasp the
concept of abstract numbers. Two logs, yes; but the difference between "three" and "many" was nonexistent.

Kanna, the boy decided, was quite stupid.

He had come from a race of inferior minds, men so limited
that for hundreds of years—or perhaps thousands, since
Kanna could not discern the difference—not one of them had
questioned the improbability that the old man would continue
to live while whole generations of valley dwellers aged and
passed into dust. Not one of them had dared to take the Stone
from him. Even much later, when the climate changed
noticeably and the vast plains which had held giraffe and
antelope and elephant dried into lifeless deserts, when the
limitless expanses of fresh water in which hippopotamus had
waded dwindled into two muddy rivers, when the hunter-
tribes fled the valley or died with sand in their mouths, not
one of them had sought to steal Kanna's power.

When they were gone, the New People came to the valley.
They were not hunters, but farmers who lived in the parts of
the valley that had once been swampland. They irrigated their
fields from the muddy rivers. They built their houses of mud
brick and burned animal dung for fuel. They wove their
clothing from fibers grown near the rivers. They created art
and spoke a language which used a precise grammar, so that
it was not necessary to augment it with gestures.

Into the midst of this advanced society had walked Kanna,
reeking of the animal skins he wore.

"Kanna was empty." He clasped his hands over his heart to
indicate his loneliness. "Here. Kanna see New People."

Saladin nearly laughed at the clownish mask of sadness that settled on the old man's features as he remembered the encounter.

"New People many. One, two, many. Throw spears. Many wounds." He pointed to the places on his ancient, unblemished torso where the weapons of the Sumerians had struck.

Saladin tried to picture the faces of the civilized men when the old hermit had plucked the spears from his body and walked away without a scratch.

"That's when you became a god to them," Saladin said, maneuvering a thick piece of wood onto the fire that warmed the dank cave where the old man and the boy made their home.

Kanna looked at him uncomprehendingly.

"The New People worship you as a god. A white god with sapphires for eyes, who rides on moonbeams." He told the old man the story of the farmer who had seen Kanna fishing at night.

The hermit laughed, the firelight accentuating the deep folds of his brow. "Kanna run. Kanna think New People man try to kill." When his laughter subsided, his gaze settled into the hypnotic flames of the fire. "Bad to live so long."

"Not as bad as dying, I imagine," Saladin said dryly.

The old man smiled. "After New People throw spears, Kanna come to mountain." He patted the rocky earth as if it were a favorite cow. "Kanna stay. Kanna . . . empty." He accompanied the word with the same gesture he had used before.

Then the corners of his eyes crinkled. "But boy come." He could not pronounce Saladin's name. "Boy come, not empty."

His hand touched his heart. His eyes welled with tears.

Saladin sighed and turned away. The old fool's sentimentality bored him. For seven years he had lived with Kanna's apelike stupidity, because there was nowhere else for him to go.

There still wasn't. He had no future back in the valley. In Kish, he would be executed as a runaway slave if anyone recognized him. Back at Elam—if there still was an Elam—he would be a stranger with no status or property. No, he would not return in disgrace to the land his father had once ruled.

Two cities, and beyond them the deserts and the mountains and the void of world's end.

Suddenly he started. He was *in* the mountains. Since childhood he had heard that the Zagros was the end of all life, and yet he had lived here with Kanna among all manner of living things for seven years. They had roamed the mountains for miles and had not yet approached the abyss.

He whirled to face the old man. "Kanna," he said, his pupils dilating with excitement, "is there a land beyond the valley?"

The hermit nodded. "Many lands."

Saladin thought his heart would burst from his chest. "In which direction?"

Kanna pointed first to the east, then described a large circle with his arm. "Many lands."

"But the desert lies to the east."

"Past the sands," Kanna said. "Along dry river, past a tree of stone. A great valley. Many New People."

"Past the sands . . ." Saladin's voice was barely audible. The priests had declared that the mountains lay at the end of the world. "But there cannot be . . ."

Kanna nodded stubbornly.

For a moment, Saladin allowed himself the luxury of a dream. A new land, filled with people like himself. There, he would not be killed as a slave. And perhaps he would not have to go as a servant. He could trade on his knowledge of healing. Kanna knew every plant and root and rock within a hundred miles and had shown Saladin how to use their medicinal properties to treat wounds and sick animals.

"How can I go there?" he asked hesitantly. "What route do I take?"

The old man shook his head. "Boy not go. Boy die in sands." Then he smiled. "Stay. On mountain." He took the boy's hand and placed it over his own chest. "Stay. With Kanna."

Saladin yanked his hand away. He could not bear the touch of the old man.

"Do you think I'm going to stay here forever?" he shouted. "Stay here as the pet of an old monkey man?"

Kanna drew back in alarm, which only fueled Saladin's anger.

"Don't pretend to be afraid of me! You know I'm going to die here an old man while you go on with your worthless life. You shouldn't have the Stone! It should belong to someone worthy, not—"

He stopped short, his breath suddenly halted by the magnitude of the idea.

The Stone.

With the Stone, he could cross the desert. With the Stone, he could accomplish anything, possess anything, learn anything.

With the Stone, he could live forever.

"Give it to me," he said in a low voice.

Kanna backed away, toward the damp walls of the cave where they slept. "Boy bad."

"The Stone," Saladin said.

The old man's lips drew into a tight downward semicircle. He looked like a child about to cry. His eyes flickered down to his waist, where he kept the Stone inside a snakeskin pouch.

Saladin's young, strong hand reached out to grab the thong suspending the pouch.

"No!" Kanna howled. Saladin yanked it, oblivious to the old man's efforts to push him away. He forced Kanna against the stone wall. "No!" The hermit's eyes darted wildly around the small cave.

"You pathetic old bore," Saladin said. He spanned his right hand around Kanna's neck while he continued to pull at the leather thong at the old man's waist.

Then, like an animal forced by desperation to action,

Kanna burst through the boy's stranglehold and butted his head against Saladin's.

The boy reeled backward; the old man's skull was thick as rock. He had barely had time to regain his vision when he saw the firelog coming at his face. Kanna swung it savagely, filling the cave with the ferocious, atavistic cry of the ancient hunter facing a beast.

The blow sent Saladin sprawling on the packed earth in a fountain of blood. Kanna wept, his shoulders heaving uncontrollably. He took a step forward toward the body, then stopped. If the boy was alive, Kanna knew, he would heal him with the Stone, and it would all begin again.

Their time together had come to an end.

Kanna waited. The boy would not live without him.

Shutting his eyes tightly, the old man stumbled out of the cave into the sunlight. He would go far, far into the desert. He could live there. He could live anywhere. He would live, even though he wanted to die.

The old man began his descent down the familiar mountain. He said nothing, but as he walked he placed his clasped hand over his heart.

# CHAPTER THIRTEEN

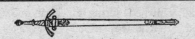

When Saladin regained consciousness, it was night. He could barely make out the embers of the cooking fire with one eye; the other had no vision at all. The blood on his face had dried into a thick crust. His right shoulder throbbed with a dull ache that grew into a screaming, searing pain when he touched it. His arm hung uselessly, the joint smashed by Kanna's terrible blows.

Who would have thought the old man would be so strong? Of course, he was a different sort of man. An older species, made for the work of beasts. Saladin spat out blood and broken teeth.

*I shouldn't have forced him to fight me*, he thought. He had underestimated the old elephant. All men, even those with no desire to live, possessed the instinct to survive.

Slowly he got to his feet, fighting the dizziness that threatened to overwhelm him, and rummaged through the stock of leather pouches that contained the old man's medicines. He would need a poultice of some kind for his shoulder and something to prevent infection in the head wounds. Some saltwater, painful though it was, cleared the blood and mucus out of his good eye, but the other was utterly blind. Yellowish fluid seeped constantly out of the socket; and the eyeball itself, when Saladin could steel himself to touch it through the lacerated lid, had flattened. He had seen the condition only once before, on a hare which had been attacked by some larger animal. A shard of bone from the hare's shattered skull had pierced the eyeball and deflated it. The hare had convulsed for two days before Kanna killed it out of pity.

He felt himself trembling. His wounds were too great. The fever would come soon, and he would be unable to care for himself. Without the Stone, he would die.

He thought frantically. His legs were still strong. He could walk back to Kish, find a doctor. He would say he was a wanderer, lost from his tribe; no one would know him for the boy who had vanished during the earthquake seven years before. Then, after he was healed—if a doctor existed who could treat such wounds—he would escape once more, come back . . .

*Come back here*, he thought. Back to the mountain, to live like an animal. To wander alone among the rocks until some wild beast killed him for food. To become Kanna, but without Kanna's assurance of everlasting life.

A low wail escaped from his lips, growing, echoing through the cave until it became a scream of rage and despair.

"Kanna!" he shouted.

But Kanna was gone. To another part of the mountains, to . . .

Saladin's head snapped toward the wall. The medicines. The old man had left the medicines. Some of them had taken years to gather and distill. Some were made from plants that no longer existed. Some were taken from animals that had not lived in the valley for millennia. Whenever they had moved in search of game or water, the medicines had been the first things Kanna packed in his animal-skin bundles. He would never leave without them.

But they were here, in the cave. His other belongings, too, were still here. The old man had taken nothing. Yet Saladin knew he had left for good. Kanna would no longer trust him. The boy would attack again. Kanna had to know that.

*But he loves me.*

That knowledge was as sure as the fingers on his hand. Kanna regarded Saladin as his son. The old man had not moved; he had fled, brokenhearted, from his child's betrayal.

He could have killed Saladin, but he had not. He had left his medicines for him.

And he had gone to the one place where the boy would not dare follow.

*Along the dry river, past the tree of stone* . . .

He had gone east, into the desert.

By the time Saladin reached the remains of the petrified tree, the fever had already been upon him for two days. His eye had begun to fester and stink in the baking heat beneath the reed bandage he had fashioned, and his shoulder joint was swollen beyond recognition.

The landmarks Kanna had spoken of had been a virtual map. After Saladin could no longer follow the outlines of the ancient riverbed, he had spotted the speck on the horizon which was the tree of stone.

And he had been lucky. A day before he reached the tree, it had rained. The desert was no longer the lush grassland it had once been, but neither was it the trackless waste of windblown sand it was destined to become in the centuries ahead. The hardscrabble earth still sprouted clumps of hearty weeds that held enough moisture to keep rainwater from evaporating. In the stretches between the weeds, the rain sat on the drying earth like a cloak, turning only its thin surface to mud before baking hard again in the sun.

Saladin was lucky, because it rained at night, although he did not feel in the least fortunate. The desert was cold at night. When the rain came, there was no shelter. Saladin stretched out an antelope skin to replenish his water supply, then sat down shivering in the mud. He dared not walk without the light of the moon to illuminate the speck on the horizon. If he lost sight of that, he would surely die.

*But I'll die anyway,* he thought miserably. He was too tired to feel the shock of fear that had propelled him on this journey; too tired, even, to give much thought to the terrible pain of his body. It was dying in segments. His eye was already dead. His melon-sized shoulder would go next. As the rain fell he took a stone knife from his pack and lanced the obscene boil of his shoulder. As it spurted, he screamed mindlessly into the emptiness of the night. Then he slept, trying to keep the new wound away from the mud.

In the morning, the earth steamed. The sun drew the water out of the ground so quickly that Saladin could see it rising all around him like smoke. He stopped short, staring at it in wonder. If Kanna had not told him that there was a land beyond the desert, he would surely have believed that this place was the end of the world.

His shoulder worsened during the day. The fluid that wept from it was no longer red, but a thick greenish yellow. Hot air streamed from his nose. Chills racked him, despite the unrelenting sun.

The second day was worse. He could not bring himself to eat even a scrap of dried meat, but he drank thirstily. Before noon, his water supply was gone. He threw his gourd away without a thought, his legs moving automatically, his blistered, seeing eye fixed and unblinking on the speck which had become the shape of the massive petrified tree.

The tree was the end of his journey. At the beginning, he had felt certain that he would find the old man before he reached it. Kanna walked slowly, and hadn't had much of a head start on Saladin. The boy had not given thought to the possibility that his own injuries would slow him down.

Now he had found the tree of stone, but the old man was nowhere in sight. He had moved on, or perhaps had never come this way at all.

Saladin sat down woodenly. He stared off toward the limitless horizon, where the sandy earth crested in an unending ridge, took the filthy bandage off his ruined eye, and laughed, softly at first, then wild and racking.

*What if Kanna had never come to the desert?*

What if he was back in the cave in the Zagros Mountains, tending to his medicines, wondering what had happened to the boy who had so angered him for a moment? The old fool had no intellect to speak of; he might have forgotten the entire episode by the next day. And here was Saladin, his face disfigured like one of the clay masks the priests in Kish would don before they climbed the ziggurat to the gods, his fifteen-year-old body disintegrating before his own eyes, dying in the sands for nothing.

He laughed until he shrieked, pounding the back of his head against the trunk of the fallen tree, then pitching forward to vomit out the last of his water. When he was finished, he lay on the ground. He would die here, he decided. It was as good a place as any. He touched his finger to an indentation in the dirt and closed his eyes.

And then opened them.

The indentation was a footprint.

Saladin whimpered as he scrambled to his knees, touching the sunbaked outline of Kanna's foot. The old man had halted here, at this very spot, to shelter from the rain. And after the rain stopped, he had gone on, leaving his trail in the mud.

Luck had given Saladin another signpost, the next section of the map. He looked overhead. The sun was directly above him, blazing in full heat. Kanna was only a day and a half ahead of him, and the old man walked slowly.

He crawled to the next footprint, and the next, then staggered to his feet and began to run on the dry, hard earth. He paid no heed to his shoulder, which jolted with pain at every footfall, nor to the thirst that already caused his tongue to stick fast to the roof of his mouth. He had a chance to live, and he would take it.

By midafternoon he could barely see the footprints. The sun had dried the mud quickly. Ahead of him lay a stretch of empty brown land. But the footprints had followed a straight line from the stone tree, and Saladin concentrated all his thoughts on staying on course. He picked up some pebbles and tossed them one by one ahead of him to focus his mind on the invisible straight line of the old man's path. He forced away all pain, all suffering, all fear of death. The old man was near, beyond the ridge, perhaps . . .

Near nightfall he stumbled and knew he could not rise. He raised his head, then dropped it once again onto the ground. If he slept this night, he knew, he would be dead by morning.

With wildly trembling fingers, he pushed himself to a sitting position and took out the knife he had used to lance his putrid shoulder. Barely feeling its touch, he drew the chiseled blade across the back of his hand and drank blood from his own body.

Then, with an effort greater than he had ever known, he willed himself to stand and move, one foot after another, toward the top of the ridge.

"Kanna," he whispered without moving his blood-caked lips. "Kanna . . . Kanna . . . Kanna . . ."

He was there, at the bottom of the bare hill and to the east, but near enough so that Saladin could make out the unmistakable figure of a man.

The boy stopped and blinked. The night came quickly here and played tricks with one's eyes.

He was no longer certain of what was real and what he imagined. He wanted to see Kanna, surely, wanted it so much that his heat-boiled brain might have invented him. Or the figure below might be death himself, come to claim him at last.

"Ka . . ." It was no more than a croak, but the old man stopped and turned.

With the last of his strength Saladin held his arms out in supplication. His knees buckled beneath him. He fell to the earth in the position of a beggar, arms outstretched, head back, eyes closed. He rolled, insensate, to the bottom of the ridge while the old man loped toward him.

Kanna knelt before the boy, moaning softly over the festering wounds. The starry night was cold, but Saladin was burning with fever. His eyes were half-open and glassy. His breath was coming in ragged gasps, rattling with the grotesque music of death.

Hurriedly, the old man pulled the small metal bowl from its pouch in his belt and filled it with water from a skin slung over his back. He cradled the boy's head in his arms and tilted the Stone against his lips.

The first stream of water spilled from the sides of Saladin's mouth, but soon he began to drink. Kanna parceled it out in small sips, so that the boy would not choke on the water he so needed. When he finished one bowlful, the old man refilled it and wrapped Saladin's wasted fingers around its smooth sides.

Slowly the boy's eyes opened. He sat up, sucking air through his teeth as the wonderful Stone did its work. His shoulder shrank to normal proportions as the green poison inside it dried and disappeared. The deep wound where Saladin had pierced it narrowed to a thin line, then vanished. The marks on his hands and face were replaced by soft, perfect skin. His blisters faded to nothing. Inexorably, the ruined eye in his face rounded, filled, and healed. And through it all the Stone sang its song, thrumming through Saladin's blood with its own powerful heartbeat.

He looked up. The old man was nodding happily, smiling like a little dancing troll.

"Thank you, Kanna," the boy said. He bent forward and kissed the hermit's cheek. "Will you forgive me?"

The old man's eyes welled. He touched the boy's face with his gnarled hands. He lowered his head.

"Good," Saladin said softly, a moment before he threw the Stone into the night.

Kanna looked after it in bewilderment, but before he could rise to fetch it, the boy took the knife from his belt and drew it across the old man's throat.

The hermit's arms flailed in the gush of blood. He pulled himself to one knee before tumbling onto his back where he lay twitching, his eyes wide with confusion and fear.

"It won't last long," Saladin said.

Kanna clasped his hand on the boy's wrist. He was trying to speak, but he no longer had the means.

"I know," the boy said gently. "You would have wanted me to have it." He smiled, then pried the old fingers loose and rose to find the Stone.

When he got back, Kanna was dead. Saladin removed the belt and pouch from the body and strapped the metal cup around his waist. Then he slung the old man's water-skin over his shoulder and continued east, to the land beyond the desert.

That had been so long ago, Saladin thought from his perch above the city of Kowloon. He had scarcely given Kanna a thought for years. He smiled. Dr. Coles would have loved to hear about him.

He uncoiled himself from the white wicker chair and stretched his long arms with a sigh. He would miss China. During his incarceration, he had dreamed often of its teeming cities and boundless enticements. Revisiting rural England was the last thing he wanted to do, especially so soon after fleeing it. But there was work to be done. The cup—Kanna's "Stone"—was missing again, and he knew he had to act quickly. He had been lazy once, during a holiday with a woman, and had lost the cup for more than twelve years as a result.

This would not be so difficult a quest. He could probably pay the American boy for the cup and have an end to it.

He crinkled his long nose. No, that would be a bore. He had spent four years in a single room with nothing but an occasional novel to distract him. He would give himself a small adventure. Some horses, some costumes . . .

He laughed out loud.

A servant scurried out to check on him, cocking his head with curiosity.

"Some traveling clothes, please," Saladin said.

The servant nodded and left.

Yes, yes. It was good to be free again.

# CHAPTER FOURTEEN

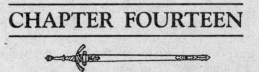

Hal felt out of place in London. Not because of the black eye, which had faded to a ripe yellow and which had been planted on him personally by Benny the barkeep, after Hal explained that the Grand Prize he'd won on the now nationally famous episode of "Go Fish!" could not be exchanged for ready cash to pay Hal's bar bill. After the episode with Benny, Hal had wisely chosen to hide out from his other creditors until his travel arrangements could be made.

It was June, and his room at the Inter-Continental was stocked with a vase filled with fresh flowers, a bottle of Moët et Chandon, and a complimentary breakfast for two.

Those, essentially, were the reasons he felt strange. The room was too clean, the vase too fragile, the champagne too expensive. He had pompously given a five-pound note to the porter, who registered no sign of surprise at the large tip, and had made what he hoped were appropriately ceremonious sounds as he sniffed the cork from the Moët in imitation of what he believed sophisticated people did with champagne.

But after the porter left, he took off his shoes, rubbed his travel-swollen feet, wished for a beer, and felt like a hick.

What the hell was he doing in *London?* He had never set foot out of New York City until he was twenty-three years old and then it was to the FBI training facility in Quantico. After that, he had traveled wherever the Bureau sent him, but he had never lingered to visit those places, and he had never been alone.

That was it, he supposed. The complimentary breakfast for two was the kicker. The double bed. The two glasses set on the table by mistake. Human beings traveled in pairs, at least when they were supposed to be enjoying themselves. The Grand Prize had been a trip for two.

And Hal had considered taking someone along with him, until he realized that there was not one individual among his entire lifelong circle of acquaintances whose company he could tolerate for two solid weeks. Except perhaps for the pimp from O'Kay's; but he would have gotten both of them arrested within twenty-four hours of their arrival.

So Hal sat alone in his flowery hotel room until the champagne was gone and his big toe had stopped pulsating and his hunger forced him back onto the street, where he felt more at home.

He settled on a small pub with a basket of dirty plastic flowers in the window and a clock advertising Guinness Stout over the bar. It wasn't Benny's, but it didn't have ferns, either, and the two sausage-and-onion sandwiches he wolfed down were magnificent.

"Nothing like it this side of Little Italy," he said. "But you wouldn't happen to have a cold beer in the place, would you?"

The barman shook his head and smiled politely as he wiped off the bar in front of Hal. "Enjoying your stay, sir?"

"Just got here."

"Business?"

Hal grunted. He did not want to elicit the barman's pity by proclaiming himself a pleasure seeker.

A bell above the door tinkled, announcing the arrival of a new customer.

"To tell you the truth . . ." The rest of the sentence was forgotten. An elderly gentleman walked in a stately manner toward the bar. Hal recognized him at once.

"It's you," he said as the Englishman sat down beside him.

"Indeed," the old man said with a noncommittal smile and a nod of his head. Clearly he didn't remember Hal.

"I think we've met. In New York, a couple of weeks ago. You were going to a game show."

Slowly the light of recognition came into the Englishman's eyes. "I say, it's Mr. Woczniak, isn't it?"

"Hal. Sorry, I'm not good at names."

"Taliesin." He offered his hand. "Bertram, but no one calls me that."

"Taliesin," Hal repeated in a whisper. An ancient name. "That's right, I remember. Like the bard." He saw the man's hand and shook it quickly.

"Ah. So you're a student of medieval literature."

Hal laughed. "I guess the people at 'Go Fish!' think so." He related his experiences as a contestant on the show, leaving out the weirder parts of the story. He did not mention that he'd had no idea where his answers came from.

"Anyway, I ended up winning the grand-prize trip to London. So here I am."

"Jolly good!" Taliesin said, chuckling heartily. "And our paths cross again. I'd hoped they would."

"Yeah." The smile faded from Hal's face. "It's funny."

"Funny?"

Hal shrugged. "I meet you on the street, you give me a ticket to a game show, I win. That's funny. Peculiar. And now I'm in England for maybe four hours, and I meet you again."

"Coincidences happen."

He felt uncomfortable inside his skin. "Yeah. I guess so." He shook the feeling off. "What's your line of work, Mr. Taliesin?"

The old man sipped from a mug of warm Guinness. "By

training, I am an archaeologist. By inclination, an historian. By the infirmities of old age, a pensioner."

"I thought you were in New York on business," Hal said. "You had to meet somebody at the Museum of Natural History."

"Ah, yes. I do some consulting work for the London Museum from time to time. The people in New York were planning to reconstruct a Medieval English town, and I was sent to assist."

Hal felt a low-wattage jolt of electricity course through his entire body. "Your specialty is Medieval English history?"

Taliesin nodded. "I've always felt particularly at home in that era. They call it the Dark Ages, but it was only considered dark in comparison with the fireworks of the Renaissance. Actually, it was quite an interesting time, bringing about the amalgamation of the Celtic tribes with the influences left by the Romans . . ." He stopped abruptly and smiled. "What an old bore I am, lecturing in a pub . . . I say, Hal, are you ill?"

Hal forced himself to swallow. "No, it's just . . . just another coincidence, I guess."

Hal didn't like coincidences. He didn't like all the coincidences that had been occurring since the first time he'd met Taliesin. If he'd still been with the Bureau, he would have had the man investigated.

But for what? Hal Woczniak didn't have a nickel to his name, and his penurious condition was obvious. He had no secrets, not anymore. Anyone associated with the Bureau would disavow any knowledge of him. Even the Chief had written him off two months ago.

Taliesin ordered another pint for Hal. He drank it down. It tasted like dog urine, but it did the job. And truthfully, despite the vague sense of unease brought on by seeing the old man again, Hal hadn't been in such interesting company for a long time.

What the hell. Coincidences *did* happen.

Sometimes.

"You might be interested in a project I'm working on

now," Taliesin said, several glasses later. He had kept up with Hal drink for drink, but was apparently unaffected except for a slight blossoming at the tip of his patrician nose. "A student at Oxford—an 'archaeolobaby,' we call them— has made a claim announcing that the ruins of a medieval castle in Dorset may have been Camelot." He raised his bushy eyebrows in amusement. "The museum has asked me to go out to the site tomorrow. Care to come along?"

"Camelot?" Hal said thickly. Even through an alcoholic haze, the name was still magic to him. "King Arthur's Camelot?"

Taliesin laughed. "Dear boy, I assure you we won't find anything of the sort. Every village with a pile of moss-covered rocks on a hill claims to be Camelot, and every archaeology undergraduate in Great Britain hopes to find it. But it's a lovely bus trip, and I know of an excellent inn near the area. Will you join me?"

Hal slogged down the contents of his glass, and while the barman refilled it, he thought of how much he disliked London. "Sure," he said. "Why not?" He hoisted his drink. "To Camelot."

"To Camelot," Taliesin said, laughing.

The old man came by the hotel at eight the next morning. Hal had managed to shower and shave so that he bore at least a minimal resemblance to a human being, although his brain felt as if it were in the process of shorting out.

Taliesin understood. They walked in silence to Victoria Station, where they boarded a decrepit old bus along with three other passengers. Once inside, the Englishman offered Hal a thermos of coffee.

Coffee was the last thing Hal wanted. The weather was getting warmer by the minute and the bus had obviously been built when air-conditioning was the stuff of science fiction novels.

"It would be wise to drink it now," the old man said. "The roads on this route deteriorate considerably once out into the countryside."

Hal drank the coffee. It was strong and sweet, just the way he liked it, and the open windows shot a cool breeze onto his face. Within a half hour his hangover had disappeared.

"So," he said, leaning back in his seat like a new man. "Where're we going?"

"Dorset County, near the Hampshire border. A place called Lakeshire Tor. There's an old hill fort on an abandoned farm."

"The one the archaeologist thinks is Camelot."

"Not an archaeologist. A student. They're always finding Camelot, or the tomb of Charlemagne, or other equally impressive things. Unfortunately, their findings are almost always false."

"What'd this one find?"

"A rock."

"A rock?"

Taliesin sighed. "He claims it's got an inscription of some kind on it."

"What's it say?"

"He doesn't know. It seems he spotted it during an outing of some kind. Picnic with his girlfriend, most likely. Archaeolobabies like that spot, even though it's clearly marked as private property. He spent a whole blasted day clearing away brambles. By the time he might have been able to see the rock clearly, night had fallen, and the little twit was so woefully unprepared that he had to go home."

"So? Did he go back the next day?"

"An Oxford student? Of course not. He went straight to the head of the archaeology department and demanded a university-sponsored team to retrieve the rock for study." He laughed. "That would be quite premature, of course, as well as illegal."

"Then why are you going?" Hal asked.

"Insurance. If Oxford mounts any sort of investigation, the popular press will be crawling all over the university and printing stories about 'CAMELOT FOUND!' To avoid any such embarrassment, the archaeology department head has asked the museum to look over the student's rock and dismiss any connection to the Camelot theory."

"But . . ." Hal was bewildered. "Why would he connect the rock to Camelot in the first place?"

"Because *everything* on Lakeshire Tor connects to Camelot, at least according to the people who live in the area. They're quite insistent, despite an almost complete lack of evidence."

"You mean the place has been explored before?"

"Countless times. Archaeolobabies adore Lakeshire Tor. There was even a preliminary exploration of the ruins in 1931. A cutting of earth was taken. Some interesting artifacts were uncovered—Saxon, mostly, on the upper layers, but there were some Celtic-style articles below them. Jewelry, pottery shards of the Tintagel type, as well as Roman tiles and even earlier, Bronze Age items. Apparently the castle was built on the site of several previous fortresses from different eras. But the archaeologists found nothing to warrant a full-scale excavation." He studied the passing countryside.

"But the Arthur legend has always been popular in the villages around the Tor. The locals even claim that children can sometimes see the castle."

"Only children?"

"Oh my, yes. That's always part of a good legend. That children, in their purity, can understand things quite beyond the ken of their world-weary elders." He gave Hal a wry look. "It's how they explain the fact that no scientific study has ever been able to find anything."

The old man nestled back in his seat, his eyes sparkling. "And yet the legends persist," he said quietly. "One maintains that on St. John's Eve in midsummer—just a few days from now, actually—the knights of the Round Table ride their ghostly horses around the countryside, searching for their king."

"Do the children see *them* too?" Hal asked, smiling.

"No. The villagers *hear* them. Or they hear something. Tape recorders have picked up the sound."

"Are you kidding?"

The old man shook his head. "After receiving hundreds of tapes of the same noise, the museum sent its own team to record the hoofbeats. And that is what they are, according to the most sophisticated analysis. I've heard them myself, back in the late fifties."

Hal realized that his mouth was agape. "Well, what do you think it is?"

Taliesin shrugged. "An acoustical anomaly, most likely. Sound traveling from another source, perhaps from a riding school or stable. There are many in the area. It could be that at that time of year, when weather conditions are right . . . "

"Then no one's heard the horses during, say, a rainstorm."

"Some claim they have. Some of the villagers swear they've felt the ghost knights pass through their very bodies on their midnight run." He laughed. "But of course that's no more than the imaginations of some country folk with little else to entertain them. At bottom, there is not a shred of fact to establish Lakeshire Tor as Camelot. Or even that Arthur the King existed, for that matter."

"But the legends must be based on something."

Taliesin's laughter pealed. "My boy, you are the romantic."

Hal blushed. In all his life, no one had ever described Harold Woczniak as romantic.

"Forgive me, Hal. It's a compelling story. A boy, guided by destiny and aided by a beneficent sorcerer, who comes to begin a reign that will unite the world in peace and justice. It's the kind of tale we all want to believe. We all want to think that Arthur will come again, and so we keep the old legends alive." He was smiling kindly, every inch the gentle teacher.

Hal grunted. "I guess you're right."

He busied himself with the rest of the coffee and looked around the bus. Several people had boarded since Victoria Station, but his gaze was drawn to one man sitting in the first seat, opposite the driver. He was a swarthy, dark-haired man with biceps like hams bulging out beneath a blue polo shirt.

There was nothing particularly unusual about the man, who sat chatting amiably with the driver and smoking occasional cigarettes, but all the same something put Hal on guard.

It was a sense he'd developed during his years with the FBI, an almost psychic ability to spot a criminal. All experienced cops had it and relied on it heavily. They never included any mention of it in their reports, and even among themselves they used words like "hunch" rather than what it was, because what it was could not be defined.

*The guy's probably just stolen some cash out of the register at work*, he thought. *Or he beat up his girlfriend.*

He screwed the lid back on the thermos. *Or I'm just a jerk.*

That, he decided, was the most likely possibility. He didn't have the sense anymore. Booze had washed it away, the way he'd seen it erase the edge in other cops. The man had never even turned around to look at him.

*Jerk.*

"Feeling better now?" Taliesin asked.

"Huh? Sure. Fine. Thanks." He gave the thermos back to the old man. "So look at the bright side, Taliesin. Maybe this time you'll find something. Maybe you'll *really* discover Camelot."

"It would be quite a nice thing to have in my obituary notice, wouldn't it?" Taliesin said. "Of course, I would be long-dead before any such discovery could be announced."

"I don't understand," Hal said, his eyes wandering involuntarily toward the dark man at the front of the bus.

"Science works slowly, my friend. First, surveys of the land would have to be made, aerial photographs. Something like wheat would have to be planted to show the exact sites of previous habitation. They would show up dark in a photograph after the wheat grew. Then a series of earth-cuttings would be made . . . But it won't come to that."

"Why not?"

"Oh, a number of reasons. For one thing, the land is privately owned."

"I thought you said it was already explored."

Taliesin nodded. "The Abbott family gave the museum

permission to excavate the preliminary cutting sixty years ago. We'd always assumed they would grant it again, if any new evidence turned up. Unfortunately, the last of the family, Sir Bradford Welles Abbott, died earlier this year in an automobile accident and willed the Tor property to a complete stranger."

"Wouldn't the new owner give permission to excavate?"

The old man shrugged. "We've no idea what he'll do. The sod may build a shopping center on the Tor, for all we know."

A pair of wide blue eyes swiveled over the top of the seat in front of them. Hal stared back. Suddenly he felt horribly uncomfortable.

A boy, about ten years old, craned his head above the seat back. He had red hair. He would have fit the profile of Louie Rubel's murder victims perfectly.

"I wouldn't do that," the boy said. "Build a shopping center."

Taliesin smiled.

"I think the place you're talking about belongs to me." His accent was American. A woman who had been dozing beside him woke up then and crankily urged the boy to turn around. "Don't bother people," she snapped.

She was small, Hal saw, but formidable-looking. Her brown hair was pulled back into a severe schoolmarm bun, and the only adornment on her face were a pair of thick glasses. Underneath them, she might have been pretty, but her scowl made it difficult to determine.

"They know my castle," the boy whispered excitedly.

She gave him an exasperated look. "Haven't you learned anything?" she said, her voice shrill. "Don't talk to strangers."

The red-haired boy looked back at Taliesin, studying the old man's face. "He's not a stranger," he said finally. "At . . . at least I don't think so." Two frown lines developed between the bright blue eyes. "I know you, don't I?"

Taliesin crinkled his eyes kindly.

"Maybe it's your voice. You sound just like Mr. Goldberg."

"Arthur, that's enough!" The woman grabbed the boy's shoulders and forced him to sit straight in his seat. "I'm sorry he bothered you," she said, blushing. "It's been a long trip, and boys sometimes get restless."

",Quite all right," Taliesin said.

The boy peered around furtively to steal another glance behind him. This time he was concentrating on Hal.

"You, too," he said, his soft voice filled with wonder. "I know you, too."

Hal forced a grin. "You do, huh?"

"Yes." The boy smiled at him, his face filled with innocent trust. "You were the best."

Hal felt as if a cold fist had just punched him in the gut. "What did you say?"

"Get over here," the woman commanded. She rummaged in her handbag and pulled out a prescription bottle filled with enormous lozenge-shaped pills. She shook one out and held it up for the boy. "Take it."

"No, I'll miss everything." He shielded his face.

"Lady—" Hal interrupted, but she wasn't listening to him.

"I said, take it." Fighting the boy all the way, she finally stuffed it into his mouth.

He spat it out, then ran down the length of the aisle to the door of the bus.

"Arthur!"

The driver screeched the bus to a halt. He looked back at the woman, then leveled a stare at the youngster and jerked his thumb toward the rear. "Better go back to your seat, lad," he said.

The boy didn't move.

Hal saw the pill lying in the aisle and picked it up. "Just what is this?" he asked the woman.

"None of your damn business." She rose to move toward the boy, but Hal blocked her path.

"I'd like to know what kind of stuff you're forcing down the kid's throat," he said.

Blushing furiously, she peeked beyond Hal's big frame and pleaded to the boy with her eyes. The driver and the other passengers were silent, watching the scene with interest. The swarthy man in front smiled and winked at her.

"You don't understand," she said, her voice quavering, her eyes not daring to look at Hal's implacable face.

"No, I don't. Why don't you explain it to me."

She began to tremble. She covered her face with her hands, and a great sob welled up inside her and burst out.

Hal felt extremely awkward. The lady's wire was obviously stretched to the limit. She looked like some kind of bird quivering in front of him, or a little girl playing dress-up in her too-long dress and clunky shoes.

The boy finally broke the silence. "It's Seconal," he said quietly, walking back toward them. "I haven't been sleeping well." He took the pill out of Hal's hand and swallowed it dry. "This was my fault."

Then he squeezed past Hal and put his arm around the woman, who was no more than a foot taller than he was, and led her gently back to her seat. "Sorry, Emily," he said. "It won't happen again."

The woman kept her hands over her face, but allowed him to seat her. Then the boy chose another seat for himself, directly across from Hal's, and slumped into it.

The bus started up. Hal sat down quietly. When he glanced across the aisle, the boy was watching him.

"Will you wake me when we get to the castle?" he asked.

Hal nodded. "You bet."

The boy smiled and closed his eyes.

*You were the best.*

There was no mistake about it: He had used those very words.

*You're the best, kid. The best there is.*

Hal shuddered. He looked over at Taliesin, but the old man had also dozed off.

He stared out the window. He wouldn't sleep, he knew. Not now, not tonight, maybe not for a long time.

Things had gone far beyond coincidence. The chance

encounter with Taliesin, the strangeness of the game-show questions, the boy quoting from his dream . . . They were all connected somehow. He believed this with the same instinct that had singled out the dark man in the first seat as trouble. He believed, but he didn't understand a damned thing.

No, he wouldn't sleep. The dream was too close to the surface.

# CHAPTER FIFTEEN

A few minutes after the boy fell asleep in the seat beside Hal and Taliesin, the woman with him came over from her own seat to cover him with a jacket. She touched him tenderly, Hal saw, smoothing the red hair on the boy's forehead. When she turned to face Hal, her eyes were glassy with tears.

"I apologize for my rudeness," she said quietly. "My nephew and I have been under a strain for some time. I was afraid that you might try to harm him."

Her hands were still trembling. Probably chronic, Hal thought. His own hands shook for months after Jeff Brown's death, until he discovered the no-worry of the bottle after his release from the hospital.

"I thought the same about you," Hal said.

She nodded. "That's understandable, I guess. The Seconal—I wasn't forcing it on him. He hasn't been able to sleep. He has nightmares . . . ."

She stopped abruptly, as if sensing she'd said too much. With another tight, controlled smile, she stood up.

"Hal Woczniak," he said, extending his hand.

She shook it. "Emily Blessing."

"Vacation?"

"Yes," she answered. Too quickly, Hal thought.

She was about to scurry back to her own seat when the bus suddenly veered off the road into the parking lot of a country inn with two small, old-fashioned gasoline pumps outside. Emily thumped back onto the seat next to Hal.

"Oil light's on," the driver called out with a sigh. "It won't take but a few minutes to set things right." He pulled up to the rear of the old stone building, turned off the engine, and rose. "Sorry for the inconvenience," he said, "but we want to assure your safety. Go on inside for a cup of tea if you like. I'll let you know when we can be off again."

He dashed out before the passengers could start complaining. Slowly, they stood up and stretched, murmuring in futile protest. Taliesin woke up, blinking.

"I say. Has there been an accident?"

"Oil leak, I think. The driver said to go inside."

Taliesin looked out the window at the old stone building. "Oh, I say, the Inn of the Falcon. This is the place I told you about. It's quite nice inside."

Hal turned back to Emily. "Will you join us?"

"No, thanks. I don't want to wake Arthur. We'll just wait here."

Hal and Taliesin followed the other passengers into the inn, where most of them made a beeline for the rest rooms. The place was quaint but sweltering. Almost immediately Hal felt a thin trickle of sweat running down his back. Just his luck, he thought, to come to cool, bonny England and run into a New York City-style heat wave.

The old man seemed unaffected by the heat and chattered amiably about the structure of the place. Hal pulled up a chair at one of the small tables and waited for Taliesin to sit down.

"Oh, my, no," Taliesin said. "We've been sitting for hours."

"Sit down," Hal commanded.

Taliesin complied, raising an eyebrow. "As you wish."

"I want to know what the hell's going on," Hal said. "Right now."

"What on earth . . ." Taliesin was visibly relieved by the appearance of the waitress and kept her attention for as long

s possible, contemplating and rejecting a number of teas. He
finally decided on Earl Gray, smiling as if he had made a
momentous decision.

Hal leaned back in his chair, his arms folded over his chest,
his face dark and blank. When the waitress asked for his
order, he only shook his head. His eyes never left the old
man. "Start talking," he said once they were alone.

"I'm sure I don't have the slightest idea . . ."

"Cut it, Taliesin. The 'coincidence' theory isn't holding
water anymore. You wanted to meet me. You set it all up. I
don't know how you did it, but you fixed the game show
somehow, just like you somehow managed to have that taxi
show up out of nowhere. This trip of mine is your doing. So's
that boy outside who knows more about me than he should. I
want to know why."

"The boy? Which boy?"

"The one who looks like a dead kid in New
York . . . enough like him to be his brother. His picture
was in all the papers. Mine, too. Don't say you didn't know
who I was the minute you staged that pratfall in Manhattan."

"You're speaking gibberish."

"How's the kid involved?" Hal went on flatly.

"*Involved in what?*" Taliesin asked.

"The woman's a wreck. The kid's on Seconal. Exactly
what is going on here?"

"Hal, you really ought to hear yourself . . ."

"And the cops ought to hear you. But I'm going to let you
tell me first."

The old man sputtered. When the waitress brought their
order, he fairly melted in gratitude. He sipped his tea and
smiled. "Now," he said at last. "Suppose we talk reasonably
about your apprehensions."

"Apprehensions, my aunt's fanny. You brought me on this
trip for a reason, and I want to know . . ."

His train of thought left him. The bus driver came in, his
hands covered with oil. As he took his place at the end of the
washroom queue, the swarthy man who had been sitting in
the front of the bus rose slowly from his table and put on a

jacket he'd been carrying. It was an innocuous piece of business, except that the air inside the inn was hot enough to explode dynamite. Why put on a jacket?

The dark man placed some coins on the table, then casually walked out the front door.

"This is utter nonsense," Taliesin said, but Hal had stopped listening to him.

He stood up and followed the dark man outside, slowly and at some distance. The man walked quickly up to the bus and climbed aboard. Instinctively Hal reached for his gun. It wasn't there. He hadn't carried a gun for more than a year. For the first time in all the liquor-soaked months since his resignation, he felt afraid.

He cast about for a weapon. The best he could come up with was one of the fist-sized decorative rocks around the juniper bushes that lined the inn's foundation. He wrapped his fingers around it and ran in a crouch to the side of the bus.

The dark man was slowly making his way up the aisle, toward Emily and Arthur Blessing. Emily saw him and stiffened. When the man slid a gun out of his jacket, she moaned.

"Take it," she said. "It's on the seat, in the red lunch box." She pointed to the seat she had occupied.

The man looked over at the place she'd indicated, then back to her. The movement took less than two seconds, but during those two seconds Hal understood worlds. He knew the man was going to kill Emily Blessing, and probably the boy, too, whether or not he got what he wanted. He also knew that he was not in a strong position to stop him. If Hal shouted, the gunman would shoot him first, then go after the woman. If he tried to storm the bus, he would be giving the man even more time.

All he had was the rock. That, and the good fortune of a bus without air-conditioning. The open windows gave him a chance, if he could find a line of sight. But the man's head was above the window edge. No matter how well he threw, Hal wouldn't be able to do any real damage. A tap to the man's gigantic upper arm would have all the effect of a feather.

"Please don't kill us," Emily pleaded.

The man straightened up to fire, and Hal threw the rock.

It was as good a shot as he could have hoped for, hitting square on the man's elbow. The gunman leaped in surprise. His gun fired. By the time he got his bearings, Hal was in the bus, hurling himself up the aisle as Emily screamed in terror.

He kicked the weapon out of the man's hand. Then, using the counterforce of the same movement, he yanked on the gunman's leg to send him toppling onto the rubber mat of the aisle.

Hal planned none of his moves. They had all been drilled into him for so many years that they came as automatically as breathing. Once the man was down, Hal slammed him on the underside of his jaw, kneed him in the groin, then swarmed over him to pull one of the hugely muscled arms into a hammerlock.

"Are you all right?" he asked Emily. She nodded and he said, "Yell to someone to call the police."

She bobbed her head but did not move. Next to her, Arthur started to pull himself out of a deep, drug-induced sleep. Suddenly, Emily's eyes widened as she looked toward Hal.

"My God, what are you doing? He's turning blue."

The gunman began to convulse in Hal's arms. Immediately Hal switched the position of his arms to span the man's wide chest and jerked on the solar plexus with his fists in the Heimlich maneuver, hoping the man would spit out whatever was choking him. But the dark man's seizure worsened. Within seconds, his chest bucked feverishly and his eyes were bulging.

"Give me something to prop his mouth open!" Hal yelled. Emily handed him a pen. He shoved it sideways into the man's mouth, then reached in with two fingers to get at whatever obstruction was in his throat. He could find nothing. The man made a rattling sound. His body quieted and stilled. By the time the police siren could be heard, the dark man was dead.

\* \* \*

The local constable and a doctor arrived first. The constable was a young man in his twenties who swaggered up to the bus with a self-important air.

"Please remain where you are," he ordered the passengers who were gathered around the scene. He pointed to Hal, Emily, and Arthur. "You. Out."

*Ten to one the guy's never seen a stiff before*, Hal thought, rubbing the knuckles of his right hand. The dead man's jaw had been like a rock. Hal had hit him hard, he knew, but not hard enough to kill him. Not even hard enough to break his jaw.

The policeman emerged a few minutes later with the gun in an evidence bag and placed it in his car.

"Now then," he said, turning back to the crowd. His lips were white.

"You feeling okay?" Hal asked.

"You'll have your chance to speak," the young officer snapped.

While the doctor examined the body in the bus, the constable worked his way around the crowd of passengers, all of whom had run out of the inn in time to watch the man expire.

"It was the left hook to the jaw what done it," an elderly man volunteered.

"The big Yank tore him limb from limb."

"He had a gun. I seen it."

"Oh, there was a gun, sure enough. We all heard it go off."

"All right, all right," the constable said officiously. "I'll hear you one at a time."

"And when'll the bus be leaving, officer?"

"We'll be keeping it at least overnight."

There was a collective groan from the passengers.

"But you'll not be detained that long. Another bus is being routed here. You'll be on your way soon."

The constable interviewed each of the witnesses in turn, beginning with Emily Blessing.

"I never saw him before we left London," she said. "My

nephew and I were waiting in the bus. He was asleep, and I didn't want to disturb him. And then that man got on, and pointed a gun at me."

"Was he attempting to rob you, ma'am?" the officer asked.

"No. I don't know what he wanted."

Hal had been looking around at the crowd. At Emily's blatant lie, he turned around in disbelief. Her cheeks were bright red.

*She's the worst liar I ever saw*, Hal thought. *And this dickhead cop isn't even looking at her.*

"Did he make any move to attack you physically?"

She shook her head. "No. That is, I don't think so. He didn't have a chance. This gentleman stopped him." She indicated Hal. "He threw a rock through the window. The gun went off, then he got on the bus and the two of them started fighting."

"Thank you, ma'am," the policeman said. "A CID—a detective—is on his way from Bournemouth. He'll want to speak with you as well, if you don't mind."

"Of course."

He turned to Hal with a completely different demeanor. "How is it you happened by the bus when you did?" he asked, hooking his thumbs into his belt.

"Oh, brother," he muttered.

"What was that?"

"Officer . . . Constable . . . I just didn't like the guy's looks. I followed him outside."

"You didn't like his looks, you say."

Hal sighed. "That's right. Now, when's the detective coming?"

"I don't see what that's got to do with you."

It was going to be a long, long day.

"Now suppose you tell me what happened after you allegedly removed the weapon from the victim."

"The *victim?* He was going to shoot the lady!" Hal shouted.

"Are you forcing me to use restraints on you, sir?"

"Oh, Jesus."

He was rescued by the doctor, who emerged from the bus
and came straight for them.

"Gunshot?" the constable asked.

The doctor shook his head and gently pulled the constable
away from Hal and the witnesses.

"Broken neck, then," the constable suggested.

"Cyanide."

"What?" The policeman made a face and stared at Hal
accusingly.

"There's a metal capsule inside a tooth. I've left it in place
for the M.E., of course. He'll confirm it."

"Are you saying he was poisoned?"

The doctor made a facial equivalent of a shrug. "The
postmortem will determine the cause of death, of course, but
the cyanide capsule had been recently broken. The odor of
the poison is still in the fellow's mouth."

"Could the bloke who hit him be responsible?"

"It's possible. The seal may have been accidentally opened
during the brawl, but it's unlikely. My guess is that the
pathologist is going to rule this death a suicide."

# CHAPTER SIXTEEN

It was late when Hal got back to the Inn of the Falcon. Emily
and Taliesin were waiting for him in the small downstairs
lounge.

"You should have left with the bus," he growled at the old
man.

"The castle's only a few miles distant. And I wouldn't just
go off and leave you alone here," Taliesin said.

"Why not? Think I might find out what you're up to?"

"Now, really, Hal—"

"What happened?" Emily interrupted irritably.

Hal looked at her for a long moment. "The guy killed himself."

"*What?*"

"The M.E. just phoned in the autopsy report. That's why they let me go. They gave me back my passport. They'll bring yours in the morning."

"Why would he kill himself?" Taliesin asked.

Hal laughed. "I guess you'd know the answer to that better than I would."

"What's that supposed to mean?"

"Nothing. Forget it."

"Mr. Woczniak . . ."

"Look, whatever you've got going is none of my business, okay? I want to keep it that way. When's the next bus back to London?"

"Tomorrow morning," Taliesin said.

"You've got to be kidding. *Tomorrow?*"

The old man shrugged. "It comes by once a day. I've taken the liberty of renting a room for you here."

"Thanks, but I'd just as soon get as far away from both of you as I can. Where's the next-closest hotel?"

Taliesin's eyebrows raised. "There isn't one. This isn't America, you know."

"Great," Hal sighed, plopping down on a sofa. "Just great."

"Mr. Woczniak, what's wrong with you?" Emily demanded.

"Oh, nothing. I get into a punching match with a guy who's got a cyanide capsule in his teeth, I spend all day at the police station, I haven't had anything to eat in twenty-four hours, my fist feels like a bag of broken bones, and I come back to you two lying sacks of sewage. Everything's just fine."

Emily stood up in outrage, cheeks blazing, but she was interrupted by the high-pitched scream of a child in an upper room.

"Arthur!"

Hal's heart started pounding immediately. "Which room?" he shouted as they ran for the stairs.

"Number Eight," she said breathlessly.

He took the stairs three at a time.

The boy screamed again.

*Just a second, Jeff, just hold on . . .*

He was sure the railing was going to collapse and a shard of window glass was going to come down out of the sky to cut open his cheek and inside the boy would be waiting for him, tied to a chair, tied down and not breathing . . .

He kicked open the door.

The red-haired kid leaped out of his nightmare with a gasp.

Hal could only stand and stare, speechless. There was no chair. No smoke. The kid was sitting up in bed, rubbing his eyes.

Emily ran past Hal to take the boy in her arms. "We heard you screaming," she said.

Taliesin brought up the rear. "Everything all right here?" he asked gently.

"I guess I had a bad dream."

Hal turned away, sickened with relief.

"It's all right," Emily said.

"No, it's not. They're still after us. They're still—"

"Arthur, stop it."

His thin shoulders shook.

"Who's after you?" Hal asked quietly.

"No one," Emily said. "Arthur's just—"

"I asked the kid."

Emily put a restraining hand on Arthur, but the boy only stared at Hal. "He's all right, Em," he said. "He fought the man with the gun."

"But we don't even—"

"He's come to protect me." The big blue eyes passed from Hal to the old man. "They both have."

"You don't know what you're—"

"Who's after you?" Hal repeated.

The boy wet his lips. "We don't know who they are. But the man today was one of them."

"How do you know?"

"They look the same. They all have the same eyes."

"What do they want?"

Emily stiffened.

"I'll tell him," Arthur said quietly. "I'll tell him alone."

Taliesin nodded and touched Emily's elbow.

"Arthur, don't . . ." she began.

"We have to trust someone," the boy said. "I choose him."

When they were alone, the boy bent under the bed and took out a red plastic lunch box. He opened it and sifted through his childish treasures.

"How long have you known the old man?" Hal asked as casually as possible. "Taliesin. Or Goldberg. You called him Goldberg."

"He isn't Mr. Goldberg," Arthur said, not looking up. "Mr. Goldberg's dead." He stopped what he was doing for a moment, then rubbed his pajama sleeve across his nose. "Mr. Taliesin reminded me of him. He reminds me of a lot of people."

"Like who?"

Arthur sat back, leaning thoughtfully against the wall beside the bed.

*He's a little kid*, Hal thought. *Except for the eyes. His eyes are old.*

"Like when we were in Pittsburgh. Two men tried to shoot us."

"Tried to shoot you and your aunt?"

The boy nodded slowly. "But they couldn't, because someone fell in front of us. The police said he jumped from a window in the building we were walking in front of. They said if we'd taken three steps forward, he would have landed on top of us."

"So the guys with the guns ran away before they could shoot."

"They did shoot. The bullets hit the guy who fell out the window."

Hal took a deep breath.

"I won't tell you more if you refuse to believe me," Arthur said. The old eyes were somber.

"That's a tall order," Hal said.

"I know. That's when I started not being able to sleep. But it's the truth."

"Okay. I'm trying."

"Well, here's the strange part. The guy—the dead guy— looked just like Mr. Taliesin."

Hal stood up. "Is this some kind of joke?" he asked angrily.

"It's not a joke."

"Half the guys you see look like Taliesin, and the other half look like the guy on the bus. Do you expect me to believe that?"

Arthur didn't answer.

Hal exhaled noisily. "I think you've been taking too much Seconal."

The boy looked out the window. "I said I'd tell you the truth, and I have." He blinked rapidly. "But I guess I can't force you to believe me."

Hal put his hands on his hips. "You're a hell of a strange kid."

Arthur shrugged. "I'm not strange. I've just been put into circumstances nobody my age should be in."

Hal smiled despite himself. "What's your aunt say?"

"She's losing it," the boy said simply. "This is hard for her. Really hard."

Hal thought for a moment. There was no way this kid could be telling the truth. And yet there was something compelling about the cool, intelligent eyes and the mind behind them.

"Got any idea why all these guys who look alike would want to kill you?" he asked.

"Yup." He took out the dull metal cup and tossed it to Hal. "That's why."

Hal looked at it. It wasn't much, a baseball-sized sphere with the top sliced off and the inside hollowed out. Even if it were solid gold, it wasn't big enough to warrant the kind of action the boy was describing. And any fool could see it wasn't gold.

And yet there was something extraordinary about it. Hal felt that as soon as he touched it. It was warm, for one thing. Its warmth spread in fat, pleasurable waves through his body. And it was . . .

*floating* . . .

It was a strange color. Bronze, but greener.

*And it passed by, floating, draped in white samite. I did not see it again until the day of my death.*

Hal squeezed his eyes shut.

"You okay?" the boy asked.

"Yeah. Fine. I could use a sandwich," Hal said.

"My aunt says your name is Hal. I don't remember your last name."

"Hal's okay." He held the cup out to Arthur.

*For you, my king, I thought. They were the last words in my mind before the darkness. Covered with silver and precious stones, it stood in the abbey, the chalice of the King of Kings. I reached out for it, to be certain that my longing had not created another vision, like the magician's trick at Camelot.*

*The cup floating above the table had been an illusion, the sorcerer's enticement to the Quest. But here it was, true and splendid, and I touched the cup of Christ with my own hands.*

*"Thank you," said a man's voice behind me. It was rich and liquid, the voice, and on the verge of laughter. There was no reverence in it. "I knew that you, of all the High King's lackeys, would find it."*

*The man was as tall as a tree. I had heard of him, the Saracen knight who had come to Camelot to claim a seat at the Round Table; his arrogance had sent him straight to Hell.*

*But he had somehow returned. I do not claim to understand the ways of God or the Devil. I knew only that without the Grail, the Great King would die before his mission was complete. And so I moved to fight the black knight for the cup, but I was weary and sore, wounded from my long journey, and he was upon me before I could draw my blade.*

*I failed. The fate of the world had hung on my skill, and I could not summon it in time. The knight's blade flashed silver in the sun for a moment, then pierced through my neck.*

*It was finished: the King, the land, the dream, all gone, spilling away with my blood. Perhaps, I remember thinking, I was struck down for daring to touch the holy relic with my unworthy flesh.*

*For you, my king.*

The boy took the sphere. "You look like you're having a problem, Hal," he said somberly.

Hal stared at him for a long moment, weak and drained, sweat coursing down his face.

"Can I do anything for you?"

"No." He stood up to go.

"Please," the boy said. "I need your help."

"You need the cops. Get your aunt to tell them the truth."

"It isn't that easy." He looked down at the sphere in his lap. "Those men are going to kill us whether or not we have the cup."

"Why?"

"Look at your hand."

Hal held both hands out. The bruises on his knuckles were gone. "Jesus," he whispered. "Are you telling me—"

"I'm not telling you anything. You're seeing it for yourself."

"How do you do that?"

"I'm not doing it. It's the cup."

*The Chalice.*

Hal let out an involuntary cry.

"Hal?"

With an effort, he pulled himself together. "How did you find it?"

"By accident." He touched the sphere. "At least I think it was by accident. I'm not sure about anything anymore."

"You . . . you could give it to the police," Hal offered.

"Do you think that would stop whoever's trying to kill Emily and me? Considering what we already know?"

Hal looked into the wide blue eyes. "No," he said truthfully.

"Then will you help me?"

"Kid, I can't—"

"I need to get to the castle."

Hal wiped his hand slowly across his face. "What?"

"My castle. The one I inherited. I know it's probably just a pile of rocks, but I have to get there. I don't know why, exactly, but I have to see it. At least once."

Hal sniffed. He wanted to be out of the room, out of the country, away. "What's that going to accomplish?"

"Nothing, I guess. But I won't mind dying so much."

A jolt ran through Hal. "Don't talk like that," he said.

But the boy's eyes remained level. "I've thought it through pretty well," he said. "I'm going to leave the cup at the castle. I don't want Emily to go along. If I make it back, we'll both try to get lost in London."

"And if you don't?"

The boy took a deep breath. "If I don't, I want you to get her home safely. She's very smart, but she's naive. Do you know what I mean?"

Hal nodded.

"There are ways to get a new identity. I've written everything down." He rummaged through his box of treasures and came up with a small spiral notepad. "It's all in here." He gave it to Hal. "Will you see that she's all right?"

Hal blinked.

"I'm running out of time," the boy said quietly.

"How do you plan to get to the castle?"

"I'll walk. It's only a few miles from here. If I leave at four in the morning, I can get there by dawn."

"What if you're followed?"

"That's a chance I'm willing to take."

Hal looked out the window at the stars in the clear sky. "You're crazy," he said.

"Okay. Whatever you say. Will you do it?"

He sighed. "I'll go with you to the castle."

"You may be in danger."

"I said I'll go. And we're telling your aunt."

"She'll want to go along."

"Nothing's going to happen."

"Something might." The boy paused. "Hal, this quest is just for us two."

There was an earnest sound in his voice that made Hal reconsider. Finally, he nodded.

"All right. We'll go alone."

The boy smiled. "Good." He leaned back on his pillow. "Thanks."

Hal walked toward the door, then stopped.

"Arthur?"

"Huh?"

"Does anything happen to you when you touch that . . . cup?"

"It feels good."

"Yeah. But do you think things? Imagine things?"

"No. I just get a good feeling. Like it belongs to me. Did you feel it, too?"

*I have touched it with my unworthy flesh* . . .

"No," Hal said. "It doesn't belong to me. Get some sleep." He opened the door. "I'll be around."

"Be valiant, knight, and true," Arthur whispered.

Hal whirled around. But the boy was lying peacefully, his eyes already closed.

# CHAPTER SEVENTEEN

It was still dark when Arthur knocked on Hal's door.

"It's time to go," he said. A small drawstring pouch containing the cup dangled from his belt.

Hal stumbled back to bed. "You've got to be kidding."

"You said you wanted to go with me." The boy waited,

somber-faced, for a moment. When Hal didn't show any inclination to rise, he turned away. "See you," he said softly.

"Oh, for crying out loud." Hal lumbered out of bed. "What time is it, anyway?"

Arthur looked at his watch. "It's four-oh-four," he said. "We'll have to hurry."

"For what?"

"I need to leave before dawn."

"Art, nobody's chasing you. Not here, anyway. If they were, they'd have come during the night."

"Are you coming?" the boy asked stolidly.

Hal sighed and pulled on a pair of trousers over his boxer shorts. "Yeah, I'm coming."

It was nearly pitch-dark outside, with only the sliver of a new moon and a scattering of stars. "How far is it?" Hal asked.

"About ten miles."

"Great. That's just great, Arthur." He eyed the shiny chrome of a Volvo in the inn's parking lot. The driver's-side window was open a crack against the heat of the day. He could get inside with a coat hanger in less than a minute, then hotwire the engine . . .

"Hal, would it be stealing if you took something that you needed and brought it right back before the owner ever missed it?"

Hal's eyebrows raised. "Well . . . no, not really. I mean, not if it's for a good cause."

"That's what I think, too."

"Good. I'll get a coat hanger."

"What for?"

"For the . . ." Arthur patted the handlebars of two bicycles leaning against the porch. "Bicycles?"

"We'd make good time. We'd be back before daylight," Arthur said.

"I guess the rap isn't as bad as it is for car theft."

"Did you say something, Hal?"

"No. Nothing." He climbed on one. "It's been a long time

since I rode one of these," he said as he steered in a wobbly circle.

"Hey! Mine's got a light!" A pale circle shone down on the roadway ahead of Arthur as he zoomed onto the blacktop road, his wheels humming.

"How do you know where it is?" Hal called, struggling to catch up.

"The lawyers sent me a map. We turn left at a crossroads near here, then it's straight ahead."

Hal pedaled furiously for more than an hour, keeping his eyes focused on the circles of light on the otherwise empty road.

Sweat poured off him. It stank of ale from the night before last, transformed through time and the mysteries of the human body into effluvium. He had not had a drink since then, or anything to eat. The night before, after his strange meeting with Arthur, he had gone back down to the lobby in hopes of raiding the inn's kitchen and possibly liberating a drink or two from the bar's locked cabinets. But Emily had been waiting for him.

"Look, I've been through a lot," he began crankily.

"I understand, Mr. Woczniak," she had said. "Can you help us?"

"I don't think so."

"I see."

"I'm sorry."

Emily nodded.

"For what it's worth, I told the kid I'd go to the castle with him tomorrow. Afterward, I'll take you both back to London. We'll talk to the cops there."

"That won't do any good," she mumbled.

"Is that why you lied to the police?"

She looked away.

"I saw you offer the thing . . . whatever it is . . . to the guy who tried to attack you."

"Then you saw him try to kill me anyway," she said. "And they're going to keep trying. If we tell the police, we'll be asked to stay in one place, and those men will find out about it and they'll kill us for sure."

"You can't keep running forever."

"I've thought about that. When we get back to London, I'm going to mail the cup to the Katzenbaum Institute. That's where I work. The scientists there will know what to do with it. And Arthur and I will get lost until the killers lose track of us. In time, there'll be too much publicity about the cup for them to bother with us for what we know."

Hal nodded. "Sounds good." He decided not to mention the young boy's plan to leave the cup at the old castle ruins.

"I should have thought of it before we left, but everything got out of hand so fast." She shrugged. "I'll try to rent a car tomorrow to return to London. Will you come along?"

"Sure. What about the castle?"

"Arthur can go. The castle's taken on great importance for him. I think he should see it. I'll feel safe if you go with him."

"He'll be all right. And by the way, I think I've been misjudging you."

Emily shrugged. "I'm used to it."

He hadn't eaten after that. And he hadn't even tried to steal a drink, though the small lock on the bar would have been easy enough to pick.

Instead, he'd gone to bed, hungry and sober, like an athlete fasting before his trial. And for the first time in a year, he had not dreamed.

Now, gasping for breath on the bicycle, he no longer felt like an athlete. He felt like a grunting, suffering, aching imbecile. "How much farther?" he panted.

"I think I see it." Arthur switched off his light and swung his leg over his bicycle. "Over there." He pointed to an outcropping of rock in a field nearly a half mile from the road.

"You sure? It doesn't look much like a castle to me."

Arthur ignored him, wheeling the bike onto the rocky ground. With a sigh, Hal followed him.

The sky was just beginning to lighten. As Arthur approached a long, broken line of rocks, he set down his bicycle and stared off toward the scattered boulders beyond.

"We're here," he whispered.

For a long moment he said nothing more, his small face silhouetted against the cobalt sky.

"This looks like it used to be a wall," Hal said finally.

Arthur nodded.

"Do you suppose there could be a moat?"

Arthur shook his head. He walked over the ankle-high "wall" toward a large flat area dotted with stones and red clover. He picked up a pebble. "It's all gone," he said.

Hal's heart sank for the boy. "Your aunt tried to tell you it wasn't a real castle."

"But I thought something would be left. Some trace . . ."

With a single motion, Hal swept the boy to the ground and rolled with him back toward the wall. "Someone's here," he whispered.

A figure stepped out from behind a high mound of earth and waved cheerily. "I say, what's brought you here?" he called.

"It's Mr. Taliesin," Arthur said.

"I noticed." Hal stood up irritably and walked toward the old man. Arthur trotted behind. "What are you doing here?" he demanded.

Taliesin smiled. "I've come to see the dawn break," he said. "It's June the twenty-second. The summer solstice. The druids placed great stock in this day. They viewed it as the beginning of the good times, so to speak. And it's the date the locals say that children can see the castle." He chuckled. "Beautiful morning. Marvelous."

"How'd you get here?"

"I walked."

"Ten miles—to see the sunrise?"

"It keeps me young. Actually, I was anxious to see the stone."

"I thought you said it was worthless."

The old man shrugged. "Even the most jaded archaeologist can't help being excited at such a lovely fantasy."

"Well?" Hal asked. "Did you find it?"

"Not yet."

While they spoke, Arthur wandered around the field, picking up rocks and casting them away.

"I don't think this place is what the kid thought it would be," Hal said quietly.

"He was no doubt expecting a castle with banners flying and knights clanking around in armor."

"Who could blame him? He's ten years old, and he's traveled a long way." Hal walked over to Arthur.

"There's nothing left," the boy said. "Not even the tower."

"Nothing lasts forever," Hal mumbled lamely. "Come on. Do what you've got to do, and we'll go."

"Hal! Arthur!" Taliesin called, motioning them toward him. "Over here!"

Arthur took off at a trot.

By the time Hal arrived at the bramble-covered spot on the edge of the woods, Arthur was already exclaiming excitedly, "Look at it, Hal!"

It was an enormous boulder which was painstakingly set upon another, even larger boulder. The earth had been dug up around them and now the snowmanlike structure was balanced precariously on a mound of dirt that rose some four feet off the ground.

Taliesin shone the beam of a flashlight on it. "This must be where the student was digging. There's an inscription, certainly," he said, "but it's far too faint to read."

"Maybe we could make a rubbing," Arthur offered. "Like people do with the tombstones of kings."

"Intelligent boy," Taliesin said. "I plan to do just that."

He took a thin sheet of paper from inside his tweed jacket and unfolded it. "Hal, would you mind? My old bones are a little brittle for this work."

Hal climbed on top of the boulder, balancing carefully as Taliesin handed him a long, thick piece of charcoal.

"Okay, what now?" Hal asked.

"Just rub it back and forth, the way detectives in films do when they're discovering a telephone number on a used notepad. Keep the paper steady, boy."

Arthur held the two lower edges of the paper while Hal bent over the rock, tracing the outline of the ancient inscription. Slowly, as the words were uncovered, Taliesin read them by the light of the flashlight:

"*Rex* . . . Well, it's something about a king, anyway. And that looks like a *Q*. Q,U . . . *Rex Quondam* . . . Oh, no."

"Oh no what?" Hal asked. "What is it? My arm's breaking in this position."

"You can stop," the old man said flatly.

Hal straightened up. "What's it say?"

"*Rex Quondam Rexque Futurus.* 'King once and king to be.' "

"The once and future king! Holy . . ." Hal turned, wild-eyed, to the old man. "That's right out of the legend."

"Unfortunately, it's right out of *La Morte d'Arthur*, published by Caxton in 1485," Taliesin said dryly. "A thousand years after Arthur's death."

"Oh." Hal felt ridiculous at his own disappointment.

The old man walked close to the rock and peered at it. "It doesn't even look very much like a rock, actually," he muttered. "More like mortar of some kind."

"Why would anyone inscribe mortar?" Hal asked.

"I wouldn't know. Particularly with all the true rock around here."

The first rays of dawn struck some boulders a few feet away. "Well, we'll be able to see it more clearly in a few minutes," Taliesin said.

"Why did they call him the once and future king?" Arthur asked.

The old man smiled. "Legend has it that the great King Arthur, for whom you or one of your ancestors was probably named, was destined by God to unite the world. But he failed, because he was killed before he could fulfill the prophecies. When he died, the story sprang up that the king would live again one day to finish his work."

"At the millennium," Hal said.

"Correct. But 1000 A.D. came and went with no sign of any such king."

"Then he never came back," Arthur said.

"No. It's only a legend."

At that moment, Hal, who had been leaning against the big, man-made boulder, let out a sharp cry and toppled off the narrow edge of the supporting rock. In reaction, the great boulder tipped southward with a creak.

"It's going to fall!" Arthur yelled.

Hal sprang to his feet, but it was too late to stop it. The rock tumbled off and thudded onto the sloping ground, where it rolled with ever-increasing momentum toward the pile of sunlit boulders at the bottom of the small valley and then collided with them in a thunderous crash.

The three of them watched, speechless, as a small cloud of dust rose into the patch of light.

"I . . . I'm sorry," Hal managed at last.

The old man's lips tightened into a thin line. "That inscription may have been six hundred years old," he said with deep annoyance. He worked his jaw. "Ah, might as well take a look at it. See if there's any of it left."

Grimly they walked toward the fallen rock. The sunlight slashed across it in strips. "It's damaged," Taliesin said accusingly.

Hal leaned over it. An enormous crack ran down the length of it, through the ancient inscription. "Maybe it can be glued or something," he said, feeling miserable. He touched it. A big slab of the mortar fell away.

"For God's sake, man!" Taliesin barked.

Hal jumped back. His fingers were covered with gray powder. "I didn't think it'd be so fragile."

"It's medieval mortar that's been buried for centuries," Taliesin shouted. He touched the broken piece himself, then looked at his own fingers. "No doubt its only protection was the earth the student dug away."

Hal straightened up. He cocked his head.

"The only consolation is that it's of little historical significance." The old man was rattling on, though neither Hal nor Arthur were listening to him. "Except, of course, for the questions it raises about why it was placed here, of all—"

"When's St. John's Eve?" Hal asked suddenly.

"I beg your pardon?"

"St. John's Eve. Isn't that when the ghosts of the Round Table ride around the countryside?"

"Oh, that. It's not for two more days yet. What made you ask?"

"Listen."

All three of them stood in silence as a distant rumble from the north grew louder.

Taliesin cleared his throat. "As I said, there are several riding academies . . ."

A rider shot out of the woods. He was followed by five others, all coming toward them at full gallop.

The leader was a giant of a man, so tall that at first Hal thought he was standing in his stirrups. He was dressed strangely, in the finery of an ancient Persian prince, and carried a broad curved sword that blazed silver in the new sunlight.

"Something tells me they're not from the local dude ranch," Hal said.

He looked to Taliesin. The old man's face was frozen in horror.

He said only one word.

"Saladin!"

# CHAPTER EIGHTEEN

Hal wheeled toward the old man.

"What?"

"Protect the boy."

"With what?"

The old man grabbed the boy and pushed him toward the center of the castle ruins.

"Stay inside!" he called as he ran back across the low piles of stones that might once have been castle walls.

"Forget that!" Hal shouted. "Get Arthur into the woods! Go hide in the woods!"

But the old man paid no attention to him as the horsemen drew nearer.

Hal cast about. Once again, he had no weapon except the scattered stones on the ground. The riders were coming closer, their strange curved swords poised.

"Tell me this isn't real," he muttered, frantically picking up an armful of stones.

The cartoon riders bore down on him. Taking aim, Hal pelted the leader with two of the rocks, but he deflected them with his long sword arm. His expression never changed as he raised his weapon to strike.

Hal dropped the remaining stones and fell to the ground, rolling out of the way of the singing blade.

"Hal!" Arthur cried. Hal was struggling to stand up. He did not see the second rider coming straight for him, attempting to crush him beneath the pounding hooves of his horse.

Arthur stood up inside the old fortification and hurled a rock the size of his fist at the rider. It struck him on the forehead, and he toppled off his horse. The rider got to his

feet and staggered toward Arthur, his sword flashing. The
boy took aim again, but missed. The fallen man came at him
with a menacing grin on his face, tossing the sword to his left
hand and pulling out a short dagger.

"Hal . . ." the boy said softly, backing away.
"Hal . . ."

Hal leaped at him in a flying tackle, flattening the man.
They rolled, fighting for the short knife, oblivious to the rider
who had swooped around them in a big curve and was now
riding toward them. His sword was drawn, and his gaze was
directed at the boy.

Taliesin saw the tall man galloping toward Arthur and
shouted, "No!"

Hal's head shot up at the sound. The man struggling
beneath him saw his opportunity and thrust upward with the
knife, jamming it into Hal's shoulder. Hal jerked back with a
cry of pain as the man with the knife scrambled on top of
him.

And still the rider galloped toward Arthur.

Taliesin loped directly into the rider's path. "Give me the
cup," he shouted over his shoulder.

The boy blinked.

"The cup!" the old man screamed.

Deftly, Arthur unhooked the pouch from his belt and
tossed it to Taliesin.

The rider drew back his sword and let it fly downward.

It split the old man's skull. A fountain of blood shot out
from Taliesin's white hair as the old man's features seemed to
crumble beneath the weight of the heavy blade. Arthur
screamed.

But even as his body fell, Taliesin's arms remained
outstretched, reaching for the metal cup.

He caught it, somehow, as his knees crashed to the ground
and his bloody head smashed against the small stones at his
feet.

Everything seemed to happen in a split second: the
approaching rider, the swinging sword, the old man suddenly
standing in his path, the blade coming down to cleave

Taliesin's skull, the flying metal cup, Arthur's terrible scream . . . And then, suddenly, a blinding flash on the exact spot where Taliesin had fallen.

It was as if lightning had struck him. White light, dazzling and blinding, filled the meadow for a moment before being replaced by a cloud of thick white smoke.

When it cleared, the old man was gone.

The horsemen looked uncertainly to their leader, who had come to a stop. The tall man's face betrayed nothing. It was as if all the figures on the meadow were frozen in a tableau.

Arthur was the first to move. He leaped over the low wall and ran toward Hal, sobbing.

His movement broke the tension. Whispering in a frightened voice to his gods, the man with the knife shrank away from Hal and slid onto his horse like water streaming upwards. Following him, the others regrouped around their leader.

Blood streaming from his shoulder, Hal rose to a kneeling position. He held out his good arm to Arthur, but his eyes never left those of the tall horseman, the man Taliesin had called by name.

*Saladin. His name was Saladin.*

Saladin paid no attention to his men. His gaze had only wavered for an instant toward the place where the old one had vanished. He had lived too long to be surprised by even the strongest magic.

He sat perfectly erect, his eyes resting intently on the small red-haired boy.

"It is he," Saladin whispered.

For the first time since his arrival on the meadow, he showed a trace of expression. His lips curved into what might have been a smile. Then, almost lazily, he charged at full speed toward the boy.

Hal struggled to his feet. Desperately, he saw how close the swordsman was to Arthur and surged forward.

"No!" he called out hoarsely.

Saladin paid him no attention. Bending low in his saddle, he scooped the boy up in his long arms.

"Hal . . . Hal . . ." Arthur cried as the giant horseman beckoned to the others. Hal saw Arthur implore him with one outstretched hand while the rider turned expertly.

Saladin's eyes met Hal's. For the briefest moment, with a look of mocking amusement in his eyes, the horseman acknowledged him with a nod.

Then, in a precision maneuver, the horsemen all wheeled away from the ruins.

"Come back, you bastards!" Hal screamed. He ran after them, but before he was even halfway across the meadow, they had disappeared into the woods.

Hal dropped to his knees.

He had failed. He stared vacantly out at the open field, remembering the look of terror in the boy's eyes as the tall horseman carried him away.

He felt so numb that he did not notice that the birds had stopped singing. He did not see the shadow which rose beyond him, reaching almost to the distant line of trees. He remained staring fixedly at the ground until he heard the music.

Slowly then, he looked over his shoulder toward the castle ruins, and gasped.

The ruins were gone. Enveloped in mist stood a castle made of rock and timber, with ramparts and parapets, and on its great towering keep fluttered a flag bearing a red dragon.

His mouth agape, his throat parched with fear, Hal stood up and walked slowly, warily, toward the apparition.

The music was the sound of a lute, coming from inside. There was the sound of laughter with it, and the barking of dogs.

At the top of a flight of stone steps, a huge wooden door stood open. Although he wanted to run away, knew it would be best to run, he could not. Not from *that* door. He climbed the steps and walked through the giant entranceway.

He blinked at the scene within. As if a tapestry had come to life, the huge drafty hall was filled with boisterous people from another world: bearded men wearing tunics of leather and rough cloth and women in long shifts covered by togalike gowns, pulled in at the waist by wide jeweled belts. They wore their hair long, to their waists, or twisted into strange configurations of braids. They were all seated at long wooden tables laden with platters of meat and tankards of drink. Around them milled the servants in their dirty aprons along with dozens of dogs fighting over scraps of food.

No one looked at Hal when he entered. It was as if he had stepped into some ancient painting in which the subjects carried on their fictional lives while he looked on, as detached and invisible as the eyes of the artist.

*But of course*, he thought. *That's what it is. None of these people are real.*

A rib-skinny mongrel dog trotted up to him, sniffed the air around Hal's feet, and moved on.

*Did he see me?* Hal shook his head. *Don't be a jerk.* Of course the dog hadn't seen him. He wasn't really there. He was still in London, asleep on the the big bed in the too-pretty hotel room, the dregs of a bottle of champagne wetting the sheets. This castle was his version of Oz, and like Dorothy, he was seeing it all inside his own mind.

Hal was certain of this; yet to confirm it, he walked up purposefully to the table and placed his hand on the head of one of the diners. It went through both the man and the chair on which he was seated.

"Ha!" Hal gloated. Air. They weren't real.

But the smile faded from his face. What about the horsemen? What about the dark man on the bus?

*Were they apparitions too? Was the red-haired boy who had asked him for help? Was Arthur real? Was Emily Blessing or the British police?*

*Am I real anymore?*

Maybe he wasn't still in bed, he thought. Maybe he was out there in the field somewhere, knocked unconscious against a rock, maybe dying with a blade in his chest . . .

*And maybe I'm already dead.*

He shivered. Dead? Was this place not Oz, then, but some purgatory where Hal Woczniak was doomed to wander forever, alone among ghosts?

"Hey!" he shouted. He could barely hear his own voice above the din from the vast room.

"Somebody has to be able to hear me!" he screamed, running to the far side of the hall in a panic. "Get me out of here! Get me out!"

Someone laughed. A low chuckle, but Hal could hear it.

"Good heavens, man, get a grip on yourself. You haven't even tried the door."

Hal stopped suddenly, squinting through the sweat running in his eyes. Someone was walking down a curving stairwell. The bottom of his garment—a blue robe that reached to the floor—came into view.

"You talking to me?" Hal asked, his voice barely a whisper.

"Yes, Hal."

The old man appeared at the bottom of the stairs. Except for his costume, which was even stranger than the medieval clothing the other dream people wore—the blue robe was embroidered with silver moons and stars—he looked exactly the same as he had a few minutes ago out in the meadow.

"Taliesin," Hal said.

The old man inclined his head. "My name by birth. But here I am known as Merlin." He smiled and bowed with a graceful flourish. "Welcome to Camelot."

# BOOK TWO

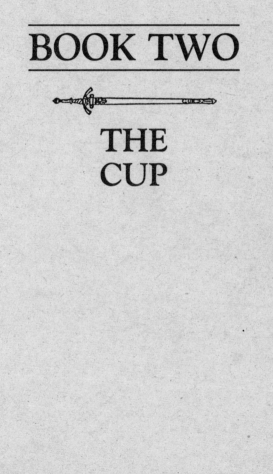

# THE
# CUP

# CHAPTER NINETEEN

"Oh, God, I *am* dead," Hal said miserably.

The old man laughed. "I assure you, Hal, you're very much alive."

"But I'm with you."

"And?"

"And . . . well . . ." He made a gesture of discomfort.

A look of recognition came into the Englishman's face. "Ah, yes. The blackguard with the scimitar. Well, set your mind at rest. I'm not dead, either."

Hal regarded him for a long moment, then poked a finger into the old man's midsection.

"Oof."

Hal withdrew his hand quickly.

"I don't mind, if you need the proof. Care to check my teeth?"

Hal touched him again. "But . . . out there . . ."

The old man smiled. "Who is to say what is illusion and what is not?"

"But I saw it," Hal sputtered. "That joker split your head open. Saw it with my own eyes."

"Pah," said the old man. "You saw it, so you believe it. You see this castle and you do not believe it. So much for both your eyesight and your logic. Come."

He turned on his heel without waiting for an answer, crossed the great hall, and held open an arched wooden door decorated with a metal cross. Hal walked inside and froze.

The room was bare of furniture except for a large, round oaken table a dozen feet in diameter. Surrounding it were thirteen chairs. Only two seats were empty, yet the room was completely silent. The men who occupied it sat at their table dressed in battle regalia, tunics of chain mail and helmets of beaten metal, as still and erect as statues.

"They look like . . ." Hal whispered. "But they couldn't be . . ."

The door closed behind him. Without the din of the dining hall, the room seemed tomblike, cold and forbidding. Hal waited for a moment, unsure of what to do. Then, hesitantly, he stepped toward the immobile knights.

He stood behind one, a big man, fair and blue-eyed, with muscles that bulged beneath the linen shirt covering his arms.

"Sir Bedivere," Hal said, remembering the stories which had come to life in his imagination as a child. "Arthur's master of chivalry."

Next to him, and just as lifeless, sat a young man with a boy's face, his light eyes filled with the passion of innocence. "Tristam," Hal whispered. A few chairs away sat a middle-aged man with ruddy, weather-beaten cheeks and intelligent eyes. He was dressed entirely in green.

"Gawain?" He looked to the Englishman who now called himself Merlin. The old man nodded.

Hal walked a few paces, then stopped alongside a knight of almost shimmering presence. He was dark-haired and handsome, and shaved his face in the Roman manner. His clothing was impeccable, and over his coat of mail he wore a heavy silver cross.

"This must be Launcelot," Hal said. "He looks just like I thought he would." He reached out his hand to touch the man's broad shoulder, but there was nothing there. The knight was an illusion, insubstantial as air.

"They are spirits," Merlin said quietly. "Like the castle. Only on special days do they approach the visible plane. Even then, not everyone can see them."

"But I can."

"Yes. I've arranged that."

"By coming into my dream."

The old man colored. "Damn it, man, this is not a dream! How many times do I have to tell you?" His white moustache worked up and down agitatedly. "I wish it were. I've had just about all I can bear of this eldritch old place. Dash it all, that's why I've brought you here."

"Whoa," Hal said. "Go back a few light-years. You brought me here to get you out?"

The old man sighed. "Exactly."

"Are we trapped in here?"

"*We're* not trapped. *I* am." He sighed. "I passed into this realm when I took the cup from Arthur. It was the only way to keep it from those thieves."

"How about these guys?" Hal passed his hand through Sir Gawain.

"Them?" Merlin rolled his eyes. "Well, of course *they're* confined here. What would they do in the outside world?"

"I don't get it. They're not real, but you are."

Merlin grunted.

"But you're stuck in here, and I'm not."

"Yes, yes," the wizard said impatiently.

"And I saw you drop dead, but that doesn't mean anything."

"Precisely."

"And you're Merlin the Magician."

"At your service."

"I'm getting out of here." Hal headed for the door.

"Come back this instant!" the old man snapped.

"Then stop conning me!" Hal shouted. "I want to know what I'm doing here. What *you're* doing here. What the hell all this is . . ."

"I'm getting to that," Merlin said with a placating gesture. "You're just going through a shock of disbelief. You'll have to get over that before we can talk reasonably."

Hal laughed, thin and hysterically. "Disbelief? I guess you could call it that. I just happen to walk in on the knights of the Round Table shooting the breeze on a summer day. No big deal. Happens all the time."

"Now, Hal—"

"And you're just a regular guy, I suppose. You get killed, you vanish in a puff of smoke, you pop up again . . ."

The old man looked down his long nose at Hal. "In case

you hadn't noticed, I am nothing resembling a regular guy. I am a wizard. Or I was. I seemed to have used up all my juice out on the field. Dying is a difficult feat for anyone."

He shuddered. "The ways we go! Being exploded into bits inside an automobile. Getting shot while falling from a thirty-story building . . ." He shook his head. "A ghastly business, believe me."

"But you said you weren't dead, remember?" Hal reminded him acidly. "Here you are, in the flesh and twice as pretty."

"Oh, why did you have to be the one?" the old man muttered. "I don't die *permanently*. Still, it's no picnic to have one's brains cleaved in." He touched his head. "Goldberg had a considerably easier death."

Hal stared. "Goldberg? The kid thought you were someone named Goldberg."

"The disguise was one of my best." He smiled. "But then, Arthur was always able to see through me. But I'll get to that soon enough." He walked around to the far side of the Round Table, between two empty chairs. He touched one of them.

"This is the Great King's place," he said. "It has been kept for sixteen hundred years, until his return. And the other—"

"The Siege Perilous, I suppose," Hal said mockingly. "For none but the pure of heart."

"Galahad's seat," Merlin said with tenderness.

"So why isn't he here?"

The old man's eyes sparkled. "Now you're starting to be intelligent about things. The Siege Perilous is empty because Galahad's place is with the king. He was a knight in the most real sense. Valiant and loyal and clean in his soul. He could not rest until he found the king again."

The old man looked up to the narrow windows letting in arrows of light. "I felt his presence in generation after generation as I slept through the long ages in my crystal cave. He was the soul of Richard Coeur de Lion, of Charlemagne, of Thomas à Becket, St. Francis of Assisi, Joan of Arc, Martin Luther, John Locke, Benjamin Disraeli . . . and more others than I could recount to you. Often he was someone ordinary, not famous, a soldier, a shoemaker. He never knew that he was searching for the Great King, but something drew him toward greatness—and disappointment, ultimately, because the king did not come in any of those lifetimes.

"I felt these stirrings in those men, that one soul. I felt it calling to the king. But the king did not come. And so I slept."

He looked gravely at Hal. "And then, after sixteen centuries, I awoke. Because the king at last was born again."

Hal felt his breath coming shallowly. "He's alive? King Arthur is alive *now?*"

Merlin nodded slowly. "I've been with him since he was a year old."

Hal couldn't help smiling. "Just like the old days, huh?"

"Almost. The boy didn't need to be educated this time around. He had that from another source. But he needed a friend." He smiled. "I became Milton Goldberg."

"Oh my God," Hal said. "Arthur. *That* Arthur."

"He is the one."

Hal sat down, oblivious that he had superimposed himself on one of the insubstantial knights. "Wait a minute. Arthur's not even British. Let alone a king."

"His nationality is of no importance."

Hal stared at him a moment, then pinched his eyes closed with his fingers. He had almost begun to believe that he was awake. "What's he going to be king of?" he asked sarcastically. "His junior high school class?"

Merlin shook his head. "His work will begin at the millennium, as foretold. The *coming* millennium."

"The . . ."

"Not 1000 A.D., as people thought," Merlin went on delightedly. "Things would have been too similar to the way they were in Arthur's time. The world had to change, don't you see? The time for him had to be right."

"But the millennium . . . That's only eight years from now."

"Exactly."

Despite himself, Hal was beginning to take the conversation seriously. "Is that why those men took him?"

Merlin shook his head. "I don't think so. They only wanted the Grail."

"The what?"

"The cup. Arthur isn't aware of its full power, but Saladin is."

"Saladin," Hal repeated. "He was the leader of the Halloween Brigade."

"Don't joke about him, Hal. Saladin is a dangerous man, more dangerous than you know. He has possessed the Grail, and he will not give it up lightly."

"You keep calling it the grail," Hal said. "You don't mean . . . the *Holy Grail?*"

"Christians have ascribed its power to their God. I do not know its true source, although I suspect that it existed long before the coming of Christ."

Hal remembered the peculiar warmth of the cup in his hands, the strange images it evoked. "It couldn't be the Grail."

"Why not?" Merlin asked, arching his eyebrows.

"Because the Grail that King Arthur's knights went looking for was this gorgeous thing, wasn't it? A silver chalice."

"Now, now, Hal. Jesus of Nazareth was by all accounts a poor man. Do you really think the fellow would have been drinking out of a silver chalice?"

"No, but it wouldn't have been a high-tech teacup, either. It was probably some nondescript clay bowl. And four hundred years later, when the knights from Camelot went looking for it . . ."

"It would have vanished into obscurity."

"Right. Or been ground into dust somewhere along the way."

"So it was most peculiar that the knights insisted upon finding it," Merlin said.

"They didn't insist. Merlin—you, I guess—insisted. Arthur didn't even like the idea. But you kept hammering away at them, hinting, nagging . . ."

Merlin laughed. "You're a fine student, Hal. You've studied your history well."

"It's something I used to think about. If the knights hadn't left on the Quest, King Arthur would have had more men around him when the crunch came."

The smile left the old man's face. "The battle of Barrendown," he said thickly.

"Whatever. When Mordred brained him."

Merlin was silent for a moment.

"Hey," Hal said awkwardly. "Don't think I'm blaming you or anything. It was a long time ago."

"Yes. A long time," Merlin said. "He needed the Grail. I thought that if I could only get it to him in time . . ."

"*Why?* Why the Grail? You just said it was probably just a plain clay bowl . . ."

"There was something within the bowl," Merlin said. "Something containing such magic that, with it, a great ruler might live not only through one battle, but for all the ages of the world."

Hal could not speak. He was remembering how the bruises on his hand had healed at the touch of the cup.

"It bestows the gift of immortality, Hal," Merlin said softly.

He opened his hands. In them, or rather, above them, hovered the small metal cup Arthur had thrown to the old man before the horsemen swept him away.

"By touching this, I banished it to the spirit realm where we are now."

Hal tried to touch it. His hand passed through. The cup faded from his sight.

"Since I made it disappear, only I can bring it back into the real world. But here, in Camelot, I may not leave without permission." He looked around the room, at the immobile forms of the spirit knights. "Like them, I cannot live again in the world of men until summoned by the Great King."

"You mean Arthur? Arthur has to call you?"

Merlin nodded. "And Arthur's life is in danger. I cannot protect him from here. Only you can do that."

"Me?" Hal asked. Then he saw the cup again, almost transparent, covered with a film of billowing white samite.

"Do you remember it, Hal?" the old man asked, his voice no more than a breath. "It wasn't covered with clay then, when you found it . . ."

*The Chalice shone with jewels. Its silver was white as sunlight. I reached out my hand . . .*

"For you, my king," Hal whispered. He closed his eyes as the memory came crashing in on him again.

Merlin touched him gently. "Rise," he said.

Hal obeyed. The tears in his eyes half-blinded him.

The old man raised himself up to his full height and gestured slowly to the empty seat beside the king's. "Take your place, Galahad," he intoned. Then his expression softened. He looked on Hal with a gaze of profound love. "For your time, too, has come at last."

Hal closed his eyes.

*The waiting is over*, a voice inside him spoke. And now, for the first time, he knew that this was no dream. Some part of him had been longing for this moment for a thousand years and more. In this place, this netherworld of spirits and illusions, he had found the truth.

His head lowered humbly, Hal sat down in the Siege Perilous.

Suddenly the dark room was infused with iridescent light. Trumpets sounded. The very air was charged with a crackling, vibrant power. A swirl of moondust rose out of the chair and enveloped Hal. When it cleared, the ghost knights were standing, saluting him, proclaiming his name.

"*Galahad!*" they chanted, soft as summer air, then growing louder, louder, until the sound seemed to shake the walls.

"Galahad!"

*Gawain. Bohort. Gaheris. Launcelot. All of them, all of them back again, my brothers . . .*

"He has come," Merlin proclaimed.

Hal rose and knelt before the old man. "Tell me what I must do," he said, his voice choking.

"Saladin has our king. Find him," Merlin commanded. "Find Arthur and return him to his rightful place with us."

Hal looked up. "I will," he whispered hoarsely. "I swear it."

A light fog snaked inside through the narrow windows. The walls grew misty.

The old man looked around sadly. "The magic is leaving," he said.

The knights, still standing in their salute, softened to dim silhouettes. Merlin himself was disappearing.

"We are returning to the plane of Avalon to await the call of the Great King. Until then, it will be only you, Galahad."

Hal reached out to him in a panic, but there was no substance to the vision. The old man was no more real than anything else around him.

"But how . . ." Hal struggled to his feet. "How will I find the boy?"

The mist was thick now, obscuring everything. Hal felt as if he were in the middle of a heavy cloud. "Tell me!" he shouted.

Faintly, the voice came. "Saladin has taken the boy to a place of darkness," it said. "A place fearful to you. A place you will remember."

Hal could barely hear the last words.

"A place I'll remember? New York? Is he taking him to New York?"

There was no answer. "Wait a minute!" Hal yelled. "What's that supposed to mean, a place I'll remember? I've never even been in this country before!" He stumbled around in the thick fog. "Don't go, damn it! Tell me what I'm supposed to do! Don't go! Don't go!"

But it did go, the castle, the banners and trumpets, the knights, the old man himself, vanished into the mists. Hal blinked and found himself standing in the middle of a pile of ancient rubble on top of a grassy hill.

He looked around for a trace of the castle, but there was nothing left of it but moss-covered ruins.

The meadow was the same. The rubble was the same. But

nothing else would ever be the same, he knew, not for Hal Woczniak, reborn in this single moment of time as Galahad, champion to an ancient king.

"Hal!" It was Emily Blessing's voice, shrill and frightened. "I've been looking for you for hours. Where's Arthur?"

"He's been . . ." He rubbed his forehead. "He's been . . ."

"Did you see it, too, mister?" piped a high voice nearby. Hal turned to see a little dirty-faced urchin dressed in a ragged shirt and a pair of cotton pants too short for his gangly legs, standing barefoot on the hillside.

"What?" Hal said groggily.

"The castle. I seen it," he said proudly. "I come here every day to see it, but most of the time it ain't here. But sometimes it is. I ain't told anybody about it." He looked up apprehensively. "You did see it, though, didn't you?"

His eyes met the boy's. "You saw it?"

The boy nodded.

"Hal, you're bleeding!" Emily cried hysterically.

Hal touched the place on his shoulder where the horseman's blade had sliced into the flesh. It was the first he had noticed the wound since he'd watched Saladin ride into the woods with the boy.

"Arthur's been taken," he said.

Her hands flew to her mouth. Hal's legs buckled.

"Get a doctor!" she commanded the boy. "Get the police, as fast as you can!"

"Yes, ma'am," the boy said, white-faced, and took off at a run.

Emily knelt beside Hal. "How did it happen?" she shrilled.

"Saladin," Hal said. "His name is Saladin . . ."

"What? I can't hear you."

Hal turned to her. "I'll find him," he said. "I promise you I'll find Arthur."

Emily stifled a sob and sat a little straighter. "What about Mr. Taliesin?" she asked quietly.

Hal looked over to the spot where the old man had died, disappeared, and then reappeared again in a world that had vanished before his eyes, in a dream that was not a dream.

"We'll see him again too," he said. "I'm sure of it."

# CHAPTER TWENTY

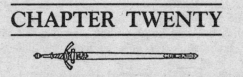

The red-haired boy lay asleep on a brocaded divan in a country house near the English Channel, some twenty miles away from Maplebrook Hospital.

The house had lain vacant for almost fifty years before Saladin issued instructions from his cell for his men to buy it. For the duration of his incarceration, it had served as headquarters in the operation to free him.

It was a rambling stone manor, one of many homes Saladin owned all over the world. Like the others, it was kept immaculately clean inside. Saladin could not abide filth. But the exterior of the place was decrepit and forbidding, poking out of the overgrown lawn like an immense tombstone. It was a place for hiding.

He sat in a straight-backed chair opposite the boy and gazed with patient wonder at the sleeping child.

"So the king has returned, after all," he said.

He did not lower his voice; the boy had been drugged to keep him quiet after the horses were taken away to the stables behind the house, which also sheltered a sedate Mercedes-Benz sedan. But there were no neighbors to see any of those things. That was one of the reasons the house had been chosen in the first place.

"This place suits you." Saladin stood up and walked to a window and looked out toward the dark woods.

"It resembles Tintagel, where you were born. I made a pilgrimage there after your death, Arthur." He laughed softly. "I wanted to see the land you came from. I wanted to know what rough winds had produced a man who could come so far in such a short life."

The breeze from the sea ruffled his dark hair. "I was young myself then, even though you'd caused me to lose twelve years."

Twelve years. Most of the legends had put the Quest at much longer, decades upon decades, but that had not been the case. The cup had been lost to all of them—Arthur, Merlin, the foolish questing knights—but none had felt its loss as acutely as Saladin, for only he had truly understood its power.

He had been fifteen years old when he stole the cup from Kanna, and twenty-five when he arrived, centuries later, in Britain. The ten intervening years of his life had been lost all at once, during a sojourn in Rome. Some thieves had stolen the cup while he slept in a doorway on a darkened street. He had chased after them, but he was not familiar with the meandering streets of the city and soon lost them.

The thieves were apprehended by Roman soldiers that very night, and the odd metal ornament confiscated. The foot soldier who took the cup had considered turning it over to his superior officer, but decided that it was not of sufficient value.

Or that was what he told his comrades. It would have embarrassed the soldier to say that he kept it simply because he liked the *feel* of the thing, that its pleasant warmth filled him with an inexplicable sensation of well-being.

He kept it as a charm. When he was sent to Jerusalem with half his garrison, he wore it on his belt, attached by a thong, much as Arthur Blessing would nearly two thousand years later.

The soldier never had the opportunity to ascertain just how lucky the cup was, since occasions for battle in Jerusalem were few. The Romans had little trouble quelling the occasional unarmed uprisings of the Jews. More often, the soldiers were called upon to police violence between one sect of the contentious locals and another. It was during one of these, a brawl in a tavern, that the Roman lost his talisman.

He had not noticed that it was missing until he was walking back to his barracks; then he turned around immediately and went back to search the place, but it was nowhere in sight. Even beating the tavern owner did not yield any results. Finally, with a sense of immense irritation, the soldier gave up the metal hemisphere as lost and in time forgot about it completely.

During the scuffle in the tavern, a panicked man had yanked it off the soldier's belt. The cup, wrapped in a leather pouch and secured with a thong, had rolled out the open door, where a dog picked it up and carried it back to his master, a young potter's apprentice.

"What's this?" the boy asked, grabbing the metal oddity from the dog.

Aaron was fifteen and quite bored with the endless stream of plain clay bowls he had to turn out each day for the master potter. What was worse, he knew that his task would continue for several more years before he might be permitted to work on more interesting projects, since the plain glazed bowls were the staple of the potter's business. All of the inns and households bought them in quantity. It did not matter if they were imperfectly formed; so long as they were not cracked, they would sell.

The boy had a gift. As a child, he had sculpted animals from stone with a piece of flint. His father, who was a laborer, had beaten him for his lazy, time-wasting ways, but nothing seemed to stop the boy from his carvings. Then once, when the father found a secret cache of stone figures hidden inside a hole in the wall of their house, the idea had come: He would sell the child. He was of little use in a household with four other sons and not enough food to feed them all, and the right buyer might even have use for Aaron-Good-For-Nothing.

He extolled the boy's virtues to the master potter Elias. Taking a chance, he even showed the potter the carvings he had found.

"Is this not the work of a genius?" he rhapsodized, though he himself had no idea if the carvings were good or not. "My wife and I had hoped that our son might one day become a fine craftsman like yourself, but alas . . ." At this he shook his head sadly. "We are too poor to give the boy the attention he needs."

Elias looked at the stone pieces indifferently. "How much do you want for him?" he asked, whereupon the boy's father set to a lively dispute about Aaron's worth.

He settled for a modest sum, but at least he was rid of the boy. And Elias the potter had a new slave who might, if he lived up to the promise of the childishly crude but interesting sculptures, eventually become a real asset to the potter's business.

On the day Aaron took the metal cup from the stray dog which had slept with him in Elias' outbuilding for the past year, he had already fulfilled his quota of plain clay bowls and had some time to play. Elias was gone for the day, delivering merchandise to the innkeepers who were his regular customers.

Aaron examined the object carefully. It was a strange shape, almost a ball, except that the top had been sliced off. Making a bowl from it presented a marvelous challenge. He set a fat wooden block on the wheel and placed the cup on top of it.

As the wheel spun, Aaron applied wet clay to the metal cup with both hands, covering it evenly. As he approached the inward-curving lip, he first pulled the clay in, following the shape of the sphere, then flared it out and eased it in again so that the final effect was of gently rippling waves growing from a central pedestal.

It pleased him. When he was finished with the exterior he covered the inside painstakingly, using a stiff brush to apply the almost-liquid clay slip. Then he fired it in the bellows-fed kiln and painted it immediately with a motif of fish swimming through ever-darkening tiers of water.

As he fired it again to make the designs permanent he realized that it was fully dark outside. In his pleasure at working with a piece on which he was able to employ his talent, he had lost track of the time. Indeed, he thought briefly as he lit the small oil lamp in the workshop, it had not seemed as if time were passing at all.

The bowl was beautiful. He was admiring it when old Elias came in to see why the kiln was running so late at night.

He spotted the painted bowl in the boy's hands and took it from him with a scowl.

"I fired all the bowls," Aaron explained, gesturing toward the pile of plain glazed pottery he had made. For even in his zeal to finish his creation, he knew that Elias would not have permitted him to use the kiln for only one object.

The potter cast an eye at the new bowls, then returned his gaze to the fluted fish bowl. "And this?" he asked.

"It was an experiment."

Elias turned the bowl around in his hands. "What is inside it?"

"A metal cup I found."

The old man hefted it from one hand to the other, judging the balance of its weight. "The ware was not clean when you painted it," he said.

The boy frowned. He did not know what the old man was talking about.

"For work like this, you have to clean all the nubs and specks of clay off the object before you fire it the first time, so that it will be perfectly smooth. You feel this?" He took the boy's hand and passed it over the side of the bowl. It felt just like all the other bowls he had fired.

"Rough."

"But—"

"All right for common bowls," the potter said, raising one shoulder in a shrug. "But for a decorative piece . . ." He made a face. "No one would want such a thing."

He tossed it into the pile of plain bowls. "You've wasted my paint."

Aaron hung his head. At least old Elias hadn't broken it in a rage. The bowl would be sold as part of a mass shipment.

"I'm sorry, master," he said.

The old potter looked at him sternly. "You've missed your supper," he said.

The boy did not answer.

"Go to bed. You're using valuable oil." As he left the workshop, Elias said, "Tomorrow I'll teach you how to clean the ware."

Aaron could not believe what he had just heard. Trembling with joy, he went over to the pile of pottery and picked up his bowl. It was weighted perfectly. Even the master had found no fault with that. The ripple design, too, was good. And, if the truth be told, the fish were quite pretty.

He laid the bowl back where Elias had put it and blew out the lamp.

The next stop for the cup, now disguised as a drinking bowl, was an inn in Jerusalem, where three years later it was placed on a long table where thirteen men gathered together for the last time.

The innkeeper set the fluted fish bowl—his own personal favorite—before the leader of the group, because although the man was only a carpenter by trade, he had achieved some prominence lately as a prophet and teacher. Some even claimed that the fellow had performed miracles, including turning water into wine and bringing a dead man back to life. Of course, those tales were undoubtedly false, but who knew? A man who could inspire such stories might well become rich. If an innkeeper were to prosper, he had to pay attention to things like this.

Although the innkeeper was disappointed that his famous guest declined to eat that evening, he brought the group the best wine he had to offer when they asked for it and loitered near their table as the man called Jesus of Nazareth performed a strange ritual.

He poured the wine into the beautiful rippled bowl, then passed it around to the other men at the table, even though they had wine of their own.

"Drink," he said in a gentle voice. "Do this in remembrance of me."

And as the innkeeper watched Jesus pass the bowl with his long, expressive hands, he was suddenly filled with a terrible sense of desolation. For there was something in the man's calm eyes that bespoke an utter resignation and a sadness beyond knowing.

This man would never become rich.

Jesus looked up at him. The innkeeper bobbed his head and withdrew.

He was glad he had given him the fluted fish bowl.

# CHAPTER TWENTY-ONE

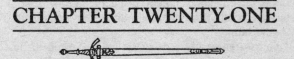

Saladin had almost despaired of ever finding the cup again when he heard about a Jew in Jerusalem who had risen from the dead after some kind of ceremony involving a cup.

The Jew had apparently been a politician of some sort. He had promised the gift of eternal life to thousands and, as an example, had already brought at least one dead man back to life before he was arrested and crucified for his wild talk.

Saladin could only shake his head at the news. This was exactly the sort of person who should never have had possession of the cup. For what if the authorities had believed him? Its priceless magic would have passed into the hands of some dictator, who would keep his position for countless ages. As Saladin himself would not feel the urge to rule for several centuries to come, he viewed this possibility as a disaster of great proportions. Politicians were bad enough; immortal politicians would be a catastrophe beyond contemplation.

At least the loose-lipped fellow seemed to have learned his lesson. According to the talk around Rome, Jesus of Nazareth had been quietly buried after his execution. Then, after three days, his body had disappeared from the vault where he had lain. Now, God knew, he might be anywhere.

Still, it was the first inkling Saladin had had concerning the whereabouts of the cup in ten years, and he had to follow it.

Feeling less than hopeful, he packed a few things and made plans to travel to Judea.

He had been working as a physician in Rome. During his wanderings in the Arab world, he had pursued the healing arts which he had begun to learn from Kanna. In the growing civilization of Assyria and Babylonia, he learned much about the workings of the human body, about which the Romans, for all their political sophistication, were still ignorant. Despite his ostensibly young age—still a teenager—the doctors in the city soon came to respect the knowledge of the mysterious youth from the East and often sent their own patients to him.

Of course, since the physicians only referred to Saladin those cases which they themselves could neither diagnose nor treat, a good number of Saladin's patients died. Before long, he became known as a healer of last resort, and was even referred to, behind his back, as "Doctor Death."

Saladin did not mind the reputation. His practice brought him a good income without many social obligations, as the foreign doctor of the moribund was not considered sprightly company in fashionable circles. As he grew older, he took to wearing black, which set off his now-imposing height as well as his melancholy air. In his way, he had been accepted into Roman society. It was the first time in some twenty-five centuries that he was considered a respectable man.

As he boarded the ship sailing eastward, he actually felt a twinge of indecision about leaving. Was it necessary, he mused, to live forever? If he remained in Rome, he would have a reasonably good life. He had already lived for nearly three millennia. Perhaps it would not be unpleasant to grow old. The last ten years of aging like a normal human being had not been troublesome to him, and he had met many men well beyond their middle years who spoke of their "long" lives with affectionate memory.

Even death, from his experience with his patients, was not so terrible. During his life, he had endured pain far worse than death. Had he not been tied to posts and left to die in the desert sands after the death of the Pharaoh Ikhnaton? Had he not, immediately before his arrival in Rome, been tossed into a burning funeral pyre by a mob of barbaric Macedonians?

No, death was not so fearful. And yet, he had tasted life. Endless life, such as only one other being before him had known. The white-skinned, half-beast Kanna had had no appreciation for it; indeed, at the moment of his death, the old creature had seemed almost relieved. But Kanna had done nothing with the timeless ages that had been his. He had stayed on his mountaintop scratching for roots while mankind was leaping up all around him, performing wonderful feats. He had seen nothing of the world, learned nothing, achieved nothing. Saladin had used the cup as it should have been used. He savored life; always, he wanted more.

His moment of indecision had passed by the time the ship set sail. He would find the cup again. He would find another life. He would never let go.

Once in Jerusalem, Saladin went straight to the tomb which had been vacated by the allegedly immortal Jew. It was not difficult to find; since the bogus death, the place had been surrounded by superstitious peasants, many of them lame and sick, seeking a cure for their ailments in the stone where the "miracle" had taken place. Most, Saladin saw, were more in need of simple medical care than miracles. If he'd had the inclination, he could have set up a practice on the spot that would have kept him busy for years to come. But these were poor people who would not know how to appreciate a physician's skill even if they saw it in practice; whatever he did would be attributed to the miracles of the vanished charlatan anyway. Besides, he did not have the time.

He pushed himself through toward the senior officer among a small group of Roman soldiers guarding the tomb from the mob. In their zeal, Saladin supposed, the wretches who'd come seeking miracles might set up a shrine right in the tomb. Saladin did not involve himself much in politics, but it was common knowledge that the Jews were an unruly lot who had never taken well to Roman rule. Unlike the Britons, who openly fought the occupying Roman forces, the

Jews talked meekly and officially submitted. Then they just went on doing whatever they wanted.

Converting them to the Roman religion was out of the question, at least for the moment. They would never give up their vengeful, solitary god in favor of the convenient pantheon of Roman deities. It was the only point the Jews were really adamant about, so Rome, in her wisdom, let it go. As they became more civilized, it was thought, the Jews would eventually abandon their strict religious code and come around to a less demanding mode of worship.

But the "miracle" cults were a problem. Not only were the Jews themselves annoyed with them, but the disruption these radicals caused made the administration of the province hellish. It seemed to Saladin that the Nazarene who had escaped the tomb had inadvertently created yet another troublesome cult.

"Who was he?" Saladin asked pleasantly.

The soldier looked him over, noticing Saladin's fine Roman clothes and perfect speech. "A nobody," he answered with a smirk, pushing back a woman who was keening like a harpy. The woman had long red hair and a face that in a bedchamber might have seemed wanton.

She seemed to be oblivious to the soldiers' barrier, throwing herself again and again at them in an attempt to enter the tomb.

"I don't envy you your job," Saladin said.

The soldier smiled grimly. "I've had better postings, that's sure."

The woman flung herself at him once more. In exasperation, the soldier swatted her across the face with the back of his hand. "They're like lunatics," he muttered, massaging his knuckles. "This is the worst, but they're crawling all over the city, following the blackguard's footsteps. They're camped up on the execution grounds like ravens. I've heard the cross itself has been torn to pieces." He shook his head. "By Jupiter, even the tavern where the poor devil took his last drink is overrun."

This time the woman threw herself at Saladin, clutching the sleeve of his black robe with her spindly fingers.

"Do not listen to the Roman!" she exhorted, her eyes glassy. Apparently she took Saladin to be one of her own people. "Jesus is the Christ—the anointed one sent by God. The Romans killed him, but he lives again. I have seen him with my own eyes . . ."

Her words tumbled out in a wild rush while the soldier methodically loosened her grip on the tall stranger.

"Where have you seen him?" Saladin asked, but the soldier had pushed her away and drawn his sword.

"Get the woman away before I have her flogged!" he commanded. The crowd screeched in protest.

"Where have you seen him?" Saladin repeated, shouting.

It was no use. He could hardly hear his own voice above the noise. Craning his neck to see over the heads of the people, he watched someone take hold of her and lead her, sobbing, out of the crowd.

"See what I mean?" The soldier put his sword away. "Lunatics."

Saladin pushed his way toward where he had spotted the woman. "Wait!" he called. But when he finally freed himself from the press of bodies, she was gone.

He questioned the others at the tomb, but none could identify the woman he described. Nor had any of them seen the vanished Jesus of Nazareth. Several, though, were able to give him the location of the inn where Jesus had last been seen publicly before his execution.

It was probably a waste of time, Saladin thought as he walked the dusty road into town. The people here were feebleminded. They would believe anything. Had such a thing happened in Rome, he would have found a dozen men within a half hour who would tell him the man's location for a price. But what could one expect in this backwater, where the buildings were constructed of mud and even the roads were unpaved?

The inn was at least a start. People there might have known the man and where he was living. He groaned inwardly as he approached the place. It was overrun with noisy people, clamoring at the door for a peek inside. Once again Saladin had to muscle his way through the crowd.

It was jammed inside with tables—some of them nothing more than crates or blocks of stone—pushed so tightly together that he wondered how anyone could move among them. The innkeeper, a rotund man who sweated profusely, shouted orders at his help. When Saladin tapped him on the shoulder, he turned irritably, then softened as he appraised the tall stranger's moneyed appearance.

"Yes, sir. In one moment we'll have a table for you and a meal like you have never tasted!"

"I'd like to have some information about the man they call Jesus of Nazareth," Saladin said.

"Yes, yes, of course. This is where he took his last meal. Lamb, it was. The finest, prepared with leek. It is the specialty of the house. Shall I order some for you? It will be ready by the time you're seated."

Saladin leaned close to the man. "Were you a friend of his?"

The innkeeper looked up, startled. "No, sir!" he pronounced vehemently, shaking his head so vigorously that his jowls trembled. "I am an honest tradesman. How was I to know he was a criminal?"

At this, Saladin was somewhat taken aback. "I only meant—"

"I knew nothing of him," the fat man insisted, sweeping his stubby hands in front of him as if to erase all doubt as he backed away. "Or his friends. They have not been back." He turned, but Saladin grabbed his arm. He could feel the man tense.

"I mean you no harm," he snapped. "I am a stranger here and wish only to learn his whereabouts."

"His whereabouts?" The innkeeper looked at him askance. "He is dead, sir." The frown left his face. "You did not know?"

"I heard his tomb was empty," Saladin said cautiously. If the man knew anything, this was the time to negotiate the price of his knowledge. "I understand he was a great teacher. I would be willing to pay a considerable sum to see him . . . or one of his followers."

The innkeeper sighed. "I'm afraid it's too late for that," he said. "They've all been arrested, or gone into hiding. As for the man himself . . ." He spread his arms in an elaborate shrug. "They say he rose from the dead. What can I tell you? Now, if you'll just be patient a few minutes more, I'm sure I'll be able to find a table . . ." He was anxious to be about his business.

"You heard no discussion when he was here?"

"No, sir, except for the ritual of the cup."

"What?"

The innkeeper suddenly beamed. "Ah, you have not heard about that? It was in this very room that he passed his wine bowl to all at his table, asking them to remember him. It was as if he had a premonition of his own death, you see. I heard that with my own ears," he said proudly. "Would you care to see it?"

"I . . . All right." At least it would give him a moment to talk with the man privately. He may have heard more than he remembered.

"Splendid. Wait in the storeroom around the corner. I'll be with you in a moment." He shouted for someone to bring wine to the table. "The fee for viewing it is small . . . only three shekels." He smiled ingratiatingly and bustled back into the dining room.

Saladin made his way slowly around the corner. To his annoyance, the storeroom was also crowded with after-dinner loiterers willing to pay three shekels for a look at a worthless bowl. He joined them, bending almost double to pass through the low open doorway.

Inside were stacks of ceramic bowls, casks of wine, and assorted litter, including an old trunk of some kind. The repository of the sacred cup, no doubt, Saladin thought irritably. The ceiling of the earthen-floored room was too low for him to stand erect, forcing him to lean against the wall like a lazy schoolboy. The air in the small place smelled of leeks and sweet wine.

This was ridiculous, he thought. The innkeeper knew nothing, except how to squeeze a little extra money out of his customers. But where would he go next? Back to the tomb, perhaps, to see if the crazed woman might return? Or should he wander about the city, as he had for so long in Rome, asking discreetly if anyone had seen a man with an odd sphere-shaped metal ornament?

He sighed. Such a search might take another ten years, and again yield nothing. He did not think he could bear ten years in Judea. He swallowed to hide his dismay. Back to Rome, then. Back to the life of ordinary men, lived in the shadow of death. He felt like weeping.

"Move aside," he murmured as he passed through the crowd on his way toward the exit.

"Forgive my tardiness," the innkeeper cried, the solid bulk of his belly pushing Saladin back into the fetid chamber. "Three shekels, please. To defray the cost." He held out his apron, which had a large pocket in the front, as the sightseers dropped coins into it.

Saladin was about to leave in disgust when the apron opened in front of him. "You won't be sorry, sir," the innkeeper said with a wink.

With a resigned sigh, Saladin dropped in three coins.

The fat man briskly unlocked the chest with a key he brought from beneath his apron. Puffing from the exertion of bending over, he lifted the lid and produced a blue-green bowl. Some of the women made "oohs" of appreciation, although Saladin could not imagine what for. It was an execrable piece of pottery, garishly decorated with primitive-looking fish.

"Some called him Messiah, some heretic," the innkeeper said in a mysterious whisper, as if he were a pagan priest reciting an incantation as he raised the bowl ludicrously above his head. "On the night before his arrest, Jesus of Nazareth passed this very bowl to twelve members of a secret society and gave them his final orders."

He paused dramatically.

"What were they?" a woman asked finally. "The orders."

"That I cannot tell you," he said, maintaining his theatrical voice. "But he told his men to remember him while they carried them out."

The woman gasped.

"A plan to overthrow the Romans," someone suggested.

"Each man drank solemnly from the bowl, then passed it to the next." Slowly he handed the fish bowl to the nearest onlooker. "Careful."

The bowl was passed reverently from hand to hand.

*This is worse than the cheapest street carnival show*, Saladin thought. He was almost embarrassed to accept the bowl, but when he did, he noticed its weight. It was too heavy to be made of clay. The ripple, too, was unusual. The indentations were too deep. He ran his fingers along the grooves.

Saladin had spent a number of years as an artist, most notably in Egypt during the Eighteenth Dynasty, working in the tomb of the Pharaoh Ikhnaton. He had produced a great deal of pottery, as well as the quasi-realistic sculpture and painting which were the hallmark of the period. And so he realized, as he studied the exaggerated ridges in the innkeeper's crudely painted bowl, that something was inside its base.

He turned it over and tapped on its underside. The sound produced was different from the dry click of his fingernail upon the fluted sides of the bowl. The base itself could fit easily into a man's hand, and if one listened, if one paid very careful attention, he could hear the faint *thrum-thrum* of his own heartbeat in his ears.

And then it grew warm in his hand.

"Sir, please, everyone would like a chance to . . ."

Saladin smashed the bowl against the wall.

A woman screamed. "Sir!" the innkeeper shouted, his face beet red as he parted the crowd imperiously.

It was his. Saladin closed his eyes as his long fingers wrapped around the warm metal of the sphere and felt its ancient magic coursing once again through his body.

"The authorities will be called, I assure you!"

Saladin laughed aloud. He took a bag filled with gold Roman coins from his belt and dropped it into the innkeeper's hand. "For your loss," he said, and swooped through the low doorway like a bird of prey, his black cloak billowing behind him.

For a moment the people crowded into the storeroom were silent as they watched the tall man leave the inn. Then the innkeeper, with his practical turn of mind, opened the drawstring of the pouch and peered inside.

"Look, a fish, whole," a woman said as she picked up a broken piece of the bowl. Others followed suit, scrambling for the pottery shards on the floor.

"Please, please," the innkeeper said exasperatedly. "Those are precious relics from the true cup of Christ." He opened the pocket of his apron and smiled. "Thirty shekels."

Outside, the spidery figure of Saladin fairly danced toward the stables. He would ride out of this cesspool and buy passage on the first ship he found headed for Rome.

What luck! He had found the cup on his first day in this godforsaken place. Encased in a bowl covered with fish, of all things!

Then he stopped, so suddenly that an elderly man bumped into him from behind.

He squeezed the metal sphere in his hand. So the man called Jesus hadn't kept it, after all. He probably hadn't even known of the cup's existence. For all his talk about eternal life, he had literally let the opportunity to live forever slip from his fingers.

And yet the tomb was empty.

Saladin shuddered.

When he arrived back in Rome, he did not speak of his journey to Judea. After thirty years, he vanished to India, where he worked as a trader in silk for a time before returning to Rome.

By then the Christians had been recognized as a danger to

the Empire. They met in secret, known to one another by the symbol of the fish, which they displayed in clever ways.

"Lunatics," an acquaintance of Saladin's said as they sat together in the Colosseum watching a group of Christians kneeling in prayer while a lion mauled one of their number. "They won't fight. They're even proud to be crucified."

"Perhaps their belief is strong," Saladin offered.

"What belief? That a man can live forever?" His friend laughed harshly and pointed to the dead man at the lion's feet. "It didn't work for that poor fool."

"Some things are beyond the logic of our eyes and ears," Saladin answered. But the lion had attacked another of the Christians, and the crowd was on its feet, hooting and cheering.

No one heard him.

# CHAPTER TWENTY-TWO

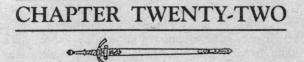

The next time Saladin lost the cup, a woman was responsible. She was a barbarian, even by the Britons' standards, which were far below his own. If Saladin had thought Judea backward, he was aghast the first time he set eyes on the northern island of Brittania.

There were no roads at all here, except for the highways the Romans had built during their long occupation, and these were crumbling and fallen into disuse. Now the grassy countryside was crisscrossed with a series of dirt footpaths.

Since the Roman legions had left, the entire country seemed to have reverted to barbarism. Saladin thought of a neglected garden that had been overrun by thorns and bramble. The villas of the nobles had become ruins, replaced by primitive thatch huts. The cities and villages, once efficient centers of trade, had degenerated into rambling slums where none but the most scrofulous peasants dared live. Even the military garrisons themselves had been taken over by filthy locals who lived in the tumbledown barracks with their animals, surrounded by offal.

There were no laws here. Everyone was illiterate. The great concepts of government brought by the Romans had been utterly forgotten. The British did not even understand the rudimentary skills of plumbing.

It was a horror. Saladin sat astride his horse—which, fortunately, he had brought with him, since these pale-skinned northerners did not even have decent animals to ride—and wondered how soon he could get out of this place. Ships seldom came to the island. He might be stranded here, he thought with dismay, for six months or more.

And then, too, there was the question of where he would go. He was finally weary of Rome. The Visigoths had invaded some years before and actually sacked the great city itself.

The invasion had come as an unspeakable shock to the Romans, although Saladin himself was not much surprised. The decadence and corruption of the nobility—which, he had to admit, had provided a number of quite enjoyable evenings for him over the years—had not made for good government. The Romans had in fact become so cynical that the barbarian Visigoths even tried to negotiate with city officials. They had offered to keep the peace, for a price. The emperor's representatives had condescendingly refused to pay "protection" money to the nomadic horde, but they did not bother to fortify the city, either. The parties just went on amid a spate of fashionable jokes about the Visigoths, until the Romans found themselves at the mercy of foul-smelling warriors who dressed in boarskins.

Saladin himself had seen the wind shifting and took the opportunity to absent himself from the city before the attack. But to his dismay, he found that similar atrocities were occurring in practically every center of civilization in the world. Vast confederations of horsemen from the plains of Eurasia were attacking the civilized centers of China, Persia,

India . . . even the stodgy Greeks in Athens were falling beneath the barbarians' massive numbers. There was really nowhere to flee from Rome, unless one chose to wander into the wilderness.

It was extremely tiresome, Saladin had decided as he returned to Rome during its death throes.

Actually, it had proved to be one of the more interesting periods in his endless life. Rome in those final years reminded him of a venerable noblewoman who had taken leave of her senses in her old age. There was nothing—no pleasure, no sensation, no experience—that could not be had for a price. Saladin had lain with senators' wives, a Nubian prince . . . even one of the sacred vestal virgins on one occasion. Feasts were held at which common townspeople, in imitation of the nobles, ate until their bellies were about to burst, then staggered away to vomit in the street. The spectacles at the Colosseum grew ever more shocking and contrived, mixing depraved sex with gruesome violence whenever possible.

But the Romans could no longer be shocked. "Rome has seen it all" became the city's jaded motto. For the Romans knew that their time was quickly passing. Soon they would all be killed in their beds—and their civilization with them. It was the end of the world, and the Romans accepted it—to their credit, Saladin admitted—without a trace of sentimentality.

After the city was sacked for the fifth time, and he had watched his own house go up in flames, Saladin decided to leave the Eternal City. It had not been eternal at all, he thought sadly as he rode northward, away from Rome, with nothing more than a saddlebag filled with gold, the metal cup, and, out of habit, a small pouch of medical supplies. The city had come and gone in what seemed like the blink of an eye.

He had not intended at first to travel to Britain, but as he moved steadily northward, an idea began to form in his mind: If Rome was done for, perhaps its provinces were just beginning to flourish. He had heard that the Romans had built cities on the northern island and had sufficiently tamed the wild Celts to the point where many of the British landholders had become Roman citizens. Their sons learned Latin, and they lived in Roman-style villas. Some of the wealthier ones were even granted the title of senator.

These reports, he now saw as he looked over the desolation of the country, had been utterly false. Whatever gains the Romans made during their occupation had been lost completely. Entrusting barbarians with civilized government was like giving gold to an infant, he thought angrily. If they couldn't eat it, it was of no value to them.

*Now where?* The thought hung heavily on him. The climate in this place was cold, colder than anywhere he had ever lived. Even though it was only September, he wrapped his cloak around him for warmth. He certainly wouldn't stay in one of the so-called cities; they were pestilential. There were farms in the area where he supposed he could buy a night's lodging, but the prospect of living under the same roof with not only barbarians, but their livestock as well, was daunting.

He decided to spend the night in the forest. For although Saladin had become a creature of civilization, he had not forgotten his childhood years in the Zagros Mountains with Kanna. He had no fear of the wilderness and knew how to live off the land. That night he killed a young deer and roasted it over a high fire.

That was the night, too, when he met Nimue.

It must have been the fire that drew her, or the smell of food. Saladin had cooked the whole deer and sat on its skin while he picked at a haunch. He longed, absurdly, for fruit. Food supplies had been low in recent times even in Rome, due to the constant invasions, but there were still peaches or melons to be had, if one knew where to look. But here . . . He sighed. In this cold place, he would be lucky to keep from starving.

He would go back to the docks tomorrow, he decided, and every day thereafter until he could find someone with a boat to ferry him and his horse across the channel back to Europe. There, he would live out whatever time he had to until the world settled into some kind of order.

He tossed the piece of meat aside, his appetite gone. Never in more than thirty centuries had he seen anything like the disaster that was sweeping the world. If he had been a superstitious man, he would have agreed with the Romans that mankind's time had come to an end. The statesman Cicero had been right when he warned the nobility against giving in to the mass of common men, the rabble: Now the barbarians were taking over the earth.

Saladin leaned back in disgust on the deerskin which was still stinking of fresh blood. It was that or the bare ground. He closed his eyes and tried not to think.

In the stillness of the forest, the noise made by a broken twig sounded like a thunderbolt. He leaped up from his place and drew his dagger at once.

The animal stopped, silent, but in the light of the fire he could see its eyes, glassy and shining, surrounded by a cloud of glowing hair. It made a sound, almost a cry, then sank to the ground.

Cautiously Saladin made his way toward the creature. It did not move. It was lying facedown in a patch of dried leaves. As he reached it, he prodded it with his toe to roll it over. He saw with some surprise that it was a woman.

Or, rather, a girl. She could not have been more than sixteen, Saladin thought, staring at her in distaste. Yet, with her filthy white flesh and clothing made of animal skins, she reminded him uncannily of the ancient mountain man Kanna.

When she did not move, he bent over her to see if she were still alive. Aside from a lot of scabs and bruises, which seemed normal, judging from her physical appearance, there were no signs of mortal wounds. He opened one of her eyelids. From the look of the eye, she had fainted. The iris, he saw, was blue.

He had never gotten used to blue-eyed, pale-skinned people, even though he had known many. Alexander himself, the greatest warrior in history, had been fair, and Saladin had half fallen in love with him at one time, but that was more despite the man's appearance than because of it. Even the Greeks, for all their learning and elegance, had seemed physically repugnant to Saladin. That was why he so preferred life in Rome. For while there were blonds there, too, they were not of the type he so disliked—pasty and weak-looking, like termites or bottom-feeding fish. Like Kanna. Or this girl.

Her skin was hot. A fever of some sort, probably brought on by whatever vermin she carried on her person in such plentiful supply. She stank.

Saladin was inclined to leave her where she was, but she posed a problem. Sick or not, she might attack him during the night. The woods were dark.

Cursing softly, he dragged her back to the fire. She would probably be dead by morning, anyway. Until then, he could prevent her from slitting his throat by keeping an eye on her.

She came to briefly, and tried to bolt. "Oh, stop," Saladin said wearily, pinning her arms back. "I'm not going to hurt you, you putrid sack of offal."

She tried to resist, but she was very weak. Her eyes opened wide. He could feel her hot, febrile breath and turned his face away from it. Firmly but without violence he positioned her in front of the fire.

"You're hungry, I suppose," he said, tearing off a piece of meat from the cooked carcass of the doe.

She looked at it, but her eyes lost their focus. Her tongue pulled loose from the roof of her mouth with an unpleasant sound. She was thirsty.

Reluctantly Saladin offered her his cask of water. He had seen a creek nearby; he would clean the cask's metal spout in the morning, after setting it on the fire to burn away the impurities from the creature's mouth.

She drank from it greedily, spilling water all over herself. She did not stop until he took the cask away from her. Then, with a last tentative look at the stranger in the wood, she curled up by the fire and went to sleep.

As the flames softened into embers, Saladin did the same.

# CHAPTER TWENTY-THREE

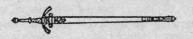

Saladin awoke to find the girl squatting on the ground in front of him, gnawing on a piece of cold meat. Her blue eyes, no longer glazed with fever, stared up at him with a mixture of awe and fear.

"So you're still alive," he said without much interest.

She smiled at him. Her teeth were good, despite her feral life. She tried to speak. It was tentative, and in a guttural language that sounded to Saladin like gibberish. He wondered how long it had been since she had spoken with another human being.

But that was nonsense, he told himself. The creature probably had a protector somewhere nearby, some great hairy male beast of her own kind who would come looking for her with a club in his hand.

Saladin stretched and rose to untie his horse.

"Get away," he told the girl. "Go on now, go." He pushed her.

She fell onto the earth with a hurt expression on her dirty face. Saladin ignored her and climbed onto the saddle.

The docks were filled with fishing boats, small craft that could not carry a horse. Saladin's horse was a good one, an Arabian stallion which he himself had brought to Rome from Persia. Even the strong animals from Gaul, used by most of the Roman officers, were no match for the swift-legged piece of living flesh that was Saladin's prized steed. The great sculptor Devinius had begged Saladin to allow him to sketch the horse, but Saladin had refused. If such a statue were made, the horse would have been stolen. The emperor himself would have wanted it.

To give up the stallion for a boat ride was not a price Saladin wanted to pay.

"When do you expect a bigger ship to dock here?" he called to some fishermen.

They looked up, but did not answer him. He called again; this time one of them shouted something in the same ugly-sounding language his forest girl had used.

Imagine, Saladin thought angrily. After almost four hundred years of Roman rule, these barbarians had lost the Latin language in less than half a century. How was he supposed to talk to these people? By the gods, his horse was more intelligent than the natives here.

He turned away, wanting nothing more than to get away from this place. The wind was cold today. Soon winter would come, and with it the certainty that no ship from any civilized place would make its way to the northern wasteland where he was stranded.

Saladin had no doubt that a British winter would be unlike anything he had ever experienced. There was said to be snow here. Not just on the mountaintops, where Roman nobles would send slaves to collect it for dessert at dinner parties, but everywhere. And, too, the land was apparently beset by other barbarians. Roman officers who had campaigned in Britain had mentioned a race of light-haired warriors called Saxons who made infrequent raids on outpost hill forts. The legionnaires had regarded them as more of a nuisance than any real menace.

"Beasts, that's what they were," one old soldier had said while recounting his experience. "They don't look like humans, they don't talk like humans." He had made a face. "And, believe me, they don't smell like humans."

It almost made him laugh. Even the Visigoths would find nothing of value to plunder in Britain. Whoever these Saxons were, they had to be truly desperate to consider looting this frozen, barren, impoverished dung heap.

The horse reared up. Caught daydreaming, Saladin brought the animal under control at the same time as he reached for his sword.

It was the girl, running out of the woods toward him.

"You again!" Saladin said with distaste.

She was carrying two dead squirrels by their tails. She came up to him, smiling timidly, and offered the two small bodies to him.

He hesitated for a moment, but the girl nodded her head and stretched out her arms.

Saladin took the squirrels. It would save him hunting later.

"How long have you been following me?" he demanded, then chided himself for wasting his time talking to her. In the sunlight, the color of her hair was extraordinary. It was curly as well as tangled, and surrounded her head and shoulders like a gigantic halo.

Why, she might be a Saxon, he thought. She certainly seemed to fit the old Roman soldier's description. But she was no warrior. Running out of the woods toward his horse had been the act of a fool. Any other man would have killed her on the spot.

He was about to ride on when she touched his ankle.

"Get away from me!" he said, jerking his foot back.

She pointed down the road, or what passed for a road.

"What?"

She pointed again, ran a few steps back toward the woods, beckoned to him, then darted into the trees and disappeared.

He listened. There were horses coming from a distance. He cantered back toward them. Once he got a look at whoever was approaching, he could outrun them if he had to.

To his surprise, the horsemen were soldiers, of a sort. They wore some kind of armor, although every man seemed to have outfitted himself in his own fashion, and they rode with no sense of rank or form.

But they did carry a banner, a rather beautifully embroidered red dragon on a field of white. Clearly, Saladin thought, this was an entourage of one of their chieftains. Even in this desolate place, there might be some men of learning who could at least speak enough Latin to direct Saladin toward a decent place to spend the night. His best chance was with these nobles.

"*Ave!*' he called when the group was within earshot.

The soldiers surrounded him at once, their weapons drawn. With a flourish Saladin bowed to them, although his great height combined with the size of the stallion he rode set him far above the Britons on their shaggy little ponies.

"I am a stranger in your land, and I beg your indulgence in granting me an interview with your liege lord," he said in his most elegant Latin.

The men murmured among themselves, again in the unpleasant language of the land. But their eyes never left his horse. One of them actually rode up and touched the animal.

Saladin had the stallion stomp a warning. The soldiers gasped at this simple feat of horsemanship.

"I demand to see whoever's in charge!" Saladin snapped. He looked down the line of riders. They all appeared to be soldiers with the exception of two, at the end of the line, one very old, the other young. The younger was common-looking, red-haired and plainly dressed. The old man appeared to be a priest of some kind, dressed in a long shapeless robe with a cloak thrown over his shoulders. Both rode the same undistinguished beasts as the soldiers. Not a litter or carriage among them.

Exasperated, he turned to go, but the soldiers stopped him with their swords.

"You really are beginning to annoy me," he said. "Let me pass."

The soldiers stayed. One of them jabbed his sword in the air toward Saladin.

"I told you buffoons to let me pass!" he roared as the stallion reared up majestically. He drew his own sword, curved and magnificent, the blade longer than his own arm, and swung it expertly over his head.

"Now, now," came a quiet voice.

The old man rode forward.

The youth shouted something in the native tongue, and to Saladin's surprise, the soldiers backed off a few feet. But the young man himself did not approach.

"Buffoons we may be," the old man said, "but we are not

in the habit of threatening an army of armed men." His Latin was perfect.

"Forgive me," Saladin said. He accorded the man the same bow he had given the soldiers. "I am stranded in a strange land where I can buy neither food nor shelter and cannot make myself understood to ask for these necessities. I forgot myself."

"It is understandable, under the circumstances," the old man said pleasantly. "What do you call yourself?"

"I am Saladin, lately of Rome and her Empire. I am a physician and a nobleman, whose name is known."

"Not here," the man said, smiling. "I'm afraid Rome has had little influence in Britain for some time."

"That I have seen for myself. I wish to return to the Continent—" *Or anywhere else*, he thought wryly. "But I am having difficulty securing passage on a boat large enough to take my horse."

The man stroked his white beard. "I believe a Roman ship is due shortly. They usually come to trade for wool and dogs before winter."

"Yes, sire," Saladin said patiently. "In six weeks' time. It is too long to sleep in the woods. I stopped your men to ask about lodging. I will pay well."

The old man looked surprised. "Lodging? with us?"

The young man said something in the local language, quite casually, it seemed, and the men all burst out laughing.

Saladin felt a flash of anger. The impudent pup! Apparently the nobles of this odious place felt no need to teach their children any manners. The little fool even had the temerity to ride up to join the two men.

Then he surprised Saladin by speaking in flawless Latin. "Your circumstances are unfortunate, sir. Please accept our hospitality for as long as you require." He inclined his head briefly, then trotted his horse back into the line, speaking curtly to the men leading the procession.

It moved forward. The old man gave Saladin a look of amusement. "Well, we'd best be going, then," he said. "Camelot is not far."

"Camelot?"

"The High King's winter quarters." He pointed toward the horizon. Some ten or twelve miles away, Saladin judged, sat what looked to be an enormous stone castle on a hill. In his reverie, he had not even noticed it.

The youth passed by on his horse. Such an undistinguished-looking youth, with his shock of red hair and plain clothing.

Saladin turned to the old man.

"Is he the High King?" he asked.

The old man nodded.

"And you are regent?"

"Oh, nothing so grand. I am Merlin. I'm afraid I don't have a title. I could be described as an old household retainer, I suppose."

A servant, and riding beside the king! Saladin was confused. He did not know whether to continue speaking to the man or not.

"I daresay we're not what you're accustomed to. But you'll get used to us."

He led his pony forward to join the young king, gesturing to Saladin to join him.

When all were gone and the dust had settled on the road, the girl emerged tentatively from the woods. The carcasses of the two squirrels had been trampled to pulp.

The stranger had left her without a thought.

# CHAPTER TWENTY-FOUR

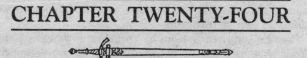

"You looked so young," Saladin said to the sleeping boy. "Yet it was clear from the beginning that your knights adored you."

It was that more than anything else, he supposed, that started the first stirrings of ambition within himself.

Saladin had never before aspired to power. Part of it may have been his youth, despite the fact that he had already lived nearly thirty-two centuries. Still, to outward appearances, he had been a fifteen-year-old boy for most of that time. Then, in what had seemed like an instant, he became a twenty-five-year-old man. Professionally useful: After his return from Judea, his fortune increased a thousandfold. People had sought him out as a physician.

To be truthful, he had been a very good doctor, even though he had never once used the metal sphere to cure a patient, not even when the patient was the emperor himself. It would have been a foolish risk. Besides, he was not particularly dedicated to keeping people alive. As someone immune to death, he understood with detachment that death was part of the natural order of things.

But he was, to say the least, vastly experienced in his profession. Had he been more dedicated, he might have revolutionized the practices of medicine and surgery. As it was, he had discovered a way to resuscitate a stopped heart—a procedure which brought him so much renown that he feared he would have to leave Rome. He was alternately hailed as a saint and castigated as a sorcerer until finally Emperor Nero tipped the scales by summoning Saladin to the royal palace to treat a recurring case of gout. After that he was well regarded, even though he was not invited back after the emperor's next attack.

His colleagues subtly chided Saladin for not making more of his opportunity to curry royal favor.

"There was nothing to be done for him," he'd answered curtly. "Not with his eating habits."

Actually, he had been relieved. If he had been selected as a personal physician to the emperor, it would eventually have become difficult to maintain the secret of his immortality. He would have remained a twenty-five-year-old man, while everyone around him, including the "divine" ruler, aged and died. No, the secret was too important to risk for a temporary moment in the sun. Why should he need power? He had life. Besides, Nero was a repulsive little pervert whose personal habits offended Saladin. He was not unhappy when Nero died shortly afterward and the name of Saladin faded from court circles.

But here, in this strange and barbaric land, things were different. This was not Rome, where holding power meant forever watching one's back. Here the High King lived as a normal man and regarded the kingship as a job.

Arthur commanded the forces at Camelot with an easy hand. Where the Roman emperors had held themselves up as living deities, this king behaved like a leader among equals. He was, they said, a great warrior, going into the thick of battle himself and living no better in the field than the lowliest of his soldiers.

At the castle, he disdained finery and diversions. Except for public ceremonies, he did not even wear a gold circlet around his head to signify his rank. Entertainments at Camelot were simple, a harper or a storyteller. The food was plain. The stone castle itself was rough, though immense. He had even constructed a round table where he met with his most favored knights. Saladin had seen it himself. The king's chair was no higher than the rest.

Such a man, Saladin thought, could not command respect for long. Love, yes. The men loved him for his very ordinariness, for his Spartan purity. He was one of them. But he was not a king, not of the sort Saladin had known.

"Do you read Celtic?" Merlin asked, interrupting his reverie. Saladin had been standing at the carved wooden bookcase in a parlor off the Great Hall. It was an odd room, furnished only with a low bench and a rush mat on the floor in addition to the small cabinet. But it was fairly sunny compared with the other slit-windowed chambers in the drafty stone keep of the castle, and considerably warmer than his own small sleeping room on the upper level.

Saladin had taken to spending most of his days there, looking through the meager collection of writings. There were copies of Plato's *Republic* and Aristotle's *Ethics*, written in Greek on pages of yellowed linen, and Emperor Claudius' autobiography in Latin, some writings of Julius

Caesar, and *The Orations* of Cicero, which Saladin knew so well he had almost memorized it. There were works in Frankish as well, folk tales he had found amusing, and several beautifully illuminated works in a language he could not read. It was one of these that he was holding when the mysterious "court retainer" named Merlin had come upon him.

Saladin nearly jumped. He had grown unaccustomed to being spoken to in the castle. No one, apparently, understood Latin except for Merlin and the king, and Saladin rarely saw either of them. As for the others, they were like a wild bunch of boys, spending their days outdoors hunting or practicing the arts of warfare. Neither activity would have appealed much to Saladin even if the weather had been warm; as it was, he thought the knights must have been mad to venture outdoors when it was not absolutely necessary. Each day grew colder than the last. The trees were almost bereft of leaves already, and at night the chill wind blew mercilessly into the sleeping rooms, freezing Saladin to the bone.

"Celtic?" He looked down at the beautiful manuscript. "Is that what you call your language?"

"No. We speak English here," the old man said, "although it may have been Celtic at one time, long ago. It's an ancient language, older even than Latin." He recited a poem of some sort, the sounds dolorous and musical. When he was finished, he smiled.

"That was beautiful," Saladin said, immediately embarrassed at paying the compliment.

"It's still spoken in Ireland, across a sea to the far north. The place is even wilder than Britain. But they love to speak and sing. The Irish have a tradition of storytelling that's as old as the sea."

"And how do you know it?"

"I've traveled there," Merlin said. "In my youth, I was a bard. My voice was never as good as some of them, particularly the Irish, who sing like angels, but I played the harp and learned the old stories. I found these books there. All of them were written by women."

"Women!" Saladin was aghast. "They waste learning on women?"

Merlin nodded. "But it's a rare art, in any case. The oral tradition is very strong. The bards themselves are quite powerful. They're regarded rather as magicians."

Saladin's eyes narrowed. There was something in what the man said that sparked his curiosity. "That's how you're treated here," he said.

"Oh, nothing of the kind." He laughed self-deprecatingly. "The king tolerates me because I had a hand in his education."

"These books are yours," Saladin said.

"Yes. I put them here so that Arthur might read them. I suppose I could have given them to him outright, but I really couldn't bear to part with them. Do you read Greek?"

"Of course." He saw Merlin's look of amusement and added, "But education is easily come by in Rome. May I ask how you achieved such scholarship?"

Merlin shrugged. "If the truth be told, there was probably more of it around in my day. The Saxons hadn't burned everything, and the cities weren't the mess they are now. . . . But I imagine all old men speak of the past as if it were a better time than the present. All it means is that we liked living better back then, because we were young."

Saladin put the book back on the shelf. "You are more right than you know. The times were better sixty years ago. In Rome, a man could walk the streets without fear for his life. Now, thanks to the mobs within and the invaders without the city, there is no safety, no peace."

"Those sound like bitter thoughts for one so young."

"Young?" He blinked. He had forgotten himself with the old man. "Yes, of course." He forced a smile, an expression with which he had never felt comfortable. "With experience comes optimism, I'm told. Perhaps I've yet to attain that."

He had almost slipped, almost exposed the secret of his life . . . for a moment's conversation with a near-stranger! Nothing like that had ever happened to him before. Yet, he thought, there was something about the old man which seemed to draw him out, as if Merlin could read his mind. . . .

"Excuse me," Saladin said abruptly, and walked away, not knowing exactly where he would go.

"Saladin." The voice was soft. "I'll teach you English if you like."

It was an offer Saladin could not refuse. He had five more weeks remaining on this miserable island before the Roman ship came. To fill the long days with learning a new language was enticing.

"I've nothing better to do with my time," he said.

"After dinner, then."

Saladin left. But for an hour or more, he could not rid himself of the feeling that he had already said too much to the old man.

# CHAPTER TWENTY-FIVE

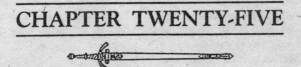

The beginning of the end was, of all things, an act of kindness.

Saladin had been at the castle for several weeks. October was cold, and it promised to be a bad winter. The sea was savage, and already a few dry flurries of snow had blown through the inner bailey of the courtyard at Camelot.

Each day for weeks Saladin had ridden to the docks to await the arrival of the Roman vessel which would take him away from this forlorn island; each day he returned, frozen and disappointed. By the first week of November, he knew in his heart that the ship would not come.

His only consolation in those days were his lessons in the native language and the attendant company of Merlin. The two men, he learned, had much in common. They were both well traveled, although naturally Saladin had visited more distant places; both were scholars by inclination; and, most surprisingly, they were both physicians.

Merlin's knowledge of medicine was not modern. During the course of their lessons, the old man had sometimes spoken of the "Old Religion," the pagan worship which had dominated Britannia until the Roman occupation, when the druid priests had been driven off or executed. The Romans' own polytheism had never taken root here among the ordinary people, and had been recently replaced by Christianity, whose missionaries were as strictly against the old ways as the Romans had been.

Yet still, the Old Religion was practiced in secret. Shrines set up long ago to gods so ancient that their names were no longer remembered were nevertheless tended with care by passersby. The stone bowls were filled with clean water, and often small sacrifices of food were left at the shrines to appease the Old Ones, the mystical deities who had watched over the land since the beginning of time. The priests of this ancient cult, the druids, still performed their rituals in secret places deep in the woods, as they had for centuries since the old ways were outlawed.

Merlin was one of these.

Not that he attempted to bring the Old Religion to the court at Camelot; indeed, he lived among the crosses and other accoutrements of the new foreign religion with as little notice as he had taken of the Roman statues during his childhood.

"Christianity," he told Saladin matter-of-factly, "is the way of the future. Arthur must maintain a Christian court, at least nominally, if he's ever to unite all the warring tribes of the island."

"I should think you'd be offended," Saladin said archly. "Or frightened. The Christians apparently wish to eradicate your religion completely."

The old man smiled. "So did the Romans. And for four hundred years, they thought they'd succeeded. As far as the Christians know, the druids have been gone for centuries."

"But what about you? You're here to prove them wrong."

"I am just an eccentric old man favored by a king who is

well-beloved," he said. "And so they call me not a druid, but a wizard." He laughed. "And they attribute my long life to magical immortality."

It was with the druids that he had learned the arts of medicine. And truly, Saladin felt, no mortal man could know more about the properties of herbs and minerals than Merlin. The two of them spent long hours in the parlor by candlelight, their respective unguents and plants spread about on the floor between them, discussing various ailments and their cures. Despite his long life of secrecy, Saladin found himself enjoying the exchange of medical information. When he told Merlin of his technique in treating heart-attack victims, the old man had listened, fascinated.

"No medicine is used?" he asked. "None at all?"

"Not during the initial attack. Only physical movements are required to stimulate the heart to beat again." Saladin showed him the movements, strong, almost rough, applied directly to the chest. "You must replace the heart's rhythm artificially until it has revived. Naturally, this does not always succeed. Your best chance is with a young man, but even this often fails."

The two men discussed the procedure for hours. In the end, they determined that the physical manipulation, combined with the essence of foxglove, a plant found in the region containing highly stimulative properties, would be a worthwhile experiment.

Through Merlin, Saladin learned how to prepare many new medicines. He bundled himself up in a fur cloak and the two walked the fields outside the castle together for long hours, searching for plants that had not already been killed by the early frosts. Afterward, Saladin always complained of the cold, but he never passed up Merlin's invitations.

"Truly, Saladin, I can scarcely believe you to be only twenty-five years old," Merlin said as they were trudging through the shallow caves of the area looking for pyrite, which Saladin claimed could be packed into infected wounds from tooth extraction.

Saladin pulled his cloak higher around his neck. "Sometimes it feels more like twenty-five centuries," he said.

Merlin smiled. He touched the younger man's back lightly, and they moved on.

"They say the hills are hollow here," he said. "It's because of all the small caves cut into the land. Some parts of Britain are honeycombed with them. In the old days, when the Romans were establishing rule here, many people fled the legions by living in these caves. Some of my ancestors were among them." He picked up a rock, studied it, then cast it away.

"Actually, they're not bad places to live. When the court travels north, I often stay in one myself, near the border of Dumnonia. It's every bit as comfortable as the drafty castle where Arthur and the others stay, and there's far less noise."

"I am acquainted with the merits of cave dwelling," Saladin said.

Merlin stopped suddenly. "Why, that's where you learned your medicine, isn't it? In a cave."

Saladin stared at him. Then the old man *could* read his mind. He felt a mixture of panic and anger rise up inside him.

"No, no, please don't bolt. It's a small gift, I assure you," Merlin stammered. "The fact is, I'm not sure it's a gift at all. I don't really read thoughts. Just a random image now and again. Sometimes it's nothing more than a feeling. It confuses me, more than anything."

Saladin relaxed a little.

"But I would like to ask you . . ." His gaze wandered down to the velvet pouch hanging from Saladin's belt.

Unconsciously, Saladin's fingers wrapped around it.

"I see that quite often when I'm talking with you. It's a ball of some kind, a metal ball. Am I right?"

Saladin was silent for a long moment. The old man seemed to be exhibiting nothing more than curiosity. "It's a talisman I carry for luck. A charm," he said finally.

Merlin frowned. "May I look at it?"

"No." He walked ahead.

* * *

The incident occurred in one of the small caves. It was not dark there, nor particularly deep, and the two men walked about without much caution, gathering rocks by feel.

"Do you dislike darkness?" Merlin asked.

Saladin took a moment to answer. "No," he said finally. "I far prefer it to rooms filled with smoking candles."

"I quite understand," the old man said. "Darkness is often solitary. There's much to be said for being alone . . ."

He broke off as Saladin uttered a hoarse cry, and Merlin heard the sound of falling rock. "Saladin!" he called, rushing toward the noise.

There was no doubt about what had occurred. Even in the hazy darkness, Merlin could see the cloud of dust that had risen from the rockfall. He cast about frantically, trying to discern where Saladin might be in the rubble.

Working as fast as he could, he lifted stones and hurled them aside. If he could uncover a part of the man, he reasoned, he would be able to approximate where his head was and possibly save him from suffocation.

"Hold on!" he shouted, ignoring the pains which had already begun shooting through his arms and chest. He regretted his age. If his guest—a fellow physician—died because his rescuer was too slow to help him, Merlin would never forgive himself.

He worked harder, hearing his own breath coming ragged and loud. At last he uncovered part of Saladin's shoulder and was quickly able to clear the area near Saladin's nose and mouth.

He was breathing. "Thank the gods," he said, gently lifting the stones from over the prone man's eyes. "Don't panic, now," he said. "You probably have some broken bones, so I'm going to clear enough of this away to make you comfortable before I go back for help."

"There's no need. I'm unhurt." Saladin blinked dust out of his eyes.

"Marvelous," Merlin said, although he knew that the man's lack of pain was probably due to shock, and he would not be surprised if he uncovered a severed limb beneath the mound of stones. "Can you move?"

"No."

"Then don't try."

He patiently continued removing rocks one by one. Before long he found the reason for Saladin's immobility: A large flat boulder had fallen directly onto his midsection.

Merlin groaned inwardly. Fractured ribs, certainly; a broken hip, perhaps two; possible damage to the spine; internal injuries. If he lived for an hour, it would be a long time.

"I've got to get this off you," he said. "I'll come back in a moment." With that, he ran out of the cave and into the woods beyond it.

When he returned, puffing with the exertion, he carried a long, straight branch, which he worked gently between the rock and Saladin's abdomen. "There's going to be some pressure," he grunted as he formed a small mound of stones beside it. "I've got to lever that thing away. I'll try not to hurt you, but . . ."

"Get on with it," Saladin snapped.

Merlin finished constructing his fulcrum, then rested the center of the branch on top of it. "Prepare yourself, Saladin," he said, then pushed down on the end of the branch with all his might. Slowly the big rock creaked.

The old man pressed down harder, his arms trembling with the effort. If he slipped, he knew, if his strength failed him for a moment, the rock would come crashing atop a man who had already suffered any number of injuries. It would kill him at once.

"It's . . . moving," Merlin said, squeezing out the words. The cords on his neck stood out starkly. His face, shaking with strain, felt as if it were about to explode.

Finally the rock gave. It tumbled over once, then thudded with a cloud of dust near the cave entrance.

"I'll get myself out," Saladin said.

"No, no." Merlin scrambled over to where he lay. "It

won't take long now . . ." He began to cough. It was deep and searing, and each spasm was worse than the last.

"Move out of the way," Saladin shouted, lifting his arm. A shower of stones sprayed out from the spot where the arm had lain.

Merlin rolled aside, unable to stop the racking cough. His breathing did not return to normal until all four of Saladin's limbs were in view and the tall man was able to extricate himself from the rubble.

"You can walk?" Merlin wheezed. It seemed incredible.

"I told you I was uninjured," Saladin said irritably. "But I refuse to stay here any longer."

He walked from the cave as if he had been sitting on a soft cushion rather than buried within a mountain of rock.

Merlin himself was far more exhausted than his companion seemed to be. The physical ordeal he had been through, combined with the nerve-wracking worry about Saladin's condition, left him feeling every one of his seventy-one years.

He sat on the cave floor, his breath as audible as a donkey's bray. He tried to stand up, but a tightening in his chest forced him to sit down again immediately.

He felt light-headed. For a moment he bent forward—slowly, so as not to aggravate the pain in his chest—to dispel a fierce ringing that had begun in his ears.

"Are you coming?" Saladin called from outside.

"Yes," Merlin answered, but he knew his voice was too feeble to hear. "Yes," he repeated, louder.

He stood up. His legs were wobbly, but functional. With a shuffling gait, they led Merlin out into the light.

"You look ashen," Saladin said.

"The dirt, most likely," Merlin answered with a weary smile.

Saladin dusted off his long black robe. "Yes, I'm filthy. I'll need someone to wash my garments immediately." With an air of deep disgust, he picked a cobweb out of his hair.

"First things first," Merlin said, walking over to him. "Let me take a look at you before we head back. Sometimes injuries don't . . ." He peered closely at the tall man's face. He lifted one of Saladin's hands. "There isn't a scratch on you," he murmured in amazement. "Not even on your feet."

"I should like to go back now," Saladin said. "My fur cloak is gone, and it's cold here." Not waiting for a reply, he strode toward the castle.

Merlin barked out a laugh that turned into a cough. "But it's remarkable! I've never seen such a thing. Surely, with the amount of rock that fell, you must have suffered something . . . *something*."

His hand clutched unconsciously at the collar of his robe as he struggled to keep up with Saladin's long strides. "There isn't even a mark on your skin, such as might be left by a fingernail." He gasped for air. "Not a bruise . . . Saladin . . . ah. . . . ."

He fell to the ground.

Saladin whirled around, recognizing the choking sound of a man whose heart was undergoing a monumental seizure.

Merlin was lying on the grass, his arms and legs flailing wildly. This was no small attack, Saladin knew; those were characterized by a concerted stillness of the limbs. Men who feared they were suffering from heart attack took pains to move nothing and breathe shallowly. But those in the full throes of pain no longer cared for such precautions. The agony overwhelmed them. That had been Saladin's experience, and he knew it was what he was witnessing now.

The old man's lips were blue. His eyes were bulging, and sweat coursed off his face. Saladin knelt down beside him and began the treatment at once, pressing into the bone above the heart with the heels of both hands in rhythm.

Merlin's wild movements increased. At one point he cried out, some sort of incantation in a language Saladin did not understand. Then the old man's eyes rolled back in his head and he shuddered and lay still.

Saladin continued the movements, not knowing what else to do. Every five beats he rested briefly to take Merlin's pulse. It was weakening to nothing. Had Merlin been a patient in his practice, Saladin knew he would have given up at this point and informed the family.

For all the rest of his long life, in fact, Saladin could not answer why he had not done exactly that. Was it fear of the king and his barbaric knights, perhaps, who would surely have accused Saladin of murdering their beloved wizard, whom they believed to be immortal? Was that all? Or was it the sudden, irrational urge to preserve the life of the only man, in all his life, who had ever called him friend?

Friends were irrelevant to Saladin; people aged and died and passed into dust. Their lives were as meaningless to Saladin as those of ants. Some of them had tried to understand him. Some had actively sought his company for a time. Some had even possessed qualities worth knowing—brilliance, wit, beauty—but he had never felt even the slightest desire to save any of them from death. Why now, he would wonder for ages to come, why at this moment, on this empty field, did he take the metal orb from its pouch and hold it over the still body of a dying man?

He swallowed. He should walk away. Merlin was nothing to him. He was old; his time had come.

Perhaps he dropped the sphere. There were many times in the future when Saladin was certain that was what had happened: He simply dropped it. It fell on the old man's chest.

And the moment when he heard the great rush of air fill Merlin's lungs, he hid the ball away, cursing himself for using it.

Merlin sat up. He touched his chest with fluttering hands.

"It was warm," he whispered.

Saladin stood up.

"You used it."

"I resuscitated you by the method I explained," he answered coldly.

With an effort, the old man pulled himself upright. "I saw you," he said quietly.

"You were unconscious."

Merlin examined his hands as if they were things of wonder. "It was more than that. I was dead, or nearly so. I saw a light, Saladin, and heard the voices of a thousand people calling to me." His face lit up. "People I had not thought of in fifty years. My old nurse, whom I loved. The shepherd who first led me to the cave in the north. A young druid priest, killed by the Romans . . ."

"You've suffered a strain," Saladin interrupted. "These are delusions."

"No." The bony fingers touched Saladin's robe. "I saw myself, as if from a great height. I was lying on the ground, and you were bending over me. The ball was in your hand. You touched it to my chest." He blinked. "In that instant, I felt myself rushing back toward earth, toward the body I had left behind. And then there was a warmth, a great warmth emanating from the spot where your magic had begun its healing."

He let go of the sleeve. "You know I speak the truth."

Saladin regarded him for a long moment, his face pale. "Rubbish," he said at last, and walked away.

# CHAPTER TWENTY-SIX

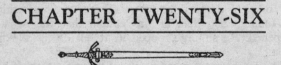

Merlin did not mention the incident again. The stranger whom the courtiers at Camelot called the Saracen Knight stayed alone in his room for several weeks, venturing out of the castle only to inquire futilely at the frozen docks, where it soon became apparent that no ship would come until spring to carry him home—wherever that was.

Saladin had spoken of Rome, but he was no Roman. From his manner, Merlin imagined that the tall physician had always been an outsider of one sort or another, looking at life through a perspective that even one of Merlin's age could not comprehend.

It was the ball, Merlin knew. Although Saladin had

studiously avoided him since his near-death experience in the meadow, the old man had been haunted by the memory. It had been no delusion, as Saladin insisted. His training with the druids had taught him to distinguish the fine line between imagination and the supernatural.

And he had been witness to the supernatural before. When the young boy Arthur had pulled out the sword that no grown knight could budge from the stone, he had known he was witnessing a miracle. The stone had lain at the Abbey of Glastonbury since time out of mind, inscribed with its ancient Celtic message: *Whoso pulleth this sword from this stone shall be named rightwise king.*

No one knew who had written the inscription, or how the stone had become fused to the magnificent sword. Some said that it had been the sword of Macsen, the great Celt who had been crowned Emperor Maximus of Rome generations before. Others claimed that the sword Excalibur had been invested of a life of its own by the ancient fairy folk in the far distant past. But no one knew. Even the druids, with their ancient memories, could not divine its mystery. And yet the boy had taken the sword without effort, and the knights had bowed down to him on the spot.

Later, after the strange story of Arthur's magical feat had traveled throughout Britain, whispers arose that Merlin himself had used his sorcery to loosen the sword from the stone. They claimed that Arthur was the wizard's son, and that Merlin had conjured up powerful spirits to gain the throne of the High King for the boy.

These stories amused Merlin, since he knew the limitations of his power. It was true, yes, that he could sometimes divine some trace of people's thoughts; it was an ability he had possessed since childhood. But it was an incomplete thing, giving him only images and intuitions. Even after his training with the druids, Merlin often thought that his "gift" may have been nothing more than the ability to observe people closely. The rest of what the common folk called "magic" was simply education, which had been in woefully short supply since the Romans left Britain.

Merlin's family had had strong ties with the Romans, as well as a history of rule in Britain. His ancestors had been petty kings since the time of the Celts. When the Romans first came to the island, Merlin's people had been among the first to be "civilized"—that is, awarded Roman status and offered Roman education for their children. His father, Ambrosius, had been reared in the Roman manner, even though the Romans themselves were long gone by his time, and in turn he reared his own children the same way.

Much of Ambrosius' schooling was lost on his oldest son, Uther, who nevertheless grew up to become one of the strongest kings in Britain. Uther had been a truculent and stubborn boy who cared little for books. He was shrewd, but not much concerned with matters of thought. Ambrosius' other sons were much the same. During their lessons they would sit numbly through their father's lectures, longing to be back astride their ponies or practicing with the lance.

It was probably his disappointment in his legitimate sons that had prompted Ambrosius to include Merlin in the lessons. Merlin was a bastard and would not normally have been admitted into the household, but, as his mother had died in childbirth, and Ambrosius' wife was already a year dead by that time, the old chief saw no reason to let the infant starve. Of course, the boy was not permitted to practice the arts of war; his half-brothers would not have stood for that. Even as a child, Uther jealously guarded his right to eventual kingship, and Ambrosius knew that to dangle Merlin in front of him would be to sanction the boy's murder.

Besides, Merlin seemed to have no inclination toward battle. He was a gentle boy with an extraordinary mind, who showed an affinity for learning from his youngest years. This delighted Ambrosius, who would not have been a king himself if he had not been born to it, and who had loved Merlin's mother deeply.

She had been a young girl when he met her just after the death of his wife, and he had never known much about her. Illya was a creature of the woods, a healer whom the peasants called a witch, but to whom they went with all their own

ailments as well as with sick animals. She had healed
Ambrosius, too, with her love, but she had never told him
about her past or her family or why she lived alone in the
forest. When she revealed that she was with child, Ambrosius
had been tempted to marry her, although he knew it would
have been a dangerous decision, frowned upon by the other
kings of Britain. But things never came to that. Illya had
refused him gently, saying that she had no desire to change
the place or the manner in which she lived.

At the time, Ambrosius had given little thought to his
unborn child. He already had three sons, and his mistress was
offering no difficulty. Indeed, during the last months of her
pregnancy, they had frolicked together like children. It had
been the happiest time of Ambrosius' life. And then, overnight, she was gone.

Every time he looked on Merlin's thin, serious face with
his sensitive eyes and tender mouth, he thought of Illya
cradling a fawn in her arms or walking through the fields, her
arms overflowing with wildflowers. Her son, he knew, would
never be king; yet still there was something remarkable about
him.

Merlin never told his father about his supernormal abili-
ties, such as they were, and it nearly broke Ambrosius' heart
when Merlin left to see the world as a bard. During his
travels, the "power" he possessed grew. The long years of
living by his wits had undoubtedly sharpened his instincts.
He found that he could communicate with animals to an
uncanny degree, as his mother had, and that he often knew
what men were thinking before they spoke their thoughts
aloud . . . and even if they spoke different thoughts. His
ability had saved his skin more than once, but he knew that
it was not developed to the point where it could be of any real
use. If he could only harness this gift, cultivate it, he knew,
he might open whole new worlds to himself.

He joined the druids to do just that. And they did teach him
many things—the healing arts, for which he had a natural
talent, and the ancient knowledge of the Old Religion. But
his extrasensory power remained rudimentary. After many

years of study and practice, he was able to levitate objects to some degree, but Merlin viewed that as little more than a parlor trick. And he was able, quite uncannily, to transform images in his mind into external visions that others could see. The druids looked upon this as an extraordinary development, but to Merlin himself, it was a small achievement. The visions were a manifestation of his concentration, he explained, nothing more. What he was looking for was something far greater.

"But *we* are the wizards and sorcerers the people whisper about," one of the priests had told him, not without amusement. "Our small powers are the things they spin into legends about men with lightning bolts shooting out of their fingers. Surely you don't aspire to that sort of thing."

"I don't know if I aspire to anything," Merlin said miserably. "I only know that I'm incomplete. It's as if . . ."

He wasn't able to finish. It would have sounded pompous. But the truth was, Merlin often felt as if something of awesome energy were growing inside him. Like a bear, which at birth is no bigger than the first joint of a man's finger, the creature within him had grown to massive proportions and was straining to get out. And Merlin had spent half a lifetime trying to find the key to release it.

Sometimes he felt as if it would devour him from inside. Even after Merlin had made his way back home and was tolerated, if not exactly welcomed, at King Uther's court as a physician and occasional ambassador to other provinces, he felt a dreadful unease, as if whatever was growing inside him were about to split open his skin and burst out.

And then, when he saw the boy Arthur—another bastard, Uther's, and thus Merlin's nephew—lift the magic sword from the stone, he realized at last what he must do. It suddenly all made sense: He was to use his small powers to protect the High King of Britain, to grant long life to the man who would rule as no sovereign had ever ruled before.

Arthur was the king, the man meant to be king, the king now and forever. Even before he claimed the sword, Merlin had seen in the boy a spark of greatness: He had possessed from the beginning a sharp intelligence combined with the capacity for leadership, and all of it was tempered with what Merlin could only describe as *grace*. Fairness, mercy, purity of heart, personal austerity, humor . . . all of these were qualities which Arthur the boy, and later, Arthur the king evinced. He inspired not awe or fear, but a fanatical loyalty among those who served him. He was born to rule, and from the moment he came to power, Arthur had known his mission: He was to unite the world in peace for all time.

Such a king had never lived, before or after. Oh, there had been rulers who sought to conquer all the lands they saw, be it for greed or for adventure, but none had seen beyond the boundaries of their own kingdoms.

Arthur was different. His vision was one so grand that it would have shocked and appalled his contemporaries, or even world leaders well into the twentieth century and beyond. Merlin himself had been stunned when he had first heard of Arthur's plan. For what he wanted was no less than a global consensus of law.

"I don't want to destroy the Saxons," he had confided to Merlin in a moment of reflection shortly after his coronation. "I just want to civilize them."

Merlin had smiled. "There are those who might view that as an impossibility."

"It's really just a matter of time," Arthur went on. "Once they learn how to farm, they'll stop attacking and come as peaceful settlers."

Merlin found it hard to hide his astonishment. "You *want* them to settle here?"

"Why not? There's plenty of space. They could bring part of their own culture here. We'd be all the richer for it."

"Arthur," Merlin said worriedly, "you've just become king. I must urge you most strongly not to bruit these ideas about to the petty chieftains—"

Arthur burst out laughing. "Can you imagine what they'd say? No, I plan to keep my thoughts to myself for the moment."

Merlin rolled his eyes in relief.

"For the chiefs to support me as High King, I'll have to give them what they want—battles and victories. Right now, that's the only thing the Saxons understand, anyway. But the time will come when our nation and theirs will live together, trade, work together for mutual benefit . . ." His eyes sparkled. "Wouldn't it be wonderful, Merlin, if we could talk with people from all the lands that lie beyond Gaul and Rome?"

"Heaven forbid," Merlin said. "They may be as bad as the Saxons."

"At first, I suppose, they would. But someday they might be allies." He sighed. "I wonder if one lifetime will be enough."

The old man smiled. "It's never enough," he said gently.

"Is that why things never change?" Arthur asked.

"Perhaps."

He had left the boy-king then, and Arthur did not mention his radical thoughts during all the years of his growing power. Instead, he proved himself in battle time and again, gaining the great respect of the petty chieftains and their vassal knights through his courage on the battlefield. Merlin had begun to think that the king had forgotten his childish dream when Arthur announced, just before leaving for one of the endless battles against the Saxons, that he had just granted settlers' rights to a band of Germans who had been beaten by Arthur's knights during an attempted attack on a northern village.

"Are you mad?" Merlin stormed. "They came to invade your country."

"But they didn't. And so instead of slaughtering them and then waiting for their neighbors to attack in a second wave, I have welcomed them and asked them to help in our defense against the Saxons."

"You've done *what?*" Merlin was aghast. "You've got one bunch of barbarians to fight another bunch of barbarians?"

Arthur only smiled. "Come now, Merlin. Many of the petty chiefs have been using German mercenaries for years to help them defend against the Saxons."

"But they were paid and then sent home. They weren't invited to take over our country."

"They're not taking over. They're settling here as farmers, subject to our laws."

"Good God, Arthur, they know no laws. They're barbarians!"

"That's a meaningless word," Arthur said. "To the emperor of Rome, we ourselves are barbarians."

"But it's . . . it's indecent," Merlin sputtered. "The whole concept is indecent."

"Why? See how it works." He pointed to the door separating his private apartments from the Great Hall. "Out there are the kings of twenty tribes. Until a few years ago, each of them was sworn by generations of blood feud to kill the others. Now they dine together at my table, working toward a common good."

"But the Germans . . ."

"Yes! And, in time, the Saxons, too. Together we'll build roads, and coin our own money, and trade in all sorts of goods. We'll read one another's books. We'll develop fair laws that apply to everyone, everywhere."

"Rome already tried that sort of thing," Merlin said.

"No, it didn't. Rome tried to make everything Roman. The laws were Roman laws. The language was Latin. The leaders of government were all Romans. Every nation under Rome's influence was a slave state, conquered by Rome and never allowed to forget it. I want something different—autonomous nations working peacefully and in concert with one another. A free world, ruled by free men."

Merlin shook his head. "Your heart is good, but I'm afraid you're still too young to understand the lure of power," he said.

"Power is only desirable to those who don't possess it," Arthur said lightly. "I don't plan to take anything away from anybody."

"How could you understand? You became king by the most extraordinary circumstance I've ever witnessed. Most don't. Most men come to power through violence or trickery.

And it's the power they want, Arthur. Oh, they may start out thinking as you do, wanting to be part of a better world, but in this consortium of kings you're talking about, you can be sure that one king will try to gobble up another as soon as he's got the chance. And more than one will be looking to the High King's throne, to gobble up everything else, including you. It's human nature, Arthur."

He was beginning to feel irritated. Romantic idealism was tolerable in a young man with nothing more to do than look after his fields, but it was a dangerous quality in a king. If Arthur was so naive as to think that he could offer Britannia to the Saxons without their seizing power, he was a fool who would lead his country into oblivion.

"You ought to be with your men," Merlin said finally.

"I suppose so. But my idea could work. With laws and a good army—"

"And an uncorruptible king who lived a thousand years," Merlin snapped.

Arthur smiled. "Do you think you could arrange that? They do say you're a wizard."

Merlin got up grumpily, bowed to the king he now thought of as a naive child, and stomped away, leaving Arthur laughing as he buckled on his chain mail.

# CHAPTER TWENTY-SEVEN

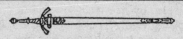

Arthur did not live a thousand years, of course; he died young, despite Merlin's efforts, without ever having fulfilled his mission.

In the centuries to come, Merlin might have forgiven himself for Arthur's early death, if it had not been for the dream.

It came on the night of their discussion about the Germans.

Merlin went to bed feeling annoyed, as one would with an adolescent son who has announced that he will spend his life in some frivolous pursuit: It would pass in time, but the passage was bound to be unpleasant. He did not understand Arthur, really, until the dream.

In it, he stood at the far end of a long table in the king's Great Hall, watching the approach of another man. The visitor was dressed strangely, in long loose robes, like the garb of an angel, and was surrounded by light.

At first Merlin took him to be a priest of some kind, perhaps a druid come bearing a gift for him, for the man held something in his two hands. But as he moved nearer, Merlin saw that the man was not a priest at all, but the one the Christians believed to have been the living god, Jesus the Christ, and above his outstretched hand floated something shiny and hard, draped in glittering white samite.

Merlin was about to speak to the man, to ask him what he was doing in the court of the king, when he noticed that Arthur was standing beside him, his eyes fixed on the approaching stranger's. Arthur's arms raised and the object moved toward him, slowly as a whisper, down the length of the table.

"Arthur, take it!" Merlin shouted.

As he spoke, the glittering cloth unfurled from the object and it hovered alone in the air, metallic and curved, the circle within the circle, the symbol of perfection, of eternity, of life without end. . . .

"Take it!"

But the cup and the man behind it were already beginning to vanish. The king reached out, but made no attempt to grasp the cup. Before it arrived at the end of the table, it was as transparent as a insect's wing. And when it vanished, so did the king, disappearing into the mists as if he had never existed.

"Arthur! Arthur!"

The old man awoke in a sweat. For surely he had just seen Arthur's death, and the means to prevent it. Saladin's cup had healed Merlin's own stopped heart. It had brought him back from the dead. It had protected Saladin from all injury during the rockslide in the cave. Saladin, the young man with the old eyes and the knowledge of a thousand lifetimes. Saladin, who was only twenty-five years old and yet knew the secrets of the pharaohs.

*It feels more like twenty-five centuries*, he had said.

But of course, he had meant that literally! The cup had the power to heal and protect the human body indefinitely.

*Saladin had lived forever.*

But the cup was not meant to be his. It belonged to Arthur, to the one man who could not be corrupted by it. To the forever king, who would use it to fulfill a great destiny and hold that destiny until the Creator Himself came back to claim the earth that Arthur had made holy for him.

The dream frightened him. While it was still dark outside, Merlin slipped away from the castle to the forest and walked through the windy December cold to the secret glen where the druids performed their ageless rites. There he stood, clearing his mind of all thought except for the image of the cup as it had touched his dying breast. He felt its warmth again, its perfection.

The Christians talked about the Second Coming, when their god would return in wrath and glory to condemn the wicked to eternal fire and lead the godly to paradise. Merlin did not know where he himself would stand in such a judgment, as he was not a Christian. Yet the dream had been clear: The cup had passed from the Christ to Arthur. The king was meant to drink from the cup of immortality.

In the darkness Merlin caused the image of it to project from his mind into the space before him. It was an illusion, but with solidity and dimension. He examined it. Could this, then, be the hallowed Grail, this common-looking object?

It had to be. And it was meant to stay in Arthur's keeping.

But what about Saladin? The man had done Merlin and the others at Camelot no harm. If he did not offer the precious cup as a gift to the king, whose place was it to take it from him? To steal the cup would be a lowly act. Arthur would never even accept the cup under such circumstances.

The image dissolved before Merlin's eyes.

There was the dilemma. To acquire Arthur's immortality, Merlin would have to cheat another man of it—a man who had saved Merlin's own life. And yet to let it go . . .

To let it go would be to see the awful dream become a reality: Arthur dying, still young, his vision forgotten, the world fallen back into chaos and savagery.

He left the grove in full daylight feeling tired and even older than his years. He would have gone back to bed if it were not for the commotion at the main gate. Horses were stamping, their armored riders covered with blood, as the servants poured out of the castle, wailing as they carried in a blood-soaked litter.

Merlin's heart quickened in his chest. He knew that this was more than the usual check of the wounded and dead after battle. He ran up to the litter, barely able to breathe.

"Arthur!" he whispered.

"He took an arrow in his back." This from Launcelot himself, the greatest of Arthur's warriors, who was said, because of his purity, to have healing in his hands. He was sobbing as he helped carry the litter inside. "I touched him. He's breathing, but there's nothing, nothing I can feel . . ." He turned his head angrily, his great dark mane stiff with the blood of his king.

"You must heal him, wizard!" he demanded, the words filled with helpless violence.

But Merlin knew he could not. He had not even known that the king had been wounded. Last night's dream had been a premonition of immediate danger, and he, Merlin, the great sorcerer, had not even recognized it.

He was overcome with self-loathing as the knights lay Arthur on the rough oaken table near the castle's well. The king's wounds, Merlin saw, were mortal.

"Shall we take him up to the sollar, sir?" Gawain asked politely. He was a rough man, used to action. In the stillness of the silent stone walls, Gawain seemed to want only to do something, anything, rather than stand by uselessly while his king died.

Merlin shook his head. The narrow curved stairs leading to Arthur's private rooms would be too difficult to negotiate. It would only hasten his death.

Then he remembered his dream again, and his breath caught. He could not save the king, but another could.

As if his thoughts had been spoken aloud, a voice answered them: "He is dying."

Saladin was standing behind him, looking down over Merlin's shoulder at the blood-covered king.

Launcelot snarled through his tears. The aging Gawain reached for his sword in his fury at the Saracen's quiet declaration.

Merlin looked up at the man silently. Saladin stared back at him. "Help him," the old man said at last. His voice was the merest whisper.

Saladin turned toward the entrance of the room. Merlin ran after him, touching his arm. "I beg this of you."

The tall man took a deep breath. "You're talking nonsense," he said.

But the old man followed after him doggedly. "The cup of Christ," he pleaded. "You must use it to save the King."

All of the assembled knights and servants were watching them now. Merlin and Saladin had spoken in Latin, so the others could not understand them, but they would learn about the cup soon enough.

It was bound to come to this, Saladin thought. In thirty-two hundred years, he had revealed the secret only once; but once, he knew, was one time too many. Now the whole world would hunt him down to possess the cup.

"How dare you do this to me," Saladin hissed. He disengaged Merlin's hand from his sleeve and flung it aside. "Let him die!"

At this, Launcelot lunged forward, his blade drawn. Saladin threw him off with a strength Merlin had never witnessed before. The big knight virtually flew away from him, crashed sprawling on the stone floor beside the well. The force of Launcelot's fall caused the well's handle to spin out of control, sending the big wooden bucket to the bottom with a splash.

"Do not set your dogs on me again, Merlin," Saladin warned. "I could kill Arthur and a thousand others like him." Slowly he walked over to the table where the king lay. He leaned across the Siege Perilous and touched Arthur almost lovingly. "Perhaps I would wish to be king myself," he taunted. "A king among your savages. I could be, as you well know. I would have a long, long reign."

With that he took a short, jeweled knife from his belt and held it above Arthur's throat. "Far longer than your precious Arthur's."

The knife came down. One of the serving women screamed. Launcelot scrambled to his feet. The other knights rushed forward.

Only Merlin did not move. At the moment when he realized that Saladin meant to vent his anger at Merlin by murdering the king in front of him, his eyes rolled back in his head. The movement was almost involuntary, as was the welling of power he felt rising within him. It was the creature, the unseen beast he had carried inside him for so long, now standing, straining, exploding to life inside Merlin's body.

The power was blinding; the wizard's eyes were suffused with an unearthly light that he could feel coiling through his viscera like a great hot snake.

Slowly his hands raised, palms up, as the power focused in them and crackled out through his fingers. He did not see the knife drop, as the others did. He did not see the look of astonishment on Saladin's face as the power pushed him backward like a wall, slow and inexorable in its force, or the light which glowed in the space between the two men like a flaring sun. Merlin saw nothing and felt nothing, not even the remnants of anger toward the tall man who would see his king dead. The power burned all emotion out of him, burned him pure. He was no longer a man, he knew, but a receptacle for this shapeless, invisible beast that had lain inside him for

more than seventy years. He was the power, and nothing—
the gods help him, not even himself—could stop it.

Saladin resisted, holding his hands up in front of his face,
squinting against the awful glare. But the light only grew
stronger, and the invisible wall pressed against him, suffocating and relentless. With a cry he slid backward, his shoes
scraping against the stone flags of the floor, until he slammed
against the side of the well. His back snapped. Everyone
heard that. And then his head lolled back, unconscious.

"He's falling in," someone said, but no one dared to
intervene in the terrible miracle they were witnessing.

A sound came from Saladin as he toppled backward into
the well, a low sigh that reverberated from the damp stones
to the water below, so that all that could be heard by the
breathless spectators was an echo, melancholy as the song of
a wild bird.

When Merlin came to himself, Launcelot was on his
knees, making the sign of the cross. Gawain still held his
hand to the hilt of his sheathed sword, the muscles in his face
working frantically.

How could Merlin explain to them what had happened? He
himself had no idea. And yet he knew that it was he who had
called the power forth and directed it at the man who had
once saved his life. In those first weak moments after he
emerged from the thrall of the power, when his human limbs
felt as if they would shatter to fragments and his heart
pounded as if it were about to explode, he felt only fear. For
there would be no rest for his soul now. He had trespassed
beyond the boundaries of everything mortal.

And yet he would not have acted otherwise. Not for the
blessings of the gods themselves.

"Bring him up," he commanded hoarsely.

The servants in the room drew away from him.

"I said bring him up!"

Gawain leapt to the well, his grizzled face registering relief
at having a task to do. He began, slowly, to bring up the big
bucket with its heavy load. Launcelot rose to help him. Soon

all the knights were clustered around the well, pulling on the long rope, shouting orders at one another.

Merlin moved back to Arthur and touched his bloody face. He was still alive, though he had long ago passed out of consciousness. The old man picked up the jeweled knife that lay beside the king and waited.

"The rope . . . It's breaking! I can feel . . ."

Three of the men fell backward, the frayed rope dangling from their hands.

"A dead man in the well," one of them moaned. "And the king not half-alive."

One of the maidservants sobbed hysterically. The steward came over to shake her.

Merlin waited.

"We'll close it up," Gawain offered gruffly. "Close it up and dig another . . ."

And then Saladin came, as Merlin knew he would, roaring with the voice of a caged beast as he clawed his way up the sheer wall and burst out of the opening, arms outstretched, fingers splayed to kill.

The knights screamed.

"Hold him!" Merlin shouted, raising the knife.

They leapt on the tall stranger, the dead man brought back to life by whatever evil demons he commanded, as Merlin cut the sodden velvet pouch from Saladin's belt.

At once he saw the superhuman strength fade. Kicking and flailing, Saladin had become no more than a man, angry, terrified, panicked. And mortal.

"You do not deserve to possess this," Merlin said, holding the cup.

The silence in the room was charged. Then softly, bitterly, Saladin laughed. "That is what I said to the man I stole it from."

The old man blanched.

"Don't be a hypocrite, wizard. You're as much a thief as I was."

Gawain snaked the dagger to Saladin's throat.

"No!" Merlin shouted.

"Let the barbarian kill me here," Saladin drawled. "I'd rather not hang, if it's all the same to you."

Gawain pressed the knife more deeply against his neck.

"Enough!" Merlin slashed the air in front of him with his hand. "He is to remain unharmed, do you understand?"

Gawain looked at the wizard in bewilderment. "But he tried to kill the king."

"Give him safe conduct to the open road."

The Green Knight's expression grew truculent. "He belongs in the dungeon—"

"Do it!" Merlin ordered.

Another knight, Launcelot, put a restraining hand on Gawain's arm, then nodded. Gawain sheathed his knife.

Saladin straightened out his wet clothing. "A life for a life, eh, Merlin? Is that what you're offering me?"

"That is correct," the old man said. "My debt to you is now paid. I owe you nothing." He gestured to the knights. "Take him. And do not return to this hall. I must be alone with the king."

The knights pushed Saladin roughly toward the entrance.

"I swear I will take back what is mine!" Saladin whispered.

*You're sure to try*, Merlin thought sadly as he watched him go.

He heard the footfalls of the servants die away as the steward led them out of the hall. He was alone now with the still body of the young man whom all called High King of Britain. But to Merlin he was still Arthur, the young red-haired boy who had pulled the sword out of the ancient stone, the warrior who had dreamed of a world order of peace. Arthur, now and forever.

He took the metal cup from the pouch. Even the cold water from the well had become warm in the perfect circle of its hollow. This he touched to Arthur's lips. Then softly, gently, he wrapped the king's blue hands around the sphere and held them there.

Before his eyes the raw, gaping wounds closed. The color

returned to Arthur's ashen face. And then the eyes opened, blue and eager as a child's.

"What are you doing with me, Merlin?" he asked, his smile twinkling.

"I am giving you your legacy," the wizard said. But his words were so quiet that he doubted if Arthur heard him.

He slipped the metal cup into the folds of his sleeve. Even Arthur could not have this knowledge yet. Let him celebrate his life first. Let him hear the stories of the old sorcerer and his battle against the evil Saracen knight. Let him be comfortable with being king before learning that he must be king forever.

"Call in your knights, my lord," he said, bowing. "They will wish to see you."

His ears were filled with the soft rustle of his gown as he left the king alone in the vast chamber.

# CHAPTER TWENTY-EIGHT

The wind whipped Saladin like an icy lash. He had not noticed the cold at first, when the soldiers carried him outside the castle. He had been half-drowned then, and besides, he had expected the British barbarians to kill him in short order. But they had only dumped him halfway down the high hill where Camelot stood and then kicked him so that he rolled unceremoniously to the bottom.

He gathered up his sodden robes and, looking over his shoulder like a thief at the taunting soldiers, made a run for the road. That was when he felt the wind.

It was December. He had not ventured out of the castle since the day he had made the dreadful mistake of saving Merlin's life. Now, shivering violently, his clothes stiffening around him, he felt nothing but regret for his folly.

Whatever had possessed him to use the cup? On a wizard, no less, a reader of minds, a man closer to the king than anyone on earth, whose ambitions for Arthur were clear? Of course Merlin would take the cup. Combined with his own powers (Had he really created an invisible, moving *wall?*), the sorcerer might well own the cup for all eternity.

White flakes began to swirl with the wind. One of them landed on Saladin's eyelash, where it remained, frozen, until he brushed it away. Snow. He had never seen snow before, except as an occasional dessert at lavish dinner parties in Rome. It swept against his face, melting against his numb flesh, blinding him so that he could barely make out the road ahead of him.

The road to where? he wondered bitterly. He had no place to go, and no possessions. The things he had brought with him from Rome had been left in the castle. He no longer even had a horse to ride. The great black stallion was quartered in the king's stables now.

He cried out in rage. The sound, muffled by the snow, died quickly. Soon he was enveloped in silence again.

He had not walked a mile when he became certain he would die. His fingers were too stiff to move. His belly ached from the cold. His hair had frozen into hard tufts. There was no way to make a fire without flint, and the flint was buried beneath the snow. He wondered what would happen to a body left in the snow. It would become stiff as wood, most likely. The cold might preserve it against rot. How ironic, he thought, that his body should be kept perfect by the very thing that killed it.

It would not be long. He might last until nightfall. But the darkness would bring his death. It was not the easy death he had imagined, growing old in Rome amidst the company of his peers. But then, what did it matter how one died?

He stumbled and fell. His face struck the hard surface of the road. Blood stained the snow.

He heard a sound, high and piercing. Had he screamed? No. He would have known. He wasn't so far gone, he thought shakily, that he no longer recognized his own sounds of anguish. But he had heard something. A wild dog, perhaps. A winter crow. As he picked himself up, he saw something coming toward him through the snow.

It was a boy, very small and strangely dressed, with a ragged cloak blowing behind him in the wind. Saladin stopped in his tracks, watching. It was not until the figure was quite close that he realized it was not a boy at all, but the wild-haired woman he had met in the forest during his first night in Britain. A deerskin was wrapped around her shoulders. This she removed and gave to Saladin. He took it without a word and followed her back the way she had come.

The journey did not last an hour, but it seemed like an eternity. After a while the woman propped herself against Saladin for warmth and wrapped his long arm around her to keep him from falling. She was wearing crude pouchlike shoes made of squirrel skins, he noticed. Unable to think or look ahead, he watched her feet move through the snow.

In time, the feet stopped before a wooden doorway. Numbly Saladin looked up. The woman was smiling, nodding. Putting her shoulder to the door, she swung it open and helped Saladin inside.

There were bodies on the floor, and pools of blood, still red. It was the last thing Saladin saw before sinking into unconsciousness.

He did not know how long he had slept, but he suspected it had been some time since he'd entered the house. It was broad daylight, and the snow outside had vanished. He was in a warm room with high ceilings. The bed upon which he was lying was exquisitely comfortable, with a mattress of feathers. Beyond it was a fireplace with three small burning logs; in front of the fireplace was a stool with his clothes draped over it.

He sat up, dizzy, remembering the bodies. They had been lying on the floor, hacked to pieces as if by an axe. The blood had still been shiny. But they were gone now. It must have been a dream of some kind, a delusion of the cold. . . .

Then he saw the strangest vision of all. The urchin who

had brought him here walked into the room. She was dressed in a toga that trailed on the floor behind her. Around her neck was a string of colored porcelain beads. Aside from the ludicrous finery, she was the same dirty-faced, wild-haired creature he had met in the woods. She still wore the fur bags on her feet.

Not noticing him, she went first to his clothes and shook them out.

"I've nothing to rob," he croaked.

She looked up in delight, tossing his things on the floor and running up to embrace him.

"Get away," he muttered, slapping her hands.

She did not seem to mind his irritation. Instead, she beckoned to the doorway. When Saladin failed to respond, she tore off his covers.

He was completely naked. He lunged to cover himself, but she only giggled. Bounding off the bed, she picked up his robes and handed them to him.

"Eat?" she asked. She made the motions of eating, but he had understood the word from his few lessons with Merlin.

"Yes," he answered tentatively.

The girl's eyes widened. "You speak," she whispered.

It was useless to explain to someone so primitive that there were other languages besides her own, so Saladin merely shooed her away and proceeded to dress himself.

The house was a good one, laid out in Roman style, although the floors were wood rather than mosaic tile. In the hallway a chest lay open, its top splintered. Fine clothes of Roman cut lay strewn across the floor, along with broken pieces of jewelry. Beyond it, in the large sitting room and in the atrium past that, lay scattered objects: a wax tablet, some account ledgers, cushions with the stuffing ripped out. The polished wooden floor was stained with large dark spots.

*This is the room I saw*, Saladin realized. *The bodies were here*.

Just then the girl beckoned to him. There was the aroma of cooking food coming from the kitchen. She led him into the dining room, where broken dishes and glassware lay all over the floor. The girl did not seem to mind the debris; she stepped carefully over it as she brought a clay pot filled with soup to the inlaid wood table. Smiling, she set a bowl in front of him and poured soup into it.

"What is in here?" he asked suspiciously.

She shrugged. "Roots. Herbs." She said something else that he could not understand. He poked around the pot and found the haunch of a small animal. So she had not used the human bodies, at least.

"Where are the people?"

"Dead. Saxons. Today. I saw them. Very lucky." She fondled the necklace she wore. "Pretty things."

Saladin stared at her. Apparently, it had not bothered her in the least to find a house filled with murdered people. Worse, she had probably seen the attack. What sort of life had she led before moving into the woods to live like a wild animal?

Distractedly, he turned his attention to the soup. He was hungry, and it tasted good. He drank the entire bowl without speaking, then held it out for the girl to refill.

"What is your name?" he asked when she brought it to him.

"Nimue," she said.

"Where is your family?"

"Dead," she answered without much concern. "Long ago."

"How did you find me?"

She smiled at him. "I waited. I looked for a place to stay the winter, and I waited for you. Am I beautiful?"

"Certainly not." He examined her appearance. "You're filthy."

She frowned, puzzled. He had used the Latin word. Unfamiliar with its English equivalent, he picked up the hem of the garment she was wearing—a man's toga—and wiped her face with it. "Dirt," he said, pointing out the black smear.

She touched her face.

"And your hair. . . " He made a move to touch it, then recoiled. Her head was swarming with lice. "You're perfectly disgusting," he said, pushing her away.

She fell into the corner of the room, her lips trembling. Then she stood up, emitted a loud sob, and fled.

Saladin rolled his eyes. It was bad enough that he was doomed to die in this wilderness; but the fact that he would be spending an entire winter of his precious mortal life with a vermin-covered girl was almost more than he could bear.

But one had to be philosophical, he reasoned. He had been fortunate to find this place at all. From the looks of things, the freshly killed inhabitants seemed to have been prosperous.

He took a look around. There was some food left in the pantry, although it was obvious that the Saxon raiders had helped themselves to plenty. Every room had a fireplace, with piles of dry logs beside each. There was furniture, and the clothing, which was quite fine and obviously imported. There was even a wine cellar, although its stock had been completely depleted.

Nimue ran past him, dressed once again in her rags and skins, bolting out the back entrance off the kitchen. He followed her with some amusement.

"Are you running away?" he asked, but she did not turn around.

As he walked back inside, he noticed the neat pile of frozen bodies stacked like logs beside the house. There was a woman, her throat cut—the lady of the house, by the looks of her elaborate hairstyle—and her husband, dressed finely, although his clothes were covered with blood. Two others appeared to be household servants. The girl must have carried them out here by herself, Saladin thought. Why, she was strong an an ox.

He looked out over the brown grass of the fields, and was suddenly overcome by despair. There was no hope at all, he knew. The cup was in the hands of a king and would never be released. He went back inside and sank into the down-feather sofa in the room stained with blood.

The loss of the cup had been his own mistake. He should not have taunted the barbarians with Arthur's death. He should have killed him silently, subtly, perhaps under the guise of examining him. But he had been too angry at the time to think properly. The betrayal of Merlin, who owed Saladin his life, had been a great blow.

The cup made men into beasts. Even Merlin, the most educated and compassionate of men, had succumbed finally to its spell. Merlin had meant to kill Saladin with his magic, without the slightest compunction. To possess the cup, a man would do anything.

Perhaps the one called the Christ had known what he held in his hands during his last supper, after all. Perhaps he had known and, because he was more than human, was able to put it aside.

Saladin knew that he, too, should try to put it aside, or else waste what little was left of his life in idle dreaming. The king would never let the cup go. Only Merlin could gain possession of it, and Merlin belonged to the king.

Only Merlin . . .

# CHAPTER TWENTY-NINE

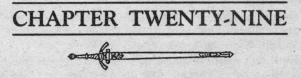

The next sound he heard was the thundering of a horse's hoofbeats. Saladin got up, blinking hard, his hands shaking. Had the Saxon invaders returned as he had dozed? Still groggy but tense with fear, he grabbed the iron poker from beside the fireplace and edged toward the door.

The horse outside whinnied. Saladin inhaled sharply. He recognized the sound. It belonged to his own horse. Before he could move, the girl bounded into the room, whooping and gesturing wildly.

"Come! Come!" she shouted. She was even dirtier than before, and smelled of horse.

The stallion was lathered with sweat. It stomped its forepaw when it saw him. The girl gentled him with a touch.

"How . . . how did you. . . . "

"I took him from the king's stable," she said proudly.

Saladin touched the horse's glistening flank. He was unsaddled. Nimue must have ridden him bareback.

"But the grooms. The knights . . ."

She laughed and ran a short distance away. Then she produced a medley of strange sounds with her mouth. The stallion's ears danced. He turned and walked directly to her.

"How on earth did you do that?" Saladin asked.

Nimue patted the animal on the rump, urging it toward the meadow. "I can talk to all the animals," she said. "To get your horse, I just opened the door of his stall and called to him. The grooms were busy. They never even saw him leave."

"You rode him out of the castle grounds?"

She shook her head. "I waited in the woods for him. I rode him from there."

"But no one saw you?"

"No," she said, as if it were a ridiculous question. "No one ever sees me."

Saladin laughed. "A wood sprite, that's what you are."

She smiled at him shyly. "Do you love me now?"

Saladin was taken aback. "Love *you?*"

He hadn't meant to sound quite so incredulous. She had rescued his horse, after all. And when her face crumpled into a mask of utter dejection, Saladin felt a twinge of remorse along with his general irritation.

"Oh, stop that at once," he said when she began to cry. "Look. Go wash your face. And your hair. Take the bugs out of it. You'll look better, at least. That is, you'll feel better."

She stared at him, pouting. "Don't understand you."

Once again he realized that he had been speaking a mixture of English and Latin.

"Well, never mind." He took her by the wrist and led her to the kitchen, where a big bar of brown soap lay on the bottom of a wooden tub. He picked it up and slapped it into her hand. "Wash yourself with this," he said, trying to enunciate clearly. He pulled her hair. "This, too."

"Aggh," she shrieked, wriggling away from him.

"Go to the river. Don't come back until you're clean."

Nimue gave him a hateful look. He opened the door and kicked her outside.

*My horse*, he thought with more joy than he could remember feeling in years. He could leave Britain, go back to Rome . . . but why bother with Rome? There were places he'd never been, islands in the China Sea where the women painted their faces stark white and the aristocracy spent their leisure hours guessing the fragrances of exotic blossoms. Places in India where holy men lay on beds of nails to clear their minds, and kings with green beards and robes of billowing silk rode elephants into battle.

His excitement rose, then sank abruptly, shattering like glass against the inexorable truth. He would not have time to see any of those pictures. When the cup was stolen, the rest of his life had been stolen from him also.

Merlin!

*Only Merlin could give it back* . . .

He looked out at the river. Nimue was standing hip-deep in it, scrubbing the tangled mass on her head. Saladin shivered to think how cold the water must be, but the girl stood stoically, performing the task he had set for her.

Well, she was accustomed to hard living, he reasoned. Even among the barbarians of this land, she wasn't quite human.

Suddenly his throat went dry. *She wasn't quite human.* Why, that was marvelous!

He couldn't take his eyes off her. From a distance, she appeared to have quite a good figure. He stood in the doorway, transfixed, as Nimue rinsed the lye suds off her hair and dressed once again in the rags she had been wearing.

"A wood sprite," Saladin said aloud.

He had found a way to get the cup back.

By the time Nimue returned to the villa, Saladin had assembled everything she needed from the smashed trunks in the hall: combs, dainty slippers, and a woman's robes, including a linen under-tunic, a white silk gown with long sleeves and a round neck, and a shorter over-tunic of palest green silk.

Nimue looked at the items arrayed neatly on the bed where Saladin had slept. Her eyes were expectant, half-delighted, half-frightened.

"You wish me to wear these?" she asked.

"Take off your clothes," Saladin commanded.

Nimue shrank away.

"Oh, bother with you," he said, ripping the filthy rags off her body and tossing them into the fire. She yelped and tried to retrieve them, but he held her back. "Here, put this on for the moment." He handed her a magnificent cloak the color of sapphires.

She wrapped it around herself, preening this way and that.

"Hold still." He pulled over the small stool by the fireplace and pushed her onto it. Then, using an ivory comb, he yanked at the wasp's nest of hair that seemed to spring out of Nimue's head like a yellow thicket. She screamed with each stroke, shutting her eyes tight against the involuntary tears that ran down her face, but made no attempt to move from the stool.

"Good girl," he said, as if he were currying a mare. In fact, the business of untangling the wretch's hair was far more troublesome than caring for any animal. Freed from its balled-up state, it reached below her waist, and was thick and heavy besides. Saladin actually felt himself working up a sweat as he tore away the knots and cast them onto the floor.

"There," he said at last. He gave a neat center part to the cascade of golden waves, then stood back to admire his work.

The effect, caused as much by the soap as the comb, was nothing less than shocking. The girl's skin was milky white, flushed with rose pink in her cheeks. It was so flawlessly smooth that Saladin almost lost his revulsion for pale skin.

Her teeth were small and even—miraculous, considering the girl's diet and lack of self-regard. They were surrounded by lovely soft lips, dark and full and well defined. And her eyes, catching the reflection of the cloak, were an astonishing turquoise blue.

"Why, you really are beautiful," Saladin said in amazement.

She smiled at him, nearly brimming over with happiness. "Remarkable!"

"Remarkable!" Nimue repeated, laughing.

"Now put on these things." He stripped the cloak off her and held out the undergarment, noticing the lithe young body. It was perfect, strongly muscled, yet too young to be stringy. Her breasts were surprisingly full, tipped by small pink nipples, and below, between her long legs, sprouted a fine golden down.

He handed her the clothes, one after the other, instructing her on how to wear each piece. When she was finished, he took a long golden string he had found at the bottom of one of the chests and wrapped it artfully around her waist.

Nimue looked down at herself, plucking at the fine fabric. "Jewels," she shouted suddenly, darting out of the room. She made no sound as she moved, Saladin noticed. That was good. That would work wonderfully.

When she came back, she was wearing the same necklace of broken pottery she had been playing with earlier, its red and yellow clay beads bouncing against her breast.

"No, no," Saladin said, yanking it off her. The beads spilled onto the floor. Nimue gasped, heartbroken.

"Don't do anything I don't tell you to do," he said.

She lowered her eyes.

"That's better. I'm going to teach you some things," he said quietly. "I want you to pay a great deal of attention, do you understand?"

She nodded.

"We'll speak English. You'll have to teach me what you know of it." He leaned against the wall and crossed his arms. "I have a plan for you."

She nodded again, waiting.

"Are you afraid of wizards?"

Nimue's eyes opened wide.

"Oh, he won't hurt you. In fact, I think he'll fall quite i love with you."

Her forehead creased. "What about you?"

Saladin smiled. "Nimue, if you do what I ask of you, shall love you for all my long, long life."

She looked up at him, the turquoise eyes welling.

"Now suppose you tell me about yourself."

# CHAPTER THIRTY

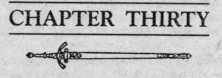

There was nothing particularly romantic about Nimue's past She was the offspring of a German mercenary hired to protec a farmstead some twenty miles inland. Her mother had been a camp follower. The mercenaries and their women traveled in packs, setting up camps outside the estates they were hired to protect, and remained for the length of their contract, o until their employers' money ran out.

Gold was scarce; only families who had hoarded it since the time of the Roman occupation could afford to pay the mercenaries, since they rarely traded their fighting service for food. Nimue's father, a huge blond warrior named Horgh had amassed quite a fortune during his twelve years i Britain, returning after each engagement to his village on the Rhine, where he kept a wife and several children.

Nimue was not his only bastard. In the camps where she grew up, several of the children bore Horgh's likeness Nimue's mother, a beautiful but feebleminded woman, neve seemed to mind it when her man took a new woman to bed or even the fact that he hoarded all his money in a distan country while she and her daughter lived on scraps cast aside by the soldiers.

The child herself had little to say about the matter. He father rarely spoke to her; at any rate, their languages were different, and she could not understand him when he did speak. Her mother was almost completely silent with other human beings. Sometimes she took Nimue into the woods, where she called to the small animals and birds, who flocked to her and the little girl as if they were beacons in the darkness.

Nimue learned all her survival skills from her mother: how to read the weather, how to shelter in the winter, how to kill a wounded animal painlessly and take its fur. In fact, it was their practice to flee to the woods when the Saxons raided their encampments rather than risk being slaughtered in camp.

It was during one of these precautionary flights that her mother was killed. A Saxon bludgeoned her with a metal-studded club while she ran with her small daughter toward the forest. Nimue screamed, but the Saxon who had killed her mother had gone on to the camp rather than chase a child into the woods. Later, when everything was quiet and the house and its outbuildings lay in smoldering ruins, Nimue went back.

The camp was deserted. Apparently the mercenaries had been warned about the size of the Saxon raiding party and, to a man, had deserted before the invaders arrived. All that was left were the bloodied bodies of the women and children. In the main house, too, the owner of the estate had been killed, along with his family and servants, and the tenant farmers who had fought the Saxons with them.

Nimue buried her mother, as she had watched the camp women bury fallen soldiers all her life. When she was finished, she listened to the song of birds in the still air. She no longer knew a single living human being.

She took what clothing and food she could salvage from the wreckage at the camp and went into the woods to live. She had been eleven years old.

By the time Saladin found her she was nearly twenty, though she looked younger, and was completely self-sufficient. This was important to Saladin.

"He'll come before spring," he told her as he set her

behind him on the big stallion. She was dressed beautifully and he did not want to mar her appearance with a long walk. "Find food if you have to, but keep clean."

The girl could find food, of that he had no doubt. In fact it annoyed him somewhat to be losing her hunting skills. For the past several weeks, while he taught Nimue the things she would need to know, she had kept the table well stocked with pheasant and quail and had even brought down a deer with nothing more than a rope and knife. She had proven to be an excellent cook, too, flavoring the wild meat with herbs she collected from the countryside. In addition to hunting and cooking, she also made herself useful by chopping wood and keeping the house fires lit. She had even buried the bodies of the former tenants.

The only task she had not mastered was keeping the house clean. Saladin had been appalled that she could walk repeatedly over the piles of broken pottery in the dining room without bothering to pick any of it up. She exhibited the same indifference when it came to matters of simple hygiene. On more than one occasion she had served the dinner on plates still crusted from an earlier meal. In the end, Saladin had given up berating her for her squalid ways—she didn't do a good job of cleaning even when forced to—and had taken on the responsibility himself. He was tidy by nature, and cleaning was not a task he particularly disliked, although it offended him to have to pick up after a woman.

But, he thought resignedly, it would not be his problem for long. One way or another, Nimue was going. If Saladin was lucky, his investment in her would have been worth the effort.

"Do you remember what to say?" he asked, trying not to seem anxious.

"Yes."

She rode along behind him, breathtakingly beautiful in her shimmering silk clothing, her golden hair streaming behind her. The hands resting on Saladin's chest were small, like feathers. But they were trembling. He could feel her whole small body shaking.

"What on earth is wrong with you now?" he snapped.

She pressed her forehead to his back. "I don't want to leave you."

He made a sound of disgust. "Don't be a fool."

"I can make you happy."

"Hardly," he said, though there had been times when, because of the long, cold winter, he might almost have believed it. Nimue was quite beautiful; there was no denying that. Under Saladin's tutelage she had learned some basic tenets of civilized behavior, which had rendered her quite agreeable. She could now eat properly, without covering her face with food, and had learned to control her facial expressions somewhat, so that she no longer stared dead-eyed with her jaw slack and open when she had nothing particular on her mind. She had learned to smile prettily and to speak in a low voice. Saladin had even taught her a few songs from Egypt, which no one would recognize, to show off her lovely voice. She already knew how to walk with such grace that she made no sound and left no tracks. Her general competence and basic intelligence were impressive, and her warm disposition made good company, even for someone as easily annoyed as Saladin.

All in all, she was becoming a most desirable woman. Under different circumstances, Saladin might have been tempted to make love to her, but that was out of the question. He had examined her thoroughly to confirm that she was a virgin. That, too, was important. No, she was a gift for someone else. Someone who would pay a very high price for her.

He brought the stallion to a halt near the caves where he and the old wizard had gone to gather rocks.

"Wait in there," he said.

"But what if he doesn't come?"

"Sing," Saladin said. "Sing one of the songs I taught you. He'll come."

"And then?"

"Let things happen as they will, Nimue." He watched her vault off the horse, her fine things swirling around her like shimmering mist, and felt a twinge of sadness. For what he planned was not likely to happen, and he had grown almost fond of the girl. "If you are still alone by spring, come back to me," he added in an impetuous moment.

Nimue beamed. "Oh, I will!"

He grabbed her by the wrist and squeezed hard. "But never mention my name, Nimue. Our lives will both be forfeit if you do."

"I swear I'll obey you," she said.

She waited for a moment, perhaps expecting the tall, elegant man from a far, distant land to kiss her, but he made no move toward her.

"Go quickly," Saladin said. He mounted his horse and rode away.

The bells from the small chapel inside the walls at Camelot were ringing brightly, but they failed to lift Merlin's spirits. As the king and his knights prepared themselves for the morning's church service, the old wizard skulked around his rooms like a shadow of gloom. He wouldn't be expected to attend, of course; everyone at Camelot knew that Merlin followed the Old Religion, and though many of the knights believed wholeheartedly in Christianity and professed to spurn the workings of sorcery, they were all grateful to the old man for using his magic to heal Arthur's terrible wounds.

Merlin himself had rarely given a thought to the Christian chapel or its bells. Yet today he thought they would drive him mad with their cheerful noise.

For weeks now, since the expulsion of the "evil Saracen Knight"—as the men called Saladin—and the king's miraculous recovery, Merlin had shut himself up in his rooms like an invalid, not even answering the king's summons.

Arthur and the others attributed the old man's withdrawal from society to the sorcery he had used. It had drained him, they said. The magic had caused him to draw too near to death, in order to do battle with it.

They could think what they liked, for whatever they imagined would be better than the truth.

The chapel bells made him want to scream. Slamming the door behind him, he stalked from his rooms and out of the castle, ignoring the greetings of those he passed.

It was Christianity, he told himself. The new religion had taken root like an unwanted weed. With its confounded promise of eternal life, it had taken people away from nature and the natural order. He would go back to the grove where the druids used to meet. He could think there, away from the ceaseless pealing of the bells.

But the grove brought him no solace. The spring of Mithras, where the priests cleansed themselves before their rituals, had dried to a trickle. The sounds of the forest, once pleasant and welcome, now seemed deafening. They blotted out his thoughts. They made his soul boil over in confusion. There was no place for him anymore, not since the magic had spilled out of him. It had changed him forever.

But it was what he'd wanted, wasn't it? To perform real magic, to give vent to the power he had stored up for a lifetime? To cease to be human?

Merlin folded his arms over his knees and wept. "Gods forgive me," he whispered.

For he knew it was not any of the things he sought to blame that had caused the agitation of his spirit. It had not been the new religion, or the disuse of the sacred grove, or even the magic he had somehow summoned out of himself on that frightening day. It had been the evil in his own heart.

He had called forth the magic with his anger and had used the magic to try to kill a man who had once saved his life.

Oh, it had been for a good cause; no one could doubt that. The king could not have been allowed to die, not if there were any possible way Merlin could prevent it. And there had been only one way—to take the magic cup from the Saracen. Had the man not tried to kill Arthur with his own hands? Would the king not surely be dead now, if not for Merlin's actions?

Yes, yes . . . He pounded his head against his arms. He had gone over it all a thousand times. It was all sensible, understandable, all for the *good*. And yet he could find no peace. The dream still haunted him, the dream in which the

Christ held out the chalice of eternal life. If He was the manifestation of the true God, why had He taken the cup away?

And Merlin's own magic still frightened him. He remembered little about it. The power had simply boiled out of him, blinding and numbing him. But he remembered the feeling afterward, that terrifying certainty that he had somehow changed completely, that he would never again find death, or release, or peace.

Was that the meaning of eternal life? Had that been the meaning of the dream—that life, lived beyond its normal span, was a curse far worse than death?

Yet it could not be. Saladin was not an unhappy man, particularly. And he surely did not want to part with the cup that Merlin had stolen from him.

*It has already caused me to steal*, Merlin thought. *It nearly caused me to kill.*

What would it do to Arthur?

He heard a sound and looked up. A lovely sound, like a woman's voice, singing a strangely beautiful song. It was distant, faint; when it disappeared, Merlin thought he must have imagined it. But it began again, high, soft, filled with mystery.

Almost unconsciously he stood up in the grass of the grove and walked toward the music.

Ancient, it was, ancient and perfect, serene yet somehow hopeless. It came from the caves.

He walked faster, half-expecting whoever it was to vanish before he arrived, but the music grew louder as he drew near to the cave.

He stopped short. It was the same cave where he had taken Saladin. He was standing almost on the exact spot where his heart had ceased to beat. He would have died there, if the stranger had not saved him with the cup.

*A life for a life*, he thought. The debt was paid. He had the cup. Now he would have to learn to live with it.

The music stopped for a moment. Merlin felt himself

covered with perspiration. He would never be free from his own guilt, he knew. Even death would not release him.

But the singing came again, and it washed over him like cool balm. How long had it been, he wondered, since he had heard a woman sing? Certainly none had ever sung to him. His mother might have, he imagined, if she had lived longer. But in all his long life, he had never heard a woman's tender voice even speak his name in love.

Slowly he walked into the cave. Shafts of sunlight streamed in behind him. His shadow filled the space momentarily, then he knelt in wonder. For sitting inside the sun-dappled tunnel, the crystals sparkling like diamonds around her, was the most beautiful woman he had ever seen.

She was not shocked by his sudden appearance. She did not even cut off the haunting refrain of the melody she was singing, but sang on until it ended. The last note hung in the cave like a promise.

He could think of nothing to say. Her beauty was unearthly. He blinked, thinking she might vanish like a thought.

"Who are you?" he whispered at last.

"I am Nimue," she said. "Come to me, Merlin. I have waited for you."

She held her arms out to him.

The old man hesitated. If she was not imaginary, she must have been sent for some ill purpose.

Saladin. Saladin was using her to get back the cup.

"Why are you here?" He tried to make himself sound stern, but could not disguise the quaver in his voice.

She rose, as gracefully as a plume of smoke. "If you cannot trust me, I will wait until you can," she said softly.

She ran to the back of the cave, through the dark tunnel where there was no light.

Merlin followed her, but he did not find her. He even went back to the castle and returned with a candle, but she was gone.

# CHAPTER THIRTY-ONE

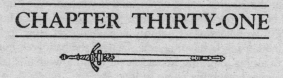

Merlin looked for the mysterious woman all that day and the next, feeling like an old fool. He tried to convince himself that he was merely conducting an experiment: He wanted to find out how a fully grown, flesh-and-blood human being could have vanished from the cave without a trace. Other men might have stuck on the point that the individual who called herself Nimue was a human being at all. She looked human, certainly, but it was well known among the common folk that nymphs, wood sprites, and other ethereal creatures could appear quite human under the right circumstances. Merlin did not believe in the lore of the fairy folk. He was an educated man, and a bona fide sorcerer, besides. People did not simply vanish.

In the early afternoon of the third day of his search, he found a back entrance to the cave. It was not much bigger than a badger's hole, situated in an outcropping of rock a few hundred yards from the cave's main entrance. It was neatly covered over with a broad flat stone.

So she was human after all, Merlin thought, somewhat annoyed with himself that the discovery had disappointed him. He waited near the opening for an hour or two, then gave up and returned to Camelot.

The castle was in a topsy-turvy state, with preparations under way to move the court north to the summer residence at Garianonum. During the long winter, local food supplies had been nearly depleted, and the lavatories and sewage moat were full and stinking. It was time to vacate the place, so that the permanent staff could clean up and begin restocking for the following autumn.

In his anguished state of mind of recent weeks, Merlin had

forgotten completely about the move and was quite astonished to see the wagons already being loaded in preparation
for the journey.

"When do we leave?" he asked a passing page.

The boy winced. "The day after tomorrow, sir," he answered, cringing. Even before the incident with Saladin and the
well, most of the castle residents had been reluctant to speak
with the sorcerer for fear he might turn them into frogs or toss
them into a bubbling cauldron of witch's brew, and now it was
worse since the tale had been spread about how he had cast the
evil Saracen Knight down to hell.

"Isn't it rather early for the summer residence?"

"Yes, sir," the page acknowledged. "But it's the king's
orders." He ran away without waiting for any more questions, making the sign to ward off the evil eye behind his
back.

Merlin sighed. It was pointless living here. In spite of the
crowd of people, the king's court was a lonelier place for him
than the deserted grove of the druids. And with the noise and
the stench it was a far less pleasant place, besides. He had
remained only because of the king, but Arthur was now a
grown man who no longer depended on Merlin except for
advice in matters of diplomacy, such as it was in a land that
was still woefully lawless. He was certainly not needed to
help the king plan his war strategies; no one in Britain was a
better leader on the battlefield than Arthur.

And increasingly, during the past few years, the battlefield
was where the king spent his time. Despite Arthur's plans for
a united world, the Saxons had been attacking more and more
frequently, each year with larger and more organized armies,
and the king had no recourse but to fight them. There was no
diplomacy to speak of, except between Arthur and the other
British chieftains, and they were all too busy warding off the
growing hordes of invaders to argue much with the High
King, or even with one another. Merlin's only contact with
Arthur in the past five years had been the rare conversations
they had during brief periods of peace.

They were wonderful conversations, though. Arthur had

grown into a fine man, humorous and wise, though still as straight as an arrow in his personal discipline. He always spoke Latin with Merlin, although with no one else, as a gesture of respect. Together they discussed philosophy and poetry and passed the time like gentlemen of leisure.

Merlin smiled. He had not realized before how difficult those quiet hours must have been for Arthur, the High King of a country now virtually under siege. Yet it was part of the man's towering self-discipline that he would give his precious time to his old mentor out of remembrance and gratitude.

Merlin had always thought of Arthur as a son, but he was a grown son now, a son who had exceeded even his father's wildest expectations. It was time to go. It was time to show Arthur his destiny and then stand aside to let him fulfill it.

Arthur was in the sollar, being helped into his chain mail.

"I must speak with you," Merlin said.

The king laughed. Whenever he laughed, he still looked like a boy, but his red beard, Merlin noticed, showed a few strands of gray, and fine lines were beginning to appear at the corners of his eyes. "It had better be quick, I'm afraid," he said. "The scouts have spotted a Saxon ship thirty miles to the north. If we don't stop them, we're likely to be besieged here in Camelot, with barely a chicken among the lot of us."

"It *is* urgent, Your Majesty."

The king's smile left his face. The old man almost never addressed him as anything except Arthur. He dismissed his servants. "What is it, Merlin?" he asked.

"I don't believe I'll be going with the court to Garianonum. There is a small house on the lake I plan to buy. The owners are moving north. They fear the Saxons have struck too often in this part of the country . . ."

He realized he was babbling, and silenced himself abruptly.

"You aren't ill?" Arthur asked gently.

"No, I'm fine, Arthur. It's just that I've had enough of court life. Garianonum is no more than two days' ride, should you need me, and when you're here—"

"Of course. That won't be a problem. But I'll miss you. I suppose I've taken you for granted. I always assumed you would be with me until the end of my days, like my arm or my leg. Or my brain." He grinned, and suddenly all the signs of age were wiped out. He was a child again, the frightened, skinny boy standing before the rock with the great sword Excalibur gleaming in his hands.

He walked over to Merlin and put both arms around the old man.

*How strong he is*, Merlin thought. *How frail I must seem to him.*

"There's something else," he said. "I had planned to tell you later, when there was more time, but since I won't be going with you . . ."

He saw Arthur glance toward the door. The king was in a hurry, and would not be able to listen to an old man's prattle for long.

He took a leather pouch from the folds of his robe and opened it. Inside was the metal sphere he had taken from Saladin. He handed it to Arthur.

"What's this?" the king asked, unconsciously opening and closing his fingers around the object.

"It's what cured you when you were wounded," Merlin said. "You were dying, Arthur. There was no way to save your life."

"Yes, they said you'd used magic to heal me." He laughed again. "Well, perhaps I shouldn't allow you to leave the court. It's not every king who can boast a proven wizard among his friends."

"Don't joke, Arthur. I had nothing to do with it. Not the healing, at any rate. The other. . . ." He fluttered his hands in dismissal.

When the king did not answer, Merlin went on irritably, "The cup . . . the thing in your hands. It heals wounds." He swallowed. "It will make you immortal."

The king stared at the cup. It was singing its song through his body. His eyelids fluttered. "It's warm," he said softly.

"It carries the gift of life," Merlin said. "Eternal life. Please do not doubt me, Arthur."

Arthur watched a bruise on his wrist disappear. "I don't," he whispered. Then, with a deep breath, he tore his eyes away from it and gave it back to Merlin. "Use it well," he said.

Merlin was appalled. "It's yours!" he shouted. "I stole it for you!"

"But I don't want it," the king said calmly.

"You don't want it!"

"Good heavens, if you yell any louder, the servants will come in and beat me with sticks," Arthur said.

"But . . . but . . ." Merlin shook his head like a dog who'd been drenched. He forced himself to quiet down. "You are the greatest king this land has ever known," he said softly. "Your life is important."

"Yes." The king's eyes flashed. "My life is important. To me. Because it is short, and precious. Because each day may be my last. Because if I don't squeeze every drop of wonder from it that I can, I will be forever diminished. That is why I am a good king, Merlin. That is why my life is worth living. Do you think I could bear to live through endless ages of endless days, knowing that there was no urgency to anything I did? Why, it would be worse than eternal Hell!"

"Those are personal considerations. Think of Britain."

"I do think of Britain, every moment. Britain needs many things, but what she doesn't need is some despot kept alive forever by sorcery to rule as he likes by whatever whim takes him at the moment."

"You wouldn't do that, Arthur."

"Oh, no? Not for the first hundred years, perhaps. Or two hundred—how long will you give me, anyway?"

Merlin made a dismissive gesture.

"One day I would bend, Merlin, as anyone would." His voice was very low. "And I would keep on bending until my soul was as twisted and corrupt as a dead tree. No. I don't want it."

"But your plans . . ."

"I've begun them. The Round Table is part of my plan. No man holds his head higher than any other at that table. All may speak and be heard. No one is punished for his thoughts, only for his actions."

"But that is a small thing. A transient thing."

"It is an idea, Merlin. And even the smallest idea is never transient. Sometimes they take years—or centuries—to become reality, but they never die. There will be men after me who understand, and they will keep my idea."

"Who?" Merlin asked belligerently. "You have no heir." He hadn't meant to be so blunt. The subject of the queen's barrenness was a sore one to almost everyone, exacerbated by rumors of a bastard son of the king's somewhere in the north.

Arthur was silent. "I had hoped I wouldn't have to defend myself on that count with you," he said finally.

Merlin did not know whether the king was referring to his refusal to discard the queen, or his repeated claim that there was no such son.

In truth, Merlin was inclined to believe Arthur, both on account of the king's austere personal ways and because at this point, even a bastard would be more helpful to him than no offspring at all, yet Arthur continued to deny the charge. He said that the child's mother—a distant kinswoman—had had trouble explaining the boy's appearance to her husband, whom the child did not resemble in the least. In order to spare herself, she named the king as the child's real father, since her husband could hardly put the king's son to death, or the child's mother, either.

"I'm only thinking of your future, and the future of Britain," Merlin said. "If you die before your time, much will be lost."

Arthur only smiled. It was not his boyish grin this time, but a sad smile, full of age and knowledge. "When I die, it will be my time," he said.

Merlin stood, stunned. "You really have become a Christian," he said at last.

Arthur laughed. "Perhaps. However, if I'm in any real

danger of dying, I'll probably call on you to remedy the situation."

*No, you won't*, Merlin thought. *You wouldn't cheat death, the way I have. You'll die bravely, and we'll all be the worse for it.*

But he said none of these things. "My gods and yours be with you on your journey," he whispered as they left the sollar together, Arthur helmeted and ready to do battle.

Behind the metal slit of his visor, Arthur's eyes shone with joy.

# CHAPTER THIRTY-TWO

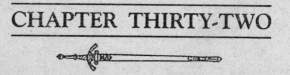

Merlin said his farewell to the king early in the morning. He did not wait at the castle for the knights to ride out with Arthur in their midst, followed by the women and then the wagons and retainers, but stood watch instead on the outcroppings of rock above the crystal caves.

Some of the entourage looked away from the sight of the old sorcerer who seemed, in the sunlight, to be floating above the rocks. Others were mesmerized by the sight. Several of the servants made the sign against his power.

Arthur felt only sadness. Merlin was his mentor and, despite the difference in their ages, the best friend he had ever known. To leave him was to say good-bye to the last vestige of his own youth. But worse than his own sadness was the sadness he felt for the old man.

Merlin, to his knowledge, had never known a woman. Not that the subject had ever come up between them; the old man would not have appreciated Arthur's prying into his personal life. But the king knew that his old teacher was a lonely man. Few dared to become close to a sorcerer, and now even the druids who had understood some of Merlin's power were gone. He was as alone in this world as it was possible for a man to be. And with his new plaything, he was assured of being alone forever.

Arthur had no doubt that the metal sphere could do what Merlin claimed. He had felt it himself, its power almost irresistible. That was why he had given it back. He was not a wise man; perhaps that was what made him a king. There were times when it was not helpful to see all sides of a question. There were times when one needed to see only black and white, good and evil, survival and death. Merlin would never see those distinctions clearly again.

He raised his arm in farewell. Far away, through the cloud of dust thrown up by the slow-moving caravan, he saw Merlin's hand lifted in salute.

Then the king turned and rode on. The past was done, and time was precious.

The wind blew the last billows of dust away. Now the rutted road stretched empty over the far hills. Merlin stepped off the boulder, feeling a twinge in his hip.

The cup would take care of that, he thought with bitter amusement. He would never suffer an ache or a pain again. The king had rejected his gift of eternal life, but he himself would go on plodding long after his protégé's bones had turned to dust.

*Arthur had refused.* The old man had never expected that. What man would refuse to live forever? The thought made Merlin angry. Arthur had never given much thought to the future, but to spurn *this* . . .

He hobbled back toward the castle, working the stiffness out of his joints. Then he remembered that the castle was deserted, except for the small staff that was busy cleaning up the mess from the court's presence all winter. They certainly wouldn't appreciate having a sorcerer in their way.

The cottage by the lake was only a few miles away. He had moved most of his possessions into it the day before. The few items that were left were packed into the saddlebags of his horse and mule.

He looked back at the crystal cave. If he hadn't loaded up
the horse, he would just as soon have spent the rest of the
morning there. It was dark and cool in the cave, and with
Arthur gone there wasn't anything he cared to do at the new
house or anywhere else.

His mare whinnied. "All right," he said. He would ride to
the cottage. He would unpack his things. He would take a
look at the small garden behind the house. And then he would
wait to die, he supposed. He would wait for the next thousand
years to die.

"It's about time."

Merlin looked up, startled at the voice. He was even more
surprised when he saw Nimue astride his mule. "What are
you doing here?" he asked.

"Keeping you company, old man. And your health would
fare better if you didn't frown so."

"My health is fine," he said crankily, hoping to disguise
the fluttering of his heart and the trembling of his fingers. "I
don't need company."

"Too bad," the girl said blithely. "I've chosen to spend the
day with you."

"I thought you weren't planning to reappear until I learned
to trust you."

"Have you?" she asked.

"No."

She shrugged. "Suit yourself." She threw a leg over the
mule.

"Wait," he said. "That is, what difference does it make
whether I trust you or not?"

"None at all to me," she said, sitting more comfortably.
"But I wouldn't want you to fear for your life every time I
talk with you."

"Have you been sent to murder me?"

She shook her head. "I'd be a fool to try to kill a wizard.
There's no telling what you'd do in return. Change me into a
worm. Turn my eyeballs to dust." She shuddered.

Merlin grunted. "Well, try not to forget it," he said,
mounting his horse. She was the strangest person he had ever

met. Her speech was good, almost cultured, yet she seemed completely unconcerned with ladylike behavior. It occurred to him more than once during the short journey that Nimue just might be the wood nymph he had sworn she wasn't, but he forced the idea away each time.

Once they reached the cottage, she proved to be quite helpful in unpacking the mule and taking care of the mounts. Nimue seemed to have a natural gift with animals. When Merlin asked her about it, she said only that she was accustomed to communicating with them.

He had carried a few provisions with him in the saddlebags. These Nimue ate with the appetite of a soldier. Later, she disappeared for a half hour and returned with a sackful of frogs, which she dismembered with ease as Merlin looked on in distress.

"We can fry these up, if you've got some grease," she said.

"I don't eat meat," Merlin said.

"What? Well, no wonder you're such a frail old thing. These frog legs are just what you need."

He declined politely, but watched in fascination as she devoured the entire panful.

"Perfect," she said, licking her fingers.

Merlin smiled. "Where do you live, child?" he asked.

Nimue looked around. "What about here?"

He blinked. "Well, I hardly think . . ."

"Don't be silly. I'll cook and clean for you—although I'm not a very good cleaner—and you can teach me your wizardy things."

"I'm afraid it's not that easy," Merlin said.

"Why not? People make things harder than they are. I'm young and strong—"

"And I'm old and male," Merlin said.

"Yes." She smiled. "That should work out fine."

Merlin shook his head and smiled despite himself. He had no doubt that she had been sent by someone, but the reasoning was beyond him.

"Why have you come?" he asked quietly. She flung her

hair and began to speak, but he held up his hand. "Now, none of your pat answers, if you please. I need to hear the truth."

Something in his manner seemed to deflate her. "I can't tell you the whole truth," she said, subdued. "I promised."

"Ah. But someone did send you. Tell me why."

"Don't you like me?"

"I think you're wonderful."

"Then why are you asking so many questions?"

Merlin looked into her large blue eyes, saying nothing.

"I'm supposed to make you fall in love with me," she said finally. She smiled uncertainly. "Have I?"

The old man laughed. "My dear, I'm enchanted with you."

The uncertain smile spread into a grin. "Good. Then I'll stay." She sucked on a frog bone.

"Not so fast."

"Well, what else matters?"

"I'd like to know why I'm supposed to come under your spell."

"My spell?" She giggled. "You're the sorcerer." She extracted the last of the marrow from the bone and set it down. "I don't know why he had me come. It wasn't to kill you, though. I wouldn't have done that."

"Well, that's something, anyway," Merlin said wanly.

"And he wouldn't kill you, either."

"Oh? What makes you so sure?"

She laughed. "Who could kill a wizard?"

"I imagine it can be done," he said dryly. "How well do you know this man?"

She looked away. "Well enough." Then she added quickly, "I'm a virgin, though. You can check if you like."

Merlin cleared his throat. "Unnecessary," he managed. "But this fellow is your friend?"

"Well, not a friend, exactly."

Merlin waited.

"He found this pretty dress for me."

Merlin still waited, unimpressed.

"He taught me to speak. Well, I could speak, but I got out

of the habit of having conversations. I didn't know anyone else."

"Anyone . . . at all?" Merlin asked.

"No. Isn't it funny? After my mother was killed, I was too afraid of people to let them see me. But the animals like me. They always have."

*And the only person she's let into her life is Saladin*, he thought sadly. He knew perfectly well who Nimue's unnamed master was. Saladin was not a man who loved easily.

"Child . . ." he began, but Nimue had already sprung to her feet.

"Shall I exercise your horse? I ride much better than you do."

She waited expectantly for his reply, a child yearning to go outside to play. "Certainly," he said at last.

Saladin was using her, of that he was sure. But the man's mind was subtle, honed by ages. Merlin could not fathom what his embittered enemy had in mind, except that it somehow involved the girl. And the cup, of course. Arthur's cup.

When she left with the horse, he went outside and buried the cup in the woods behind the house.

# CHAPTER THIRTY-THREE

By April, Nimue and Merlin had become inseparable. With Arthur now grown and gone, the wizard's books had become dusty with disuse. He brought them out for Nimue.

She learned quickly, eager to study everything, but she was particularly interested in Merlin's knowledge of plants and animals. The young woman already knew quite a bit about the local wildlife, but she asked questions relentlessly about every new bit of information he offered her.

Nimue took to wearing men's breeches and an old shirt. They were far more practical than silk for tramping in the woods to examine mushrooms, or for exploring caves.

"This is where you first came to see me," she said as they walked into the crystal cave.

Merlin broke off a finger-length piece of violet quartz. "I had been coming here for some time before then," he said.

Since she'd first moved into the cottage on the lake, he had not brought up the subject of Saladin or his intentions. Whatever they were, Merlin had no fear of them. He'd had a good long life and did not fear death, if death were possible for him. And in truth, even that specter had begun to vanish. It had been eight weeks; if Saladin planned to kill him, he surely would have tried by now. The man was still a mystery to him.

But whatever Saladin might have hoped to accomplish by sending the girl to Merlin, it had not worked. Nimue was not a seductress by nature, and Merlin certainly had no intention of turning her into one. He liked her just as she was, wild and bright as a poppy. The two lived like an eccentric father and his equally eccentric daughter, experimenting with strange new foods and making do in a house neither of them cared much to clean. The house was only for sleeping in, anyway. During the days, the two of them lived outdoors, riding and walking, talking, laughing, teaching, learning, gathering flowers, catching fish, studying insects, reading, and pouring out their thoughts.

Merlin had not been so happy since Arthur was a boy, and perhaps, he thought more than once, perhaps he was even happier. Arthur had delighted him, but Merlin had known the boy's destiny even before Arthur himself had. He had never guessed that the lad would become king in a blinding moment of magic, but he did know that Arthur would one day rule. It had made him circumspect in some ways. Arthur's education had been geared toward his destiny as king. Merlin had taught him philosophy, navigation, Latin, geography, history above all.

There was no need for such care with Nimue. He taught

her everything she was interested in. She learned to play the harp, and he taught her the old ballads he had sung during his traveling years. She didn't care for Latin, so they never studied it. Instead he recited to her the long poems in ancient Celtic, and she repeated them, savoring the strange sounds and pressing for their meaning. She was apt at mathematics and geometry, insofar as they related to her own life, but had no use for abstract applications.

"What do I care how far it is to the stars?" she scoffed. "I'm never going to go there." She stared up at the night sky. "Tell me again about Perseus and Medusa and Pegasus," she whispered.

And Merlin repeated to her, night after night, the ancient Greek tales of heroes and monsters and unlucky lovers, shining forever above them.

"Do you think that we become stars when we die?" she asked.

"We might. It's as good a theory as any, I suppose."

"Where will you be, Merlin?"

"I beg your pardon?"

"When you die. Tell me where you'd like to be, and I'll look for you there. I'll wish on you every night."

He smiled at her sadly. "I don't think I'll be a star, Nimue. I haven't got enough belief."

"And I'll bet you won't die, either."

The declaration made him shiver. "Why would you say that?"

"You're a wizard. A real one. I've seen it for myself. You can read my thoughts."

"That's hardly a feat, Nimue. You're the most transparent person on earth."

The round yellow eyes of an owl gleamed eerily from a tree near the lake. Nimue made owl sounds. The bird swooped into the starlight.

"You've scared it away," Merlin said.

A moment later, the owl dropped a dead mouse onto his lap. He gasped, then stood up, cursing, brushing the thing off his robe. Nimue laughed. "By Mithras, you're twice the wizard I am," he said, embarrassed.

"No, I'm not. And when I die, I'm going to be right there, in the center of that lion." She pointed up to a cluster of stars near the west side of the moon.

"What lion? I don't see any such thing."

"That's because you have no imagination. But the lion's there, and I'm going to be the heart of it."

He looked at Nimue, her skin glowing like a pearl against the light of the full moon. *Yes*, he thought, *she ought to be the lion's heart*. A sudden feeling of sadness came over him. "You must marry, Nimue," he said softly. "You can't go on living this uneventful life with me."

"But I like you," she said. "I'll marry you if you want."

Merlin smiled. "Thank you for the offer, but I'm afraid I'm past that sort of thing."

"Don't you like women anymore?"

"Not the way I once did. Feverishly, you know. That's become far too tiring."

"Did you ever love a woman?"

Merlin was glad that she could not see the flush come to his cheeks. Still, he did not mind talking with her about such things. Nimue had had too little experience with people to judge their actions on anything but the most primitive level of kindness or cruelty. Like the forest creature she was, she accepted all things about her fellow living beings with serene equanimity. Merlin felt he could tell her anything.

"A few," he answered. "I never had a great love, except for the magic. I wanted the magic so badly, I could never devote my whole mind to the love of a woman. Still, there were a few."

"But you got the magic."

"Yes."

"That's something, anyway."

Merlin smiled. How he had grown to love her, he thought.

"I'd like to marry," Nimue said after a silence.

"He won't marry you."

She covered her head with her arms. "There you go again, reading my mind."

"Most likely he's forgotten all about you."

"He hasn't!"

"Nimue, listen." Gently he drew her arms away. "The man you're waiting for is no ordinary knight."

"I suppose he is foreign," she admitted. "But what of it? He's nearly as educated as you are, I'll wager."

"No, that's not the difference. The difference is . . ." He struggled for the right words, and could not find them. "He cannot love you, child. He has lived too long. It means nothing to him. He's very like me, only a thousand times more bitter, more afraid. A thousand times older, if you will. You must believe me, Nimue. You will not be happy with him."

She stood up, her eyes blazing. "How would you know? Who have you ever made happy? Those ladies you ran away from to do magic?"

Merlin could not answer. She was trembling, her long hair curling darkly against the brightness of the moon. "You can't be right," she said. "You can't be."

"Nimue . . ."

"Because you're the only two living people I know in the whole world. If you don't want me, and if he doesn't want me . . ." A sob burst suddenly out of her, and she ran off into the night.

At first Merlin meant to let her cry herself out in privacy, but something caught his attention. Far away, he could hear the approaching hoofbeats of a horse. "Nimue?" he called uncertainly. He listened again. It was not his horse. He knew its sound.

Then the horse stopped suddenly, and a woman screamed.

"Nimue!" Merlin called, running as fast as he could toward the dark road.

The horse was riderless. On the hill above the road, illuminated by moonlight, were two struggling figures.

"Stop! Stop it, I say!" Merlin shouted to no effect. Nimue was defending herself valiantly, squirming and kicking, but she was clearly no match for the man who pinned her to the ground. Merlin picked up a rock, the only possible weapon at hand, wishing he was the sorcerer the local folk thought him to be. It would be far more satisfying to turn the blackguard into a tree than to smash in his head. Nevertheless, he had to do something to help. He crept nearer, hoping fervently that Nimue could hold the fellow in position until he got within hurling distance.

"Don't you dare bash me with that rock," a man's voice said.

Merlin dropped it instantly. "Good heavens, it's Arthur."

Arthur sat up, holding Nimue by her hair. "I found this baggage creeping around your property," he said. Nimue lunged at him with both fists, but Arthur clapped one of his hands around both of hers. "And a fine thief she is, no doubt."

"Arthur, do let go," Merlin said, stunned.

The king looked up at him, wide-eyed. "Do you know her?"

"Ah . . . Your Majesty, may I present . . ." He tried to think of an appropriate title for the girl, or even a last name. He knew neither. "Nimue," he said at last. "Nimue is my . . . my ward."

Arthur let go of her hair. He stared at Merlin.

"Nimue, I present Arthur, High King of Britain."

She stood up, sniffling, and offered her hand to the king. When he took it, she pulled him upright. "I'm glad you tried to protect him," she said. "Hope I didn't hurt you."

Merlin winced, but Arthur, having regained his wits, roared with laughter. "Your ward, you say!" He clapped the girl on the back. "I was once Merlin's ward myself."

"Please come inside," Merlin offered.

"No, really," the king protested.

"You needn't suppose you've interrupted us in the middle of some improprietry," Merlin said grouchily. "You can see the girl's young enough to be my granddaughter. What brings you back here, anyway?"

"I was lost," Arthur lied. "Now that I know where I am, I really must be going. . . ."

"Oh, be still," the old man said. "Now come inside. That's the last of this discussion, Arthur. I mean Your Highness." He stomped toward the cottage, forgetting that he was walking in front of the king, and far too annoyed to care.

# CHAPTER THIRTY-FOUR

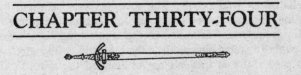

Merlin's mortification had lessened somewhat by the time he led the king into the cottage, although he was still dismayed by Arthur's knowing smile.

"It's not what you think," the old man insisted as he lit the fire. Nimue had gone to fetch the king something to eat and drink.

"There's no need to explain, Merlin. You're old enough to do as you please."

"Those years are far behind me. Now I'm so old I can only *think* as I please. And you're not that old yet, so keep your thoughts to yourself."

"As you wish," Arthur said genially. "She's quite pretty, though."

Merlin harrumphed.

"Does she take good care of you?"

"Damn it, I don't need anyone to take care of me! What sort of doddering fool do you think I've become?"

"You just said you were too old to do anything except think."

"Yes. And when I can't manage that any longer, I'll let you know."

Arthur laughed. "It's good to see you again, old friend."

Merlin's face softened. "Yes. Yes, Arthur, it's good to see you, too. The winter's been a cold one."

The king nodded.

"No heir." Merlin startled himself. He hadn't meant to speak the words which had burst into his mind. "Forgive me," he muttered.

"It's all right," Arthur said. "I could never keep anything from you. All the same, it's nothing to worry about."

The old man kept the images that thundered into his brain in check this time, but still they swirled and swooped, agitated as wild beasts. The thoughts were coming from Arthur, he knew; they had spent so much time together that Merlin no longer even considered it mind reading. Arthur's thoughts traveled almost instantly to Merlin, with an intensity so powerful that they all but obliterated the wizard's own thinking.

No heir. A barren queen, or a king without good seed. Either way, it was the end of the Pendragon dynasty, and possibly the end of all Arthur's plans as well. Launcelot . . . anger . . . guilt . . . the petty kings threatening to revolt . . . Everything was tossing around in a jumble. The king's mind was in a terrible state. Merlin's head began to throb with the effort of trying to contain the wild thoughts.

"Arthur," he said. He was feeling nauseated. If the king could not control the bombardment of his terrible emotion-laden visions, Merlin would have to leave the house. He needed distance if he were ever going to understand what was going on behind the king's noncommittal eyes. "Arthur, please stop it."

And then, the one image, crashing down like a hammer, which obliterated all the others and allowed Merlin to understand, at last, the roiling cauldron of Arthur's mind. "Oh, no," he said. "The queen."

Arthur covered his eyes with his hand. "I've put her aside," he said.

The silence seemed to fill the room.

"I'm sorry," Merlin said at last.

"I had to do it for the tribal chiefs," Arthur said, his voice heavy with misery. "Several of them have threatened to secede unless I appoint one of them my heir. Of course, that would be the end of the kingdom. The factional fighting would be as bad as it was before . . . before . . ."

*Before the miracle of the sword in the stone*, Merlin thought. The act which had proven Arthur's right to govern beyond a doubt.

"They can't be blamed," Merlin said gently. "Most of them didn't see it with their own eyes. So many legends have already sprung up about you. They may think the miracle no more real than the other stories."

"The Saxons are winning."

Merlin tried to put his arm around him, but the king stood up to escape his touch. He did not wish to be comforted. His face was haggard, with the blotchy look of many sleepless nights.

"Don't jump to conclusions, Arthur. The Saxons are barbarians, with primitive weapons. They have to cross the channel in crude boats—"

"They're taking over our country!" the king shouted. "Oh, we stop a band here and there, when we see them. But there are too many of them, coming in all over the coastline. They'll outlive me, and the petty kings know that."

"So the kings are asking for an heir from you."

"Asking!" He threw back his head and laughed bitterly. "Some of them have already vowed to support the so-called bastard prince in the north. His name, I gather, is Mordred. He's twelve years old, for the love of God!"

Merlin frowned. "Why would they do that?"

"As a result of some clever drum-beating on the part of the boy's father—excuse me, 'Guardian' is the title he grants himself, since I am supposed to be the churl's father."

"King Lot of Rheged," Merlin said. "He always was an ambitious one."

"Exactly. If he can attract enough support for the boy to take over the High Kingship after my death, Lot himself will effectively rule. And he'll suck every part of Britain dry for his own gain."

"But surely the petty kings know that."

"Of course. But some of them will profit from an alliance with Lot. Those are the ones who are going over to him now."

"And the others?"

"The others will remain loyal—so long as I produce a legitimate heir."

"I see," Merlin said.

He saw more than he wanted to. For in the king's thoughts he saw the memory of Queen Guenevere, white-faced and trembling, as the knights led her away to the nunnery in which she would be imprisoned for the rest of her life.

"Launcelot hates me," the king said quietly. "He was the queen's champion, you know, and a Christian. He thinks I've broken my vows to God by bending to the chiefs."

He sat down again. "And I have, I suppose."

"It is never easy to rule," Merlin said, hearing the hollowness of his own words.

"Launcelot's last words to me were that he could no longer serve a king he did not respect. He left the next day."

Nimue entered and Arthur immediately changed the subject. He tried to keep his voice light and good-humored.

"But we have a new knight, and this one, I think, may well sit in the Siege Perilous."

"What is his name?" Merlin asked.

"Galahad. He is really exceptional, Merlin. Absolutely the best. Guards me like a giant dog and won't let me out of his sight. Much like Launcelot used to." He chuckled sourly. "Of course, now there are rumors that he is Launcelot's son. God, is there anyone in this island that someone else is not calling a bastard?"

Nimue placed a cask of wine and some bread and meat on the table but, aware of the king's distress, she did not speak and left the cottage immediately. Merlin was grateful for the consideration.

"Drink some of this," Merlin said, handing Arthur a glass. "It's dandelion wine. I made it myself last summer."

Arthur smiled. "It's the Roman in you. You never cared for mead." The king drank a sip. "Where's the girl?"

"She's gone."

"I'm sorry. I've disrupted things. She'll be angry."

"No," Merlin said. "Nimue wished to help. That was why she left."

"She'll gossip."

Merlin shook his head.

"Do you love her?"

"In a way. As a father. The way I love you, Arthur."

The king's lips tightened.

"Yes, I wish I were her age again, too," Merlin said gently. "Where did Launcelot go?"

Arthur drank his wine. "Back to Gaul, I suppose. He didn't tell me. The rumors have already started, though. That he's gone into the forests to live as a hermit. That he died of a broken heart for love of the queen. The most popular story, as I understand, is that Launcelot and the queen were lovers. I'm sure that one was started by my own supporters. It gives me a reason for discarding Guenevere, you see," he said bitterly. "If she was unfaithful, then I had a perfect moral right to put her away. The lie has been so well received that some clans are calling for me to burn the queen at the stake."

He tried to laugh but, to Merlin's consternation, began to weep instead. "Isn't that the biggest joke of them all? Guenevere reviled because I broke my marriage vows to her."

He closed his eyes and sat in silence for a long moment. "I'm so tired, Merlin. So damned tired."

Merlin put his hand on the king's shoulder. This time Arthur did not move away. "I'd like you to stay the night," the old man said.

"I can't." He sighed. "If I did, I might never go back."

"You'll go back," Merlin said. "You are the king."

Arthur took a deep breath. His eyes were half-closed with exhaustion. "I never thought I'd be the sort to sacrifice my soul to stay in power," he said wearily.

"We have already covered that ground, sire," Merlin said. "I still have the cup of the Christ. You need only speak the word."

"I have already spoken the word," Arthur said sternly. "The word remains no."

Merlin nodded. "Then never think that you go back to hold onto your power. You return because it is your obligation."

"To whom? Britain? Britain will be a Saxon country within fifty years. Not to God, surely. Not after what I've done to my wife."

"To history, perhaps," Merlin said softly.

"To history." Arthur's lips curled in a thin mockery of a smile. "It doesn't matter now, anyway." He wiped his brow with the back of his hand. "I've been riding all day."

"Rest, Arthur."

The king leaned back on the soft straw-filled cushion, his glass still in his hand. Merlin took it from him and sniffed at the dregs, then walked outside.

"Nimue," he said softly.

The girl appeared from behind a tree.

"Why did you drug the king's drink?"

"He needed to sleep. It's harmless, anyway. It wouldn't have affected him if he weren't dead tired." She turned to look through the small window at the sleeping man.

"You were probably right to do it," Merlin said. "Nevertheless, don't take liberties with the king."

She didn't hear him. She was staring at Arthur. "Was he always so sad?"

"No," Merlin said. "He was a happy boy. Serious, but happy." He looked up at the moon. "I've never seen a happy king."

"Then why did you let him become king?"

"I had nothing to do with that."

"You could have stopped him."

The old man thought once again of the boy who had freed the ancient sword from the stone. What might his life have been if the miracle had not occurred? Would he have been spared this misery?

"I had no right to keep him from his destiny," Merlin said.

Nimue went inside and loosened the king's shoes, then

covered him with a thin blanket. "Go to bed, Merlin. I'll sit with him," she said.

She did, through the night, stoking the fire when it grew low, and staring at the copper-headed man who slept as if it were his only escape from the demons that plagued him.

*This is the lion*, she thought. When this man died, he would surely shine through the darkness of night.

She felt her heart melting. Perhaps it was all men, she thought. Since she was a child, she had only met three people on earth, and she loved all three of them. Were they all so wonderful as these three?

Nimue heard a great sigh escape from her lips. What a marvelous thing life was.

# CHAPTER THIRTY-FIVE

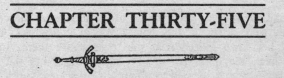

When Arthur awoke, Nimue was there, smiling. And before his troubles could crash through the barrier of sleep to hurt him, even before he could look about his strange surroundings in the moment of disorientation before realizing that he had fallen asleep in a bed other than his own, he smiled back at the sheer joy in her.

"Don't wake Merlin," he said. In the dim predawn light, the king saddled his own horse and mounted.

Silently, Nimue gave him a loaf of bread for his journey.

"Be well," Arthur said.

Nimue nodded. In another moment he was galloping down the dirt roadway.

As Nimue watched, a knight came out of the forest and turned down the road to follow Arthur. The knight—a young man with an angelic face—had spent the night on his horse, watching Merlin's cabin.

This must have been the Galahad she had heard the king

speak briefly of the night before. How wonderful to have someone who loved you so much that he would be on constant guard for your safety.

Or was it wonderful?

She watched until Arthur disappeared into the still-dark western sky. "Good-bye, my lord," she said softly. She had met the king of Britain and would not change places with him for all the gold on earth.

The first rays of sun appeared behind her, making the dew on the grass shimmer. Nimue took a deep breath. This was her favorite time, when a new day broke over the land. Beside the cottage, the small lake was awash in silver. The wet grass tickled her bare feet as she walked toward it, then ran. She clambered up a pile of rocks that served as a lookout for boats. Then, with a whoop, she dived into the bracing water.

She emerged on the far side of the lake, near the caves. They were surrounded by wildflowers and tall grass. A doe and her fawn grazed near the rocks above them. In the distance, the high towers of Camelot rose into the pink morning sky. It seemed to Nimue like a scene from a fairy tale. She wiped her wet hair back from her forehead and breathed in the fragrance of the clean spring breeze.

As she walked toward the caves, the deer looked up, startled, and bounded away, their white tails bobbing. Nimue frowned. No wild animal had ever been frightened by her presence before. Had her life in the world of men taken away her ability to live among the animals? Did they somehow know that she had become one of *them*, the enemy?

She called to them. The big doe stopped for a moment and looked back at her, then turned and leaped into the forest.

"It's afraid of me, not you," a voice behind her said.

She whirled around, gasping. "Saladin!"

He smiled at her sadly. "I thought you might have forgotten me."

"Forgotten? Never!" She wrapped her arms around him, but he offered no response. She drew back, embarrassed. "Have you been waiting for me?"

"Every day for more than a week."

"I'm sorry. Time seems to go by so fast."

He smiled, but there was no joy in it. "Yes," he said. "I know."

It was an awkward moment. "Where have you been?" Nimue asked finally to ease the tension.

"I've traveled," Saladin said. He looked older, although only two months had gone by since they had parted company. "I went back to Rome. Everything's dying there. The fountains are filled with algae and the bloated carcasses of dogs." He stared at an indefinable point for some time, then closed his eyes and inhaled deeply. "Have you done what I asked of you?"

Nimue frowned, puzzled. "I've gone to live with Merlin," she said.

"Good."

"He's not in love with me, though." She laughed. "Actually, he's become like a father to me."

"That's good, too," Saladin said. His big stallion stepped out of the bushes. "Call him."

She looked back at the cottage across the lake. "I think he's still asleep. We could go there."

"To a wizard's home? No."

"Oh, it's nothing like that," Nimue said gaily. "He's really just an ordinary person—"

"Call him!" Saladin demanded. She heard the edge in his voice. "Stand on the rock. He can see you from there." He prodded her toward the big outcropping of boulders above the caves, then climbed up after her.

"Merlin?" she called tentatively. There was no answer. "I can go back and bring him to you," she offered. "I'll swim over—"

But Saladin was not disposed toward more conversation. He drew a long dagger from his belt and, swift as an adder striking, slashed across her face. "Call him!"

Nimue was too stunned to cry out. Blood dripped onto her wet clothes as Saladin yanked her arms behind her. "Merlin!"

he shouted, and his voice echoed across the water. "Come see what I have, sorcerer!"

The old man came out of the cottage and froze.

"Bring the cup," Saladin commanded. "I am ready to negotiate with you."

Merlin arrived on horseback within minutes. His expression was grim. "The girl will bleed to death," he said.

"A facial wound is never as serious as it looks," Saladin answered. He jammed Nimue's arms higher on her back.

She winced. "Why are you doing this to me?" she asked plaintively.

"It's nothing to do with you," Merlin said. "Your friend wants something that I possess. He's using your life to bargain with."

Nimue tried to look behind her at the man who had first brought her back into the world. "Is it true?" she asked.

Saladin said nothing.

"It's true," Merlin said. "That was why he sent you to me. He knew I would love you." He added softly, "And I do."

From the folds of his robe he took the small metallic sphere. Saladin inhaled sharply.

"Surprised that I have it?" Merlin said, holding it up to catch the sun.

"Why, you even kept it from the king," Saladin said with a smile.

"I offered it to him. I begged him to take it. But Arthur wouldn't have it. He knew, more than I, what it might do to a man. But now, looking at you, I see for myself what sort of monster one's dreams can make." He closed his fingers over the ball. "Release Nimue, and the cursed thing is yours."

Saladin pushed the girl away, but kept his dagger trained on her as she sprawled onto the rocks. "Give it to me!" he whispered raggedly.

Merlin threw the cup on the rocks. "Get away!" he hissed to Nimue.

The young woman sprang to her feet. But instead of

scrambling off the rock, she turned and dived for the cup.

"What are you doing?" Merlin screeched. The young woman paid him no attention.

"Your greed has just cost you your life, child," Saladin said calmly as he raised the dagger over her back.

Merlin ran toward her, screaming, as Saladin savagely brought the blade down.

It struck rock.

For an instant the two men froze in place, Saladin clutching the dagger, Merlin with his arms outstretched. No one was there. The girl had disappeared.

It was Merlin who first saw the bit of scrub bush bobbing over the spot where Nimue had vanished. *The hole*, he remembered. When Nimue had run away from him inside the crystal cave, she had escaped through an opening in the rocks above. This was the opening.

"What sorcery have you taught her, wizard?" Saladin demanded hoarsely.

Merlin smiled. "Who could teach her anything?" he said softly.

"I'll hunt you to the ends of the earth, old man," Saladin said. "And after you're gone, I'll kill her. And your king. And everyone else on this island, if need be. But I will get what I want."

Merlin knew that the man spoke the truth. "Does life mean so much to you?" he asked quietly.

"Don't try your foolish philosophizing with me, Merlin. You would do the same to keep the cup. And the girl, your . . . succubus, or whatever she is, is gone. Now that she has the treasure of life, you'll not see her again."

At that moment, Nimue burst out of the mouth of the cave like a bird in flight. With a raucous laugh, she leapt upon Saladin's waiting stallion and kicked it into a run. "Catch me if you can, traitor!" she called out behind her.

Saladin scrambled off the rocks, his dignity forgotten. The girl was riding toward the lake, where the shore was covered with boulders. Even a good horse—and Saladin's stallion was the best—would have to slow to a near crawl. He would have time to catch up with her. And when he did, he would savor each moment that it took to kill her.

Merlin, too, saw the danger. "Nimue!" he shouted. "Get off the rocks! Head into the woods!"

But to his dismay, she continued on her way until the stallion was balanced precariously on a mound of stone rubble. Then she stopped completely.

"Swim it!" Merlin called desperately. "Swim the horse."

Nimue appeared not to have heard him, or to notice that Saladin was approaching dangerously close. The dagger was still in his hand. He would not hesitate to kill the animal, Merlin knew, to get to the girl and the precious object she was now flaunting.

She held both hands high above her head, palms flat, as if offering the cup to the sun. A series of loud, shrill shrieks poured from her lips.

*This is some kind of incantation*, Merlin realized with wonderment. *One of her animal sounds*. But what was she calling? There was the occasional wolf in the forest, but the noises she was making in no way resembled the howl of a wolf. Besides, surely she knew that the presence of a predator would cause the horse to bolt on the slippery rocks.

Saladin had nearly reached her. The stallion sensed his rage and skittered a little, but Nimue held him steady with her legs, all the while chirping her strange sounds.

And then Merlin saw it: a flock of birds, thick as a cloud, screaming down from the trees. They were birds of all varieties, from tiny brown wrens to brilliant red cardinals. There were crows and sparrows and elusive bluebirds that rarely left the dark safety of the forest. There were scarlet tanagers and wood finches and bluejays, all of them converging on one point at the side of the lake.

Merlin could only watch in amazement as they came, their wings making a sound like thunder, their calls melding into one high, piercing, terrifying scream.

A few pecked at Saladin. He swatted them away, dropping his dagger, covering his face. But most of them flew directly to Nimue. They covered her with their soft, moving bodies for a moment, then rose into the sky above the lake.

Saladin peered over the torn sleeve of his robe. Her eyes were closed. Her lips were silent and parted in a gentle smile. And her hands were empty.

High above, a flash of light glinted off a metal object in the midst of the flying birds.

"No!" Saladin screamed. "Come back!"

Nimue laughed. "Your treasure will be where the wild birds go," she said.

"And where is that, sorceress?" Saladin spat.

"I didn't ask." With that, she reared the stallion up on its hind legs. It kicked out toward Saladin, who backed away and fell.

"Whatever it was, I doubt your prize could bring you anything greater than the love of a true friend," Nimue said. "You've lost that with me, Saladin. You will not find such a friend again."

She brought the stallion back from the shore to where Merlin stood. "Mount your horse, old man," she said, "and travel with me. For I will not leave your side, now or ever, and will love you well until the end of my days."

Saladin closed the draperies against the harsh sun. "Who would have thought the creature capable of such loyalty?" he mused aloud.

Nimue had been as good as her word. She had remained with Merlin until his death—or what was believed to have been his death—until whatever call alerted his sorcerer's spirit that Arthur had returned after almost seventeen centuries.

How had it felt to wake after so long, he wondered. To live, knowing that everyone you had known and loved in the past was long dead, their bones rotted into nothingness?

How had it felt? But of course, Saladin already knew. He had outlived everyone. Everyone on earth, the great and the small. The Sumerians, the Egyptians, the Greeks, the Macedonians, the Romans, even the invincible Persians whom he himself had led during the twelfth century, in one of the most stunning reigns on earth—he had outlived them all. He had been a king and a pauper and a merchant and an artist and a physician, and done all manner of work to pass his endless days. He had watched history unfold and reform and repeat again and again, because human beings never learned from their short pasts. He had met millions of people, so many that they blurred in his memory like dots of color on a spinning pinwheel. Some of them remained, whole and intact, in his memory: Kanna and Merlin; the fool of an innkeeper in Jerusalem; handsome Alexander of Macedon; and Nimue . . .

*She might have been mine*, he thought, and the vision of her face stirred in him an actual physical pain. In all his years of life, only Nimue had truly loved him.

Nimue. The Lady of the Lake. When Merlin died, she lay his body inside the crystal cave and had it sealed shut. The legends had sprung up instantly, of course: Everything connected with Arthur managed to reach the realm of myth before long. The locals, who had thought the great sorcerer Merlin incapable of such an ordinary act as dying, claimed that Nimue had stolen the old man's magic and used it to imprison him.

In her old age, the common folk had come to her to cure their fevers and poxes, although they never quite forgave her for banishing the king's royal wizard.

It was only decades after King Arthur's death that a few of the more imaginative among them began to perceive Nimue's role in the whole fantastic history: that she had preserved Merlin for the time of the Great King's return. For above all the legends, the belief that Arthur would come back to reign again was the most persistent and universal. "The Once and Future King," they called him; Arthur, the man even death could not destroy.

"And here you are," Saladin said, lightly touching the young boy's red hair. "You really did come back."

Arthur Blessing had been asleep for hours. Several times servants had peered into the room, worried about their master who sat hour after hour with the unconscious child, but each time Saladin waved them away impatiently. The boy who lay before him was a living miracle, just as his other life had been filled with miracles, and he wanted to be alone with him.

How odd, he thought. Only two people in the whole history of mankind—the Jew named Jesus who had risen from his very grave and this boy who had somehow been restored to his identical past self—had overcome the finality of death. And they had both rejected the cup of immortality.

"Why did you not take it while you had the chance?" Saladin whispered.

In the end, Arthur had been slain by an inexperienced boy, the puppet of an ambitious petty tyrant. His death had been agonizing, humiliating. More than half of his supporters had deserted him when he refused to take another wife. Of those who remained loyal, only a handful had been present during the battle in which Mordred's sword inflicted its mortal wound. The rest, the best of the Round Table, had gone hunting for the cup.

The Grail, they called it by then, Christ's holy cup. Some of the knights claimed to have received instructions to find it from the ghost of Merlin himself. Personally, Saladin believed that Arthur must have told some of the older knights about the miraculous properties of the sphere after it was irretrievably lost, and the Great Quest had been, for many of them, a search for personal treasure which ended in faraway places long before Arthur's death.

Of them all, only one knight had pursued the Quest wholeheartedly for the full twelve years of its loss: Galahad, the newest knight, reputed to be the son of Launcelot and the one that rumor said was allowed to sit in the Siege Perilous.

At the outset, Saladin had not intended to follow the young knight. But wherever he went with his questions, he found that another had come just before him seeking the same answers. It seemed, he had conceded at last, that Galahad's mind worked much like his own. During the final years they saw one another frequently, though they had never spoken together. The first time Galahad heard Saladin's voice was when the dark Saracen had thanked him for leading him to the cup, a moment before he sliced into the young knight's neck.

Even then, Saladin remembered with irritation, the myths had sprung up like weeds. Upon seeing the Grail, the legends insisted, Galahad's spirit was lifted to heaven by a host of angels.

*Not by angels, but by the blade of my sword*, Saladin thought pettishly. Why was it that everything connected with Arthur took on dimensions of grandeur? Every small fact associated with his life had become so interwoven with the fabric of history that it would never be forgotten.

Yet what had Arthur done, really? The nation over which he ruled was savage and sparsely populated. He had not given it glory, nor improved the sorry lot of its inhabitants. In the end, he had not even been able to stem the tide of the invading Saxons, who eventually overran Britain.

Mordred, the dubious "heir" to the Pendragon dynasty, was himself killed in the same battle in which Arthur died—by Arthur's own sword, the legends said. The petty kings who had fought so long among themselves were all wiped out or displaced within a decade or two by the Saxons. Camelot itself was taken over as a Saxon stronghold. Nothing about Arthur, king of the Britons, had endured for long after his death.

And yet the legends were told again and again.

"He will come back," they said. "The king will come again."

"What was your destiny?" Saladin whispered. What was the imperative so overwhelming that this failed king had not been permitted to pass into obscurity?

Saladin had thought about the magic surrounding Arthur for centuries. For a time, he had become a king himself. His reign had been longer, his feats more glorious than any of Arthur's accomplishments. And yet he was not remembered as Arthur was. He had never been considered immortal.

And now, Arthur was back. To try again, to fulfill the mission interrupted by his death so long ago.

"I wish I didn't have to kill you," Saladin said.

But he would kill him, of course. The boy, his aunt, the American . . . all of them would have to die before the whole world found out about the cup.

It was a pity. Saladin stroked the child's forehead. "You might have made a glorious king," he said.

# BOOK THREE

## THE
## KING

# CHAPTER THIRTY-SIX

The constabulary in the village of Wilson-on-Hamble had not seen anything quite so exciting since the time Davey McGuinness, the local veterinarian, had gone to old Eamon Carpenter's farm to treat two sick milk cows and found that they had been poisoned.

"One of them rolled over and died right in front of Davey," Constable James ("Call me Jack") Nubbit explained as he escorted Hal and Emily to their car. Though the boy who had come upon Hal in the meadow had called the police immediately and reported that a man was bleeding half to death near Lakeshire Tor, Nubbit had been unable to come until his assistant arrived back with the village's only police vehicle. By that time, Emily and Hal had already found their way to the doctor, who had stitched and bandaged Hal's shoulder.

They met Nubbit on their way out. With the constable was the young officer who had questioned the bus passengers the day before, while Nubbit had gone fishing. "Hooked a three-pound speckled trout," he'd told them proudly before launching into the saga of Mr. Carpenter's dead cow. Nubbit was a red rubber ball of a man, with a beet-colored nose, florid round cheeks, and a bald, sunburned head. He wore the expression of a lapdog lusting to have his throat tickled. His companion stood stolidly behind him as Nubbit regaled Hal and Emily with the criminal history of Wilson-on-Hamble.

Hal saw the despair on Emily's face as they parked the borrowed car at the inn. The aging police cruiser pulled in beside them. "We'll find Arthur," Hal said.

"It's been more than two hours," Emily said flatly.

"Ah, the Inn of the Falcon," Constable Nubbit exclaimed as all four doors slammed at once. "Good choice. Katie

Sloan always made a fine apple tart. Have you met Mrs. Sloan?"

"She lent me her car," Emily said with a sigh.

"Well, it's just like her. Salt of the earth, Katie is. Why, when that cow of auld Carpenter's died on Davey McGuinness—oh, it was a terrible thing, vomiting something fierce—it was Katie sent her husband, God rest his soul, to go help clean up the mess. Had to bury the cow, don't you know. Can't send a poisoned cow to the knackerman. Why, the hole they dug for the beast must have been—"

"Excuse me, Constable," Hal interrupted. "A child has been kidnapped, and the perpetrators are armed."

"Yes, right," Nubbit said, his face flushing even redder as he took his notepad from his uniform jacket. "Blessing. Arthur, it is."

"Yes," Emily sighed wearily. They had already gone over the broad outlines of the situation with Nubbit but had felt as if they were forcing the information on a man who had other, grander things on his mind.

"The lad who called told us you'd been wounded."

"Nothing serious," Hal said.

"Gunshot?"

"No. They were carrying swords."

"Swords, you say?"

"That's right. Six men on horseback. Arabs, I think. They were dressed in some kind of costumes—balloon pants, turbans, that sort of thing. And they used swords."

"No guns," Nubbit said, writing carefully. "Well, we can be grateful for that, at least."

"What? That they didn't have guns? They had swords, for God's sake!"

"Now, Mr. Blessing, we realize you've been through a bad patch—"

"My name's Woczniak. The boy is Miss Blessing's nephew."

"Spelling, please?" He poised his pencil over his notepad.

"What are you going to do to locate Arthur?" Emily said exasperatedly.

Nubbit came to attention, as if he were taking an oral examination in school. "We are proceeding on the assumption that the man who tried to kill the Blessing boy yesterday on the bus was somehow connected with today's events."

Hal grunted in sarcastic dismissal.

"Because the man on the bus was identified as an Arab by several different witnesses, we have sent his fingerprints and a morgue photograph to Metropolitan Police headquarters. They haven't got the material yet—"

"Of course not," Hal grumbled.

Nubbit cleared his throat. "However, I've spoken with people in London personally. Scotland Yard will send the prints and photograph on to Immigration and to Interpol." He glanced down at his notes. "Also, we've talked with residents of the area."

"About what? A man riding on a bus from London?" Hal could feel his irritation approaching the breaking point. "What did you think the locals would be able to tell you about him?"

"Well, I . . ." Nubbit shook his jowls. The young officer with him gave Hal a sour look and mumbled to his superior, "What did I tell you about him?"

"Sir, I assure you we are doing the best we can," Nubbit said indignantly. "This may be difficult for you to understand, but generally these cases are solved because someone has seen something. Now, we're going to go back to the residents of the area and ask . . ."

"We were alone," Hal said loudly. "It was dawn. There were no witnesses."

Nubbit cocked his head and squinted at him. "You seem very sure about quite a lot."

Hal raised his fists in front of his chest. *This moron doesn't believe me*, he thought. He forced himself to open his hands. Hitting the cop in charge of the investigation wasn't going to help matters.

Outside, the darkening clouds of a thunderhead were looming. Rain was on the way. "I think you ought to make castings of the hoofprints of those horses before the rain comes," he said as calmly as possible.

"Hoofprint castings? In a farm meadow?"

"The prints would be fresh." Hal said, forcing out the smooth if mechanical words. "Seal off the area. Then, after you've made the castings, check with local stables, breeders, saddlers, feed stores—anyone who might have had contact with these people. Try trucking companies for rentals. Unless the kidnappers rode those horses through the streets, the animals were brought in some kind of van, or else kept at a stable. Make a search of the field where we were assaulted. Maybe one of the horsemen dropped something . . ."

Nubbit held up his hands, smiling. "Now, now, those are all fine ideas, sir, but you've got to remember we're a small constabulary."

"Then get some help," Hal said coldly. "Christ knows you need it."

"I've told you that our report has gone to Scotland Yard."

"Are they sending someone?"

"Well, I'm sure that's up to them," Nubbit said defiantly. "But as I've told you, we are prepared to do everything we can to retrieve the child."

The woman who ran the inn peeked into the parlor where Hal, Emily, and the two policemen were standing. "Can I get anyone a cup of tea?" she asked.

Nubbit turned toward her with a warm grin. "Well, now, Katie Sloan, since you're asking . . ."

"Nubbit, get out of here," Hal said quietly.

The constable's round head whipped toward him sharply. It was nearly glowing in its redness.

"You heard me," Hal said.

"Mr. Woczniak," the innkeeper began. Hal ignored her and spoke directly to Constable Nubbit.

"I can't make you do your job," he said. "But I'll be damned if I'll let you sit on your fat ass while a bunch of killers get away with a ten-year-old kid. Now get out before I throw you out."

The young constable flexed his shoulders. "That goes for you, too, Einstein," Hal added.

The two policemen bustled out with great dignity.

Mrs. Sloan watched them leave and then shook her head. "I've heard what happened to you out on the Tor," she said. "I wish we had a better police force to offer you."

"Me, too," Hal said quietly. "May I use your telephone? It's long distance, but I'll pay for the call."

"Certainly." She brought a black rotary telephone out of a cupboard and set it on a small table near one of the sofas. "Just let me know if you'd like some tea or a bit of something to eat."

Emily nodded at her as she left.

"I want to call the United States," Hal spoke into the phone. "Washington, D.C. The Federal Bureau of Investigation. Assistant Director Fred Koehler. My name is Hal Woczniak." He spelled it for the operator, than thanked her and hung up.

Emily was seated on a hard chair, staring blankly across the room. Hal put his hand on her shoulder and kept it there until she looked up suddenly, as if she were surprised to see him.

"We'll get him back," he said softly.

She nodded slightly, the gesture of someone who did not believe what she had just been told but no longer wanted to talk about it. Then her eyes drifted away from him, again looking toward the window.

When the telephone rang, Hal bolted across the room to answer it.

"Yes?"

"Mr. Woczniak? Hold on for your party, please."

A moment later another voice crackled over the line. "Hal? That you?"

"Right, Chief. I'm calling from somewhere in the south of England."

"What the hell are you doing there?"

"I'll tell you about it sometime. Right now I need a favor."

There was silence at the other end.

"I'm sober, Chief," Hal said.

There was another silence. "Then I'm listening," the Chief said finally.

# CHAPTER THIRTY-SEVEN

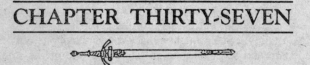

Inspector Brian Candy arrived from Scotland Yard with a tweed suit, a pair of socks that did not match, two assistants, a gray van filled with equipment, and a businesslike approach to his trade which Hal found both familiar and comforting.

Candy climbed the three flights of stairs to Hal's room on the top floor of the inn and arrived without being out of breath. Quite a feat, Hal thought, considering the man's size. Candy was well over six feet tall and as broad as a bull. He nearly filled the room with his girth and quiet energy.

"Constable Nubbit has already filled me in with most of . . . what he knows," Candy said graciously.

Hal snorted. "About this case? Or was he still going on about auld Eamon Carpenter's dead cow?"

Candy ducked his head and sneaked a smile. "He was kind enough to meet us on the road. My men have gone to the meadow to make the castings you suggested."

Hal looked out the window. "It's been raining for forty minutes," he said quietly.

Candy tightened his lips. "Unfortunate," he said. "Still, they may find something."

*At least he's not lying to me*, Hal thought. "Thank you for coming," he said.

"No thanks necessary," Candy said. "When my superintendent gets rung up by one of his old friends in the FBI and he tells me to march, I only ask how far. Now suppose you tell me what's going on here."

Hal nodded. He was perched on the windowsill and saw

Candy take not one, but three ballpoint pens from inside his jacket pocket and lay them on the table in front of him as he opened up a large spiral-bound notebook and looked up at Hal like a man with all the time in the world.

As Hal went over the details of the morning ambush, he studied Candy's broad face. It was a face he liked instinctively, beefy and hard, with a bushy moustache and auburn hair that Hal guessed had, in childhood, earned him the nickname Red. He gave the impression of earnest competence, and it was easy for Hal to see him as a member of a regimental boxing team somewhere; probably a middleweight in those days, with a technically correct, plod-ahead style that—so unlike the flashy antics of American boxers—quietly piled up points and won him a lot of bouts by decision.

The only thing that belied that impression was Candy's eyes. They were dark and quick and darting, the eyes of a casino pit boss watching a new dealer work.

They were not the eyes of a man Hal wanted to lie to. Still, he wasn't about to tell anyone, let alone a police officer, about Camelot revisited and Merlin the magician disappearing in a puff of smoke while holding the Holy Grail. There were some things he had to keep to himself if he hoped to get any cooperation from the authorities.

So he gave a truthful story, but carefully, not the whole truth. He described how he had met both Taliesin and young Arthur Blessing and his aunt Emily on a bus while on tour. Very matter-of-factly, he told how he had disarmed someone who was trying to kill the boy.

Candy looked up sharply and Woczniak knew why. If there was someone in custody who had been involved in an earlier attempt against the boy, the mystery was almost solved already.

Hal shook his head. "No survivors, I'm afraid," he said. "The bastard bit down on a cyanide pill and was dead before the cops could question him."

Recognition dawned in the inspector's eyes. "Right you are. I read the reports on that this morning. Didn't realize you were talking about the same boy. Some photographs and fingerprints were sent to headquarters, but they haven't arrived yet."

"Of course not," Hal said. "Constable Nerdnick sent them."

"The prints should be identified tomorrow. I'll have the results called in to me as soon as they come in. We'll be working out of the constabulary."

"Can you keep the locals out of the way?"

Candy smiled. "I think so." He checked over his notes. "The boy was willed this property by his mother, you say. Was she British?"

He was looking at Emily, but she only stared straight ahead. She had said nothing since Candy's arrival.

"Emily?" Hal prompted gently.

Her eyes panicked, then focused on the Scotland Yard detective. "I'm sorry," she said.

Candy nodded sympathetically and repeated the question.

"No, she was an American," Emily answered. "Dilys— that's Dilys Blessing—was included in her . . . in Arthur's father's will. But since she wasn't alive at the time of the man's death, the property went to Arthur. That was a stipulation in the will."

Candy wrote constantly, but never took his eyes off Emily. "What was the father's name?" he asked.

Emily's face worked. Finally she pulled herself together enough to answer. "Abbott," she said. "Sir Bradford Welles Abbott. He was never married to my sister."

"I see," he said noncommittally. "I understand you saw nothing of the episode this morning?"

She shook her head numbly. "I went to the meadow to see what was taking them so long. I arrived too late."

"It's just as well," Candy said quietly, then turned back to Hal.

*He's good*, Hal thought with admiration. Candy had sensed that Emily was walking a thin wire and didn't push her too hard. In the end, he would get more out of her that way, Hal knew.

"And the old man who was with you?" the inspector asked. "Taliesin. Odd name. Welsh. Where is he?"

"He took off," Hal said.

"Took off?"

"The perps left with Arthur, and he chased them," Hal said.

"On foot?"

"Right."

"Might he have been working with the kidnappers?"

"No. They . . ." *They cut off his head.* "They wounded him. He was hurt."

"Badly?"

"No. I don't think so."

"What was his first name?"

"I don't know," Hal lied. The last thing he wanted was for Scotland Yard to begin a manhunt for the old man. It would waste what little time there was to find Arthur. "I met him on the bus."

"Do you know anything about him? Where he worked, where he lived?"

Hal shook his head, and folded his arms across his chest in an unconscious gesture of defiance. Candy looked at Emily, but she was no longer paying any attention to the inspector or his questions.

"Excuse me," Candy said. "I need to make a telephone call."

When he left the room, Hal let out a slow sigh of relief. Then he spotted the beer in an old metal bucket beside the small table where Candy had been sitting. Anticipating the inspector's arrival, Mrs. Sloan must have placed it there. There was even ice in the bucket.

Slowly Hal walked over to it. There were three bottles. He took out two. He had wanted a drink all day, and especially wanted one now. The bottle was cold and sweating. He could imagine the taste of it on his cigarette-dried throat.

"Care for a beer?" he asked Emily, but she didn't hear him.

He sighed and put back both bottles. He couldn't risk it,

not while Emily was in such bad shape. What was it they said about drunks—that one drink was too many and a thousand weren't enough? If he had one now, he knew, he would have a thousand. And when he woke up, stinking and lost, Arthur would be dead and Emily would be in a nuthouse. No, he wouldn't have one. Not yet. Not just yet.

Soon he heard Candy's heavy footfalls coming back up the stairs. "I thought the Yard might have made some headway with the dead man's prints, but they've got nothing so far," he said. He added, "They're still working, though. If the fellow's ever been arrested and booked anywhere in Britain or the Continent, we'll know about it."

*And what if he hasn't?* Hal thought. But he already knew the answer to that.

"Suppose we go on to the kidnappers," Candy suggested. "You say they were Arabs?"

"That's my guess. But it may have just been their clothes."

"Fairy-tale costumes," Candy said noncommitally.

Hal nodded. "Turbans, silk harem pants . . . Right out of the Arabian Nights."

"Why do you suppose they were dressed so fancifully?"

"I really don't know," Hal said.

Candy wrote. "Did any of them speak? Call out a name, perhaps?"

"The only one who talked was . . ." Suddenly he recalled what Taliesin had said. "There was a name. Saladin."

"Which one was he?"

"The leader."

"The tall one."

"At least seven feet," Hal said. "He had this devil's face and weird eyes, pitch-black. His skin was white, but not as if it was supposed to be white. It was unwholesome-looking, like a dark-skinned man who'd been out of the sun for years. In the states, we called it 'prison pallor.' He had a goatee."

Hal glanced over at Candy and saw that the Scotland Yard inspector was staring hard at him.

"What is it?" Hal asked.

"Nothing."

"Don't tell me that. You recognized him from my description, didn't you?"

"No. I don't know any Saladin," Candy said crisply. "The description did remind me of someone, but it's not the man you're talking about."

"Why not?"

"He's dead."

A crack of thunder shook the windows.

"Gracious, it's getting bad."

Everyone turned to see Mrs. Sloan in the doorway. She was panting and out of breath from the long climb up the stairs.

"Sorry to disturb you, but there's a telephone call for Inspector Candy downstairs." She snapped at the bodice of her housedress to cool off. "Terrible muggy, it is."

Candy got up. "One thing to say for those boxy motels you Yanks have," he said. "Telephones in the rooms."

Mrs. Sloan laughed. "I expect the exercise is good for you."

Candy smiled at her ruefully and headed down the stairs with her.

Hal and Emily sat in silence while the rain pelted the windows. He knew what Candy's call would be about.

"Call off the search?" he asked when the inspector returned.

Candy nodded. "Too much rain. But they did get some castings. And they picked up a few scraps of fabric. Looks like silk." He smiled hopefully, then walked over to the table and snapped his notebook shut. "If you think of anything else, give me a ring." He replaced the three ballpoint pens in his pocket, nodded, and lumbered toward the door.

"Inspector?"

Candy paused at the door.

"You said the description I gave you reminded you of someone. Who?"

"A murderer. Psychopath. I had a hand in arresting him."

"What was his name?" Hal asked.

Candy grinned crookedly. "No one knew. The chap wouldn't tell anyone, and he had no identification."

"A homeless guy."

"No, quite the contrary. He lived like a king. But he had no bank accounts, no credit cards, no driver's license."

"What about the place where he lived?" Hal asked, professionally curious.

"Rented. He signed the agreement with an X." Candy chuckled. "That's how the press referred to him during the trial: Mr. X."

"Wait a minute. Somebody must have known who he was. Neighbors . . ."

"Only the servants. Dozens of them."

"Well?"

"None of them would talk. Not a word. They all served time for contempt. Still, none of them cracked."

"He must have paid them well." Hal looked at Candy. The inspector was chewing the inside of his lip. "You want to tell me something?"

Candy shrugged. "What?"

"They were all Arabs, weren't they."

The inspector stared at him for a moment, then nodded. "I was told you were very good at your work. But you're wrong on this. The man's dead."

"How?"

"Fire. The sanitarium where Mr. X was serving a life sentence burned to the ground a month ago. His body was found."

"Who identified it?"

Candy smiled and shook his head. "He's dead, Mr. Woczniak."

"Hal. Who came for the body? The servants?"

"No one came," Candy said with a sigh. "The body was seven feet tall. It was found in Mr. X's cell in Maplebrook's basement. He was the only prisoner down there."

"Was there dental I.D.?" Hal persisted.

Candy frowned. He was thinking, Hal knew. The inspector

was beginning to doubt. "There must have been," he said, but his face was still troubled.

"Can you check?"

The two men stood face-to-face for a moment. "I'll check," Candy said finally.

# CHAPTER THIRTY-EIGHT

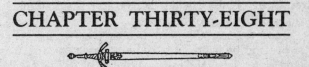

After Inspector Candy left, Hal led Emily downstairs to the small pub.

"A soda will do you good," he said, directing her toward one of the stools at the empty bar. They were the only customers in the place, and Mrs. Sloan was nowhere in sight.

Emily stared glassily ahead. The whole business of their flight from Chicago and the repeated attempts on her own and Arthur's lives had taken their toll on her even before this latest, most crushing blow. She had been a nervous wreck on the bus; now it seemed that whatever sanity she had managed to hang onto up until that morning had evaporated. She just sat, staring, like a porcelain doll made up to look like a schoolmarm.

Hal believed it would pass. He had seen people emerge from emotional stupors deeper than Emily's. His own had been worse, he realized, but he had come out of it only so he could crawl into a bottle.

He wanted a drink badly. Seeing the bottles lined up and sparkling in the now-opened cabinet was a lot more difficult than he would have thought possible during his I-can-quit-anytime days.

"Mrs. Sloan!" he called out at last. After another minute, the innkeeper leaned out through the kitchen door.

"Oh, my, and there you are," she exclaimed, wiping her hands on her apron. "I was just making tonight's soup."

"I'm sorry to bother you, but I wanted to give you back the keys to your car. Thank you."

"Think nothing of it." She took them and threw them into a battered metal cash box just below the liquor bottles. "Now, what can I get you to drink?" She lumbered behind the bar, filling the space like a battleship in a canal.

"I'll have a . . ." Hal stopped, unable to squeeze the words out of his mouth. "Maybe just a soft drink," he managed at last. "For both of us."

"Right you are." She went to a large locker at the end of the bar and brought out a bottle of grisly-looking orange liquid with a label Hal had never heard of. "Will this do?"

"Fine," Hal said.

"Have the police been of any help in finding the young one?"

"They're looking for him."

"It's truly sorry I am for you both," Mrs. Sloan said, and the plain, blunt features of her face showed that she meant it. "What a world."

"Yeah," Hal said.

Emily started to cry. She sat stock-still in front of her untouched drink, her arms dangling at her sides, sobbing quietly.

"Oh, now, I'm sorry, missus." The woman held out two cocktail napkins for her. When Emily made no move to take them, Mrs. Sloan thrust them under her nose and commanded, "Blow."

Emily obeyed, and the older woman wiped up her face. "But the little lad's going to be fine, you'll see. Why, didn't a Scotland Yard inspector come himself? If anyone can find him, they can."

Hal marveled at Mrs. Sloan's gentle authority. *I'll bet she's raised ten kids*, he thought.

She took another wad of napkins and forced them into Emily's hand. "The lady wouldn't be feeling so poorly if you hadn't had to put up with that fleabrain Nubbit first," she said with a trace of annoyance.

Hal smiled. "Funny. The constable seems very fond of you."

"Hah. Always begging for a free apple tart, that one is. My sainted husband had the misfortune to be born cousin to him, but I wouldn't set him out to track down a missing kitten."

"I don't know," Hal said. "I hear he's a great man when it comes to big cases like poisoned cows."

"Oh, he told you that, did he? His moment of glory. His one and only major crime. It happened ten years ago and he's still looking for the one that did the poisoning. And if you ask him about it, he gets all dark and official-looking and says, 'The case is still open. The investigation is still proceeding.'"

Her imitation was so good that Hal laughed out loud. To his surprise, Emily smiled, too.

Hal took a sip of his drink. It was ghastly. And warm.

"Oh, you'd be wanting ice," Mrs. Sloan said, gliding back toward the locker.

"No, it's all right. Mrs. Sloan, have you lived here long?"

"All my life. I was born right where Albert Carson's hardware store is, back when that whole part of the village was nothing but sheep farms."

"Have you ever heard of a psychiatric hospital named Maplebrook?"

"The asylum? Oh, yes. We called it the Towers around here. That was its name, you know, before it got fancied up. But it was still the same place inside." She shuddered. "A bad place."

"I heard it burned down."

"Aye. Never found who did it, neither."

"It was arson?"

"Whatever you want to call it. But it was no accident, and that's the truth."

"Who would want to burn down an insane asylum?"

Mrs. Sloan wiped a glass idly. "Ghosts, maybe," she said casually. Hal smiled in disbelief. She caught him. "Oh, you Yanks think you know so much, coming from your new country. That's because you haven't seen what we have. You haven't seen the castle rise up out of the morning mist, or heard the hoofbeats of the ghost horses as they ride."

"The castle?" Hal felt his heart skipping. "You've seen it?"

"As a girl. We all have, one time or another. It's been a while, though." She smiled. "It's like the fairies, they say. Once you stop believing in them, they won't come to you no more."

*I wouldn't bet on it*, Hal thought. "Is the asylum far from here?"

"Not more than twenty miles. There's not much left of the place, though, and good riddance, I say. Oops, I hear the soup boiling over." She turned and fled, with a certain rhinoceroid grace, into the kitchen.

Hal leaned across the bar and dumped the rest of his orange drink into the sink. He walked to the door. The rain seemed to be lessening and the skies appeared a little lighter.

"There," Mrs. Sloan said, flinging open the hinged door with a whack of her mighty hand. "Leek-and-potato soup. Will the two of you be staying for supper?"

"I think so. I'd like to take us out for a drive first, though. Is there a place around here where I could rent a car?"

"Oh, Wilson-on-Hamble's too small for that sort of thing. How far do you need to go?"

"Not very far," Hal said evasively. "Just a drive around the countryside."

"Well, use mine, then." She took the keys out of the cash box and tossed them over to Hal. "Just don't be getting into any more bother with it."

"No, I couldn't . . . not without paying you for your trouble, anyway."

She laughed. "Hell's bells, anything you could pay would be more than it's worth. Fill up the petrol when you bring it back. That'll be a bargain for both of us."

Hal picked up the keys. "It's a deal." He stood up, then helped Emily off her stool. She gave him a puzzled look but didn't ask where they were going. Hal didn't suppose she cared, really, as long as she wasn't alone. "Thank you," he called to Mrs. Sloan.

She was wiping the bar clean. "It's due south. Turn left out of the parking lot and follow the signs to Lymington," she said without looking up.

"I'm sorry?"

"Maplebrook," she said.

# CHAPTER THIRTY-NINE

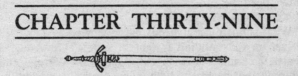

The small Morris Minor lugged heavily up a steep hill, seemed to gather power at the crest, and then went into a long glide down into a lush verdant valley. Then, to the left of the spot where the road leveled out in the glen, Hal saw the remains of Maplebrook Hospital, several hundred yards back from the roadway.

The damage to the old building had been extensive, even worse than he had anticipated. The roof had fallen in and three of the four outside walls had entirely collapsed. The interior of the one partly standing wall was a crazy quilt of scorch marks, broken-off stairs, and bits of flooring.

*No accidental fire can do this*, Hal thought. He wondered why Inspector Candy hadn't told him that the sanitarium had been destroyed by arson.

He slowed down at the bottom of the long hill, then pulled into a paved driveway past a small, discreet sign reading:

MAPLEBROOK HOSPITAL
ALL VISITORS AND PERSONNEL
MUST SHOW IDENTIFICATION
AT FRONT GATE

Candy had mentioned that the fire had occurred only about a month before, but already the driveway was grown over with the rough weedy grass that seemed always to thrive in

England's damp climate. The bald tires on Mrs. Sloan's car skidded a few times on the long, twisting drive up to the high wrought-iron fence with its abandoned gatehouse.

The gate was open now, flung wide for the fire engines and police and never closed. Hal didn't blame them. It was pretty obvious that there was nothing left of the place to vandalize. He drove on until the driveway was too torn up to negotiate, then stopped the car.

"We're here," he said.

"What is this place?" Emily asked slowly.

"Just an old building I want to snoop around in." He opened the trunk and took out a long coil of rope and a high-powered flashlight with a handle he'd bought in a hardware store on the way.

"What are they for?" Emily asked.

"Precautions," Hal said. "Don't worry. We're in no danger, believe me."

The driveway's blacktop was split into craze-lines, with big chunks of asphalt missing. Hal stooped down and picked up a piece. "The pavement exploded," he said. "This was one hell of a hot fire."

The pile of rubble surrounding the wall was massive, though not particularly interesting: pieces of roof slates, ceiling plaster, stone, chunks of timber beams. The police had undoubtedly gone through it all thoroughly for any personal items or office records. But Hal was not looking for anything so obvious.

He picked up a three-foot-long piece of charred wood and poked around in the debris, being careful about where he walked. There was a basement here someplace, and the floor hadn't entirely caved in on it. When the piece of wood sank through the rubble, he began to poke and kick until a man-sized hole opened up.

Next, he held one end of the wooden post and slammed it onto the ground as hard as he could. It stayed in one piece.

"This might do," he said. With a block of stone, he hammered it into the ground, then tied the rope around the post.

"Are you going down there?" Emily asked.

"Yup."

"Hal, no—"

"Just try to hold it in place for me while my weight's on it. Can you do that?"

She looked up at him. Then, hesitantly, she nodded.

"Good." He put his arm around her and gave her a squeeze. "You're doing better already, you know that?"

She went over to the post and braced it with both hands.

"Perfect." He tossed the rope down the hole. "I'm going down," he said. Then he put the handle of the flashlight between his teeth and lowered himself through the hole into the basement.

"I'm in," he shouted when his feet touched bottom.

It was cool here, almost cold. The air still reeked of smoke. He was not able to stand up straight, due to the twisted and burned wooden beams crisscrossing overhead. In the beam of the flashlight, he could see piles of plaster that had fallen in from the upper stories.

*What the hell am I doing?* he thought. *One sneeze and five floors' worth of crud is going to come down on my head.* He looked up, through the beams and shattered plaster, at the gray sky before going on into the labyrinthine waste of the basement.

He heard one of the timbers squeak as it rubbed against another. He shuddered and crouched low and tried to pick his way toward one of the interior walls that still remained in the subterranean structure. The wind was whistling through the debris that surrounded him, twisted, jagged, like a cage built by a madman.

He reached the wall. There was room to move along it. Timbers were propped against it, but there seemed to be some small passage possible if he stayed close to the ground.

His hand hit something metallic on the wall. When he shone the flashlight on it, he saw that he had touched an electrical outlet. The wall was white plaster, but there were black singe marks around the outlet. The plaster crumbled under his hand. With his fingertips he dug around the outlet.

The electric wires leading to the socket were burned but otherwise intact. Yet he could see that there had been some kind of flash fire inside the wall by the socket. He reached his hand far in and felt a dry crumbly substance, brought it out, and examined it in the flashlight beam.

It felt like dried putty, but when he touched his tongue to it there was the distinctive etherish taste of plastic explosive. He put the little pea-shaped piece of plastique in his pocket and continued down the wall.

He had to double up to get under one beam that was pressed against the wall, and when he struggled to get past it, he could feel the beam groan and slide an inch lower down.

*Get out of here, Hal*, a voice inside him commanded. He pushed it out of his mind. There was no way he was leaving now.

There was another electrical outlet some fifty feet beyond. Again, the metal fixture itself had blown loose from the wall into which it had been fastened. Another explosion.

*They've all been packed with plastique*, he realized. Every socket. That would be enough to bring down a structure as big as Maplebrook.

Someone had sabotaged the place. Someone with enough time to wire every wall socket in the building.

A few yards farther the passageway turned at a right angle. The ceiling here was a little higher and he could almost walk upright. But behind him, timbers creaked as they continued to settle. He didn't think that he could go back the way he had come without some beams working loose and crashing down on him.

*And it would only take one to cripple me and pin me here forever*, he thought.

Another timber shifted, closer, by its sound. Sheepishly, he remembered his fire-and-arson training at Quantico in which the instructors had relentlessly driven home the axiom that a building destroyed by fire never really finished falling down. For weeks and even months after the initial blaze, it kept crumbling in on itself. Only heavy equipment could finally level the thing so that the ruins stopped shifting by themselves.

As if the building had read his mind, a shower of plaster and cement poured down from the ceiling less than ten feet behind him. Immediately afterward, a big timber groaned and then gave way with a tremendous crash. Hal dived headfirst into the tunnel and crawled as an avalanche of debris spilled into the space.

*You flunk, Woczniak.*

Somewhere overhead, he heard Emily scream, but Hal could not respond. The cloud of dust created by the falling timber was so thick he could barely breathe. He squirmed along the stone floor on his belly, keeping the beam of the flashlight ahead of him even though his eyes were tearing and blinded.

While he was crawling, his wounded shoulder bumped against something hard. He gasped with the pain, then coughed violently. He wouldn't be able to stay down here much longer, he knew.

Then he trained the beam of his flashlight on the object he had crashed into. The dust was settling, and he could see the outlines of bars.

*Bars. A cell.*

Mr. X had been a prisoner on this floor. The only prisoner. Still keeping low, he hurried down the corridor, sweeping the light across each charred and empty cell, until he came upon one with its door open.

There he stopped. The cot in this cell had a sheet on it and a neatly folded blanket, burned black at one edge, at its foot.

*He was here.*

Hal studied the bare cell carefully with the flashlight. There were no pictures on the wall, no photos or letters, no cigarette butts, nothing to indicate that a human being had occupied this space. He checked the plumbing behind the toilet. Nothing had been taped there.

He shook his head. He had never seen a cell so clean, so utterly devoid of the personality of its occupant. Then he saw on the floor near the bed a series of dark stains. He knelt over them with the flashlight. They looked like drops of blood, dried black with time. On his knees he followed them to the door and beyond, into the corridor.

Hal sighed. So the man had died in here and had been carried out . . . *No, wait a minute.* Inspector Candy hadn't said anything about Mr. X dying of wounds. He had gone down in the fire, along with the rest of the inmates. From asphyxiation, most likely, judging from the relatively untouched condition of the basement cell.

Hal's mind worked frantically. In a panic, Mr. X might have banged his head against the bars . . . But there was only one trail of blood drops, and it led outside the cell. He followed them back inside. There were stains next to the bed, but not on the sheet. Then he picked up the hard pillow and turned it over. There was a large, stiff smear of blood almost coating one side.

It was puzzling. The trail was clear, from the corridor to the cell floor to the pillow. Yet Mr. X had not died of wounds. He followed the droplets of blood again. From the corridor into the cell . . .

Suddenly he whirled. Of course, he thought. Mr. X hadn't been carried from the cell to the corridor. It had been the other way around. *The bloodstains are leading from the outside in.* He knelt down to examine them again. There was a faint smear still visible through some of the dried blood droplets, and the smear extended in the direction of the cell.

Someone had dragged a bleeding man into the cell, waited for him to die, then turned the pillow over to conceal the blood.

But why hadn't they cleaned up the blood on the floor? Or replaced the pillow?

The answer came to him in a rolling wave: *Because they knew the fire was coming.*

And whoever had died in this cell, it wasn't Mr. X.

Hal strode to the bed and tore open the pillow. Balls of hardened foam spilled out. Then he stripped the sheet off the bed. He opened the rolled blanket and then lifted the thin mattress.

There was a book underneath it, resting on top of the flimsy springs.

Hal picked it up and fanned through the pages. No loose paper. From the card in the front pocket, it looked like a library book. It was written in a language he could not read. He stuck it in the waistband of his trousers and continued searching the room, but there was little else in the cell that could conceal anything. He wished he'd brought a knife to slit open the mattress but had to settle for a check of the seams. They appeared to be intact, and there were no hard lumps inside.

Just as he was finishing up, another rumble sounded from down the corridor. Hal looked over to see the dust rising from another section of fallen ceiling. After the heavy rain, the weight of the crumbled plaster, now soaked with water, was too much for the frail, fire-damaged structure to support. Before long it would all come down, and if Hal wasn't lucky, he was going to go down with it.

He left the cell and followed the corridor around another bend, only to find that it ended in what seemed to be an impenetrable barrier of rubble, twisted wood, plaster, lathwork, and sharp shards of roof slate. His way was blocked, but to his left, the rubble sloped up at a forty-five-degree grade. He could not see any sky at the end of the ramp, but if he got there he might be able to push his way out through the debris.

He dug into broken strips of plaster and slate and began to scramble up the incline. He seemed to slide back as far and as fast as he moved forward, and around him he could hear the creaking of boards and beams, sounding almost angry for having been disturbed.

Trying to swallow his panic, he climbed harder, digging his feet into the shifting debris to push himself upward. He could feel his fingers bleeding as he forced them into the loose rubble.

But he was moving forward. Moving upward.

And then he was at the top of the grade and could move no more. Something solid had closed the escape route.

He twisted his body around so that he was jammed into the

small area in a sitting position, supported by his back and his legs, then reached over his head and tried to work the obstruction loose.

It was a large section of plastered wall, and it was too heavy to move. He was trapped again.

He paused and took a deep breath.

*Not so damned fast.* He looked around and found a yard-long chunk of wood, possibly a broken two-by-four from a wall stud.

He held it with both hands and then began hammering upward on the plaster itself. First it creaked, sending choking powder down into his upturned face. He spat it out, squinted hard, and kept hammering at the plaster above his head.

Suddenly the wooden post broke through. The gray light of the cloudy sky dazzled Hal's sore eyes, which had adapted to the dark. "Emily!" he shouted.

"Hal?"

"I'm over here."

Before he could tell her to stay out of the way, her hands had reached through the hole and were clawing at the loose stones from the top.

"Watch it. You'll fall through."

"I'm not as stupid as you are, damn it!" she shouted.

Hal grinned. Her shock at Arthur's disappearance was giving way to anger. Good. People could live with anger. When they were good and mad at the world, they didn't shrivel up and die like worms in the sun. She was going to make it now, he knew. "Well, clear the area for a second, anyway, so I can loosen some more of this crap," he shouted up to her.

He hammered at the white sheet of the fallen wall until he chipped away another chunk. "All clear," he shouted, and Emily's hands once again appeared, bleeding but working frantically above him as he pulled the loose plaster down.

"Once more," he said.

Another voice answered him. "Hold on, Yank. Move clear if you can."

"Candy?"

The big Englishman responded with a grunt as he hoisted a huge piece of sheetrock and threw it like a giant discus onto the grass. Hal shielded his head with his arms while debris poured down on him. When it stopped, there was a hole big enough for him to drag his body through.

Emily threw her arms around him. "Thank God you're all right," she said.

Hal smiled. "I was just thinking the same thing about you."

"And I was thinking what a horse's arse you are," Candy said, slapping the dust from his suit.

Emily laughed. It was the first time Hal had ever heard her laugh.

It sounded beautiful.

# CHAPTER FORTY

The inspector was laughing too. "You look like Frosty the Snowman," he said.

"When did you get here?" Hal panted, trying to catch his breath.

"I arrived just in time to see you buried alive. Sorry I couldn't be of more help, but you didn't tell me you were going spelunking. I went back to the inn, but you'd gone. Fortunately, the perceptive Mrs. Sloan guessed your destination."

Hal saw that the door of Candy's Ford was wide open. The inspector had probably come at a dead run. Hal might have felt some semblance of gratitude toward the man if he weren't so annoyed with him.

"Why didn't you tell me the place had been sabotaged?" he said accusingly. He took the piece of plastique out of his pocket and slapped it into Candy's hand.

"What difference would that have made?"

"We might have known from the beginning who we were dealing with. This building was destroyed from inside. By an inmate. Your Mr. X never died in that fire." He told Candy about the bloodstains in the cell. "Someone carried a seven-foot-tall man into that cell and killed him there. What I can't understand is, why didn't anyone notice that the corpse had been shot or stabbed?"

"He wasn't," the inspector said. "He died of asphyxiation. According to the report, the body showed all the right signs."

"Then how did the blood get all over the pillow?"

Candy looked at the ground. "His teeth were broken."

"His teeth?"

Candy nodded. "After I left you, I called headquarters for a check on the body's morgue report. Seems all the fellow's teeth had been broken."

"To prevent an identification."

The inspector sighed. "I doubt if much effort had been made in that case, anyway," he said. "There was only one inmate in the basement, and he was seven feet tall. A seven-foot-tall body was recovered from the inmate's locked cell. That was probably enough, under the circumstances."

"No one noticed the blood leading into the cell?"

Candy shook his head. "The place was filled with smoke when the bodies were retrieved."

"And no one from Scotland Yard thought to go into the basement since the fire?" Hal asked angrily.

"We're not a national police force," Candy said evenly. "We only come into most cases when we are requested to. Apparently the local investigators on this case saw no need."

He had been careful, Hal noticed, to indicate that he himself had not been involved with that investigation. "Well, they should have seen the need," Hal said.

Candy looked ashamed, as if any lapse of judgment on the part of British people anywhere reflected poorly on his own reputation.

"I found this under his mattress," Hal said, handing Candy the book.

The inspector leafed through it, frowning in bewilderment. "It's from the library in Bournemouth. That's the nearest big city. But what the blazes is the language?"

"Urdu," Emily said.

Both men turned to her at once. They had nearly forgotten she was there. "I beg your pardon?" Candy said.

"Urdu," Emily repeated. "It's a dialect of Hindi, with an essentially identical grammar, although it's written from right to left in the Perso-Arabic script, whereas of course Hindi is written from left to right, in the Devanagari style—"

"Excuse me, Miss Blessing," Candy interrupted. "Can you read this?"

"I think so," Emily said. "It was one of the languages I studied in graduate school." She squinted at the title. "*Social Movements of the Punjab During the Late Nineteenth Century*. That's a rough translation."

Both men looked at each other. "It'll do," Candy said, handing the book to her.

"All right," Hal said. "Now that we're officially involved in this investigation, I'd like to see a picture of Mr. X. Do you have one?"

"We could arrange to get one. As to your being a part of the investigation . . . ."

"Would you rather deal with Constable Nubbit? Come on. I'm a civilian here, but you know I'm trained. I can help. And I'm going to be involved with you or without you. Wouldn't it make more sense for us to work together?"

Candy thought about it for a moment. "I suppose you make a case," he said finally.

"Good."

"As long as you remember who's in charge around here."

"You're the boss, Inspector."

Emily closed the book and looked up at both of them. "Just find Arthur," she said quietly.

Arthur awoke with the setting sun splashing into his eyes. A tall man as thin and angular as a spider was standing at the window, looking out.

The boy leaped up from the sofa, blinking wildly. The tall man turned, smiled, then turned back to the window. "English sunsets are lovely," he said.

"Who are you?" Arthur demanded.

"An old friend," Saladin said, touching the lace edge of the draperies. "No doubt you don't remember me."

Arthur ran for the door, but it was locked. "Why'd you bring me here? Where's Hal? Did you kill him too, the way you killed Mr. Taliesin?"

"Taliesin? Is that what the old fox is calling himself these days?" He laughed.

It occurred to Arthur that this madman who had grabbed him on horseback must have confused him with someone else. "Look. My name's Arthur Blessing. I'm from Chicago . . ."

"Yes, yes," Saladin said. "I know exactly who you are. Do you have to use the toilet? If you do, it's over there." He pointed to a corner of the large, elegantly appointed room. "If not, please calm yourself. I assure you there is no way for you to leave this room."

Arthur sat down. Suddenly his head seemed to be crammed painfully full of memories—the horsemen in the meadow, the shining sword that sliced through the old man's head, the bolt of lightning that washed everything in its dazzling light and seemed to sweep Taliesin away with it . . .

And before that, the other memories, the nightmare memories of the man in the bus and the others who had followed Arthur and Emily from Illinois.

All for the cup. Emily had wanted him to give it up, but he'd insisted on keeping it. And now the old man was dead, and Hal and Emily, too, for all he knew.

"I don't have it," he said quietly.

"Don't mumble, Arthur."

Arthur scowled at the remark, but spoke up clearly: "The cup. The metal ball. I don't have it."

"Yes, I'm aware of that. The man you refer to as Taliesin took it."

"He's dead," Arthur said angrily. "You guys killed him."

Saladin only smiled. "One doesn't kill a wizard, boy. Especially not that one. He'll be back."

"A wizard? Mr. Taliesin?"

"Cornflower," Saladin said.

"What?"

"The color of your eyes. I'd almost forgotten. They're cornflower blue." He sighed. "It's been so long."

"You're crazy," Arthur said.

Saladin sat down in a straight-backed chair opposite him. "I suppose it must seem that way. But you'll understand. We have some time."

"Some time before what?" he asked with as bad an attitude as he could muster.

The tall man shrugged. "I'd prefer not to talk about that just now, Arthur. Tell me, when did you meet this Mr. Taliesin?"

Arthur looked at him sideways. He didn't want to give the impression that he was willing to be friendly to the man who had kidnapped him.

"Long ago?" Saladin prodded.

"Yesterday," Arthur said sullenly. "On the bus."

"Ah. And did he remind you of anyone else?"

"No. Well—" Arthur waffled.

"Who?" Saladin leaned forward in his chair.

"Just Mr. Goldberg. Sometimes."

The tall man sank back into a slouch.

"He used to live in my building back in Riverside. He didn't really look like Mr. Taliesin, and he didn't talk like him either. But once in a while Mr. Taliesin reminded me of him. I don't know why. Mr. Goldberg was Jewish. I think he was born in Germany. . . ."

"I'm not interested in Mr. Goldberg," Saladin said acidly. "Was there nothing at all familiar about the old fool? Nothing that . . . called to you?"

Arthur frowned. "Why should he call to me? I just met him."

"Fascinating," Saladin said. "You're a completely new person. Yet you look exactly the same."

"The same as what?"

"The same as you were, you little twit! You don't have any idea who you were, do you?"

Arthur struggled to understand for a moment, then gave up. "Nuts," he muttered.

Outside, the sun settled into a warm red line on the horizon, nearly flat except for the rise of one hill on which a partial wall stood among piles of rock. Arthur's heart beat faster.

*The castle.* So the horsemen hadn't taken him far. If he could escape, he could walk to the castle, and from there he could find his way back to the inn.

The tall man went to the door and spoke to someone outside, in the hallway.

*He's got the room under guard*, Arthur thought. Escaping might not be so easy.

"Are you hungry?" Saladin asked.

"No," Arthur lied. He was ravenous.

Saladin laughed. "Perhaps you could force yourself."

"I wouldn't bet on it."

In another few minutes a servant appeared with a tray. Arthur was startled to see the man's eyes. They were the same as the tall man's. And then all the memories came into focus:

*All the men had had the same eyes.* All the men who had chased him and Emily, who had tried to kill them so often.

"What do you want from me?" he asked quietly.

"From you? Nothing." He had the servant uncover the tray. On it were a steak, a heap of french-fried potatoes, sliced tomatoes, a few stalks of green asparagus, a hard roll, a glass of milk, and an enormous piece of chocolate cake. "Please," Saladin said, gesturing toward the plate.

"I want to know why you've got me here."

"For the cup, of course. It belongs to me, and I intend to get it back."

"I told you, I don't have it. It disappeared with Mr. Taliesin."

"And it will reappear with him when he comes to trade it for you."

"What makes you so sure he's not dead?" Arthur asked.

"That would be difficult to explain just now. But take my word for it. He's alive. Do eat, Arthur. Keep up your strength."

Arthur smelled the aroma of the steaming steak. "I don't want it," he said.

Saladin smiled. "You always were stubborn. Very well." He rose and knocked on the door. Immediately the same servant appeared to remove the tray. Arthur felt like weeping to see it go, but he kept his face impassive.

"What if he doesn't come?" the boy asked. "I only met him yesterday . . ."

"And he may have figured out what the cup can do?" Saladin finished for him.

Reluctantly, Arthur nodded.

"Do you really know what it can do, Arthur?"

"It can heal wounds."

"And therefore . . ." He gestured for Arthur to continue.

*Therefore what?* "Whoever owns it won't ever get hurt."

"Or?"

"Or what? I don't know what you're getting at."

"Don't you? Don't you really?"

The boy only stared, puzzled.

"Come, Arthur." Saladin led him to a small table inlaid with an onyx–and–mother-of-pearl chessboard on which sat two armies of playing pieces, one silver and one deep gold. "Do you play?"

Arthur was silent for a moment. Then he pulled out a chair and sat down.

"I thought you might," Saladin said. He took the seat opposite the boy, on the gold side of the board.

"What happens if you don't get the cup back?" Arthur asked. He pushed a pawn forward.

Saladin countered his move. "I'll kill you," he said pleasantly.

# CHAPTER FORTY-ONE

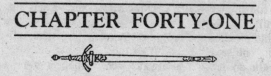

Hal dropped Emily off at the inn, where she could concentrate on the translation of the book, then followed Inspector Candy back to the constable's office. The team from Scotland Yard had set up its own headquarters, using both the office and a big unmarked van parked behind the station. In deference to Constable Nubbit, Candy's two assistants tried to do most of their work from the mobile unit.

Their names were Higgins and Chastain. Higgins was a young, scholarly type with shaggy hair, an aristocratic jaw, and big, unspeakably filthy glasses. Hal wondered how he could see anything through those nearly opaque lenses.

Chastain, on the other hand, was clean as a new kewpie doll. Well past the retirement age for regulation gumshoe detectives, he obviously held on to his job by being the best on-the-scene analyst on the force. He had the abstracted air of someone who'd had very little to do with the everyday world for a long, long time.

Neither seemed to Hal much like policemen. They hardly batted an eye when Candy announced that Mr. Woczniak, formerly of the FBI and the principal witness in the Blessing kidnapping case, would be working closely with them. Most cops Hal knew would have bristled and complained immediately that an outsider was going to mess with their work, but these two seemed beyond that.

Looking at their equipment, Hal could guess why. Most of the materials they worked with were too exotic for Hal to name, let alone discuss. These two were like creatures from another planet, content to observe the inanimate evidence of the sweating, suffering, dying species called human beings from the confines of their tiny technological cell.

They made Hal wonder at the changes in police work since he'd first entered the Bureau's training camp. But then, he thought, why not? The personnel in every other business was just as specialized these days. True, Higgins and Chastain didn't look as if they could hit the broad side of a barn with a stack of tommy guns between them, but the machines and chemicals and fine tools they used with such casual mastery would be far beyond the ken of most field investigators, including himself and probably Brian Candy.

While the inspector spoke on the phone with Metropolitan headquarters, Higgins handed Hal a heavy white object that looked like a postmodernist sculpture.

"Before the rain got to be too heavy, we were able to pull plaster hoofprints on two of the horses that were in that field," he said. His voice was so soft that Hal had to strain to hear him. He was probably keeping his voice down so as not to disturb his superior's telephone conversation, Hal knew; yet it seemed so natural for Higgins, as if he had spent his life in the rarified atmosphere of a mobile laboratory and rarely had to raise his voice to a normal speaking level.

Hal turned it over and was able to make out the imprint of a horseshoe.

Chastain, the older technician, did not even bother to speak. He just held another plaster casting in front of him with a look of quiet triumph on his face.

Hal smiled wanly. "Do these tell you much?" he asked finally, figuring that since his ignorance of their esoteric work was bound to come out sooner or later, there was no point in delaying the truth.

"Oh, yes," Chastain said, smiling avuncularly.

He did not seem inclined to continue. Fortunately, Higgins took up the slack. "We know that the print you're holding is from a very large horse, for one thing," he said in the near whisper that came so naturally to him. "Large but delicate, judging from the shallowness of the imprint and the spread of the hoof. Bred for sand. An Arabian, most likely. And the horse wasn't shod locally."

"How can you tell that?" Hal asked.

"From the heads of the nails," Higgins breathed. "We checked with the stables and the blacksmiths around here. It is common in this area to use rounded nails, you see. But if you look carefully, you'll find that the nail heads on that horseshoe are triangular." He raised an eyebrow in a significant manner.

Chastain did, too. The same eyebrow. Hal took that to mean that both casts evinced the same anomaly.

"And they came from different horses, I guess," Hal said. The older assistant frowned deeply and nodded.

"Nearly two millimeters' difference in size," Higgins explained, "along with variations in weight distribution."

"Different riders," Chastain enlarged.

"Ah. So if they weren't shod here, then where?"

"We have that on the wire," Higgins said. "If anybody in any department in Great Britain knows any blacksmith who shoes with that kind of nail, we'll have it."

Hal nodded. He hated to ask the obvious, but someone had to. "What if they weren't shod in Great Britain?"

Higgins only stared at him through a large thumbprint. Chastain shrugged.

"Right," Hal said. "I don't suppose anybody saw the horses coming through town?"

Chastain took the cast from Hal as he shook his head.

"No," Higgins said. "But we found tire tracks on the other side of the woods, near the first evidence of equine activity. The tracks belong to a truck with a probable weight of twelve thousand kilograms or more."

"Big enough for six horses," Hal said.

Chastain lowered his eyelids and nodded.

"But no imprints, unfortunately," Higgins continued. "We can conjecture about the weight of the vehicle because . . . well, because of a number of factors. But the rain washed away much of the imprint before we could cast it. We have photographs, however. They're developing now."

As if on cue, Chastain opened a small door resembling the entrance to the lavatory on an airplane, and emerged a moment later with a still-wet photograph of a tire track.

It was a large wheel, Hal could see that much, with a long scar running diagonally along it.

"I couldn't quite recognize the make of tire," Higgins apologized.

"Michelin," Chastain said, deftly relieving Hal of the photograph.

"Okay. It's a start. Has anyone sold any large amounts of hay or horse pills or whatever?"

Both men blinked. "Horse pills?" Higgins asked blankly.

"Well, they've got to eat, don't they?"

"Quite," Higgins said. "No, nothing of that nature."

"Horses eat grass in summer," Chastain suggested. It had been his longest sentence so far.

Inspector Candy saved Hal from further embarrassment by hanging up the phone. "Sorry, Hal," he said. "There's no match for the prints of the dead man on the bus. We've even checked with Interpol and Israeli intelligence, in case the bloke was a terrorist of some kind, but everyone's come up blank."

Hal sighed. "Then the guy had no history."

"And we never turned up the body of the old man, either."

"Who?"

"Taliesin. You said he was wounded when he ran into the woods after the horsemen."

"Oh. Yeah," Hal said.

"So he might still be alive."

*Oh, yes,* Hal thought. *Maybe not in any form that Frick and Frack could identify, but the old troublemaker is definitely alive somewhere.*

The question was where. The castle was gone. Just where did disembodied spirits go when the places they haunted vanished into the air?

"Care for some tea?" Candy asked.

Chastain smiled. Higgins had already lost interest in their visitor, and was looking through a microscope at a thread from a piece of muddy cloth.

"No. No, thanks," Hal said. "You seem to have done everything possible." It was hard not to sound disappointed.

The scientists, after all, had done an excellent job given what they'd had to work with. It had just been too damned little.

"The Maplebrook files will be here in a couple of hours," Candy said, understanding Hal's despair. "Maybe you'd like to come back then."

Hal nodded. "All right. I'll see how far Emily's come with the translation of that book. Thank you all for your information and time."

Candy nodded. Chastain didn't hear him. He was huddled beside Higgins. Through a wordless mixture of grunts, facial gestures, and written notes, they were marveling over the treasure beneath the microscope.

Hal left the van and drove Mrs. Sloan's Morris back to the inn. He walked through the door just in time to hear Emily screaming.

# CHAPTER FORTY-TWO

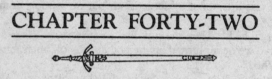

"Lord, what's wrong?" Mrs. Sloan leapt up from her stool behind the bar when the shrill scream filled the inn. "She just went up not one minute ago."

"Call Inspector Candy," Hal said as he ran up the stairs.

Emily was huddled in the far corner of the bed. Her face was wreathed in terror. "Someone was here," she said, her voice quavering.

Hal went to the open window. Careful not to touch the sill or frame, he leaned out and looked outside. It was night now, and he could see only the lower slate roof of the old inn building. The peak of that roof was just three feet below the window of Emily's room. But there was no sign of anybody on the roof. Whoever it was had probably slid down the steeply angled slate and then dropped the short ten feet to the ground below.

He listened carefully. In the distance, he heard the faraway drone of a motorcycle which gradually died away.

"I went downstairs to have some tea with Mrs. Sloan. When I got back, he was in the room. He threw me onto the bed. I thought he was going to kill me, but he just turned and jumped out the window."

"What'd he look like?"

"A lot like the man on the bus. They could have been brothers."

On the small writing desk where Candy had taken his notes, the library book lay facedown. Beside it was a postcard. Hal picked it up by its edges. It was a faded color photograph of an amusement park dominated by a Ferris wheel filled with people wearing dated clothes from the sixties. In the foreground, a man with sideburns and a woman wearing a french twist pushed a baby in a stroller toward a carousel.

*Every day's a holiday at Heatherwood!* read the caption at the bottom in red script. On the back, someone had written a message with a black fountain pen:

> *The boy is safe. Wait for my communication. When it comes, bring the cup.*

"What is it?" Emily said, walking up to the desk.

"Don't touch it. There may be prints. It's the ransom note. They'll trade Arthur for the cup."

Emily's shoulders slumped. "Where is it, Hal? Arthur always kept it with him. If he doesn't have it . . . We've got to go back to the castle and look."

"It's not there," Hal said.

Her face colored. "How can you be so sure?"

*Because I know where it is*, he thought. *It's in some other goddamned dimension with a vaporized sorcerer.*

But he couldn't tell her that. "I'll go tomorrow and look again," he said.

Emily was silent for a long moment. "They'll go through with the trade, won't they?" she asked. "I mean, they did send the note. If we can get the cup to them . . ."

Hal knew what she was getting at, but had no answer for her. "Sure, they'll trade," he said. "They don't have any reason to keep Arthur."

She chewed her lip and nodded. She wanted to believe that as much as Hal did. "I just wish . . ." She grimaced to keep herself from crying. "I wish I'd been better to him."

"Emily—"

"I always treated Arthur as if he were interrupting my life," she whispered. "But I wouldn't have had any life if it weren't for him. He was the only human warmth I ever knew, and I pushed him away, again and again . . ."

"Don't do this to yourself," Hal said, taking her hand. "The kid's tough. You've helped make him tough. He's going to come through this."

Candy knocked on the door, then strode in. "What's the trouble?" he asked.

Hal pointed at the postcard. "Emily had a visitor. He left that."

Candy picked it up carefully and read it. "Did he say anything?"

"No," Emily said. "He came through the window. I walked in on him."

"Did he try to harm you?"

"He knocked me onto the bed, but I think that was just to get me out of the way."

"She says he looked just like the dead man from yesterday," Hal said.

Candy nodded, reading the note through again. "What's this cup?"

Hal shrugged. "It's something Arthur brought with him from the States. A lucky piece." He described the hollow sphere. "From what he told me, it's made of some kind of weird metal."

"Weird? In what way?"

Emily looked up. "We don't know," she answered. "I did some laboratory tests on it. It wasn't anything I'd ever seen before."

"Would it be valuable?" Candy asked.

"If it were truly a new element, then yes, of course. It

would have immense scientific value. But I haven't run nearly enough tests to make a claim like that."

"Apparently someone thinks it's valuable enough to take the boy for it." Candy stared at them both, blowing air out of his nose like a bull. "Why didn't you tell me about this before?"

Neither answered.

"Well, where is it?"

"It disappeared," Hal said truthfully.

"Where did it disappear? In the meadow?"

Hal nodded. "Arthur might have dropped it."

"He might," Candy said. "It's unlikely that Higgins and Chastain would have missed such a thing during their search." He stepped back and fixed Hal and Emily with a terrible look. "Unless you've got the thing, and you're holding it back."

"No!" Emily screeched. "I wouldn't sell Arthur's life for a piece of metal!"

Candy's eyes left hers and settled like death on Hal's. "How about you, Yank? How many pieces of silver would you need?"

Hal clenched his jaw. The inspector knew he was lying about something, but Hal could no more tell him what had happened than he could tell Emily. Or anyone else. He barely believed it himself, and he had seen the bowl and the old man vanish with his own eyes. "I don't have it," he said.

The inspector nodded perfunctorily. Whatever good relationship they might have had, Hal knew, was now destroyed. Candy would not trust him any longer. "Any idea why he chose this card?" He held up the photo of the amusement park.

Hal shook his head. "It looks old. It might have just been lying around."

Candy grunted in agreement. He started to leave, then turned around and faced Emily. "How far have you gotten on the book?"

"I've skimmed almost halfway through. It seems to be a

treatise on the final days of English rule in the Punjab before
it became Pakistan. Pretty dry material, really."

"You find out anything about the book?" Hal asked.

Candy shrugged. "It *is* from Bournemouth."

"Who was it checked out to?"

"Actually, to the librarian himself," Candy said.

"And who is he? Did you talk to him?"

"I think you can leave that sort of thing to us, Mr.
Woczniak."

"Give me the name, all right?"

The inspector sighed at Hal's mixture of bullying and
pleading. Finally he opened his notebook. "Laghouat."

"What?"

"His name is Hamid Laghouat." He snapped the notebook
shut and held up one hand. "I know, he sounds like an Arab.
We're looking for him now."

"Looking? He's gone?"

"That's right. A few days before the fire."

"Where'd he go?"

"Left without a trace," Candy said.

He let himself out.

"Come on," Hal said, taking Emily's arm.

"Where are we going?"

"Downstairs, for dinner. There's no point in worrying on
an empty stomach."

He picked up the book and they made their way into the
pub. Mrs. Sloan flung her arms around Emily.

"There, I'm glad to see you've come to no harm," she
said. "I'll have a gate put over that window tomorrow."

"No need for that," Hal said. "Whoever it was just wanted
us to know they could get in. If there had been a gate, they'd
have found another way."

"Would you like another room, then, miss?"

Emily shook her head. "Thank you. I'll be fine."

"All right. Would you be wanting some soup?"

"Soup and anything else you've got," Hal said.

Mrs. Sloan laughed. "Right you are."

They sat down at a small table. Hal immediately started leafing through the book page by page, moving it to one side when Mrs. Sloan brought their meal.

"What are you looking for?" Emily asked.

"I don't know. But the guy might have left something. This was hidden under the mattress."

Emily rubbed her face with her hands. "If you're right, if Arthur's in the hands of an escaped mental patient . . ."

"If I'm right, then we've got someone to look for," he told Emily levelly. "It means we can catch him."

"But no one knows his name."

"Only 'Saladin'. That's what Taliesin called him."

"Do you think they knew each other?"

"Yes," Hal said. "I don't know how, but the old man definitely recognized him. He was afraid of him."

Emily shook her head. "That poor man," she said. "Whatever possessed him to run into the woods after six men on horseback?"

Hal didn't answer, and they both ate in silence.

"I don't think Saladin's his real name," Emily said suddenly.

"Why not?"

"Well, you said he was seven feet tall."

"So?"

"So the Saladin of history was seven feet tall. I think Mr. X is either just copying King Saladin, or has some serious delusions."

"Who's King Saladin?"

Emily drank her water delicately. "In the twelfth century, a Kurd named Saladin conquered Egypt for the Syrians, then put himself on the Egyptian throne and turned against them. He was a great ruler, from all accounts, but he had no loyalties. A man without a country."

"Sort of a free-lance pharaoh," Hal said.

"Right. There was no one else like him in history."

"I guess he'd stand out in a crowd."

"Actually, his height wasn't so unusual back then. The Persian nobility were all very tall. Darius, who fought Alexander the Great, was seven feet tall, too."

"What else do you know about Saladin?" Hal asked. "How did he die?"

Mrs. Sloan brought their soup, along with a basketful of hard rolls, and, incongruously, two oranges. "Hope this makes you feel a bit better," she said.

"I'm sure it will." Hal bit into one of the rolls. He hadn't realized just how hungry he was. He had to force himself not to swallow it whole.

"Natural causes, I think," Emily said with her mouth full.

"What?" Hal's mind had turned entirely toward his digestive activities.

"I think Saladin died of natural causes. I can look it up tomorrow if I can find a library or a good encyclopedia."

Hal nodded and opened the book again, but he couldn't bring himself to stop eating. When he took another bite of his roll, the pages of the book flipped closed, and he found himself staring at the pocket on the inside front cover. Suddenly he dropped the roll and opened the book again. "Look at this." He turned the book around so that she could read the pocket. "The date. The date the book was checked out."

"June the first," Emily read.

"Right. But that was *after* the asylum burned down." Emily looked at him in confusion. Hal turned his hands palm-up as if looking for an answer in them. "Why would this librarian, Laghouat or whatever his name was, put a wrong date on the book?"

He looked at it again, mumbling to himself. "June the first. June one. Six-one. *Six-one!* Page sixty-one."

She opened the book. Page 61 was covered with marks.

"They're just pencil dots," Emily said.

"They're marks. And they're deliberate. What are the words under the dots?"

Emily rummaged in her handbag for a piece of paper and a pen. "I wish I had an Urdu dictionary," she said.

"Well, frankly, I don't think we're going to find one in this pub. Just do the best you can."

She began to write, occasionally gazing off into space as a translation eluded her. Finally she put down the pen. "I might be mistaken," she said. "It doesn't make a lot of sense."

"What's it say?"

She pushed the piece of paper across the table toward Hal. "It says, 'All is in place.'"

The cop's instinct in Hal came boiling to the surface. The inmate had devised a plan for his escape which had involved destroying the building that held him and everyone inside it. This message was the equivalent of an all-systems-go signal.

"What's this on the bottom?" He squinted to read her crabbed handwriting.

"That's the part that doesn't make sense. It looks like, 'Bless your name.'"

# CHAPTER FORTY-THREE

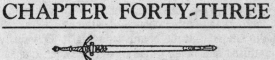

Saladin was winning the chess game. The boy had been a much more resourceful opponent than he had expected, but gradually, through the accretion of a number of tiny advantages, Saladin had gained a winning position and would soon finish Arthur off.

He looked away from the board as one of his men entered the sitting room and stood quietly inside the door, waiting.

"Yes?" Saladin said irritably. "Have you delivered the message?"

The servant bowed.

"Very well." Saladin nodded in dismissal.

"What message?" Arthur asked.

"That does not concern you." He glanced down at the chessboard. "You should concede. The game is over."

"It's not over yet," Arthur said. He was thirsty, but he would not give his captor the advantage of knowing it.

Saladin sighed. "I find nothing so tiresome as a mechanical endgame."

"I won't concede." Arthur hunched closer over the board so that Saladin could see only the red hair on the top of his head. Then he moved, sacrificing a bishop.

"That was stupid of you," Saladin said, quickly taking the piece.

Arthur said nothing. His next move was another sacrifice, then another. Saladin rolled his eyes. It was the mindless play of a tired and willful child. Without thinking, he captured each piece as it was offered until Arthur was left with only a queen and a king against ten of Saladin's pieces.

Suddenly Arthur moved his queen near Saladin's king and called, "Check."

The response was simple. All Saladin had to do was to capture the queen with his own queen to render Arthur's king defenseless. Naturally, if he did not capture Arthur's queen, if he simply moved his king away, Arthur would play queen-takes-queen with a chance of winning.

Saladin squinted at the board, studying it. Obviously the boy, confused and hungry, had missed the fact that Saladin could just take his queen. He moved his queen sideways, snapping Arthur's queen off the board with passionless contempt.

Then Arthur leaned back in his chair and folded his arms across his chest. "Stalemate," he said.

Saladin's eyes flashed back to the board.

It was true. Arthur's king was safe on the square he now occupied. But if he moved to any other square, he would be placing his king in jeopardy. That made the position a draw. Neither player could win.

"Stalemate," Saladin whispered incredulously. With a ten-year-old! It was not possible. He scanned the board, looking for a way out. There was none. "Incredible," he said.

"Next time I won't settle for a draw," the boy announced grandly.

Saladin looked over to Arthur in angry disbelief. The insolence of the pup! Nobody had spoken to him in such a manner in centuries. But Arthur met his eyes calmly, every inch the king he had once been, long ago in another life that the boy himself could not remember.

"You like to win," Saladin said.

Arthur said nothing. His young blue eyes held only amusement.

Saladin caught the look. The boy clearly loved the sweet taste of victory. Even the constrictions of his current situation could not frighten him away from it. And why not? He was a warrior, with the blood of battle running in his veins.

*Such a boy is worthy of you*, Saladin remarked to himself. *As a man, he might have been magnificent.*

He stood up. "It is late, and I have business to attend to," he said. "My servants will make up a bed for you here."

"I'm not sleepy."

"Ah, yes. That's understandable." He clapped twice, and the door opened. Saladin left for a moment, then returned with two large men who walked directly to Arthur and held him down.

"Get away from me!" the boy shouted. He kicked and squirmed, but Saladin paid no attention to him as he filled a syringe with clear liquid.

"No!" Arthur howled. He bit one of the men who held him.

"There's no need for such theatrics," Saladin said, easing the needle into Arthur's arm. "It's just something to make you sleep. You've had it before."

"I'll kill you!" Arthur shouted. "I swear I'll kill you!" He croaked out something else, but his lips were feeling blubbery and his limbs felt as if they were sinking through the floor.

"That's good, Arthur," Saladin said smoothly. "I dislike a spiritless child. You have possibilities."

They were the last words Arthur heard before he was enveloped in darkness again.

Upstairs at the inn, Hal made sure all of the windows in Emily's room were locked tight. "Don't let anyone in unless I'm with them," he said.

Emily was standing in the middle of the room, reading through page 61 of the book for the tenth time. " 'Bless your name,' " she mused. "I've gone over it again and again, and I don't think the translation's wrong. But why would someone write that?"

Hal shook his head. "We'll leave that to Candy and his assistants. It might be a code."

"You mean the Urdu words themselves might be a code for another message?"

"Could be. Or the English translation of them. Or the French translation, or Italian, or Swahili . . . We'd be wasting our time trying to figure it out. Let Candy have someone feed it into the computer at Scotland Yard."

"All right." She set down the book.

"Think you'll be able to get some sleep?" Hal asked.

"Yes, but . . . Don't leave yet, Hal." She turned away and sat on the edge of the bed.

"What's the matter?"

She shrugged tiredly and took off her glasses. "I just don't want to be alone yet." She looked up at him apologetically. "That is, if you don't mind."

Hal smiled. "I don't mind."

"I've been thinking about the cup." As she spoke, she pulled some pins out of her hair and shook it loose. To Hal's astonishment, it hung nearly to her waist.

*Why, she's gorgeous*, he thought. He had never met a woman who worked at making herself terrible-looking before. And yet, for some reason, that was what Emily did every day of her life.

"You look like a different person," he said.

"What? Oh." She blushed. "I'm just tired, I guess."

It was a strange comment, almost an apology. Hal guessed that she wasn't terribly familiar with receiving compliments. "What about the cup?" Hal prompted.

She sighed. "We left Chicago because some men came to get it. Arthur wasn't home at the time, but I was. They shot me and left me for dead. When Arthur came back, he accidentally touched me with the cup, and . . ."

"And you healed without a mark."

She blinked. "That's right."

"Arthur showed me what it can do."

Emily leaned forward on the bed. "But that's not *all* it can do." She pushed her hair away from her face. "Everything's happened so fast since the day we started running, I haven't had time to think. But when we started talking about the man named Saladin tonight, it sparked something in the back of my mind about the cup." She grimaced.

"Go ahead."

"It's going to sound crazy," she said, "but if it can reconstruct damaged tissues—heal wounds—then it can also prevent bacteria or other foreign matter from destroying normal cells. In other words, it can prevent disease. Doesn't that stand to reason?"

Hal nodded, realizing a moment before she spoke what she was going to say.

"So if the cup can heal wounds and prevent disease, whoever holds it will never be in anything other than a perfect physical state. He'll never age."

"Or die," Hal added quietly.

Emily bit her lip. "Is it conceivable?"

Hal didn't answer.

"The results of the lab tests I ran on it were unlike anything I'd ever seen. It cleaved in a curve. It showed no magnetic response. It's different from everything else on earth."

Slowly, her expression changed from excitement to grim fear. "Oh, God," she said. "No one knows about it. No one except for those men and us." Her eyes welled with tears. "They aren't going to let Arthur go," she said softly.

"We'll find him," Hal said. "Inspector Candy is close. His assistants have plenty—"

"Don't lie to me, Hal. The police don't have any idea where Arthur is. And it wouldn't matter if they did. Don't you see? To keep something as important as that cup a secret, they're going to have to kill Arthur. They're going to kill all of us, and Arthur will be first."

She was sobbing now, holding on to Hal for her life, but he

had nothing to give her. She was right, of course. He had known from the moment of Arthur's capture that the boy would never be released willingly.

Suddenly the image of the red-haired boy tied to the chair in the attic room of the house in Queens came into his mind. The red-haired boy, already dead, while the laughter of the maniac who had killed him still rang in Hal's ears.

Hal started to shake. Another child's death . . . another failure. . . .

*You were the best, kid.*

Hal stifled the scream that threatened to escape from him and held Emily, feeling as helpless as she did, wishing above all things that he had died in the hospital so that he would not have to face what lay ahead.

And then Emily's lips were on his, feverish and violent, her tears hot against his skin. "Don't think," she said in a ragged voice. "I don't want to think anymore."

She pulled him on top of her on the bed. "Make love to me, Hal. Please."

Her fingers fumbled awkwardly with his clothes. Emily was not an experienced seductress, Hal knew. But he also knew that somehow she needed him now, needed to have his body on hers and inside hers, as if that temporary union would make her entire shattered world whole again for a moment. And he needed that, too.

He opened her blouse and kissed her breasts. She arched backward, her white throat exposed, her long dark hair spilling wildly over the pillow.

He lost himself in her. He filled her with his flesh and touched her with his passion, and for that stolen time there was no fear, no guilt, no worry, no death. There was nothing but the raw sensation of pleasure and the release of something small but bright. Something almost like hope.

When it was over, Hal lay gasping, covered with sweat. Emily moved her hand to touch him, then retracted it and turned on her side, away from him. "I'm sorry," she said.

"Why?"

"Because we should have loved each other first."

Hal smiled. "It doesn't always happen that way," he said.

Her eyes glistened with tears. "We might have. At least I might have."

"There's time."

She shook her head, and the tears sheeted down her face. "No, there isn't. It's too late for us. Too late for everything."

She turned away. Hal leaned over her and kissed her cheek.

It didn't take long to get old, he thought.

Saladin sat in the darkness, waiting for his eyes to adjust to the lack of light. He had worked before like this, when he painted the tomb of the Pharaoh Ikhnaton. He had been little more than a child then, led blindfolded through the labyrinth of the pyramid with the other artists, then forced to remain inside the tomb with only candles for light and bread for food until the work was done.

How proud he had been to have been chosen! Ikhnaton himself had seen his work and selected him. Saladin had not known that his reward for painting the tomb would be death.

It had not happened quickly. First, the artists were given gold and other gifts for their work. Then, one by one, they disappeared into the desert, where the pharaoh's men buried them in the sand.

"It is the price of too much knowledge," one of the soldiers had told him sadly. And they had lowered him into the dry, shifting earth with his charm, the dun-colored cup, to protect him in the afterlife.

"Too much knowledge," he repeated quietly now. Arthur, too, had too much knowledge, and would die for it. The thought made Saladin morose. In four thousand years, he had seen only one human being return and he would have to kill that one.

He lit a match, and for an instant the large black rock beside him came into view, along with an array of paints and brushes at his feet.

*No, not just one.* Three people had come back, although Merlin hardly counted as a human being, then or now. A spirit who could vanish at will did not, in Saladin's opinion, constitute any sort of real man. Only Arthur and the other one were real.

Saladin had recognized him, of course. Stumbling around the meadow, trying to fight six armed men on horseback with his bare hands, the fool had announced who he was before Saladin ever saw his face.

And it was the same face, to be sure, albeit with a few more years on it. The knight who had so bravely—and stupidly—led Saladin to the cup had come again to champion his king.

Saladin had almost laughed aloud. Why him, of all people? He had been a failure in that life, as he doubtless was in this. Launcelot would have been a far better protector. He had been a better fighter, a better thinker, a better man all around. And yet Arthur—for Saladin felt sure that it had somehow been the king's own decision—had chosen Galahad as his champion.

The match burned his fingers. He dropped it, cursing, and its light went out.

*But then, Launcelot left him*, Saladin thought. Galahad would have followed Arthur into the fires of hell. Such had been the extent of the man's idiocy.

*For you, my king.*

Those had been the last words formed in Galahad's mind, and Saladin had heard them.

The knight had not spoken; the words were no more than a thought. But Saladin had read many of Galahad's thoughts by then.

It had been an inadvertent gift from Merlin, the ability to enter another man's mind. Of course, Saladin could not read everyone's thoughts, as Merlin could. The sorcerer's gift had been with him from birth. Saladin had practiced for years to develop his limited extrasensory faculties.

It had begun with Galahad. During the twelve years that Saladin followed the young knight in search of the cup, he had made Galahad the focus of his thoughts. He had studied him, concentrated on him, pictured him in his mind when

Galahad was not in sight, devoured him with his eyes when he came into view. He had discovered early that the two of them thought alike, but Saladin had made it his ambition to divine the man's actual thoughts as they occurred.

It was a worthless activity, perhaps. Saladin had often thought as much when, after years of trying, he could receive no mental messages whatever from the distant knight, who rarely spoke and always traveled alone. But twelve years pass slowly when one has neither home nor acquaintances. There were no books to read on his journey and few adventures to bring the pleasure of life to the surface. There was only the Quest, and the realization that each day he was growing older, and the enigmatic presence of the young knight who had vowed to spend the rest of his life searching for the Grail to bring to his king.

That was a lie, Saladin had decided after the first few years. No one would search so long for a treasure in order to turn it over to someone else. Once he was certain that Galahad's motive was greed, Saladin felt more comfortable about him. He warmed to him, in a way. And when he felt the first thought—a desire for water in a drought-stricken land— Saladin had nearly shouted in triumph.

There had been other times, although never as complete as that first powerful image of thirst: bits of thoughts, parts of pictures, the face of an old woman, a stained-glass window showing Christ on the cross. Until Galahad found the cup.

*For you, my king.*

Good God, he'd been serious, Saladin had thought with contempt. He hadn't wanted it for himself, after all. *Why, the whole journey's been a waste for the poor sod.*

And when he'd swung his sword to meet Galahad's neck, the knight's eyes had not even registered fear. They had shown only disappointment in his own failure.

*So he's brought you back with him*, Saladin thought as he lit another match. He touched it to the thick candle he'd brought with him. The flame burned steadily, without a flicker. Saladin gazed at it. *I can find you now. I've had sixteen centuries to practice.*

He brought the man's face into focus in his mind. The brown hair, the wide jaw, the beautiful features marred in this life by a scar and the ravages of too many misspent years. For this Galahad, too, had been on a quest of sorts, but without the advantage of knowing what it was he sought. More than likely, Saladin mused, the fool did not even realize that he had finally found it.

Saladin's mind ranged, searching, calling. *Hal. His name is Hal. He is a policeman. He wants to be drunk. He is in the arms of a woman. He is afraid. There was a boy with red hair* . . .

*You're the best, kid.*

Saladin smiled. By the light of the candle, he mixed some colors on a palette. Then, turning to the black rock, he began to paint.

Hal tiptoed out of Emily's room and drove the Morris to the site of the castle ruins.

The weather had cleared completely, and the moon shone bright as a lantern over the ancient stones.

"Merlin," Hal called.

His voice echoed off the mossy walls.

"Merlin, come here!" he shouted.

Nothing.

"How am I supposed to help him? I don't know where he is, for God's sake! I haven't got the cup to trade. I don't even have a gun!"

A bat swooped overhead. Nearby, a chorus of crickets began to sing all at once.

"Damn it, he'll die, can't you see that?" His voice cracked. "They'll kill him, and I don't know how to stop them!"

He sank down to the ground and sobbed. And all around him, there was no answer except the silence of the night.

# CHAPTER FORTY-FOUR

"The only fingerprints on the windows were yours," Inspector Candy said.

He stood in front of the door of the police van, squinting into the early morning sun. He did not invite Hal inside.

"Then the guy must have been wearing gloves," Hal said.

Candy shrugged noncommittally.

"How'd you get my prints?"

"We coated the plaster cast of the horse's hoofprint you were holding."

Hal sighed. So he was a suspect, too. Still, it was what he himself would have done in the same situation. "Good police work," he said.

Candy nodded. "Now, if you'll excuse us, Mr. Woczniak . . ."

"Look. I know you're pissed because we didn't mention the cup. But that doesn't really change anything about the case. The kid's still missing."

"We have cooperated fully with you," Candy said, his broad face reddening. "We didn't have to do that. It was a courtesy extended to a fellow professional. We expected your full cooperation in return."

"All right, all right. I'll level with you. I didn't mention the cup because I didn't think you'd believe me, and I knew you wouldn't allow me to help with the investigation if you thought I was a nutcase."

Candy softened somewhat. "Well, the business about a new metal does sound a bit farfetched."

*Not as farfetched as the whole truth*, Hal thought. "Besides, we didn't even know if it was a new metal or not. Miss Blessing only conducted a few tests on it. She made the assumption that it was valuable after people started trying to kill her and the boy."

"Why didn't they go to the authorities then?"

"What could the cops have done?" He answered himself. "Waited for the next attack, that's all. They were afraid. They ran."

"Then these men have been pursuing the Blessing woman and the boy since before the incident on the bus?"

"Long before, from what they've told me. Look, I'm sorry I didn't fill you in on the whole story before, but I only got it secondhand myself. Emily—Miss Blessing—isn't as wigged out as she was yesterday. She'll talk to you now. She's found some sort of code in the book from the sanitarium."

"Is she at the inn?"

Hal nodded, then extended his hand. "No hard feelings?"

Candy shook it. "I suppose not," he said grudgingly.

"Good. Now I'd like to see the file on Mr. X. Did it come?"

Candy smiled. "It came." He opened the door. "Please let Mr. Woczniak see the new file from headquarters," he instructed his assistants. Then he gestured for Hal to enter the van. "Be my guest," he said.

Higgins and Chastain were already absorbed in their work in the air-conditioned, windowless van. *Like moles who never see the sun*, Hal thought. Wordlessly, Chastain handed him the thick file and pointed to a small table where he could read it out of their way.

The first item in the file was a pencil sketch of Mr. X at his trial. "That's him," Hal said aloud. His voice sounded incredibly loud in the silent enclosure. "He's the guy I saw in the meadow. The leader of the horsemen."

Higgins came over, his eyes nearly invisible behind his smudged glasses. "Are you certain?" he whispered. "Perhaps you'd better see a photograph. There's one in here." He leafed through the papers in the file and extracted a glossy picture from near the back. It was a mug shot, showing the defendant from the front and both sides. Higgins placed it on top of the pile. "Is this the same man?"

Hal gasped. It was the same man, all right, but the detail of the photograph brought out something that he had not seen in either the pencil sketch or the face of the man in the meadow.

"What is it?" Higgins prompted nervously. Even Chastain had turned around to look.

"It's the eyes. The . . . eyes. . . ."

He had broken out in a sweat. The eyes were laughing, just as they had been laughing when the sword had come singing out of the air.

*Thank you*, the Saracen Knight had said. The silver chalice had tumbled off the altar of the abbey, and the tall stranger had caught it while blood poured over the shiny expanse of Hal's armor.

*For you, my king.*

And he had not even felt the pain of the sword, for the agony of his failure was greater.

*I knew that you, of all the High King's lackeys, would find it.*

And the dark knight's eyes shone with laughter. Like two evil lights in the darkness, they followed Hal into the spinning void, triumphant and mocking.

*My king . . .*

*My king . . .*

Higgins was holding a glass of water to his lips. Chastain had picked up the file, afraid that Hal might damage it with the perspiration that poured off his face.

"Perhaps you'd like to get some air," Higgins suggested. Clearly, neither of them wanted a sick man in their domain. Chastain was already holding a sheet of filter paper to his mouth and nose, defending himself against microbes.

"I'm all right," Hal said. He drank the water. "Give me the file."

Reluctantly, Chastain handed it back to him. The two men stood side by side, watching their visitor.

"Don't you two have something to do?" Hal snapped.

With an unspoken dialogue of wiggling eyebrows, flaring nostrils, and lip twitches, the two analysts went back to their work.

Hal, still shaking, forced his mind away from the image of the man in the photograph and read the file on the unnamed man who had created works of art out of the bodies of people he'd murdered. When he finished, he closed the file and ran his hand over his sweat-slick face. There was only one thought in his mind then:

*Oh, Christ, he's got Arthur.*

Candy was just leaving the inn when Hal got back. He was carrying the book Emily had translated. "Well?" he asked.

"He's the same man," Hal said. "I think he engineered the fire at Maplebrook."

Candy looked abashed. "I've put in a request for exhumation of the body found in his cell."

"He was a plant."

Candy nodded.

"What do we do now?"

"Give the cup to the kidnappers."

"I told you, we haven't got the cup."

"Then find it," Candy said acidly. "Or something like it. That's all we can do at this point. We'll make an arrest at the time of the trade."

"You and who else? Constable Nubbit? Or are you counting on Tweedledum and Tweedledee to wrestle that maniac to the ground?"

"I'm calling for reinforcements. We'll have plenty of men on hand."

Hal thought for a moment. "He'll expect that," he said.

"Perhaps. But it's still our best possibility."

Hal tried to fight off the feeling of despair that was beginning to envelop him. Anyone who could carry off an operation the size of the Maplebrook explosion could get around a handful of cops, he knew. It wasn't hard to kill a ten-year-old boy.

"We'll try to find them before it comes to that," Candy said.

"Yeah. Okay." Hal turned away from the inspector and stumbled into the inn. There had to be something he could do, some place he could look . . .

"Hal."

It was Emily. She was dressed in a yellow sundress. Her long hair was pulled back in a ribbon. She wore lipstick. Despite his agitation, Hal smiled at the change. "How'd you make out with the inspector?" he asked.

"I didn't tell him my theory about the ball making you live forever."

"Good."

"But I believe it more than ever. I went to the little town library this morning."

"Alone?" Hal asked. "Look, I've told you—"

"We're running out of time, Hal. I can't keep myself locked up in that room so I'll be safe while Arthur's life is in danger."

"All right," Hal conceded. "So what'd you find?"

"A history of Saladin."

"The king who wanted to be pharaoh."

"Right. You know, that's strange in itself," she said, her eyes wandering in thought. "For a Persian to become a *pharaoh*, as if ancient Egypt were somehow familiar to him . . ."

"What are you getting at?" Hal asked, a little irritably. He didn't want to spend the day in idle conversation, even with Emily.

"I'm getting at how he died," she said. "Or rather, how he was supposed to have died. It was all very mysterious."

"How's that? I thought you said he died of natural causes."

"He did. At the age of fifty-five."

"Seems kind of young," Hal said. "Which natural causes?"

She shrugged. "That's the mysterious part. There didn't seem to be any symptoms to his illness. What's even stranger is that everyone at his deathbed said he looked thirty years younger, at that. Now, most people who are dying look a lot older than they are. But Saladin appeared to be in the bloom of health when he was carried to his crypt."

They sat in silence for a while. "What are you saying?" Hal asked at last. "That you don't think he died?"

"That's exactly what I'm saying. A man who never ages is going to create suspicion sooner or later. I think that after three decades of rule, Saladin just looked too young for his age. So rather than let the secret of the cup be known, he decided to stage his own death."

"He gave up the throne . . . just like that?"

"Why not? If I'm right about the cup, he had something of much greater value."

Hal considered it. "I'm glad you decided not to tell Candy," he said.

"He wouldn't understand. But it makes everything fall into place. 'Bless your name.' Get it? It's the way someone would address a king."

Hal had to admit that she made sense, even though the concept of eternal life through the powers of a metal ball didn't. Still, very little of what had happened in the past two weeks had made much sense. Taliesin's appearance and disappearance, the apparition of the castle in the meadow, his own inexplicable sojourns into the memories of another man . . . None of it could be filed away in a drawer at Scotland Yard.

But one thing was real: Arthur was being held captive by a known murderer, and Hal had to get him back.

"Brought you two a pot of tea," Mrs. Sloan said, placing two cups in front of them.

"Thank you," Hal said. "And thanks for the use of your car."

"Oh, that's no problem," the woman said. "You might want to go see the fair, if you've got the time. It's just opening today, down at the grounds near the old amusement park."

"No, I don't think—" Emily began.

"What did you say?" Hal interrupted.

"About the fair?"

"The amusement park."

"Well, it's not much anymore," Mrs. Sloan said. "Been abandoned since 1971, when the owner run off somewheres with the butcher's daughter, and her only fourteen." She clucked disapprovingly. "The village sold off the rides and things to pay for taxes, but no one ever did get around to clearing off the site. An eyesore, that's what it is. But it turns out the place is smack in the middle between Dorset and Somerset counties, and neither one is willing to go to the trouble to clean it up. He had no kin, don't you know. The counties has been arguing about it for years."

"Was it named Heatherwood?"

"Heatherwood, that's right. I used to take my boys there when they was lads."

"Where is it?"

She told him. "But don't expect to find much," she cautioned.

He stood up. "Sorry about the tea, Mrs. Sloan. Let's go."

"Hal!" Emily called, trying to keep pace with Hal as he bolted for the door.

The motor in the Morris was already running when she caught up with him. "What was that about?"

He pulled out of the driveway. "The ransom note. It was written on an old postcard from an amusement park."

"Oh, my God. Do you think that's where they've got Arthur?"

Hal didn't answer, but he knew as soon as he saw the place that Arthur wasn't there. The grounds were accessible by three major roads, for one thing. For another, the fairgrounds were only a few hundred yards away. There was no way to hide either horses or people in the scattered, tumbledown buildings that remained.

They got out and walked toward the wreckage. The ground was deeply pitted where the rides had been pulled out like bad teeth. There was still a partial track of a kid's roller coaster rusting in the sun and the plywood silhouette of a clown rising above what used to be a funhouse.

"You can tell we're not in America," Hal said.

"Why's that?"

"Because this place closed over twenty years ago, and it's still standing. Back home, the vandals would have eaten every board by now."

"All I can tell is that you're from New York," Emily said, but Hal didn't hear her. He was looking up at the clown sign. At its base, in faded letters above the entrance to the funhouse, were the words:

## SPOOK-O-RAMA

### JOURNEY INTO DARKNESS

It was sinister-looking. There was something about the combination of clowns and evil that had always given Hal the shivers. It affected everyone the same way, he supposed; that was why so many horror movies had clowns in them.

*Saladin is taking the boy to a place of darkness. A place fearful to you. A place you will remember.*

The old man's words came back to him with a jolt. A place fearful to him? Perhaps. But he had no memory of this amusement park.

Unless it was the memory of the picture on the postcard. Could that have been the reference?

"I'm going in," Hal said.

"This place doesn't look much more sturdy than the sanitarium," Emily said apprehensively.

"You're not coming. Wait in the car."

"What if the roof falls in on you this time?"

"Then drive to the fairgrounds."

"For help?"

"No. Buy yourself a cotton candy." He kissed the end of her nose.

He walked her back to the car, took his flashlight from the glove compartment, and gave her neck a squeeze.

"Hal?" Emily was blushing. "I'm glad things aren't too awkward between us . . . because of last night," she said.

He touched her hair. He wanted to tell her how happy he

had felt to see her face in the morning, how long it had been since he'd felt comfortable in the presence of a woman. But he remembered how she had cried out in misery after their moment of love. It was too late for her, she had said. Too late for them.

And so perhaps it was. "I'm glad it happened," he said softly. He could smell the clean scent of her hair. "You're very beautiful."

She looked at the ground.

"I'll be back in a minute," he said. As he turned to enter the funhouse, he could still smell her.

# CHAPTER FORTY-FIVE

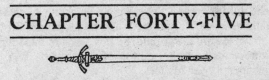

*A place of darkness*, Hal thought. Well, the Spook-O-Rama certainly qualified as that. Despite the deterioration of the building, no light at all got through.

Or air, it seemed. It was as hot as an oven inside. Hal reached up and banged on the low arched ceiling with his flashlight. The tunnel-like structure reverberated with a hollow, metallic din. Corrugated aluminum. No wonder it was so hot. During the years of the park's operation, the funhouse had probably been reasonably well ventilated, with fans blowing through ductwork, but the fans had no doubt been sold off when the place closed down.

He poked through a thick mass of cobwebs and picked up the edge of a cardboard skeleton painted Day-Glo green. It had been attached to a retractable spring by wire, but the wire had long since rusted away. Now the skeleton lay flat, in pieces, its bloodshot eyeballs furry with dust.

His feet touched something soft. The old walking-over-the-dead-body sensation, he remembered with a feeling of youthful nostalgia. At this point, if the electricity were turned on, a lever beneath the row of foam corpses would trigger a deafening noise and the sudden appearance of several garishly illuminated tombstones. This was where the girl you were with worked herself up to an almost authentic-sounding scream. It was the signal that you were allowed to put your arm around her, as long as you didn't grab her tits. There was definitely no tit-grabbing in the funhouse. That had to wait for the Tunnel of Love, although he had never actually seen an amusement called the Tunnel of Love. They were given names like Sinbad's Journey or Dream Ship, but they served the purpose: You rode on a conveyor belt covered with plastic and two inches of water, and got out with an erection that could knock over a telephone pole.

At the third "corpse," there was a wild chorus of chattering squeals that made Hal jump. When he jerked the flashlight beam down toward the ground, he saw a nest of rats scurrying in all directions from the comfort of the foam stuffing. A fat one scampered over his feet.

He recoiled in distaste, and considered turning back. Arthur wasn't here. Anyone who had come earlier would have frightened off the rats. He looked back briefly. Then outside, from ahead, not behind, he heard the sputter of a motorcycle, which told him that he had gone more than halfway through the Spook-O-Rama. He decided to head for the exit.

He hopped over the rat-infested cushion and walked quickly, scanning both sides of the twisting tunnel with the light. *Nothing*, he thought. He tried to remind himself that the picture on the postcard had been a dim lead at best from the beginning.

The rotten part of it was, it was the *only* lead. And it had led nowhere. How much time did he have left? How much did Arthur have? Was the boy's life being measured out in days now, or hours? Or minutes? Or was he already dead?

He was walking so quickly that he almost missed it. A painting on the wall, bright colors and the sort of realism one didn't usually find in funhouses. It was more like a portrait a

family would hang in their living room, the portrait of a kid
with red hair. . . .

The round circle of light stopped dead on the boy's face. It
was Arthur's, unmistakably, perfectly captured, down to the
pale blue eyes and the scattering of freckles over the nose.
The painting itself was exquisite, museum quality, but there
was something terribly unsettling about it.

The eyes, Hal decided. Something was wrong with the
eyes. They had no animation in them, no life, almost as if the
subject were . . .

Hal sucked in his breath. The boy in the painting was
seated in a wooden ladder-back chair. Only the top corner of
the chair was visible. Hal had seen that. What he hadn't
noticed until now were the ropes that seemed to grow out of
the bottom of the painting. The kid was tied to the chair.

(*A ladder-back, had it been a wooden chair up there in that
attic room oh Jeff oh no oh God . . .*)

He knew it had been. And the background of the painting,
those lovely unobtrusive gray curls, were smoke, because the
place was on fire, Jesus Jesus, and Arthur's eyes were
funny-looking because they were *dead*, just like Jeff
Brown's. . . .

Unconsciously, Hal had backed away from the painting
until he hit the far wall. He gasped, dropping the flashlight.

*No, no, leave me alone, oh help me, no*

And then he heard the gunshot outside, and his fear
exploded. Emily was in the car. Hal started running toward
the exit with the instinct of a policeman.

Two more shots had fired by the time Hal got out of the
funhouse. Between them, he could hear Emily's terrified
shrieks.

*She's still alive*. It was the only thought that registered in
Hal's mind as he barreled through the dark tunnel. When he
finally emerged, the gunman was circling the car on his
motorcycle, firing randomly through the windshield. He saw
Hal, took one shot at his feet, then sped away.

Hal memorized the license number of the motorcycle as he

ran toward Emily. She was crouched on the floor of the
Morris, her hands covering her face, screaming wildly.

"Emily, he's gone. Emily!" He grabbed her by her
shoulders and shook her. "It's Hal. Listen to me, Emily!"

Gradually her screaming subsided, and Hal was able to pry
her hands away from her face.

"He was trying to kill me," she rasped hoarsely.

Hal looked at the starred windshield. Four shots had been
fired at nearly point-blank range, and not one of them had
struck her. "No, he wasn't," Hal said. "That was just a scare
tactic."

"Well, it worked," she said as she unfolded herself out of
the car.

From the fairgrounds, several people were running toward
the source of the gunshots. "Get back in," Hal said, "or we'll
be stuck here for hours dealing with Constable Nubbit. I want
to get to Candy with this."

He started the engine. The car ran perfectly well, despite
the apparent damage. He pressed on the network of fine white
lines which was now the windshield, and it gave way.

They drove back to the village amid a sea of pebble-sized
bits of glass, and went straight to the Scotland Yard van.

"Damn it all, I knew it was a mistake letting you in on
things," the inspector said. "You could have both been
killed."

"He wasn't trying to kill anyone," Hal explained. He told
the story of his discovery in the Spook-O-Rama.

"You're sure it was a painting of Arthur?"

"Absolutely sure."

"And he was dead, you say." Candy spoke quietly, so that
Emily could not hear him.

Hal tightened his lips.

"If it's the same man I arrested four years ago, he's an
artist as well as a killer," Candy said. "We've got to accept
the possibility that—"

"He wasn't drawing Arthur," Hal blurted.

"I thought you said—"

"The face was Arthur's. The rest of it was . . ." *What? A*

*memory of mine? A nightmare I've been having for the past
year?*

"What is it?"

Hal took a deep breath. "The chair, the ropes, the
fire . . . That happened before, in another case I handled.
The last case." He spoke in a monotone about the abduction
and murder of Jeff Brown.

"So you think Arthur's kidnappers know something about
you," Candy said, trying not to let his voice betray the pity
he felt for the ex-FBI man.

"Could be."

"Is it possible we've been hunting the wrong fox?" Candy
asked. "Perhaps this Brown boy's kidnapper is involved?"

"No," Hal said. "He's dead. Blew himself up with a
grenade."

"An associate of his, perhaps?"

Hal shrugged.

*A mind reader. A man who's lived forever, who has the
power to do anything on earth he likes.*

"I'll see if I can find anything," Candy said.

"There isn't time. Saladin's going to come for the cup
soon. And I haven't got it."

"That won't matter," Candy said.

Hal knew what he meant. If the kidnappers weren't
stopped before the trade, Arthur would be killed, cup or no
cup.

"What about your reinforcements?" Hal asked.

"Headquarters thinks it's better to work with the local
authorities on this."

Hal groaned in disbelief and dismay. "Are you kidding
me? You're going to leave this operation to the likes of
Constable Nubbit?"

"They haven't left the country with the boy," Candy
explained. "They haven't even left Dorset County, as far as
we know. The locals know the area better than a team from
London, and we can get more of them on short notice." He
patted Hal's shoulder. "Don't worry. I'll be in charge, and

you'll be with me. The bobbies will only be present as a show of manpower."

"When are they coming?"

"I'll send the signal when you get the final ransom note. They're prepared. We'll have fifty uniformed men around the site within twenty minutes."

Hal sighed. "All right," he said begrudgingly.

"Take the lady back to the inn," Candy said. "And tell her to stay there. The kidnappers may be trying to contact her."

Hal nodded. "How soon will you have a make on the driver of the motorcycle?"

"We've got it," Higgins whispered, pulling a sheet of paper out of the FAX machine. "When you gave it to us, I took the liberty of feeding it into the computer at headquarters immediately. It just came in. The fellow's name is Hafiz Chagla."

"The name mean anything to you?"

Chastain shrugged elaborately. "It's just a name," he said. "But I also asked the computer to cross-reference the name with any known personal data. That's coming through now."

Hal and Candy waited as Higgins took the second sheet out of the machine. "Address, 22 Abelard Street, Wilson-on-Hamble," he read. "Occupation, electrician. . . ." He looked at Chastain before continuing. "Maplebrook Hospital, Lymington."

"I'll check out the address," Hal said.

"You most certainly will not. If you'd like to help, you can do it in the municipal building."

"Do what?"

"Find out who owns the building at 22 Abelard Street."

For the first time in two days, Hal felt some semblance of relief. Candy knew what he was doing.

"On my way, Chief," Hal said.

# CHAPTER FORTY-SIX

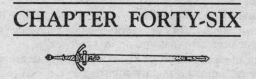

Wilson-on-Hamble, as it turned out, had no municipal building. In fact, the tax collector, village clerk, and building inspector were all the same person—a seventy-year-old woman named Matilda Grimes who had lived in Wilson-on-Hamble all her life and ran the village's very modest affairs from a table in her parlor.

When Hal found her, she was busy cooking some kind of gruel in her kitchen. She invited Hal to stay for lunch, but he declined, saying his business was urgent.

"Urgent, you say? Then you'd better go fetch the books yourself. I can't let the rennet burn." She led the way into the short hallway between two bedrooms, both of which were adorned with dolls wearing voluminous crocheted dresses, and pulled down a rickety ladder from the ceiling. "They'd be up there, marked by year," she said.

Hal thanked her and climbed up into the attic. They were all up there, deeds, tax records, every transaction recorded in the village since the early 1850s. He brought down as many as he could carry and prepared for a long session with the books, but Miss Grimes knew the place he was looking for.

"Abelard Street? Oh, my, yes. That place has been turned over a dozen times in the past ten years. And never at any profit, from what I hear. It just passes from one to another." She poured the custard into little bowls and set them carefully inside a tiny cube of a refrigerator.

"Has it gone to anyone you know?"

She shook her head emphatically. "Foreigners, all of them. England's a mecca for them, you know," she added in a conspiratorial whisper. "It's mostly London, of course, but they get in everywhere."

"Who?"

"Why, the Eastern fellows," she said primly.

"Arabs?"

She nodded, her lips pursed. "Now, I'm sure they're fine individuals, even if they are black. We don't have the sort of racial problems here that you do in America."

"No, I'm sure you don't," Hal said, trying to be agreeable, even though he had difficulty adjusting to the idea of Arabs as black people.

"But one does have to wonder about a place like Wilson-on-Hamble being sold over to foreign interests."

"Who owns the house, Miss Grimes?"

She put on a pair of glasses with outlandishly jutting rims and leafed expertly through the pages of one of the books. Hal almost laughed aloud. If a rock star wore those glasses, they would be the height of radical fashion.

"Here we are. Mustafa Aziz."

"Aziz?" Hal asked, disappointed. "Not Chagla?"

"Chagla? Oh, no."

"But I understand that a man named Hafiz Chagla lives there."

"He might," Matilda said. "It's an apartment building."

"Oh," Hal said.

"This Aziz person just bought it six months ago."

"Who from?"

She flipped the page. "Vinod Abad," she said flatly. "See what I mean?"

"I don't know. Who owned it before that?"

She thumbed the page. "Oh, it lasted four years under this owner. Must have fallen in love with the place."

"What was his name?"

Matilda squinted at the page. "Laghouat," she pronounced with difficulty. "My, that's a strange one, even for them."

"La Goo?"

"Hamid Laghouat. I'm giving it the French pronunciation. There." She pointed it out in the registry.

"Hamid Laghouat," Hal repeated, trying to remember why the name struck a chord. "Christ. The librarian," he said suddenly. Hamid Laghouat was the name of the man who had checked out the Urdu book for the sanitarium.

"I do not much care for profanity, Mr. . . ."

"Woczniak," Hal said. "Sorry."

"Woczniak? What kind of name is that?"

"I don't know. My parents changed it. Do you have an address for this. Laghouat?"

She looked at him sourly, then bent over the page. "A postal box in London."

"That figures," Hal said. "What other property does he own around here?"

"Well, I'd have to look in another book for that." It was clear from her tone of voice that Miss Grimes did not wish to do that.

"Please," Hal said, trying hard to be ingratiating. "It's very important. Police business."

The old woman sniffed disdainfully but rummaged through the pile of books until she found what he wanted. "You're going to have to put all these back, you know."

"I understand," Hal said.

"Well, here's some property under that name. It adjoins the old amusement park."

Hal closed his eyes. He had struck gold. "Are there any buildings on it?"

"Yes, a residence . . . Oh, I know the one." She looked up from the book. "An eighteenth-century manor house. It was a lovely estate back when I was a girl. A couple from London owned it. Members of the nobility." She nodded approvingly. "They used it as a summer residence."

"Does anybody live there now?"

"Oh, my, I would doubt that very much. The Londoners stopped coming back in the forties, during the war. It's been empty since then."

She found her place in the registry. "You see? It belonged to the same owner for forty-six years before this Laghouat fellow bought it. He's a librarian, you said?"

"He was. In Bournemouth. I think he's gone now."

"Odd. I never heard the name before. It would seem that

anyone with enough money to buy all this property wouldn't be completely unknown in this area. But then, I don't know everyone."

"But nearly everyone," Hal guessed.

"Most, I imagine," she answered truthfully. "And what would he be doing working as a librarian?"

"I doubt if he's the real owner."

"Well, he's the *legal* owner," Miss Grimes said pedantically. "If your name's on the paper, the property's yours."

*And if old Hamid makes a move without Saladin's approval, he turns into a statue with an axe in it*, Hal thought. "So the place is abandoned?"

"Probably. You see, it's a very unusual piece of property because it has no road access. It was built back in the days when everyone went about in carriages. But when the house stood vacant for a long time, the road—well, a driveway is what you'd call it, but it's very long, nearly a mile—it just grew over. Now you can't even see it. Or the house itself, for all the weeds." She moved her glasses down onto the end of her nose. "If someone's living there, they don't take very good care of the grounds."

"Can you show me on the map where the road used to be that led to the house?"

She drew an imaginary line with her finger. "It was right here, right behind the amusement park, through these woods," she said. "Of course, the house was here long before the park. The land Heatherwood was built on used to belong to the estate."

"Thank you, Miss Grimes," Hal said, getting up. "I'll put the books back now."

"See that you make a decent job of it," she said, padding back into the kitchen.

# CHAPTER FORTY-SEVEN

Arthur awakened late. The big Victorian room was already warm and close with the summer heat. His eyes were crusted with matter, and his tongue felt too big for his mouth, the way it sometimes got when he was younger and had to take medicine for an ear infection.

It had to be the drugs, he thought, stumbling toward the lavatory. The giant had injected him twice in one day. He ran the cold water in the sink over his head, then drank deeply from his cupped hands. It diminished his thirst somewhat, but the cotton-tongue feeling remained.

When he was finished, he stood still, blinking, trying to steady himself. His stomach rumbled. It had been more than a day since he'd eaten anything. He remembered the big piece of chocolate cake the tall man had offered him, and his own stupidity in refusing it. *A piece of cake wouldn't have hurt anything*, he thought tearily, then realized that the drugs had thrown his emotions into a tailspin. Sometimes, after taking the Seconal Emily gave him when he couldn't sleep, he would wake up on the verge of tears. This was the same thing, he reminded himself. Nothing to cry about. Nothing.

Yet it was hard to stop himself. He was alone in this place with a man who had every intention of murdering him unless he got his hands on the cup.

And the cup was gone. He had seen it vanish with his own eyes.

Arthur felt his tears welling up. Why hadn't he left it in the apartment when he and Emily ran away from Chicago? They could have given it to the Katzenbaum Institute. They could have gone to the TV stations with the story. They could have let everyone know. If they had, Arthur wouldn't be here now.

*But who would have the cup?*

He dried his tears. Sooner or later, someone would use it. There would be a dying baby somewhere, or the president of some country who'd been shot, or a thousand earthquake victims. The cup would be a miracle. For a while. And then one country or another would claim it as its own. Or someone would steal it, and sell it to the highest bidder.

Or keep it, and become something like the king of the world with it.

The thought staggered him. What would happen if a person never got hurt, never got sick, never had a bruise or a skinned knee?

*Do you really know what it can do, Arthur?* The tall man had asked him that. It healed wounds. You never got sick. You . . . what? You lived forever?

He felt dizzy. He took another drink of water, then went back into the room where he'd spent the night.

A tray of food was waiting for him: hotcakes with syrup, a bowl of fresh fruit, and a glass of milk. Arthur devoured it like a starving wolf.

"I'm glad to see you're eating," a deep voice behind him said.

Arthur ran his tongue over his upper lip to wipe off his milk moustache. "Did you poison it?" he asked.

The tall man laughed. "No. Did you sleep well?"

"Who are you really?" Arthur demanded.

"I've told you. An old friend."

"You're no friend of mine. What's your name?"

"Saladin."

"I've never heard of you."

"Then you're uneducated, as well as rude."

Arthur looked down at the empty tray. "Thank you for breakfast," he said.

"That's better. Now come with me. I'd like to show you something."

He took Arthur down several flights of stairs, past a bedroom wing, a corridor leading to a huge parlor, through a vast kitchen with three sinks, and down another flight into a large room paneled with fragrant cedar. The walls were covered with shelves and display cases, and within them was a bewildering array of artifacts, jewelry, clothing, and weapons.

Arthur looked around, astonished. "What is this place? A museum?"

"Of sorts," Saladin said. "I rather think of it as a trophy room. I haven't seen it myself for some time. I don't usually live here, but this is the safest of my homes for these things."

Everything was in perfect condition, the cases spotlessly clean. There were paintings, sculptures, even suits of armor in plain view, without ropes or other devices to keep away the curious.

The boy could not resist. He rushed forward to look at a case which held four broadswords, propped up on easel-type displays. At eye level was a sword of polished steel with a bronze hilt carved into the likeness of a snake. "Where did you get this?" he asked.

"How like you to choose the swords first." He opened the glass of the case. "That belonged to a Macedonian warrior-king. His name was Alexander."

Arthur looked at him sideways. "Alexander the Great?" he asked skeptically.

Saladin nodded. "He was little more than a boy, really. He played the harp in secret, fearing that his men would jest about him. And he had a face as beautiful as a woman's."

"Are you kidding me?" Arthur asked, knowing that he was, but still compelled by the casual ring of truth in the man's voice.

"No," Saladin said softly. "I supplied horses to his army during his march across India. In the evenings we would often share a skin of wine, and speak of the wonders of the East. He was charmingly naive. The first time he met an Indian sultan, he nearly screamed with laughter. They dyed their beards green, you know, and rode elephants. Alexander found it all hilarious. I had to intercede for him to stop the sultan from attacking his troops."

Arthur listened, fascinated. Then he frowned. "You're making fun of me," he said.

Saladin smiled mildly and shook his head.

"Alexander the Great lived three hundred years before time."

"Before Christ, you mean."

"That's right. You couldn't have been there."

The tall man sighed. "But I was. And I was old then, older than the stones of the earth." He opened the case and took out the sword. "He gave me rubies for my horses," he said. "The man had no love of riches. It was the adventure he craved. And so when I left, I took his sword. It was part of his soul."

Almost unconsciously, Arthur reached out and touched the shining blade.

"I was going to kill him, but he was asleep. He was beautiful when he slept, and I had a weakness for him."

Arthur had heard about men with that particular weakness. He stepped back from the sword. Saladin didn't seem to notice. "He died young, as I knew he would. I could have protected him with the cup, but he wouldn't have me. And now his bones are ashes on the wind."

He stroked the long blade of the sword lovingly, then put it back inside the case.

"The cup," Arthur said, finally understanding. "It keeps you alive."

"Of course. Have you seen this?" He picked up a shield-like object decorated with a geometrically stylized bird in pure gold with two emeralds for eyes. "The breastplate of Ramses the Great. And here, the knife Brutus used to slay Julius Caesar. Ah." He strode over a few paces to a small table covered with a velvet cloth. On it was a tall golden crown with three peaks in the front. "The crown of Charlemagne."

He placed it on Arthur's head. "It's a simple piece of work, but it suits you. You never cared much for finery."

The boy took it off and beheld it with wonder. It was heavy, almost barbaric. And a man had worn it, a king. "What did you say about me?"

Saladin watched him for a moment, the child with the big crown in his hands, and smiled. "Nothing," he said. He took the crown away and picked up a small curved knife.

"This was my own," he said, flipping it into the air and catching it by its bandaged handle. "It was a cobbler's tool." The gauze strips, grown fragile with age, fell away when he caught it. Saladin looked at the pieces in his hand. "There, you can still see the blood."

Despite his confusion and the indisputable creepiness of the man, Arthur leaned forward to see. The inside of the bandages were brittle with a dried black substance that cracked at his touch.

"Why is there blood on it?" Arthur asked, poking at it.

"I used it to kill someone with. Quite a few, really. All women."

Arthur pulled back his hand with a jerk.

The tall man held the half-moon blade up to the light. "That must have belonged to the first one," he mused. "There was so much blood. I always wrapped the handle after that first time."

"How . . . how many people have you killed?"

Saladin laughed. "Oh, my, I'm sure I couldn't remember." He looked at the blackened tool with amusement. "She was one of the few women, though. Odd, how long it takes one to overcome the taboos of one's upbringing. My family believed that killing women was unworthy of a man. That would mean nothing these days, of course, particularly in your country. Women are murdered all the time for a pocketful of change. But my generation viewed it as an inexplicable wickedness. That was why I had to do it, I suppose."

"Who was she?"

He shrugged dismissively. "A shopgirl, or a tart. That didn't matter. Later, of course, the newspapers made a big to-do about the girls all being prostitutes, but that was nonsense. It wasn't my intention to kill them for their profession. They were simply the available ones. In those days, ladies didn't venture out on Whitechapel streets alone in the evening."

"You're talking about . . ." Arthur swallowed. "Jack the Ripper."

"Ghastly name, that." He winced. "The newspapers, again. If it weren't for them, Victorian London would have been a marvelous place. So proper and hidden. Murder was so very shocking then."

He sighed. "I've always done my best killing in England. It means something here. In Hong Kong or New York . . . well, one might as well litter, or spit on the sidewalk. There's so little difference between crimes. But here in England, the taking of a life is still regarded as . . . well, odious."

While he spoke, Arthur had backed away almost to the stairs.

"Don't worry, child. I'm not going to kill you here. And you certainly won't be able to escape up the stairs."

"You're really crazy," Arthur whispered.

"No." He set down the curved knife. "A little bored at times, perhaps, but not crazy. You see, a life as long as mine can be rather dull. It becomes a habit, like cigarette smoking, only much harder to break. One tends to resort to foolishness now and again, to the cheap thrill."

He walked around the room, touching various objects, occasionally picking one up and setting it down again. "Sometimes I think I've lived too long." Suddenly he looked over at Arthur. "Earlier you swore to kill me. Would you? If you had the chance, would you, say, cut my throat?"

The boy met his eyes, then lowered them. "I don't know," he said.

Saladin's eyes grew bright. "Why not try, Arthur? You may develop a taste for it." He strolled over to the boy. "Death is compelling. It gives one the ultimate power over another. Have you ever killed?"

"No."

"But you will. It's part of your fabric."

Arthur didn't know what he was talking about, but he kept silent.

"Kill your enemies. It's the first principle of every ruler on earth. Humiliate them, degrade them, make an example of them for others who might dare to doubt your power."

"I'd like to go now," Arthur said.

"You're afraid because you agree with what I say. Sacrifice the small life for the important one, the defeated for the conqueror, the weak for the strong. Every great king in history has understood this idea. Every great civilization has evolved from it."

"Might makes right," Arthur said.

"Simplistic, but a start. I said you were a clever boy. Your life may become one of the important ones, after all."

"And you're dumber about me than you are about chess," Arthur said angrily. "Who decides whose life is important and whose isn't?"

Saladin shrugged. "Fate, will, circumstance . . . Who can say what goes into the creation of a great man?"

"Like you," Arthur said caustically.

"My life certainly qualifies as something out of the ordinary," Saladin said modestly. "But I have never considered myself a great man. I lived as a king for a time. I ruled well. But it grew tiresome. I was never Alexander." Lightly he touched the boy's hair. "I was never you."

He spoke softly. "Do you still not remember, Arthur?"

From behind a tall cherrywood case he brought a painting. It was the full-length portrait of a man with reddish gold hair on which rested a thin circlet of gold. He was simply dressed in black, but in his right hand was a sword of such magnificence that it seemed to leap out of the painting into the real world.

"Do you recognize it?"

"It looks like me," the boy said.

"It is Arthur of England."

The boy stood transfixed in front of the painting for a full five minutes, unmoving, breathing shallowly.

"I painted it from memory the day I heard of his death. I used glass instead of canvas, so that it would last forever. The glass is what brings the sword to life."

"You're lying," Arthur said, his eyes still on the painting.

"You know I'm not. Do you truly feel nothing? Not even the wound that killed you because you refused to accept the cup?"

Arthur made a small sound. He did feel it, the sharp, piercing pain that began in his side and burned up through his body to his heart. He held his side. His feet wobbled.

"You were a fool," Saladin said softly. "Or perhaps only young, like Alexander. Merlin wanted you to have it. He wanted it so badly that he came back from the grave to see that you kept it this time. He has it now."

"Oh . . ." The boy fell on the floor, drawing his legs up.

"I do not wish to pass another millennium alone, Arthur. You have a great destiny before you. I shall see that you fulfill it. Together we can live forever. You will rule, and there will have been no king like you in all the days of the earth."

His voice was compelling, almost seductive. "Merlin has hidden it from you," he said. "Don't you understand? He knows you belong with me, and he would rather see you die than give up his authority over you."

"No . . ."

"He knows he is too weak to rule himself. He will use you to come to power, then take it from you. That is what he did to me."

Slowly Saladin licked the perspiration from his lip as he watched the child writhe in pain on the floor. "But you can control him. Listen to me!"

He touched Arthur's chest with one finger, and the boy cried out in agony. "You can make Merlin bring the cup to you."

Arthur's eyes widened. "H-how?"

"Call to him. He must answer to his king."

Saladin bent down low near the boy and whispered. "Call him with your mind, Arthur. Call the wizard. He will come with the cup."

Arthur struggled to sit up.

"Call him. It is your time. Your world."

"What sort of world . . . will it be?" the boy moaned.

Saladin's mouth curved in a faint smile of triumph. "Whatever sort you decide to make it. With me, with the cup, your power will be boundless. Do you understand me, Arthur? Boundless."

Arthur closed his eyes. For a moment, he thought he was dying. Again.

Yes, he understood. He had come back. He had been given a second chance to right his own wrongs. But he was dying now, while still a child.

He tried to hang on to consciousness, but the darkness was overwhelming. He spun downward, down into a place so deep that there were no memories. And in that darkness he began to see the first vague, filtered images of a man walking down the length of a long stone hall. His face was filled with comfort and compassion and a light that radiated from it like the warmth of the sun, and his arms were outstretched, as if reaching for the object that floated in the air in front of him.

It was a chalice, made of silver and gold, a great treasure, surely, and nearby was a voice, Merlin's voice, oh, friend! Merlin's voice shouting, "Take it, Arthur! Take it!" And Arthur reached for the great cup, but as he did the light faded from the face of the stranger. Christ's face, dying without the light, Christ's body, fading, fading into darkness. But the chalice was still there, without the light of Jesus on it, floating closer, closer . . .

*Take it. . . .*

He came to a moment after he had lost consciousness. Whatever he had seen made no sense to him, none at all, but he remembered the fading, lightless face of Christ. And when he saw Saladin, waiting expectantly with his predator's eyes, he knew he was looking into the face of the devil.

He drew himself up to a standing position and squared his narrow shoulders, trying to will the ancient pain away.

"You're not part of the plan for me," he said.

The dark eyes flashed. Saladin stood up. He walked to the far side of the room, his jaw clenching. Finally he turned to face Arthur. "You've just forfeited your life," he rasped.

A frisson of fear rippled down Arthur's spine. His death

would come soon, he knew. And Saladin would see to it that it was not a painless death.

"Goodbye, Saladin," he said quietly.

He walked toward the stairs, aching with every step, but he kept his back as straight as that of the king in the painting, the king he had once been.

# CHAPTER FORTY-EIGHT

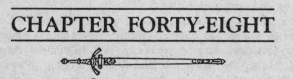

It was some time before Hal got back to the inn. After his discovery at Matilda Grimes', he went to find Inspector Candy to tell him about the mansion near the amusement park, but Candy was not in the police van. Higgins and Chastain had no idea where their superior had gone and were frankly surprised that anyone would expect them to know.

"What if the kidnappers want to trade soon?" Hal had asked querulously. "Without Candy, who've we got to go after those maniacs—you?"

"Now, Mr. Woczniak," Higgins whispered.

"There are six of them. Do you guys at least know how to shoot?"

Chastain only smiled.

"We don't use guns," Higgins said.

"Oh, great. That's just great."

"Please don't worry excessively, sir. Inspector Candy will be back soon, I'm sure."

"What about those reinforcements he was talking about? Has he called them?"

"He will. When they're needed." Higgins was edging back into the van, as if he were afraid of exposure to sunlight and unprocessed air.

Hal let him go. If it came to a confrontation with Saladin and his men, he knew, these two would be about as helpful as bunions. He cleared some more broken glass off the front seat of the Morris and drove back to the inn.

Mrs. Sloan was sweeping the front steps when he pulled up in the car. He had prepared a profuse apology, but she cut him off.

"Now, none of that, lad," she said, not missing a stroke with her broom. "I'm just thankful that the young woman wasn't hurt. She told me all about it and gave me a check to cover the breakage, besides."

"Thank you," Hal said. "Emily's all right, then?"

"Oh, she's fine. Women are like that. When they're the one getting pounded, it don't matter a fig. It's when their babies are in trouble, and them with nothing to do but fret over it, that they fall to pieces."

Indeed, Emily showed no signs of the lassitude that had overcome her when Arthur was first abducted. She jumped up from her chair inside the pub, her eyes wide, clutching an envelope in her hands.

"This came about an hour after I got back," she said. "It came with the afternoon mail. The postman didn't know how it got in his bag."

The envelope was of high-quality rag, the paper probably handmade. There was no postage on it. On the front was written the name "Emily Blessing" in the flowing script Hal recognized from the postcard. Inside, the sheet of paper contained only one word: *Midnight*.

"The trade's tonight," Hal said.

"But where? They didn't say anything about where."

"They don't want us to know that yet. Wait here for a second. I've got to let Candy in on this."

He dashed to the telephone and dialed the number of the mobile phone in the police van. Higgins answered, warily, as if he distrusted telephones and their use.

"No, Inspector Candy hasn't returned yet," he said in his barely audible voice.

"Doesn't he at least call to tell you where he is?" Hal shouted into the mouthpiece.

There was a pause in which Higgins deliberated the question thoroughly. "Usually," he said.

"Well, we've got the second note from the kidnappers. The trade's going to be at midnight tonight. I don't know where yet."

"I'll give the inspector the message," Higgins said.

"It's nearly five o'clock already."

"Yes," Higgins agreed.

Hal sighed. "If Candy doesn't get back to me in an hour, I'm going to make the arrangements myself to bring in the extra cops."

"Oh, that would be quite impossible, Mr. Woczniak. You see—"

"An hour." He hung up.

He nearly collided with the stately Mrs. Sloan as he made his way back into the pub. She was just coming in the front door, mopping her forehead with the edge of her apron. "It's going to be another hot night," she said. Then, seeing his face, she added, "Things not going so well, eh?"

"May I go into your kitchen with you?" Hal asked with as much courtesy as he could muster.

"I suppose. Long as you don't cook. The car's one thing, but I don't like people fiddling with my pots and pans, most particularly men."

"I need a bowl," Hal said.

"What size?"

"Small." He indicated the dimensions with his hands. "As big as a cup, but without a handle. Could you lend me one?"

She sat the broom in a corner. "Well, let's see what I've got."

"We're not going to fool them with a fake," Emily said.

"No, but we can't go empty-handed, either. Maybe it'll get us through the door."

In the small, sweltering kitchen, Mrs. Sloan opened a cabinet above the iron stove and pulled down dozens of bowls, all well used and in varying degrees of disintegration.

"This is about right," Hal said, picking up a small metal

measuring cup. It had a rounded bottom and a beaten metal handle. He looked up imploringly.

Mrs. Sloan gave him an exasperated look, then snatched the cup out of his hands and beat it against the stove until the handle fell off. "That's what you'd be wanting, I suppose."

"You're terrific," Hal said.

"But I want it back, handle or no."

"Yes, ma'am. Have you got some wrapping paper and a roll of tape?"

She grabbed some newspapers from a pile in the corner of the kitchen and slapped them into his hands. Then she pointed the way back to the parlor. "In the desk where the phone is," she said.

"Thanks. Thanks a lot."

Mrs. Sloan grunted in response.

Upstairs in Emily's room he wrapped the bowl in the newspaper and then sealed it with tape.

"Hal . . ."

He held up the round, mysterious-looking object. "Think we can get past the first rank with this?"

"Hal, I don't think you should go."

"What?"

"The note was addressed to me. If they see you, they might harm Arthur."

*And if they catch you with this phony cup, they'll kill you*, he thought. "We'll talk about it later. It may not come to a trade, if I can get hold of the Invisible Man from Scotland Yard."

"Inspector Candy? Is he missing?"

"The last time I saw him, he was going to check out a house on Abelard Street. That was hours ago."

"Should we go have a look at the place? Maybe he's in some sort of trouble."

Hal nodded. "I'll go. You'd better stay here. Another message will be coming before long."

Wearily, he got back in the Morris and drove to the village.

When Inspector Candy parked his car near the Spook-O-Rama tunnel, the first thing he noticed were the long strips of motorcycle tracks leading to and from the woods. It was the first time since the beginning of this investigation that he'd felt any real optimism.

The house on Abelard Street had been a waste of time, the same as every other lead he'd followed. The place was empty, tenantless, and locked up tight. Some neighbors remembered a young, dark-haired man with a motorcycle, but he had apparently been gone for more than a month, and the house had remained empty since then.

Following a hunch, he'd driven to the old amusement-park grounds where the Blessing woman had been terrorized. The ground was still damp from yesterday's downpour, and Candy had hoped for just such a tire mark as he found. But the length and clarity of the tracks were even more than he'd hoped for.

After a quick look through the funhouse, he followed the tracks on foot. They led through the woods toward a high rolling meadow almost a thousand meters away. At the crest of the hill, he found himself looking down into a verdant valley at the center of which, another mile away, was a ramshackle, old, stone manor house. The house looked as if it had been built in stages because it spread over four different levels, following the natural contours of the land. A large willow tree sat in front in the middle of a stone-walled goldfish pond, empty now except for piles of rotting leaves. There were no lights on, and no cars parked near the main entrance.

Still, it had to be the place, Candy thought. There were no other buildings nearby, except for a large barn. Candy moved closer. He found some fresh horse droppings and heard the neighing of horses from the barn.

He had them. Even if none of the kidnappers were present, he would at least be able to get the boy. He hoped that was the case. One against six were bad odds. When he called in the reinforcement officers, they could take care of the men. The only thing that mattered now was the child.

He went around behind the barn and waited for someone to come out of the house. No one did. Either he hadn't been spotted in the tall unkempt grass, or no one was home. Good. There was a chance. The house would probably be locked, but he could find a way in. He just hoped the boy was still alive.

Candy stepped cautiously onto the gravel. He was nearly at the house when he heard the barn doors swing open and saw two men on Arabian stallions ride out, screaming a high, keening wail. They charged at him, drawing long curved swords as their horses raced toward him.

"Police!" he shouted, reaching for his identification.

The men did not stop. Candy felt himself break into a sweat as the animals pounded closer. He could see their flaring nostrils and the eyes of the black-clothed horsemen as they swung their curious weapons in the air above their heads, preparing to strike.

At the last moment, Candy's nerve failed him. He dived to the ground and rolled just as the horse's hooves came down on the spot where he had been standing. While the horsemen reined in the animals to come at him again, Candy saw in an upstairs window of the house the face of a tall thin man with jet black hair and a beard and recognized him as the maniac he had arrested four years before and sent to Maplebrook.

"You son of a bitch," he whispered, and the man answered with a slight inclination of his head. His eyes were smiling.

Candy ran, but there was no place to run. He had only gone a few steps when the horsemen were on him. The first blow cut deeply into his throat. Candy felt the searing pain of it, felt his head thrown wildly back. He was even able to see the unbelievable gush of blood shoot out of his neck before the second sword smashed against the side of his head, breaking the thin bone over his right temple.

He crumpled to the ground, dead before his body touched the gravel.

# CHAPTER FORTY-NINE

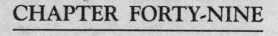

The pain in Arthur's side abated with time. He had been brought back from the basement to the upstairs sitting room where he had spent the night; the tall man himself had ordered the boy out of his sight after Arthur's rejection of him. There he waited, wondering about the strange phenomenon that he'd witnessed. He had been someone else, had actually lived as another person once, long ago, and for a time—for the briefest time, during the nonsensical half-dream that had come upon him in his imagined pain—he had remembered that faraway life.

*I was Arthur of England*, he thought. He knew that if it had happened to anyone else, he would have found the story laughable. Everyone wanted to be a king, right? Even girls. But his recollection had not been that of a king; only of a man on the verge of death. He remembered only the pain and the delirious vision of a vanishing Christ as he felt the life ebb out of his body.

Now he was no longer a king, or even a man. He was just a scared ten-year-old boy. He wrapped his arms around his knees to ward off the fear, but the fear only grew.

*You could have said yes to him*, a voice inside him said. *You could have told him you'd side with him. He would have made you a king, or at least somebody important—*

No. No, he could never have agreed. After seeing the face in the vision, it was all too clear what Saladin was.

It was better to die.

He just wished he wasn't so afraid.

"Help me," he whispered. Saladin had told him to call on the wizard. That was Merlin in the stories. "Merlin . . ."

He felt foolish. The story had seemed real in the eerie setting of the basement filled with treasures, but now . . .

"Merlin," he tried again.

There was no answer. He lay his head against his knees.

*Now I lay me down to sleep*, he thought. *I pray the Lord my soul to keep. If I should die . . .*

Suddenly the frayed cord of a lamp caught his eye. Holding his breath, he went around the room and turned on all the lamps, then watched them.

They flickered.

*Old wiring.*

The house had been built before the advent of electricity; the wiring had probably been put in later. He could picture the beautiful Victorian mansion then, illuminated by the modern miracle of electric lights.

He doubted that it had been replaced since then. All of the fixtures in the place seemed so old, as if whoever owned the house had not wanted to change them.

A short in one of the circuits might be enough to knock out most of the electricity in the house.

Arthur went quickly into the bathroom to look for a razor blade, but there was nothing in the medicine cabinet except for an old glass bottle of moldy aspirin. Working quickly, muffling the noise with a towel, he rapped the aspirin bottle against the cabinet sink until it broke. Then he took a shard of the broken glass back into the parlor.

He unplugged one of the old lamps and cut off its cord, then sliced it lengthwise to separate the two wires inside and shaved the insulation from them with small, careful strokes. When he was done, there was an inch and a half of bright, bare copper showing at the end of each wire.

With one eye on the door, Arthur folded back the ends of the wires to double them up and make them thicker, then jammed them into the slots of a wall socket. He dropped the other end of the cord, the end with the plug on it, behind the small covered table where the lamp sat. The plug was live now, and touching it would give anyone a nasty shock.

Later, when the time was right, he would push the plug

into yet another socket. If he was correct, the twisted surge of power created would short out the whole circuit. Maybe the whole building.

He hoped so. It was his last chance.

He heard someone at the door and ran across the room back to the sofa. He hid the piece of glass under a cushion.

One of Saladin's men looked in on him silently, then withdrew at once.

Arthur closed his eyes and waited.


It was 6:55. More than two hours had passed since Hal spoke with Candy's assistant, and Candy still had not arrived back at the police van.

Hal tracked the inspector as far as the empty house on Abelard Street. Several of the people who lived on the street told Hal that they had spoken with the Scotland Yard man earlier, but none of them knew where Candy might have been heading next.

*Where had the bastard gone?* In the Bureau, the head of an investigation would be suspended for taking off without letting anyone know where he was going. But then, Hal thought more kindly, Candy was probably used to working alone. Higgins and Chastain would hardly be the inspector's idea of great backup. And who else did he have? Constable Nubbit?

Hal finally resigned himself to the knowledge that, in Candy's place, he would have done the same.

There was one more thing he could do without Candy's assistance. He took out a crude map he had drawn after speaking with Matilda Grimes. It showed the location of the old house behind the amusement-park grounds.

It was right. From where the house stood, if the map was accurate, it was close enough to the remains of the castle for an easy attack through the woods. He drove to the spot where Higgins and Chastain had found the horses' hoofprints, then walked through the two-mile stretch of trees and brush.

Beyond it was a rolling meadow shaped like an enormous bowl surrounding the house. The amusement park would be to the west, he reasoned, behind another fortification of trees.

There were no people in sight at the house, but two large horses grazed in the meadow. Hal tried to remember if they were the same horses involved in the attack on the castle grounds, but he knew too little about horses to tell one from another.

He waited nearly a half hour on his belly for someone to come out of the house. No one did, and he was not about to approach the place alone and unarmed. Finally he retraced his steps back to the car and drove to the inn.

"I think I know where the kidnappers are," he pleaded with Higgins on the telephone. "With ten or fifteen men from Scotland Yard or the SAS, we could storm the place before the trade."

Higgins nearly choked. "The Special Air Service? Surely you're not serious, Mr. Woczniak."

"Damn it, these men are dangerous."

"I assure you, Inspector Candy has things well in hand."

"Candy's missing!" Hal shouted into the telephone. "For all we know, he's in trouble. He might even be in the house with Arthur."

"That hardly seems likely," Higgins said dryly.

Hal knew he was grasping at straws and tried to sound more reasonable. "Okay, maybe," he said. "But wherever he is, we can't wait for him any longer. Scotland Yard could helicopter some men down here—"

"The inspector never intended to call in men from Metropolitan," Higgins corrected him. "Officers from local constabularies will be used. That is, if the inspector deems it necessary to bring in any outside help. As it stands, however, that hardly seems to be the case."

"What?" Hal couldn't believe his ears.

"This house you claim to have located. Have you been there yourself?"

"Yes. There were horses outside."

"What sort of horses?"

"I don't know, for God's sake. Big horses."

Higgins sighed. "Big horses," he repeated. "Did you see

any of the men you encountered in the meadow by the hill fort?"

Hal was stuck. "No," he said finally. "They must have all been in the house."

"Mr. Woczniak, do be reasonable. Other people besides kidnappers live in this area. They own horses. Big horses."

Hal had reached the bursting point. "Look," he said. "We need cops with weapons to get Arthur out of that place. If you don't give me the cops, at least give me a gun, and I'll go in myself."

"That would be highly imprudent."

"I want a gun," Hal insisted.

"We don't use guns, Mr. Woczniak. I've told you that. And if we did, we would hardly issue them to irate civilians."

"What about Candy? Aren't you even worried about him?"

"No, I am not," Higgins said. His patience was evidently strained, since he was speaking almost loud enough to be heard in normal conversation. "The inspector has no doubt come across a more viable lead than yours, and is pursuing it."

"Right. Or maybe he's dead," Hal said.

"Mr. Woczniak . . ."

"Go scratch your ass." Hal slammed down the phone.

He dialed Scotland Yard next. After a quarter hour of being shunted from one disembodied voice to another, he was again told, gently but firmly, to stay out of Inspector Candy's business.

His panic rising, he tried a long-distance call to the FBI in Washington. The chief had brought Scotland Yard into the investigation in the first place; the chief would be able to kick them into action now.

The chief was aboard an airplane en route to California.

Hal hung up in despair. There was only one other man who might possibly be able to bring in enough police officers to storm the kidnappers' hideout.

"Constable Nubbit, I'm asking you to consider the possibility that something may have happened to Inspector Candy," Hal said as humbly as he could.

Nubbit chuckled. "You're an odd one. Droll. Very droll, I must say."

"May I ask what makes my request for additional policemen so very humorous?" Hal asked, feeling the air grow hot inside his nostrils.

Nubbit leaned forward earnestly. "Sir, Scotland Yard's already denied that request. I can't go over their heads."

"That's not Scotland Yard in that van outside," Hal said. "They're two scientists who wouldn't know how to stop a pack of kidnappers if they had a howitzer."

"Officers Higgins and Chastain are detectives in the Metropolitan Police," the constable said archly. "And damn nice chaps, I might add."

"What about Candy?" Hal shouted, unable to control himself any longer. No one seemed to be interested in the fact that the primary officer in the case had been missing for hours.

"Never got to know him as well as the others," Nubbit confessed. "Seemed all right. Socks didn't match. One gets to notice little things like that in this line of work, you know."

"Jesus!" He felt like strangling the man. "What I'm saying is that Candy might not be in a position to call out the extra police officers we're going to need."

"Oh, I wouldn't jump to any conclusions, Mr. ah . . . What was your name again?"

Hal closed his eyes. "Woczniak."

"Bugger to pronounce, that."

"If the inspector weren't in trouble, he'd have called."

"Oh, no, no, no. Not necessarily."

"It's after nine o'clock! The kidnappers want me to meet them at midnight. Constable Nubbit, what I'm saying is that with Candy or without him, we're going to have to pull some officers together, or those men are going to kill the boy. Can you get the word out to the other villages and towns in the area?"

"Oh, my, no." He shook his head briskly. "I'm just a P.C. Wouldn't do to have me going over the head of Scotland Yard."

"But I've explained . . ." Hal cut himself off. It was no use. He'd gone full circle with the man. Nubbit's brain simply could not tolerate any deviation from the standard routine, for any reason. "Thank you," Hal said wearily, and stood up.

"Glad to be of help," Nubbit called as Hal left the station.

Emily had heard no word from the kidnappers.

"What's taking them so long?" she asked.

"I don't know," Hal said, stretching out in an overstuffed chair in her room. He felt tired to his bones. Tired, disgusted, and hopeless. "I've talked to everyone I could, even that thickheaded imbecile at the police station. If I could only—"

At that moment, the glass in the window shattered and something sailed into the room, landing with a wet thud in the middle of the rug.

Hal jumped to his feet and ran immediately to the window. A motorcycle was zooming away down the street. He didn't need to check the license plate to know that it was the same man who had shot out the windshield in the Morris.

"Don't touch it," he said.

Together they stared at the strange package. It was vaguely spherical. The heavy brown paper had been wrapped around it hastily.

"It's . . . it's bloody," Emily said, her face white.

One side of the package was stained red. The stain was growing, oozing down onto the rug.

"You'd better get out of here," Hal said, but Emily stood frozen where she was.

"Open it," she whispered.

He knelt down beside it, tore off a strip of tape, then looked up at Emily. She nodded.

"It might be . . . something that belongs to Arthur," Hal said, trying to prepare her for the shock.

"Open it." Her voice was harsh and raspy. "Goddamnit, open it, or I will."

With a deep breath, Hal pulled aside the soggy brown paper.

It was Inspector Candy's head.

"Oh, Christ," Hal said.

Whether from shock or relief, Emily fainted. Her head hit the floor with a bang. Quickly Hal started to rewrap the grisly thing, but then he noticed that someone had written on the inside of the paper.

> *Come alone to the gristmill on Pembroke Lane, five miles south. No more police, please, or you'll find the boy's head in the next package. You must know by now that I am quite serious.*

It was signed with a large, florid *S*.

# CHAPTER FIFTY

Hal doused Emily's face with a cold washcloth. Then, when she started to come around, before she was fully conscious, he made her swallow one of Arthur's Seconal tablets. If she were awake, he knew, she would insist on meeting Saladin herself, and he was not about to permit that.

He set her on the bed with her head resting on the pillow. Then he went into his own room to find the sheet of ingenious instructions Arthur had written to assure Emily a safe life in the event of his own death. Hal attached his own note to Arthur's.

> *Emily,*
>   *Don't wait for anyone to find us. Just follow these instructions, and you'll be safe. It's what Arthur wanted most for you. Me, too.*
>
>                                 *Hal*

He wanted to say more. He wanted to say that he missed her already, that for a moment it had seemed as if he'd finally found some purpose in his life. That there might be such a thing as happiness, somewhere, and that maybe, just maybe, they could find it together, the three of them.

But he knew Emily had been right. It was too late for all of that. A few words would change nothing.

He looked at his watch. Ten-thirty. He would walk to the rendezvous. There would be no point in using a car to get away in any case.

Saladin's message said five miles south. South of what? Of town? Of the castle?

No, he realized. Saladin had been talking about the inn. He knew exactly where Hal was. He had known about Candy, and he probably knew that, without the inspector, Hal would not be able to muster enough manpower to fight.

Hal would die, of course. Saladin would never let him live with his knowledge. And Arthur would die, too, if he wasn't dead already. After tonight, only Emily would have a chance of getting out alive. It was rotten, rotten for the kid, but what had anyone expected with Hal Woczniak on the job? He had failed again. All he could hope for was to take a few of the bastards down with him.

But that was something, at least. Something he would do for Brian Candy. And for Arthur.

He knocked on Mrs. Sloan's door, awakening her.

"Lord, son, what's wrong now?"

"I'm sorry to disturb you, but I've got another favor to ask of you. The last one, I promise."

She ran her fingers through her hair. "Well, out with it, unless you plan to keep me up all night talking."

He gave her three hundred in pound notes. It was all the money he had. "I'd like you to take half of this, and give the rest to Emily in three hours. She's asleep, but I want you to wake her up. Give her plenty of coffee, and then drive her to the nearest train station and get her aboard a train for London. There's a note in an envelope addressed to her on the bureau. Please put it in her pocketbook. She'll be groggy, so she may not remember to take it."

"Good heavens, lad—"

"I can't explain any more. But if anyone comes looking for her, just tell them that she disappeared one night. That's for your own safety, Mrs. Sloan."

The woman looked flustered, then nodded. "All right. I know you wouldn't be running out unless it was a weighty thing."

"Thank you." He turned to leave.

"I'm sorry for all you're going through, both of you."

"Yeah," Hal said.

Back in his own room, he picked up the measuring cup wrapped in newspapers, then walked downstairs. He took a long knife from one of the drawers in the kitchen and slipped it in the back of his belt.

The time had come to do battle once more with the Saracen Knight, though he knew the outcome would be the same as it had been a hundred lifetimes ago.

The way to Pembroke Lane passed by the ruins of the castle. Arthur's castle, Hal thought. Camelot, where the knights of the Round Table had gathered to serve the greatest king in history.

He walked off the road and climbed the silent, dark hills for the last time. The rocks remained, moss-covered and immovable, in the places where they had fallen centuries ago. In his mind, he could see it all as it had been in the first glorious years: the grand sweep of the outer bailey, with its turrets and high walls; the courtyard where the servants tended the animals and the gardens and the knights practiced at war; the inner fortifications beyond the moat, now no more than a shallow ditch; and the magnificent keep, so tall that it seemed to touch the very stars, so strong that no enemy force could ever penetrate it. So they had thought back then, when they were the new order of the world.

It was all gone now. All but Arthur himself, come back to rule a kingdom that no longer existed, with a protector whose shortcomings had doomed them both to death.

"God, why did you choose me?" he whispered.

"Beg pardon, sir?" chirped a young voice.

Hal whirled around. Perched on the low wall behind him was the same young boy who had come to the meadow on the morning that Arthur was taken.

"I . . . I didn't see you," Hal said.

"I come to hear the horses," the boy said.

Hal looked at him uncomprehendingly.

"It's St. John's Eve, sir. The knights ride tonight. If you listen, you'll hear them coming from this very place, looking for their king till light of day."

Slowly, Hal looked around him at the ruin. "The ghost riders," he said quietly. "I've heard of them."

"Oh, they're real, all right. I come here every year. The hooves pound like thunder, they do." The boy looked up at the starry sky. "Only they don't ever find the king. I 'spect Arthur must be dead by now."

Hal swallowed. "Look, kid, you'd better get home," he said gruffly. "The cops are looking for some armed criminals around here. This is no place for you."

"But the knights of the Round Table . . ."

"Go on, get out of here." He pushed the boy toward the road, then followed him out of the castle ruins. The boy ran a short distance to keep from falling, then turned back to look at Hal.

"Go home, I said!" Hal called. The boy moved into the darkness, and Hal walked on toward Pembroke Lane.

He arrived at the mill by 11:20. Not much remained of the operation except for the skeletal remains of a waterwheel and some fallen boards. There was no place to hide here, but that didn't matter: Hal was through hiding.

Before long, he heard the sound of hoofbeats. A horse was coming near. No, more than one horse. In the moonlight he could see their shining flanks. Mounted on one was a rider dressed in black robes, holding the reins of the other animal. He stopped some distance away and gestured for Hal to approach him.

"I can't ride," Hal said as the man in black tossed down the reins.

The man did not answer. The riderless horse moved toward Hal, nickering.

Awkwardly clutching the wrapped cup from Mrs. Sloan's cupboard, Hal clambered up onto the saddle and picked up the reins. "All right," he said resignedly. "Where to?"

The horseman turned and rode away at a slow trot. Hal's horse followed him. They turned off the roadway and into the woods for a short time, then burst through into a large open field, where the mounts picked up speed.

Hal hung on desperately until they crested a rise in the field. Below, bathed in moonlight, was the old stone mansion he had seen earlier. One upstairs room was lit. The rest of the house was dark.

*I knew it was the place*, Hal thought with disgust. Everything about its location had been right. Yet no one had believed him enough to send out even a small contingent of men to rescue Arthur.

Now it was too late for that. Too late.

Arthur saw him coming.

He had heard a sound in the meadow and had run to the window, as he had run a hundred times since nightfall.

The window itself had been sealed shut. He had tried more than once to break the glass, but it was of the double-thick, insulated variety and besides, the only thing between the window and the ground thirty feet below was a narrow slate gable.

Except for the man who had come to seal the window, he'd had no visitors since Saladin's tour of the basement room with him that morning. No visits, no meals, not even the dreaded injections. It was as if Arthur had suddenly ceased to exist for the men in the old stone house.

He was relieved. Without the drugs, he could at least stay awake. That was something he knew he had to do.

Saladin had given him the option to live, and he had refused it. Whatever was planned would happen tonight, and Arthur knew he had to be alert. His life depended on that.

As he reached the window the hoofbeats became clear.

When he saw the two riders, his heart quickened. One of them was Hal. He knew it even before the moon illuminated Hal's sandy hair and light skin.

He had known it all along, he supposed. Hal would come. When he needed a champion, Hal would come.

Quickly he dashed from the window to check the wires from the lamp. A short circuit wasn't much, but it might buy Hal a minute or two.

Then he went back to the window to watch the men dismount. There was no one else around. No police. From his vantage point, he would have spotted any activity in the woods during the day. There had been nothing. Hal was alone, and probably a captive, at that.

But he had come.

"Hal! I'm here, Hal!" he shouted, pounding on the heavy glass.

Hal looked up for a moment before the other man shoved him roughly through the open door.

A few moments later, the big man who had stood outside his door since he was first brought to the house came into his room carrying a coil of rope. Arthur tried to duck him, but the man caught him easily and stuck a wad of cotton cloth into his mouth. At almost the same time, he shoved Arthur into a ladder-backed wooden chair, then tied him securely around the chest and ankles.

After an inspection of his work, the man left.

Arthur looked at the frayed cord of the lamp. Without his help, Hal would not even have a minute.

Hal almost wept with relief when he saw Arthur's face. If the kid wasn't dead, there was a chance. Never mind that he was outnumbered and had no weapons. Never mind that he had no cup to trade with Saladin or that the police had no interest in helping him. Arthur was alive, and Hal would fight with every ounce of strength in his body to keep him alive.

When his silent companion pushed him to the floor of the darkened room, Hal rolled and pulled the knife out of his belt. Then, springing to his feet, he lunged at the man.

The knife struck flesh, then bone, then an inner softness. He heard a gasp as the man struggled. Then the lights came on, and in that single, blinding instant, a swarm of bodies seemed to cover him.

When he could see once again, the bloodied knife was on the floor next to the dead man. The newspaper-wrapped cup had slid under the table. And he was lying facedown, pinned to a carpet by three men in black.

He could hardly breathe. One of the assailants had his knee on Hal's neck. With the right move—and Hal was certain the man knew how to execute it—the small bones would crack like peanut shells.

"Let him go," a deep voice boomed.

At once the three obeyed.

The man who had spoken stood in the center of the room, his arms folded in front of him. He, too, was dressed in black. His tremendous height gave him the appearance of some gigantic bird of prey at rest, its wings folded, its talons sheathed. He had only to glance sideways at the cup for one of the men to scurry over to pick it up.

But Saladin was in no hurry to see it. He looked instead at Hal, his eyes bright with amusement.

"You kill well," he said, the admiration in his voice genuine. "Most men would have thought twice about killing the messenger in a trade."

"This is no trade, and you know it," Hal said. "Now there's one less of you."

Saladin shrugged slightly in acquiescence, then held his hand out for the cup. The other man placed it, still wrapped, in his hand.

The tall man's face clouded. "What is this lie?" he growled. He threw it to the ground.

"You didn't think I'd bring the real cup with me, did you?" Hal laughed. "With all these goons hanging around waiting to slice me into bacon?" He tried desperately to sound convincing. "Look, the kid doesn't mean anything to me. I never met him until the day before yesterday. But there's no reason to kill him. Let him go back to his aunt, and I'll take you to the cup. You and me alone. Gentlemen's agreement. Okay?"

Saladin stared at him for a moment. Then his eyes softened. He smiled. "You do not have the cup," he said softly.

"Sure I do. Why would I offer—"

"Because you know I will kill you. And you would be willing to give your life for the boy." He shook his head. "You have not changed."

"Hey, I don't know what you're talking about. I'm giving you a chance to get back the thing you want most."

Saladin strode across the room. "Kill him," he said as he walked out the door.

There had to be something he could do. The lamp was not far away, and though his hands were tied, his fingers were free. Without a tool, short-circuiting the wires would mean a bad shock, maybe a fatal one. But there was no time to find a tool.

Hesitantly Arthur began to rock on the wooden chair until he wobbled precariously. At the last second, he tried to catch himself on the tips of his toes, but he knew as soon as he began the attempt that it wasn't going to work. He fell forward, managing to turn enough before he hit so that his shoulder, and not his face, struck the floor.

For a moment he lay there, perspiring with effort and pain. Then, slowly, he began to inch his way toward the lamp cord.

*Faster*, he thought, grunting as he wormed his way across the room on his side, dragging the heavy weight of the chair. If Hal was trying to fight his way out, there was no time to lose. He pushed himself harder, ignoring the throbbing pain in his shoulder.

Finally he reached the lamp cord. It took another few minutes to maneuver himself into a position where he could manipulate the wires with his hands behind his back.

*This is crazy*, he told himself. *You're going to get yourself killed.*

Carefully, because he knew the plug end was live, he

picked up the wire and reached backward toward the socket.

But what if it didn't help? What if the sudden darkness were to hurt Hal rather than help him? After all, he wasn't expecting it. What if Hal had already found his way to the stairs and was on his way to this room? He would never find it in the dark. Arthur would never get out.

*Then I might as well get electrocuted now*, he thought.

He steeled himself and jammed the plug into the socket.

A flash of blue flame spat from the metal plug. The force of the electrical jolt knocked Arthur forward like an invisible fist, flinging him across the room, the chair on his back like a turtle's shell. The chair twirled on one leg for an instant before coming to rest crookedly against the arm of the sofa.

*Oh, God, I'm still alive*, he thought, watching the muscles in his knee twitch. He didn't have enough strength left to wiggle the chair completely upright, so it stayed as it was, balanced on one leg.

He could hear shouting from the room three floors below.

"Ham-*mer*," he said weakly.

Arthur bent his head and smiled.

# CHAPTER FIFTY-ONE

If Hal had believed in miracles, he surely would have attributed the sudden darkness in the room to an act of God. All three of Saladin's men had been coming toward him when the lights inexplicably went out.

Hal reacted instantly by dropping to the floor and moving quietly in a low crouch toward the door. In the darkness, he could make out dim shapes searching the place where he had been, while the men cursed in a language he did not understand.

He put his hand around the doorknob and swung it open hard, so that it crashed against the backstop. Immediately, with an accompaniment of guttural shouts, they spilled out into the night. One, two, three black shapes.

But there had been six of them in the meadow, he thought briefly. He was sure of that. Saladin and five others. He had just killed one. That left four.

Yet he had seen only three men in the house besides Saladin. Where was the fourth?

He dismissed the thought. The man might be dead, for all he knew. Candy might have killed him in the fight that had cost the inspector his life. Or he may not have remembered correctly. It was not something to worry about.

Satisfied, he closed the door behind them and locked it, then turned toward what he remembered as being a stairway.

He had gone up a half dozen of the steps when a hand clamped around his ankle. The fourth man.

Hal hit the steps hard, cracking his head on the stone. By instinct he rolled over onto his back as the man dived onto him.

In the dark, Hal could make out only the faintest outline of a figure, but the outline was large and thick. The man raised an arm above his head and slammed it down against Hal's face. Hal felt a shuddering shock run through him from the impact. And then it struck again.

*The cup.* His face was being smashed by the steel cup that Saladin had discarded. Waves of red light washed across Hal's vision. He reached behind him for the knife, then realized that it was somewhere on the floor beneath the stairs. He had no weapon at all now.

The cup crashed down onto Hal's forehead again. Struggling to keep from passing out, Hal jerked his own arms upward and slammed both fists beneath the man's jaw.

The blow landed hard. With a sharp cry the shadowy figure above him reeled backward. Hal jabbed an elbow into his throat. The burly man fell back down the steps.

Hal did not have to follow him. He knew from the sound the man's head made as it hit the landing that he was dead.

Hal leaned against the wall for a moment, wiping the blood out of his eyes with his sleeve. Then he turned to crawl up the stairs.

He collapsed before he made it to the landing.

"The door has been bolted from inside," one of the men said. "He did not leave."

Saladin studied the house. "No, he wouldn't, I suppose."

After a long silence, the man asked, "Shall we go in after him?"

Saladin shook his head. "No, I believe there is a better way to stop him." He pointed to the barn. "Bring the kerosene."

The man looked at him in disbelief, but Saladin did not see the expression on his face. He was thinking of the treasure room in the basement, with its five thousand years of memories carefully preserved. What good were they to him now, without the cup? In the end, a life that spanned millennia was just as useless as anyone else's.

He spat, but the bitterness in his mouth remained. "Burn it down," he said.

Hal was awakened by his own coughing. The awful remembered taste of smoke was in his throat and hanging thick in the air. Through the landing window, he saw the flames licking up the side of the house.

He bolted down the stairs, tripping over the body of the fourth man, scrambling over the first he had killed, running toward the door, running . . . running to safety.

*Wait a second, Jeff, just hold on now, I'm coming . . .*

He slammed into the door, sobbing.

*No, it's not happening, not again, please God no*

The draperies were on fire. The edges of the wool carpet were smoldering, sending off plumes of black smoke.

Hal closed his eyes. Arthur was dead. He had to be. It was the way it was, the way of his nightmare, the way it had to be. He would be tied to the chair, his blue eyes glazed over, his little life gone. Oh, yes. It had come to this. And Saladin had known it all along. He had told him as much in the painting he had left for Hal in the funhouse. A special death, for a special fool.

Hal closed his eyes. "You stinking bastard," he said.

Then, his eyes washed fresh from his own tears of fear, he turned back and hurled himself up the stairway.

Arthur's panic hit him in waves. All of his senses seemed to be going haywire at once. His eyes stung from the smoke that poured in from the ventilating duct in black billows. The heat in the closed room caused him to break out in a drenching sweat. He could feel his own heart beating harder and louder. His ears rang with an eerie, high whine.

But mostly the panic was in his throat. Whenever he tried to swallow, he gagged. The smoke was filling his nostrils and lungs, but when his body tried to expel it with a cough, the wad of fabric in his mouth worked its way farther down his windpipe.

Soon he could breathe only by staying as quiet as possible, immobile, with his neck stretched up into the densest part of the smoke. But still he coughed, and with each cough, the gag went deeper and deeper.

He could feel his eyes bulging, the veins in his neck and temples about to burst. More than anything he longed to get the hateful balled-up rag out of his mouth. He pushed against it with his tongue until his jaw ached, but he could not dislodge it. And with every effort, he choked.

The choking was the most frightening thing. After a while, the constant gagging caused his stomach to churn. If he vomited, he knew, he would die. So he tried to ignore the extreme signals his body was sending, tried to sit quietly, breathing the black air, but his body would not be fooled. This was fire, he was suffocating, and every cell of his organism knew it. Foul, vinegarish fluid shot up from his stomach into his nostrils, filling them. He screamed. The sound was only a tinny muffled whisper. Afterwards, he tried to fill his lungs again, but could not.

There was no air now, none at all. Arthur felt his body stiffen and jerk. He tried to fight, but there was nothing he could do. The waves of panic crested, then began to subside, quickly, smoothly, rolling waves. An easy ride.

Easy. Yes.

He didn't bother to close his eyes. The smoke didn't hurt them anymore. His head fell back and he floated.

Water, maybe.

Easy ride.

If he stayed high, there was the smoke. It got into the lungs and cut off the oxygen and stopped the heart.

If he stayed low, there were the flames which tore at a man's flesh, piercing it like knifepoints.

Hal chose the flames.

He dropped to all fours on the landing before the last flight of stairs and scurried, like a crab, up the stairway. He could see only inches in front of him as he stumbled up the steps.

He had almost reached the top when the explosion occurred.

At first, he heard only the sound of glass breaking. The heat had caused the windows to blow out, one by one, like popcorn on a grand scale. Then there was a squealing, splintering crack and a boom like thunder as something came flying out of the darkness at him. He slid back down nearly the full flight of stairs on his belly as the object settled with a deafening crash.

It was so large that it filled the entire stairwell. By feel, he determined that it was a door, two inches thick, and solid. It had probably blown out of one of the top-floor rooms, hit the far wall, then caromed onto the stairs on the rebound. The first bounce had slowed its speed and power; otherwise he could not have moved in time to avoid it.

Hal climbed on top of it and moved cautiously, feeling splinters jabbing into the palms of his hands and his knees. When he reached the top, he turned to his right and touched the wall. It was sizzling hot. He recoiled at first, then forced himself to move along it, feeling for an opening.

He found it. Inside, because of the breeze between the broken window and the open doorway, the flames were even worse than those in the hallway, but the air was clearer. Clear enough to see the boy tied to a ladder-back chair, his head thrown back, his eyes open, his body motionless.

Hal moaned.

*You're the best, kid. The best there is.*

He froze where he stood. Slowly, as he watched, mindless and terrified, the boy's face contorted and elongated into an ugly mask. His limbs grew scales and claws. A tail formed, its razor-pointed end swishing lazily. The long snout spewed foul-smelling smoke. Its dark, mocking eyes danced with laughter.

"*Come get me, Hal,*" it said. "*I've been waiting for you so long. So . . . long . . .*"

And then it laughed, the hideous, hollow laughter of a hundred sweat-soaked nights.

*Come on, Hal, you were the best the very best kid you always come too late and it's too late now because that's what you're best at THE VERY BEST.*

With a scream, Hal rushed toward the creature and embraced it, pulling out the swollen gag, tearing off the ropes, putting his mouth on it as he ran with it in his arms toward the open window.

He kicked out the spiky shards of glass left in the frame and eased the still body onto the gable awning, dragging the rope behind him. Though they were outdoors, Hal could barely see for the smoke that streamed past them from the room.

There was no heartbeat. Hal pressed down on the scaly chest five times, then delivered a puff of breath into the monster's mouth. Five more times. Another breath.

"Breathe, Arthur," he begged. *Oh God, please let him live.*

Five more times.

*For you, my king.*

A gust of wind blew the column of black smoke pouring from the window away from them. With it flew the dragon scales, the claws, the pointed tail. They disappeared into the shimmering hot night like fine droplets of water.

The creature was gone. Hal pressed his face against Arthur's chest. He could hear a heartbeat.

*For you . . .*

He sprawled the child out on the hot roof, flinging one arm across the small body to hold him in place, hanging on to the glass-splintered window frame with his other hand, giving the breath in his own lungs to Arthur again and again.

"Please breathe," he whispered.

Another puff.

Again.

Once more.

And then the blue lips colored. A thin crease grew on Arthur's forehead, then deepened. He coughed, croupy, harsh. He gasped.

"Arthur. Arthur, it's Hal. Come back."

The boy's eyes opened. "Hal," he said, sounding strangled. He coughed again, then smiled.

Hal smiled back.

*You're the bes . . .*

The mocking voice was faint, traveling away.

*kid . . .*

Disappearing, like the dragon-creature, like all his ghosts.

*Bessssss*

The thinnest whisper, dispersing, leaving him forever.

Gone.

"What say we get out of here?" he asked softly.

Arthur rubbed the soot from his eyes. "I'm ready when you are."

Hal looked at him for a moment, then pulled him close and hugged him. He did not try to check the tears that fell into the boy's hair, salty, sooty tears of love and gratitude.

"C'mon," he said. He looped the rope below Arthur's armpits, braced himself in the window frame, and slowly lowered the boy. When Arthur was safely on the ground, Hal tied the rope around the window frame and shinnied down himself.

On the other side of the building, Saladin stood near the front entrance, his eyes fixed on the flaming specter of the house.

"My lord, the fire is nearing the barn. The horses . . ."

"Let them burn."

*Scream.*

He needed to hear them with his own ears. This man, this nobody, and an arrogant child had taken his life from him. A life so carefully crafted, woven like a fine tapestry over millennia, gone in an instant. He would grow old now. He would feel sickness and pain. And one night, his bones complaining, he would lie down and never rise.

For that, he would hear their screams as they died.

"Sire, please. The two are surely dead from the smoke . . ."

Saladin silenced him with an angry sweep of his hand.

He was probably right. They were already dead.

*But why did it have to end this way?*

Two had come back through the ages to join him. Only two, on the endless, lonely journey through time.

And he had killed them both.

Was killing all there was left, the last twisted, tortured avenue in the maze of his singular life? He had never loved. He had never ached with passion or remorse. He had never known the kindness of a friend, except for one afternoon long ago, when an old man had shown him medicinal rocks.

That had been his great mistake. He should never have befriended the wizard. If he had not, in a moment of self-indulgent abandon, given away the secret of the cup by saving Merlin's worthless life, he himself would not be dying now.

But in the end, he thought sadly, an afternoon's friendship was perhaps the only real pleasure he'd ever experienced. One afternoon, out of forty-five centuries.

He closed his eyes. He was getting soft. Thoughts of death did that to a man. They made one sentimental and ridiculous. They gave one regrets.

*I did not want to kill you, Arthur.*

*I wanted a new life, a new order. A great man to lead the world. A king. A companion. A friend.*

*I wanted Camelot.*

"Scream, damn you!" Saladin's voice rang out above the din of the fire. "Scream!"

"Sire!"

Saladin whirled on the man who had dared to interrupt his thoughts again, ready to strike him down. But the man only pointed to the far hills, toward the barn.

Its doors were open. And on the hillside, beyond the leaping flames, were two riders on horseback, heading into the woods.

Saladin clenched his teeth. "Bring the horses," he said.

Hal leaned low over the mount, trying to keep pace with Arthur's headlong gallop.

"Where'd you . . ." He winced as the horn of the saddle jabbed into his chest. ". . . learn to ride . . . like that?" he shouted.

Arthur laughed. "I never rode before!"

"What?"

"I've never been on a horse!"

"Could have fooled me," Hal muttered. The boy was a natural. He rode as if he'd spent his whole life on horseback. *Like an ancient king,* he thought.

He looked back over his shoulder, back at the burning house down in the hollow. Three men were riding out of the barn. They were leading a fourth horse, Saladin's stallion, while its owner waited, his silhouette black against the orange flames.

"They're coming after us," Hal said.

"Yes. They would."

"Maybe we ought to head into town. There are two cops, and—"

Arthur shook his head. "They won't help."

"Right . . . Well then, where are we going?"

The boy turned his smudged, blistered face to him. It was not a child's face any longer. The pale eyes were measured and determined, the mouth set.

"We're going home," he said.

# CHAPTER FIFTY-TWO

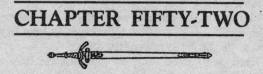

Arthur reined in his horse just short of the wall surrounding the castle ruins and dismounted.

"I don't know if this is a good idea," Hal said, looking around at the featureless meadow. "They're going to spot us here."

"I'm through hiding," Arthur said. "We're going to fight them."

"Here? Are you kidding?" Hal spoke so loudly that his horse shied. He grabbed wildly on to the animal's mane to keep from falling off. "There's no cover. We don't even have weapons, for pete's sake."

"Merlin!" Arthur called.

"What?"

"Saladin said the wizard would come if I called him." He tried again. "Merlin!"

Silence.

"Merlin! Mr. Taliesin!"

Faintly, they heard the sound of distant hoofbeats approaching.

"Forget it, kid. I tried that, too. Wherever the old man is, he can't hear you." Hal thought he could feel his heart breaking. "There's no magic. We're alone here."

"But he said . . ."

They both turned toward the sound of hoofbeats. Four horsemen emerged from the woods and were galloping across the open meadow toward them. Raised overhead, their scimitars gleamed in the moonlight.

"Then we'll fight them alone," Arthur said quietly.

Hal watched the horsemen come. Four of them, armed and battle-seasoned, against a bare-handed man and a boy.

"We'll lose," he said.

"Maybe. But we'll fight, all the same."

The boy's eyes seemed to be made of steel. Hal considered picking him up bodily and throwing him on one of the horses, but he knew that would do no good. Saladin and his men would catch up with them before long, and kill them like insects.

Arthur was right. Better to fight and die.

"No harm in trying," Hal said, trying to sound less pessimistic than he felt.

He dismounted and slapped both animals away. Being on horseback would be no advantage to someone who couldn't ride. He eyed a big pile of boulders at the bottom of a hill. "Looks like that'll be our best bet," he said, pointing to it. "Pick up all the rocks you can. We may get lucky and hit one of those jerks between the eyes."

*In the dark. Right. And maybe we'll stab one through the heart with a hickory stick while we're at it.*

They scrambled for rocks as the horsemen came on. "Wait until they get close."

"This is the rock that fell over," Arthur said. "The fake rock with the writing on it." He peered over the side to touch the long crack that ran up its length.

"Get down." Hal shoved him roughly behind the boulder, then stood up and threw a heavy stone the size of a baseball as the horsemen thundered toward them.

It hit one of the attackers in the shoulder just as he was about to close in for the kill. The force of the blow threw him backward, twisting, so that the blade swung down wildly. It missed Hal but struck the man-made boulder in front of Arthur so hard that the sword broke off at the hilt.

As the horseman rode past, Hal watched the shiny blade fly into the air and then land almost at his feet. "Mother of God, will you look at that," he said, picking it up. It was a piece of luck beyond imagining. He studied the broken steel crescent for a moment, then positioned it in his hand like a boomerang and let fly.

It hit another of the horsemen square in the chest. With a

high scream, the man tumbled off his horse. Hal let out a whoop.

He watched Saladin's men turn back and gather around their leader, apparently discussing what strategy should be taken. There was no hurry about the situation. It was understood that they would cut down the brazen American. But they had not expected him to fight so boldly.

The men grumbled, ignoring their fallen comrade who groaned and gasped on the ground beside the skittish hooves of their horses, the blood pulsing from the wound in his chest.

"Come on, you creeps!" Hal yelled gleefully. He turned to Arthur. "Three to two. The odds are getting better all the time."

"Hal, look at this," Arthur said. He had pulled a large chunk of mortar off the man-made rock. "The guy's sword broke it off. There's something inside."

Imbedded in the crumbling mortar was a cylinder nearly ten inches long, metallic from the looks of it, and studded with polished stones that looked black in the moonlight.

"What the hell is that?" Hal asked.

Arthur only grunted in reply. He was pulling at the other side, trying to break off the remaining piece of mortar that held it in place. "Help me, Hal. There's a crack in back. We can break it off."

Hal reached over and gave it a quick yank, thinking that the mortar would make a good weapon. It was big, but light enough to throw accurately. When it didn't give, he elbowed Arthur aside and braced the rock against his knees, pulling down with both hands.

"Forget it. There isn't time for—"

Just then the piece cracked off with a small cloud of dust. Hal hefted the chunk and crouched down as the horsemen began their second run. This time they split up and came at Hal and the boy from three different directions.

"Hal, it's . . ."

"Get down!"

He threw the piece of mortar at the tall leader riding

between the two others, but Saladin was too good a horseman. At the last instant before the rock would have struck, he veered his mount away. The mortar sailed past him, and he continued his charge.

He was so close that Hal saw the man's ugly smile before he felt the blade. The first blow sliced Hal diagonally, from the right side of his chest up through his neck.

Hal gasped, his eyes momentarily transfixed by the wound. The gush of his own blood was an amazing sight. It spurted from Hal's body like water from a sprinkler, pulsating with each heartbeat. Before he could even react to it, Saladin had reared his stallion, wheeled him around in a circle, and cut Hal again, this time a long vertical slice down the side of his right arm.

Saladin brought his horse to a stop. He looked down at Hal. His eyebrows arched; the black eyes registered something like mirth. Then he struck again. The third blow ran from shoulder to shoulder.

*He wants me to bleed to death,* Hal realized. Saladin had had every opportunity to make one deep, killing strike, but he had chosen instead to tease Hal, to make him dance with pain.

Far off, somewhere beyond the shock that was overtaking him, he heard Arthur scream.

Arthur! Somehow, he had to save Arthur.

Hal forced himself to stay lucid a moment longer, long enough to see the giant curved blade of Saladin's scimitar strike at him for the fourth time. He waited until it was close, very close. Then he leaped up and grasped the blade with both hands.

The pain coursed through him like a jolt of electricity. The blade was buried deep in his palms. Saladin tried to jerk it free, but Hal held fast.

*You're not getting this until you saw my goddamned hands off,* he thought. Then, screaming with the pain, he wrested the blade out of Saladin's grip and lunged toward the towering horseman.

The point of the sword dug into the tall man's leg, piercing it so deeply that the tip punctured the flesh of the horse beneath him.

The animal reared. Saladin kicked it into a gallop, retreating down the meadow. And following them, the tip of the naked steel blade growing out of his bleeding hands, ran Hal, staggering like a beheaded chicken, screaming incoherently.

"Hal!" Arthur called, terrified. But he knew Hal couldn't hear him now. Saladin had not fled. He had enticed Hal out onto the open field, away from the stones which had offered what little protection there was. Now he and his two remaining men were circling Hal, egging him to run after them, laughing at his uncontrolled dying gestures.

In the moonlight, Arthur could see the drunken tracks of Hal's movements by the black streaks of his blood on the silvery grass. Tears ran down the boy's cheeks. Unconsciously he squeezed the object in his hand.

Then, with a gasp, he saw it. The cylinder in the rock was made of gold. Blinking away his tears, he could make out the intricate carvings on either end of fine, roped bands.

It was the hilt of a sword. A magnificent sword made of gold and jewels and magic. A king's sword.

"I'm coming, Hal," he said softly.

Holding his breath, he reached into the fissure of the rock and grasped the golden hilt with both hands. He felt its power, a wild, singing energy that leaped from the metal into his body. It felt almost like the cup, strong and unearthly, pouring its magic into him; but this was infinitely more mighty than the cup. It was Excalibur, Arthur knew, free at last in the hands of its rightful master.

With a cry that began in the deepest part of his soul, he lifted the sword from the stone. And, as if relieved to be giving up its ancient treasure, the rock cleaved away in two halves.

Slowly the boy raised the gleaming silver blade.

Hal stood, wavering, in the midst of the three horsemen. Saladin's two henchmen watched as their master reached into a scabbard fastened to his saddle and drew out a long, double-bladed dagger. A knife for skinning game. His horse took another measured step forward toward Hal.

It was all over now, Hal knew. He had no strength left to fight with. He had lost again; now he would be peeled like some small animal before finally being left to find his shameful sanctuary in death.

"Come on, finish it," he gasped through his blood-filled mouth.

But Saladin did not approach. He seemed to be frozen atop his mount, looking past Hal down the meadow, to the stones where Arthur was. He turned the stallion away from the dying man and faced the boy across the field. The other men, confused, reined in their horses as well.

Seeing a faint chance, Hal tried a last blind charge toward the horsemen, but it was useless. Before he reached them, he stumbled and fell.

When he hit the ground, the scimitar's blade jarred loose from his hands. His thumbs hung down from his fingers like two strips of meat. His head bounced against the dew-covered grass. He rolled onto his side, staring hazily back toward the pile of stones and the boy he had failed to save from death.

And then he saw it, too: Arthur standing tall, holding in his hand the great sword of ages.

He forgot Saladin and his horsemen, still as statues on the meadow. He forgot the blood that was pouring from his own neck, and the useless objects that had once been his hands, and the pain that burned through his body like a living thing. He forgot that he was about to die.

"My king," he whispered.

For a moment the field was utterly silent. Not a whisper of breeze, not the chirping of a single insect. It was the silence of time turning backward. And then, ringing across the rolling hills came Arthur's command, rough with tears and pain and loss:

"To arms! Your king calls you to arms!"

The sound lingered in the air, echoing, echoing . . . Then, faintly, it was joined by another sound, the surging thunder of hoofbeats as, before them all, a great castle of stone began to materialize out of the air.

Camelot was being reborn.

It seemed to be made of mist at first, the walls and turrets, the vaulting keep that reached to the stars. But as the men in the meadow watched, they saw that it was a solid thing, as real as their own flesh. Banners flew from the ramparts. Trumpets sounded the call to arms.

From behind the high wall, the sound of hoofbeats grew louder until, with a piercing squeal of metal against metal, the great drawbridge descended and the knights poured out, hundreds of them, dressed in shining chain mail, led by eleven fierce men riding horses in full battle armor bearing the red dragon of their king, once and forever, Arthur of England.

" 'Attaboy, kid," Hal said. And then his head was so heavy that he had to let it drop. The wet grass felt cool and welcome.

# CHAPTER FIFTY-THREE

Saladin's two remaining lackeys fled, screaming, as the castle of Camelot rose out of the predawn mist, spewing forth an army of battle-ready warriors like a river of silver. The river flowed after them into the woods—all but the first eleven, the king's guard. These stopped where the tall Saracen waited astride his stallion, and surrounded him.

Saladin folded his arms and stared at each of the knights in turn. "Ghosts," he spat.

Laughing, a big, dark-haired knight knocked him off his horse with the side of his sword. Another, a grizzled old veteran, looped a rope around him and dragged him toward Arthur, who had run to kneel beside Hal. Within minutes, the others returned with the mangled bodies of Saladin's men. Then together, they all dismounted and fell on one knee to pay homage to the boy-king.

They filled half the meadow, the kneeling knights in armor. Hal propped himself up on one elbow to behold the sight. "They came," he whispered. "They came for you."

Arthur bent over him, sobbing. "Don't die, Hal. Please don't die."

"Might have to." He smiled weakly. "Hey, it's all right. I did what I could. Now it's up to you."

"No! Hal, no, don't leave me! Hal . . ."

His voice was so far away. Hal wanted to answer him, comfort him, somehow. He wanted to tell Arthur that he would be just fine without him, as fine as a man had ever been. But then, the boy would find that out for himself one day.

Hal did not regret dying. Like the lost knights, he too had waited a thousand years to find his king. Now he had found him. There would be no more demons hiding in his nightmares, no more fear. It was a good end, better than he had ever expected.

He closed his eyes and sank back, drifting. The Saracen Knight once again lifted the chalice from his hands. Once again the sword sang through the air, his blood flowed, he fell dying.

Oh, yes. The past was immutable and eternal. A man could not change a moment of it; all that was in his power was to forgive himself.

*For you, my king.*

*And for me.*

And Galahad, the loyal knight who had journeyed so far, smiled and made his peace with death.

In the village of Wilson-on-Hamble, many were already awake. Some had stayed up the whole night; others had set their clocks to arise just before dawn. It was St. John's Eve, and all waited to hear the sounds of King Arthur's ghost knights scouring the countryside looking for their fallen sovereign.

There were many among them who called it a hallucination or just a natural phenomenon, some curious auditory trick of nature's. But just the same, they expected to hear the riders again, as they did every year.

They were not disappointed. This time the hoofbeats seemed louder, more numerous than at any time they could remember. The town—every street and alley and walking path in it—resounded with the hollow beats. Every field and meadow and forest copse echoed with the roar of the ghostly cavalry.

Then, surprisingly, as quickly as the sound had come, it faded.

The villagers closed their eyes and went back to sleep, perhaps to dream of days when there were knights and warrior-kings and a world of justice and peace was struggling to be born.

But that world, each knew, existed only in dreams.

Yet in a rolling, rock-strewn meadow, separated from the town by a few miles and sixteen centuries, one knight found that death refused to attend him.

The deep, still calm that had been falling upon Hal like snow stopped suddenly, replaced by a warm buzzing feeling.

Warm . . . hot, burning hot *Oh Jesus, am I in Hell?* jumpy, fiery, red-embered hot.

He did not will it, but he felt his eyes opening. Kneeling beside him was Merlin, dressed in his blue wizard's robes. In his hands he held the cup. He pressed it against Hal's cheek.

Hal felt the blood that had filled his mouth to choking start to dry up. He felt a line of healing fire tracing over the wounds that Saladin's blade had made.

Slowly he raised his hands to his eyes. The cuts that had almost severed his thumbs were gone. His fingers had healed completely, as if the wounds had never been inflicted. There was only the memory of pain, and that was dispelled by the sight of Arthur's face, smudged and weary, smiling radiantly down at him.

He sat up and grinned at Merlin. "Took you long enough," he said.

"I *told* you," the wizard answered, bugging out his eyes in annoyance. "I couldn't get out until the king himself called me."

"Arthur called you plenty of times."

"Not as the king." He looked at the boy. "First, *you* had to believe." The old man breathed deeply. He looked back at the castle with pride. "You've brought it all back, Arthur. You and your brave, rock-headed friend."

Arthur threw his arms around Hal, who laughed and then extricated himself from the boy's grip. "All right, that's enough small talk," he said. "See to your men." He gestured toward the field of kneeling knights. "And Dracula here."

Saladin looked up at them from his position as a captive on the ground. His eyes were murderous.

"Go haunt a house," Hal said.

"He's wounded. Take care of him," Arthur commanded the knights who were nearest to the prisoner.

The big dark-haired knight tore off part of his tunic, but when he approached, Saladin spat at him. The knight drew back, reaching for his sword.

"No, Launcelot," Arthur said, holding out his arm.

*Launcelot*, Hal thought. The boy had actually spoken to him. For the first time, Hal fully realized that these were not ghosts, not the frozen, dappled images he had seen in the dream castle where Merlin had outlined the task before him, but real men, as alive as he was. Not five feet away from him stood the great Launcelot himself, sweating and breathing hard, his face flushed with fury at a sullen prisoner.

Without thinking, Hal reached out to touch the knight; then he caught himself, and withdrew his hand.

Launcelot caught the movement, and the angry features of his own face softened into a smile.

"Rise, Saladin," Arthur said.

The tall man lurched to his feet, his hands bound behind him, his black leg-wrappings wet with the blood from his wound.

" 'Kill your enemies,' " the boy said softly. "Do you remember when you told me why? 'Humiliate them. Degrade them. Make an example of them for others . . .' "

Saladin's black gaze wavered for a moment, then settled back levelly to meet Arthur's. "I remember," he said.

"You asked me if I wanted to kill you. I couldn't answer you then. Now I can."

The dark eyes blinked lazily.

"Your life has been a curse, Saladin. I figured that out during the time I spent alone in that room. I was lonely and scared all the time, but I knew there were places where I wouldn't be lonely or scared, places where people loved me and wanted me around. All I had to do was get to them. But there aren't any places like that for you, are there?" His forehead furrowed. "In the whole world, in all the time you've lived, there hasn't been anyplace where you belonged."

Saladin's mouth turned down bitterly. "You are a child. Those matters are of no importance to me."

Arthur nodded. "That's the trouble, I think. Nothing is important to you. You haven't had any reason to live for a long, long time." He turned to Launcelot. "Untie him."

As the big knight loosened the ropes around Saladin's wrists, Arthur walked slowly over to Merlin and took the cup in his own hands. "I'm going to give you a gift," he said quietly.

Saladin's voice trembled with incredulity. "The cup."

Merlin audibly sucked in his breath. "Arthur, don't be rash—" He reached for the cup himself, but Arthur cut him off with a gesture.

"No, not this," he said. "Although I was tempted. Another hundred centuries of a life like yours would be punishment enough for anyone. But I don't want to punish you."

Launcelot and Gawain looked at one another indignantly.

"That's right," Arthur said, frowning, directing his remarks to his own men. "If you were given the chance to live forever, there isn't one of you who wouldn't turn out as twisted as he is."

He turned back to Saladin. "My gift to you is a life without the cup. A real life, as painful and precious as everyone else's." His eyes bore into those of his enemy's. "Accept that life, Saladin. Learn what it means to be alive."

Saladin sneered. "And so, out of the kindness of your heart, you'll keep the cup yourself," he said. "Your generosity is touching."

Arthur didn't answer.

"You won't hide it from me forever, you know."

The boy smiled. "You aren't going to live forever," he said.

The tall man turned his back on him. Slowly, as if he were walking in a procession, he made his way through the assembled knights, who cleared a path for him.

Hal sighed with relief. Saladin was still Saladin, and Hal sincerely hoped he would never see him again, but the boy—the king, in his wisdom—had been right about one thing; Now, at least, Saladin wasn't going to live forever.

And Arthur was.

Then, as sudden as the bite of an adder, Saladin whirled around in his tracks near the rugged old knight named Gawain and clubbed him on the side of his head with both hands. Gawain tried to fight him off, but Saladin wrenched away the man's sword in the space of a heartbeat.

"Arthur! Look out!" Hal shouted.

Smoothly, without an instant's hesitation, Saladin swung the sword overhead and brought it sighing down toward Arthur.

Hal dived on top of the boy, knocking him out of the way of the blow. The metal cup rolled out of Arthur's hand. Saladin snatched at it, but Hal shot out his leg to trip the tall man.

Saladin fell, and Hal jumped on top of him. They struggled, rolling atop one another as the king's knights stood by watching helplessly, unable to strike at one without injuring the other.

Finally Saladin threw Hal off. Immediately the king's men surrounded him, their weapons drawn.

Saladin held up his bare hand. "Give him a sword," he commanded, his eyes fixed on Hal. "If I must die, I wish to die honorably. I challenge the king's champion to single combat."

The knights murmured among themselves. Single combat. Despite his wickedness, the Saracen had offered an honorable settlement. One man against another. It was acceptable.

Some of the men nodded in agreement. Even Gawain, whose sword was in Saladin's hand, reluctantly withdrew from the circle surrounding the tall, foreign knight.

"Don't allow it, Arthur," Merlin warned. "Saladin attacked you openly, after you granted him his freedom. Have your men execute the black-hearted devil now."

Arthur looked, frightened, toward Hal. The Round Table knights had all moved away from Saladin, leaving room for the two men to engage in battle alone.

Merlin's voice was shrill. "Your friend does not know how to handle a sword!" he shouted. "If you permit him to fight that monster, you might as well kill him yourself!"

Hal, too, saw the knights. They were watching Arthur as well, but the expressions on their faces were quite different from Merlin's. They were looking to their king to uphold their honor. For eleven knights in armor to attack a single man, regardless of the circumstances, would be a mockery of justice. And justice was what Arthur had stood for, back in the days when injustice was the rule of law.

That, Hal understood at last, was what had kept the legend of the once and future king alive. Not charisma, not victory, but *justice* had been the shining light that Arthur brought to the darkness of the world.

"Give me a sword," Hal said.

Quickly Launcelot passed over his great broadsword. It was heavy, heavier than Hal had ever imagined. He tried to swing it with one hand, the way he had seen actors in movies handle them. It wobbled wildly.

Saladin smiled.

The knights exchanged glances.

Merlin pleaded once more. "Arthur, he can't—"

"Stay out of this!" Hal snapped. He spoke to the wizard, but he shot a furious look at Arthur, too, and the boy responded with silence. Hal tried to steady the sword.

At last Launcelot broke away from the rest of the knights and stood behind Hal. Gently, the big man placed Hal's right hand near the base of the hilt, and his left hand near the pommel.

Hal felt humiliated. Merlin's words burned in his ears. Hal knew less than nothing about fighting with such a weapon. He would be slaughtered in minutes by a man of Saladin's skill.

Saladin had planned it that way, of course. He wanted Hal's death to be a joke, as most of his life had been. Whatever happened to Saladin afterward, he would have this one final triumph to savor.

Without exchanging a word, Launcelot seemed to feel Hal's anguish. He placed his hand on Hal's shoulder, and when Hal looked into the clear blue eyes filled with compassion, he understood that his death would not be a joke to this man.

He raised the big sword with both hands. It was a signal. Launcelot stepped back, leaving Hal alone in the clearing with his executioner. Then slowly, lowering his head in a mocking salute, Saladin advanced.

The first parries were deliberate and slow. Saladin meant to show a duel, not a murder. As in the games of chess he had once played with the doctor in the sanitarium, he allowed his opponent to feel that he might have a chance of winning. It drew out the endgame. It made the play more interesting.

Once, twice: lazy strokes. The American responded in a comical frenzy, crashing the huge sword in front of him as if it were a bludgeon. Hal's eyes were wild and panic-stricken, his muscles quivering with tension. At this rate, he would be exhausted in no time at all.

Saladin would make a game of this one, tease him, make him dance. The knights would not interfere. Single combat was a cornerstone of their quaint code. And later, after the American was dead, when Saladin once again held the boy at the point of his sword, they would trade the cup for the king's life, then permit Saladin to go free. That, too, was what the chivalrous fools considered to be noble behavior. *Yes, Hal. Try to fight me.*

*Don't want to make it a joke, I owe that much to Arthur. My life for the King's honor . . . Arthur, for you . . .*

Saladin half-closed his eyes, breathing deeply. He was listening to the man's pathetic mind now.

The American knew he was going to die.

*Oh, yes, Hal. Yes, you will.*

He could almost smell the coward's blood.

He moved in closer, the sword moving effortlessly, swinging like a pendulum, higher, higher.

*Careful, Hal. You'll lose your head.*

He could wait no longer. He thrust viciously. The sword whistled near Hal's throat. Hal stumbled backward. The sword swooped again.

Hal staggered back wildly, watching the blade in the long arms slash closer to his neck, trying not to think about the possibility of dying at Saladin's hands. The tall man was planning to cut his head off, that was clear. And though Hal tried not to think, an image stuck in his mind: *Without a head, even the cup couldn't save him.*

He panicked.

*That's right, Mr. Woczniak. But what difference would it make, really?*

Hal swallowed.

*You've always been a loser, Hal. You couldn't fight me sixteen hundred years ago, and you can't now. All you can do is die. It's all you've ever been good for.*

Saladin's eyes widened, smiling.

*Hmmm?*

"Don't listen to him!" Merlin shouted from somewhere far away. "I can hear his thoughts, too, and they're full of lies! Hal! Hal . . ."

*Come to me, Hal. I'll make it quick. You know you're going to die. You've known it all along, haven't you? The boy doesn't need you anymore. He's got the wizard. No one needs you. It's time, Hal. Come.*

Hal's back struck something hard. A tree. His legs were trembling; he felt a pressing need to urinate.

Saladin's sword came close, so close that Hal could feel its wake in the hollow of his throat. He uttered a small cry; the weapon in his hands fell to the ground. Instinctively he raised his arms to cover his face.

"Hal!"

It was Arthur's voice, ringing through the meadow like a clarion bell. Through his splayed fingers Hal saw the boy twist out of Merlin's grip and run toward him, the jeweled sword in his small hands.

Saladin turned slightly toward the child, a smile playing on his lips. His hostage was practically throwing himself at him. Yes, he thought, this was all going to work out perfectly.

"No, Arthur!" Hal shouted. "Get away, damn it! Get away now!"

The boy stopped in his tracks, but the sword did not. Bending over nearly double with the effort, he heaved the golden cross overhead.

Perhaps it was the wind. The sword should have fallen to the ground within a few yards. It should not have sailed on through the air, windmilling end over end like a gleaming silver star. It should not have fallen directly over Hal, who had resigned himself to death once again, as he had those long ages ago.

Yet it did, and Hal was so filled with wonder at the sight of it that he questioned nothing. He lifted his hands heavenward, as he knew he must, and received into them the living metal of Excalibur.

Saladin attacked him at once. The move was subtle and lethal, aimed at Hal's heart. Hal watched it come, but he did not struggle to master the sword he held. Not this sword. It sang to him, and with his body he listened to its ancient song, giving himself to it.

Excalibur danced to its own music. Filled with grace and power, it pushed back the tall Saracen like a block of wood, then struck the sword held by the long arms, again, again, shooting off sparks of brilliant light in the half- morning.

*You're nothing. You're still nothing, even with the wizard's sorcery.* Saladin's words insinuated themselves into Hal's mind. *I can outlast the magic, Hal. I can outlast you all.*

Suddenly the sword in Hal's hands felt heavier. Its blade grew duller. He fought on, but his shoulders ached with each empty swing of the ungainly object.

*It was never yours, you see. You may have tricked it for a moment, but Excalibur belongs to a king, not to a worthless drunk.*

Sweat poured off Hal's face. The muscles in his forearms twitched with fatigue. Finally, panting, he lowered the great sword.

*That's better. The magic was never meant for you.*

Saladin swooped in for the killing stroke.

"Go to hell," Hal said, and brought the great sword up to meet Saladin's with such cold force that the tall man's back arched, his arms flung away from him.

"Read my mind now, dirtbag." He struck Saladin's belly, crosswise. His eyes bulging with surprise, the dark man buckled suddenly forward, his arms reflexively trying to seal the gaping wound.

"The cup . . ." Saladin whispered. Blood poured out of his mouth.

The second stroke sliced through Saladin's neck. The severed head fell. Its eyes were still open.

*Thank you.*

Hal didn't know if the voice was Saladin's or his own.

A great roaring shout went up from the knights.

Wearily Hal retrieved Launcelot's fallen sword and re- turned it to the big knight. Then he brought Excalibur to Arthur and held it out to him.

"Is he really dead?" the boy asked, amazed by what he had just seen.

Hal nodded. "It's all over," he said. A few steps away lay the metal cup, forgotten since the start of the combat. Hal picked it up and held it out to Arthur. "He won't be coming after this again."

Arthur took it in one hand while he held the sword with the other. He hefted the small cup, feeling its warm mystery. Then, with a sigh, he offered it to Merlin.

"I want you to get rid of this," he said.

The wizard blinked. "I will put it in a safe place, naturally . . ."

"No. I don't want it hidden. I want it to be lost. No one—not me or you or anyone—must find it."

Merlin gaped at him. "Surely you can't . . ."

"I don't want it!" The boy's voice carried over the heads of the now-silent knights. "It's brought nothing but misery to anyone who's ever known about it."

"But the dream," Merlin said, his face pained. "Long ago, I had a vision in which you were offered the cup by the Christ himself . . ."

"No," Arthur said. "I had the same dream. It wasn't a gift. It was a *choice*. And I've made it."

Merlin pleaded silently with Hal to intervene.

"It . . . it saved my life," Hal said.

"Yes. And now you've got a second chance. We both have. Let's take it, Hal, for as long as we've got. But no longer. I'm not going to end up like him." He gestured to Saladin's beheaded body. "And you aren't going to, either."

His young face was drawn, but his eyes were smiling. "We're not ready for the cup," he said softly. "None of us." He fondled it lovingly, like a wild animal he had befriended and was about to set free. "Maybe in a thousand years, people will know how to handle something so wonderful. But not now."

There was a long silence. Merlin bent his head.

Finally Hal cleared his throat and snatched the cup out of the boy's hand. He tossed it to Merlin like a baseball. "You heard him," he said. "Get rid of it."

Merlin sighed. Once again he had offered the king a treasure beyond price. And once again he had refused it.

He looked up to the lightening sky. A choice, he had said.

Between a short life and an everlasting one. What sort of choice was that? Who in his right mind would choose not to live forever?

The moon was a fading crescent. The long night was over at last. Near its inner curve, to the west, was a cluster of faint stars.

*The lion*, Merlin thought. By Mithras, it had been more than a thousand years since that night, when Nimue had decided that the Greek version of eternity was the true one. He smiled, remembering. The haphazard aggregation of stars in no way resembled a lion, then or now.

*That's because you have no imagination*, she had said. *The lion's there, and I'm going to be the heart of it.*

Nimue.

She, too, had chosen not to keep the cup.

The wizard's old eyes misted with tears. What happened to a soul after it died? Was it reborn, like Arthur's, in the identical body it had occupied in another life? Or like Hal's, shifting restlessly from generation to generation, searching for something it could not name? Or did it simply vanish somewhere into the vast sea of time?

Nimue, my only love, will I never find you again?

Through his wavering vision, the stars near the moon twinkled. And one, he saw, in the center, the lion's heart, shone brighter than the rest.

He made a sound, halfway between a laugh and a cry.

"Merlin?" Arthur asked.

The old man waved him down. "It's nothing, boy." He sniffed. Then he laughed truly. "I think I know what to do."

Some distance away, he climbed up on a tall boulder. Then, deep in his throat, he began the call. It welled up out of him, a whistling, shrieking noise like the cry of eagles. He held up the cup, stretching his arms toward the vanishing stars, calling, calling until the metal sphere seemed to glow.

The trees rustled. Below them, the knights looked around in anticipation and fear. Some of them crossed themselves. The wizard was at work again.

And then the birds appeared.

From every corner of the sky they came, the great predators alongside tiny, thin-beaked avians. They came until the sky was black with them and their shadow blocked out even the light of the waning stars. They screamed and sang; the beating of their wings flattened the meadow grass.

They came to Merlin for the cup, and when he gave it up to them, they soared away and dispersed.

The men in the field looked up in silence. The birds were gone. The sun would rise soon and the day would be warm and long and sweet.

# CHAPTER FIFTY-FOUR

When Merlin came down from the boulder, the knights gave him a wide berth.

"Yes, yes, I know," he muttered irascibly. "You think I'm going to turn you all into fish."

Arthur was smiling. "Thank you, old friend," he said.

The wizard grunted.

Hal was the first to break the silence. "What happens now?" he asked. "I mean, as far as I know, England already has a monarch. I don't think she'd appreciate being usurped by a ten-year-old kid from Chicago."

"Arthur isn't going to usurp anyone," Merlin said with annoyance.

"So? What's he going to do, then?"

"Dash it all, *I* don't know! I told you in the castle that he would find his own way in the world. All I can do is to keep him safe from harm until he's ready to begin whatever it is he's going to do."

"Keep him safe?" Hal set his hands on his hips. "That was your idea of keeping him safe?"

Merlin's face reddened. "Cheeky!" he sputtered. "From the beginning, I knew you'd be . . ."

He took a deep breath to calm himself. "Perhaps you're right," he said blandly. "Things do go wrong sometimes. But you needn't worry any longer. Arthur will remain in the castle to await the millennium."

"*What?*" Hal and the boy shouted at the same time.

"Well, of course. It's the only way . . ." He shook his head emphatically. ". . . the *only* way, now that the cup is gone, to ensure the King's safety."

"Wait a minute," Arthur said. "Are you going to make me disintegrate or something?"

"Oh, it won't be like that," the old man said gently. "You'll be able to see yourself and all the others. It will be Camelot, just the way it was."

He inclined his head toward the knights. Launcelot nodded.

Arthur regarded the great sword in his hands. "Back to Camelot," he said with a faint smile.

"Exactly. You'll be able to do all the things you'd like. The only difference will be that other people—current people, that is—won't be able to see you until you're ready. It's not strange at all, really. Hal's been inside. You know what I mean, don't you, Hal?"

"Well, I wouldn't say it wasn't strange," Hal said. The knights were all watching him.

Things happened to kids, even ordinary kids. Car accidents. Muggers. Crazies. He had quit the FBI because he couldn't stand some of the things that happened to kids.

"None of those things must happen to Arthur," Merlin said quietly.

Hal looked up, startled. "No," he said. He saw Arthur's confused face. "What I mean is, it might have seemed strange to me because, hey, after all, I'm not King Arthur," he said with false heartiness. "You know, I think it'll be a blast. Do you know what most kids would give to spend a few years with the knights of the Round Table at Camelot?"

Arthur looked up sadly. "But what about you, Hal? Would you come, too?"

"Me?" He looked around at the knights standing before the great crenellated walls of Camelot. He had been there, with his heroes, seated among them in a place of moondust and magic. He had done what he had been asked to do. He had kept the faith of a slum kid with two broken legs and a head filled with dreams and had seen those dreams come true. For a time—a brief, awesome, magnificent time—he had felt the pure fire of Galahad's restless soul.

But Galahad's job was finished now; it was time for Hal Woczniak to come back. Another night at Benny's, another car to fix for the Greek pimp, another morning when he'd wake up next to a woman he didn't remember meeting. Hal's life.

"Naah," he said, shaking his head. "I don't belong there."

His eyes met Merlin's. The old man understood. The future belonged to Arthur now. There was no place at Camelot for an ex-FBI agent whose life was behind him.

Hal smiled. "Go ahead, kid. You aunt's on her way to London by now. She thinks we're both dead. I left her your instructions about what to do. But I'll find her. I'll tell her you're all right."

Arthur shook his head. "You won't find her," he said. "That's the point of the plan. No one will find her."

"There's got to be some way . . ."

"I don't think so. I worked it out carefully."

There was a silence. "I'm sorry," Hal said finally. "I thought . . ."

"You were right, Hal. I didn't think we'd come through this, either." He sighed. "Anyway, I suppose it's better that she doesn't know about this. No one should know."

"But she loves you," Hal said.

*And I love her.*

"I know," Arthur answered slowly. "Maybe that's why it's best to leave her alone."

Hal looked out over the meadow. The boy had said it all. Emily had her work. She would hurt for a while, hurt badly, but in time she would be able to go on with her life. In his own time, too, Arthur would go back to her himself. And neither one of them had any further need of Hal Woczniak.

"All right," Hal said quietly. He shrugged and held out his hand. "Well, I guess this is good-bye." Arthur's eyes welled. His lips were squeezed tightly between his teeth. "Go on. I can't hang around here forever."

"Kneel, Hal," the boy said.

"What?"

"Kneel." He stood stiffly, the sword held upright in front of him.

"Now, this is going too—"

Launcelot came over and rested his big hand on Hal's shoulder. His eyes were kind but firm as he guided Hal gently down onto one knee.

"Okay, I get your drift," Hal said. Feeling foolish, he lowered his head.

Arthur stepped up to him solemnly. Then, touching Hal first on one shoulder and then the other with the heavy sword, he spoke: "Be valiant, knight, and true; for you are the most loyal of men, and beloved of your king." He stepped back. "Arise, Sir Hal."

But Hal could not get up. Not just then. The touch of the sword left him rooted, his thoughts swirling around him, centuries of memories. He had come looking for his king in a thousand different lifetimes. In all of them he had failed; all but this last.

The king had come home. Galahad, indeed, had done well.

"Your Majesty," he whispered.

# CHAPTER FIFTY-FIVE

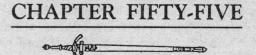

Merlin stopped them near the boulder where Arthur had found the sword.

"You can't go any farther," he told Hal. "Of course, if you'd like to reconsider the offer to come with us . . ."

Hal smiled. "No, thanks. I'll take my chances out here."

The old man nodded. "I think that's best," he said.

"Well? What say we get this show on the road?"

Arthur put his arms around his waist. "I'll miss you," he said.

"I'll miss you, too." He mussed the boy's hair, then pushed him away. "Go on, now. Be a good king, or whatever it is you're going to be this time around. Scoot."

Hal folded his arms in front of him and watched Arthur lurch away, holding on to Merlin's robes with one hand like a small child, while the other clung fast to the enormous sword. Behind them, the army of knights waited on their mounts, eager to bring their king back to his castle at last.

Then, at the last moment before they reached the drawbridge, Arthur turned and ran back.

"What is it?" Hal asked. "What's wrong?"

"I can't go, Hal."

"What are you talking about? You'll be fine in there. It's where you belong—"

"No, it's not!" His face was flushed. "Don't you see? I might have belonged there sixteen hundred years ago, but I'm not that King Arthur anymore. I'm ten years old, Hal. Whatever I'm going to do with my life, I've got to become a man first."

"So? You'll get older in the castle."

"What am I going to learn there? Everything in that place has been dead for a thousand years."

"It's the safest place for you."

"But I don't want to be safe! I want to be alive!"

They stared at one another. "Arthur . . ."

"I'm coming with you," the boy said.

"You're . . ." Hal backed away. "Oh, no, you're not."

"I won't be any trouble, I promise. I'm good with my hands, and I learn fast. I'll do whatever you say. Just take me with you. Teach me what you know."

"Teach you what? I don't know anything! Jesus, you want to grow up like me?"

"Yes, Hal," Arthur said. "Just like you."

"I'm a bum."

Slowly Arthur shook his head. "No, Hal. You're the best. The best there ever was."

He walked back to the cracked boulder and held the sword above it.

"No!" Merlin cried, running toward them. "Don't put it back! Don't . . ."

Arthur slid the sword back into the stone.

Immediately the castle began to fade. A low mist fell over it all, the towers and battlements, the courtyards, the moat. It surrounded the stunned knights, who looked at one another in bewilderment as they, too, grew as insubstantial as whispers. Horses whinnied, their manes becoming transparent, like spiderwebs.

Only one man did not flinch. Launcelot, mounted like an immovable rock on his steed, kept his eyes steadily on Hal as the mist enveloped him. His face showed no fear. Instead, it seemed to Hal, there was something like pride in the big knight's eyes. While the others around him vanished, Launcelot made his right hand into a fist and brought it over his heart in a silent pledge.

Hal frowned at first. Then he understood. The knight was asking for Hal's own promise to guard his king until Camelot rose again.

Slowly he lifted his fist to his heart.

The big knight nodded once, then faded away to nothing.

* * *

"I wish you hadn't done that," Merlin said.

The meadow was as it had been before, a ruin of blackened, moss-covered stones surrounded by dewy grass. Only one thing was missing. Hal squinted into the distance.

"Saladin's body," he said. "It's gone."

"Of course it's gone. You killed him when the castle was here. That was centuries ago, in what you call real time. His bones have turned to ashes by now."

Hal's face drained of color. "You mean we were actually . . . actually . . ."

"Back at Camelot. Yes. The King called it all back." He eyed Arthur balefully. "And then he sent it all away."

Hal looked out over the empty field. "And the cup . . . Where did it go?"

"Only the wild birds know that," Merlin said. He sighed. "Still, we may find it again." Arthur glanced at him sharply.

"At the next millennium, perhaps," the old man added with a smile.

Hal looked Merlin up and down. "Hey, how come you're still here?"

"I didn't will myself back. I can't be in two places at once, you know. As long as you two are going to be bumbling around the planet, somebody's got to keep an eye on you."

"Oh, no," Hal said. "I didn't sign on for this. I'll look after Arthur until I can find his aunt, but I'm not taking on a grouchy old man on top of that."

"Who are you calling grouchy?" Merlin snapped. He reached into a deep pocket of his robe. "Here. You'll need this." He pulled out a wad of hundred-pound notes and handed them to Hal as if they were a fistful of worms. "Filthy stuff, money. Makes your skin stink. And you can't buy anything you really need with it." He brushed off his hands.

"Where'd you get this?" Hal asked suspiciously.

The old man closed his eyes in exasperation. "I'm a *wizard*, remember? Go ahead and take it. You can exchange it for airplane rides and such."

"What about you?"

"I've got to bury that boulder before some archaeolobaby gets hold of it. Go on, though. I'll catch up with you later."

"Later when? Where? I don't even know where we're going."

"But I will," Merlin said slyly.

"I don't like it. Not one bit."

"Actually, this may prove to be fun," the old man said, ignoring Hal. "I haven't been on a good adventure for the better part of two millennia."

"You're not coming," Hal said stolidly.

"We'll see." He shooed them away with a fluttering motion of his hands.

Muttering, Hal turned and walked out of the meadow, the boy running behind him. "I suppose we're going to walk to the train station in Wilson-on-Hamble," he grumbled. "Ten miles."

"I don't mind," Arthur said cheerfully.

"I do. Well, the old haunt was right about one thing. Money never buys what you really need."

"Like a friend," Arthur said.

"I was thinking more of a taxi. My feet are killing me." They stepped over the narrow blacktop road. "Did I say taxi? This place is so isolated, we'll be lucky to find a gum wrapper here."

Just then a pair of headlights crested the hill in front of them and skidded to a stop.

"Say, guv'nor," the driver shouted. "Seem to have got myself bollixed up. Would you know the way to Wilson-on-Hamble?"

Hal looked up at the bubble on top of the black car.

"You're a taxi?" he asked.

"Right you are. Off duty, but I'll give you a lift if you need one."

Arthur climbed into the backseat. As Hal was getting in beside him, he looked back up the hill, toward the castle ruins. The old man was standing there. He raised his arm and waved.

Hal smiled and shook his head. "Thanks, you old turkey," he said. He held up his hand in a silent salute.

Merlin took a last walk among the ancient stones. Things hadn't turned out half-badly after all, he thought. Oh, the boy was willful and headstrong, and didn't know what was good for him, but he'd expected that. No one had ever been able to make up Arthur's mind for him back in the early days. It was only when he became a politician that he'd lost himself.

Maybe that wouldn't happen this time. Not if the redoubtable Mr. Woczniak had anything to say about it.

He sat down on a rock and sighed. Yes, all in all, it had been a fine night.

He was startled by the sudden appearance of a small grimy face from behind a rock.

"Who the devil are you?"

"Tom Rogers, sir," the boy said shakily. "I live down the village, sir."

"Then what are you doing here?"

"Come to hear the horsemen. You know, St. John's Eve."

"Ah. And did you?"

The boy blinked. "Why, they was all here, in the flesh," he said. "And you was in the thick of them." He waited for a response from the old man. When there was none, he went on, as if trying to jog Merlin's memory: "Killings, there was, and some bloke half-bleeding to death, hacked to pieces, and he come right back to life without a mark on him . . ." He was talking so fast that he had to wipe the saliva from his mouth with his ragged sleeve.

"And then the castle come up real as you please—I seen that before, mind you, but never like this, with the drawbridge down and all the knights charging out, why there must have been near a million of them, all in armor . . ."

He cocked his head. "You seen it, right?"

Merlin laughed. "I'm sure I don't know what you're talking about, lad."

"But you was *there*. You was . . ." He turned away,

brushing at his eyes. "It's you old ones never remember," he said despairingly.

Merlin sat quietly for a moment. "Then why don't you make us remember?" he said at last.

"What's that mean?" the boy asked belligerently.

"Why, write it down. Write all about the knights and the castle and the, ah, marvelous wizard. Write about the young boy who pulled the sword from the stone and began a new world. Start from the beginning, pay attention as you grow up, and write it down. Write it all, Tom."

The boy stood, dumbfounded. "Write? Me?"

"Why not? It's a respectable trade. Nothing like being a bard, of course. Now that was a glorious profession. But I'll tell you about that another time."

"Will you be here when the castle comes back again?"

"I wouldn't be surprised if I were."

The boy stepped back, watching him. Slowly a broad grin grew across his face. "He was a jolly marvelous wizard," he said.

"Quite. You see, you've got a way with words already." The old man stood up. "Now run along, boy, and practice. The king will need a chronicler."

"What's that, sir?"

"Look it up." He gave him a shove. The boy ran off laughing. His laughter filled the *growing day*. Then gradually it was replaced by the sound of horses' hooves, phantom horses carrying their riders on their endless search for their king. They came like thunder, galloping across the meadow, filling all the places time had emptied. They rode as they always did on *St. John's Eve*, and when they had passed, the *world* was still again except for the boy's faraway laughter.

*Write it all, Tom*, Merlin thought. *It will make a good story. A jolly marvelous story.*

# Historical fiction available from

**TOR FORGE**

## THE SINGING SWORD • Jack Whyte
In Book Two of the Camulod Chronicles, Jack Whyte tells us what legends have forgot: the history of blood and violence, passion and steel, out of which was forged a great sword…and a great nation.

## GOLDFIELD • Richard S. Wheeler
"Mixing history and melodrama with fast-paced storytelling and frontier detail, Wheeler paints a vivid picture of life in a turn-of-the-century Nevada mining town called Goldfield."—*Publishers Weekly*

## STRONG AS DEATH • Sharan Newman
The fourth title in Sharan Newman's critically acclaimed Catherine LeVendeur mystery series pits Catherine and her husband in a bizarre game of chance—which may end in Catherine's death.

## CHAPULTEPEC • Norman Zollinger
The *Gone with the Wind* of Mexico. This is a tremendous saga of love and war, and the struggle for Mexican freedom.

## JERUSALEM • Cecelia Holland
An epic of war and political intrigue, of passion and religious fervor, chronicling the fall of Saladin's empire.

## PEOPLE OF THE LIGHTNING • Kathleen O'Neal Gear and W. Michael Gear
The next novel in the First North American series series by best-selling authors Kathleen O'Neal Gear and W. Michael Gear.

# TOR
# BOOKS The Best in Fantasy